EST 1637
IN VITAM MORTEM

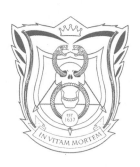

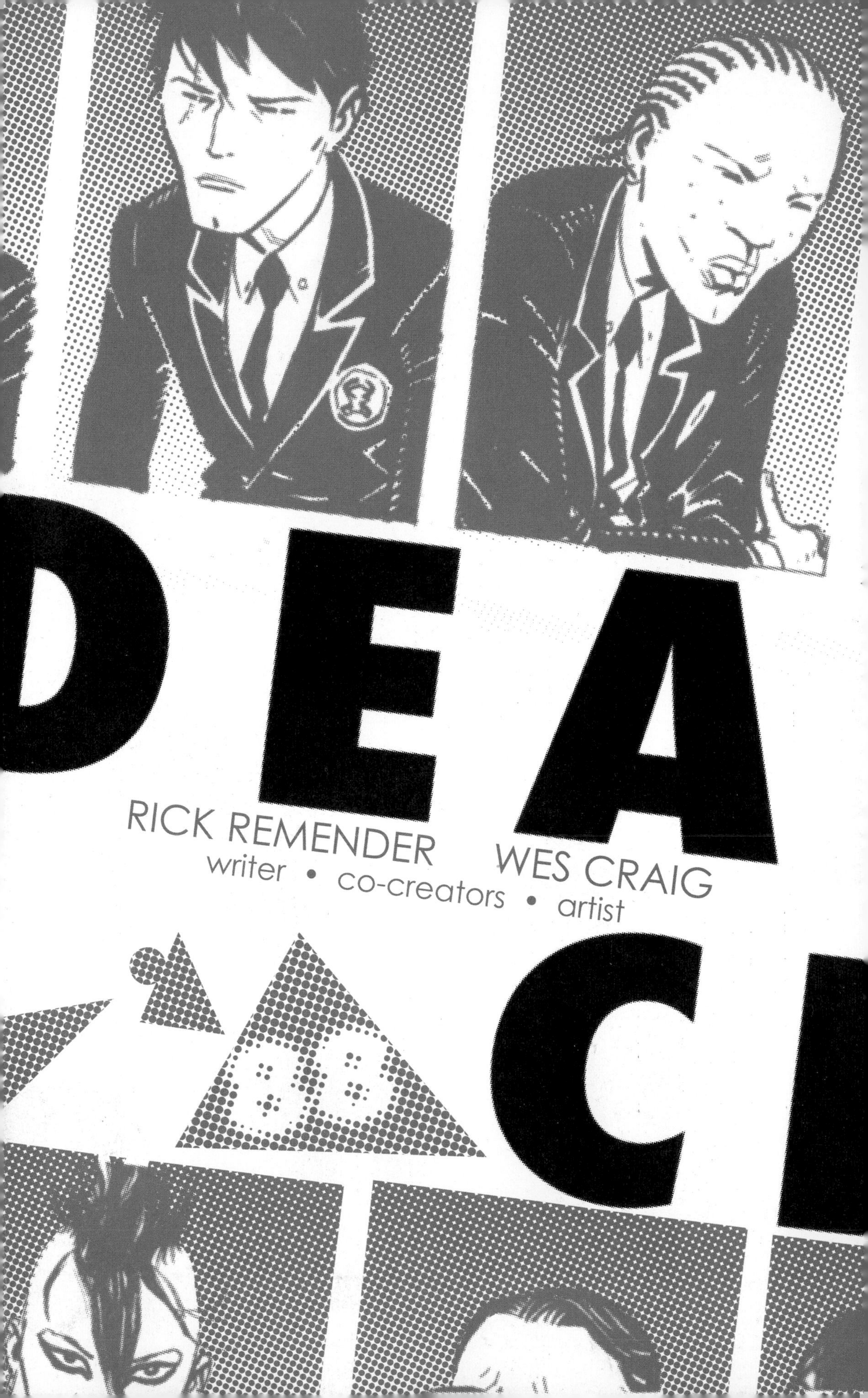
RICK REMENDER
WES CRAIG
writer • co-creators • artist

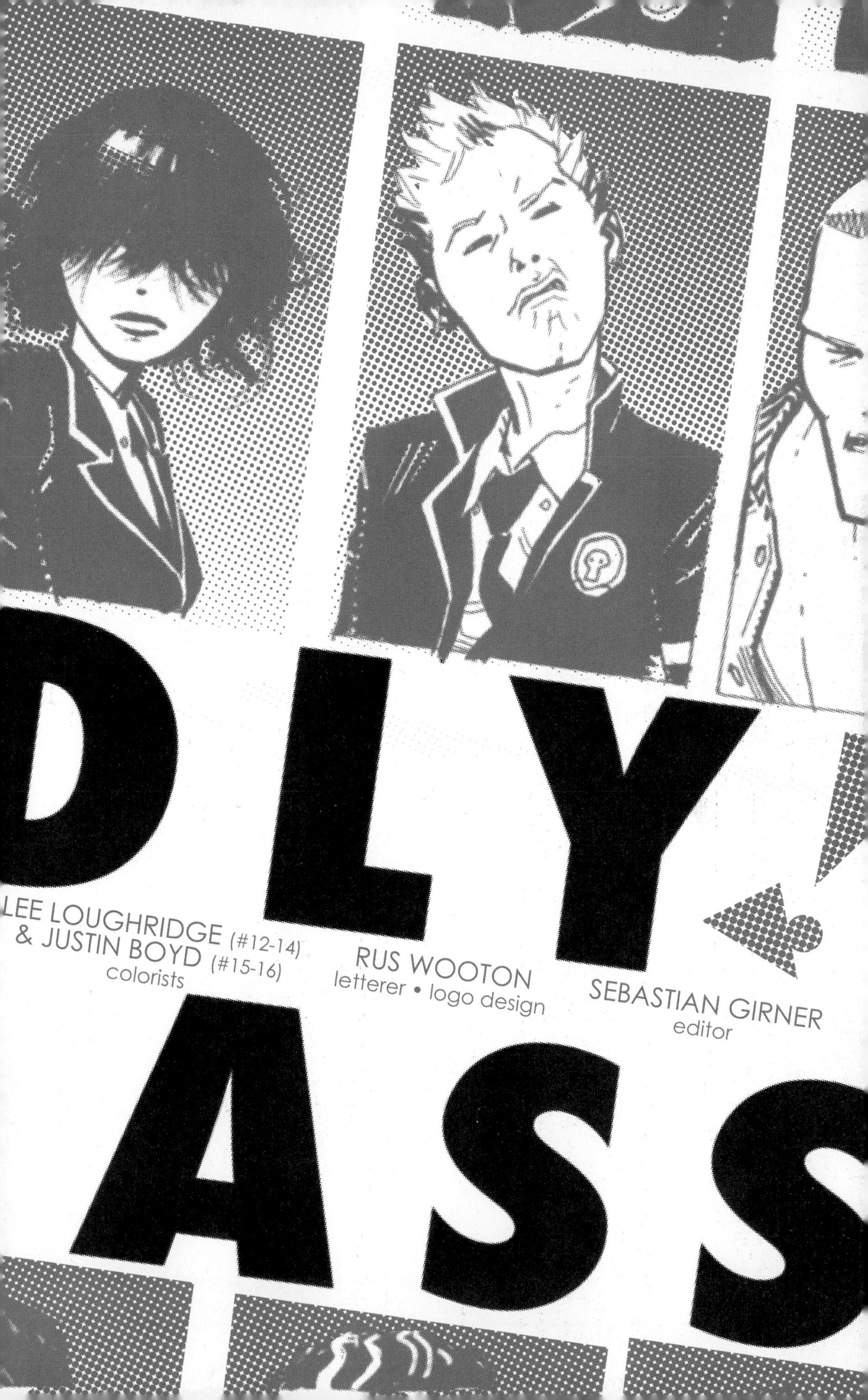
LEE LOUGHRIDGE (#12-14)
& JUSTIN BOYD (#15-16)
colorists
RUS WOOTON
letterer • logo design
SEBASTIAN GIRNER
editor

IMAGE COMICS, INC.

Robert Kirkman • Chief Operating Officer
Erik Larsen • Chief Financial Officer
Todd McFarlane • President
Marc Silvestri • Chief Executive Officer
Jim Valentino • Vice-President
Eric Stephenson • Publisher
Corey Murphy • Director of Sales
Jeremy Sullivan • Director of Digital Sales
Kat Salazar • Director of PR & Marketing
Emily Miller • Director of Operations
Branwyn Bigglestone • Senior Accounts Manager
Sarah Mello • Accounts Manager
Drew Gill • Art Director
Jonathan Chan • Production Manager
Meredith Wallace • Print Manager
Randy Okamura • Marketing Production Designer
David Brothers • Branding Manager
Ally Power • Content Manager
Addison Duke • Production Artist
Vincent Kukua • Production Artist
Sasha Head • Production Artist
Tricia Ramos • Production Artist
Emilio Bautista • Digital Sales Associate
Chloe Ramos-Peterson • Administrative Assistant

imagecomics.com

JEFF POWELL
collection design

DEADLY CLASS VOLUME 3: THE SNAKE PIT. First Printing. October 2015. Published by Image Comics, Inc. Office of publication: 2001 Center Street, 6th Floor, Berkeley, CA 94704. Copyright © 2015 Rick Remender and Wes Craig. All rights reserved. Originally published in single magazine form as DEADLY CLASS #12-16. DEADLY CLASS™ (including all prominent characters featured herein), its logo and all character likenesses are trademarks of Rick Remender and Wes Craig, unless otherwise noted. Image Comics® and its logos are registered trademarks of Image Comics, Inc. No part of this publication may be reproduced or transmitted, in any form or by any means (except for short excerpts for review purposes) without the express written permission of Image Comics, Inc. All names, characters, events and locales in this publication are entirely fictional. Any resemblance to actual persons (living or dead), events or places, without satiric intent, is coincidental. **PRINTED IN THE U.S.A.** For information regarding the CPSIA on this printed material call: 203-595-3636 and provide reference # RICH – 645871. For international rights inquiries, contact: foreignlicensing@imagecomics.com. ISBN 978-1-63215-476-7

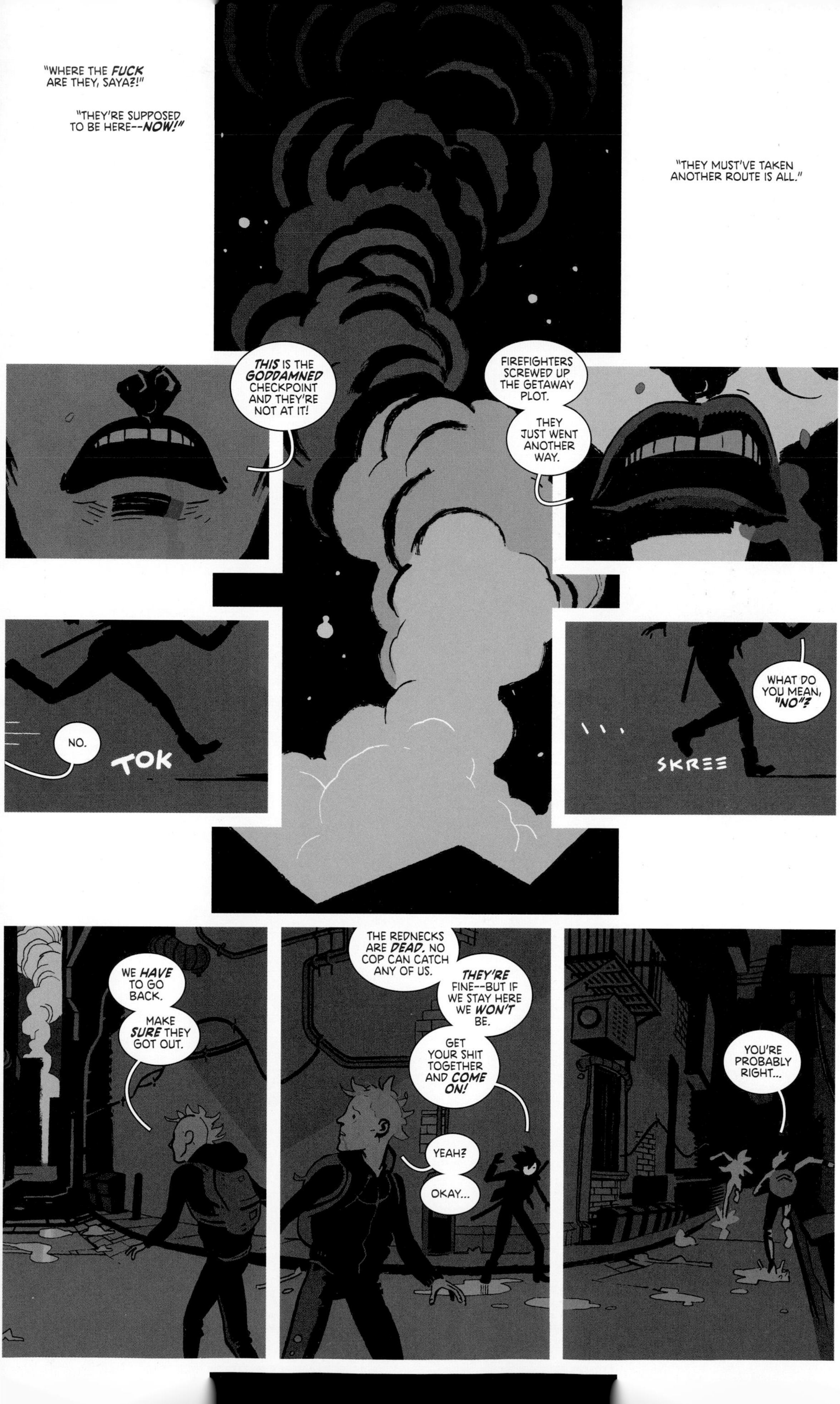
"WHERE THE *FUCK* ARE THEY, SAYA?!"
"THEY'RE SUPPOSED TO BE HERE--*NOW!*"
"THEY MUST'VE TAKEN ANOTHER ROUTE IS ALL."
THIS IS THE *GODDAMNED* CHECKPOINT AND THEY'RE NOT AT IT!
FIREFIGHTERS SCREWED UP THE GETAWAY PLOT.
THEY JUST WENT ANOTHER WAY.
NO.
TOK
...
WHAT DO YOU MEAN, *"NO"?*
SKREE
WE *HAVE* TO GO BACK.
MAKE *SURE* THEY GOT OUT.
THE REDNECKS ARE *DEAD.* NO COP CAN CATCH ANY OF US.
THEY'RE FINE--BUT IF WE STAY HERE WE *WON'T* BE.
GET YOUR SHIT TOGETHER AND *COME ON!*
YEAH?
OKAY...
YOU'RE PROBABLY RIGHT...

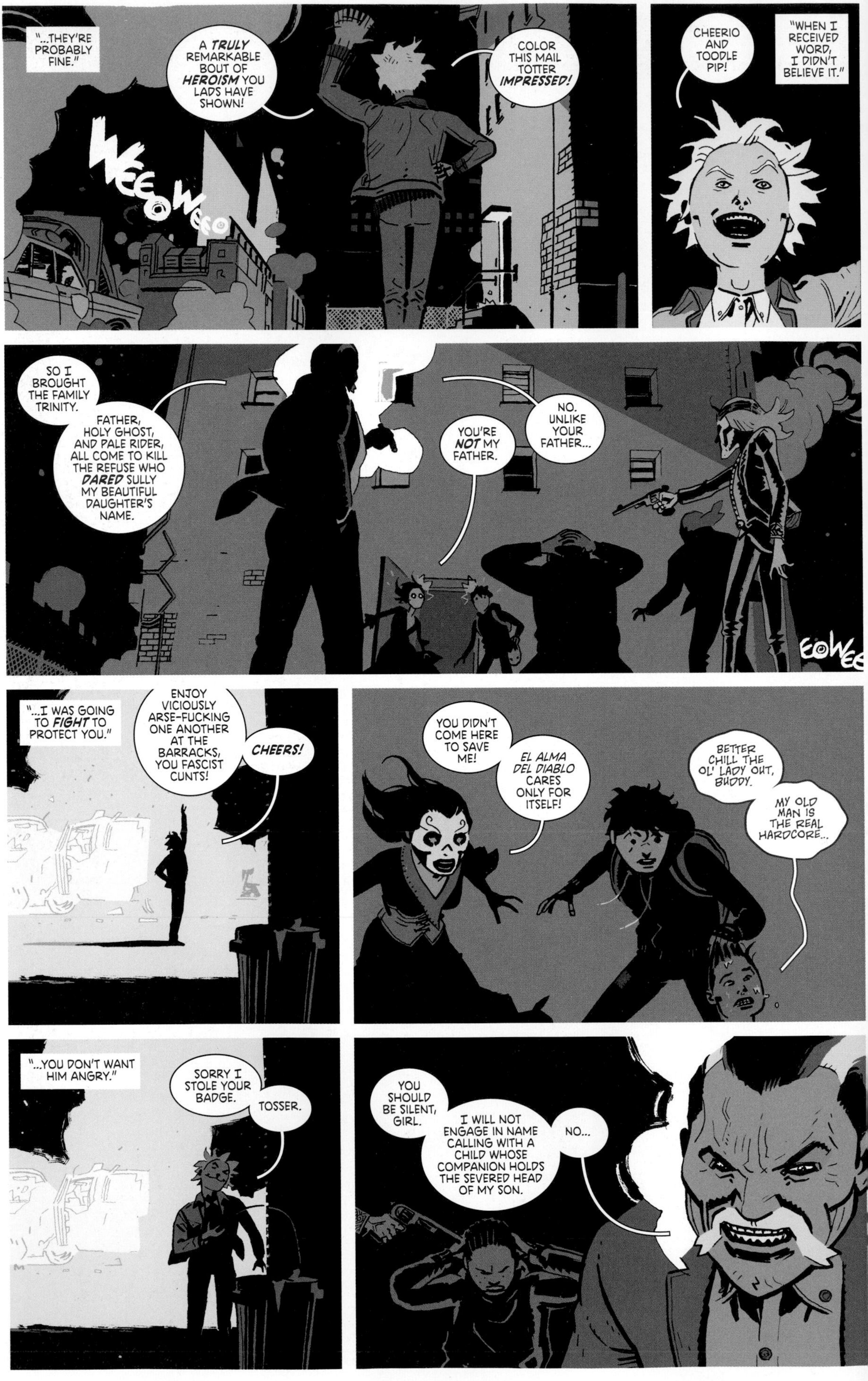

"...THEY'RE PROBABLY FINE."
A TRULY REMARKABLE BOUT OF HEROISM YOU LADS HAVE SHOWN!
COLOR THIS MAIL TOTTER IMPRESSED!
WEEOWEEO
CHEERIO AND TODDLE PIP!
"WHEN I RECEIVED WORD, I DIDN'T BELIEVE IT."
SO I BROUGHT THE FAMILY TRINITY.
FATHER, HOLY GHOST, AND PALE RIDER, ALL COME TO KILL THE REFUSE WHO DARED SULLY MY BEAUTIFUL DAUGHTER'S NAME.
YOU'RE NOT MY FATHER.
NO. UNLIKE YOUR FATHER...
EOWEE
"...I WAS GOING TO FIGHT TO PROTECT YOU."
ENJOY VICIOUSLY ARSE-FUCKING ONE ANOTHER AT THE BARRACKS, YOU FASCIST CUNTS!
CHEERS!
YOU DIDN'T COME HERE TO SAVE ME!
EL ALMA DEL DIABLO CARES ONLY FOR ITSELF!
BETTER CHILL THE OL' LADY OUT, BUDDY.
MY OLD MAN IS THE REAL HARDCORE...
"...YOU DON'T WANT HIM ANGRY."
SORRY I STOLE YOUR BADGE.
TOSSER.
YOU SHOULD BE SILENT, GIRL.
I WILL NOT ENGAGE IN NAME CALLING WITH A CHILD WHOSE COMPANION HOLDS THE SEVERED HEAD OF MY SON.
NO...

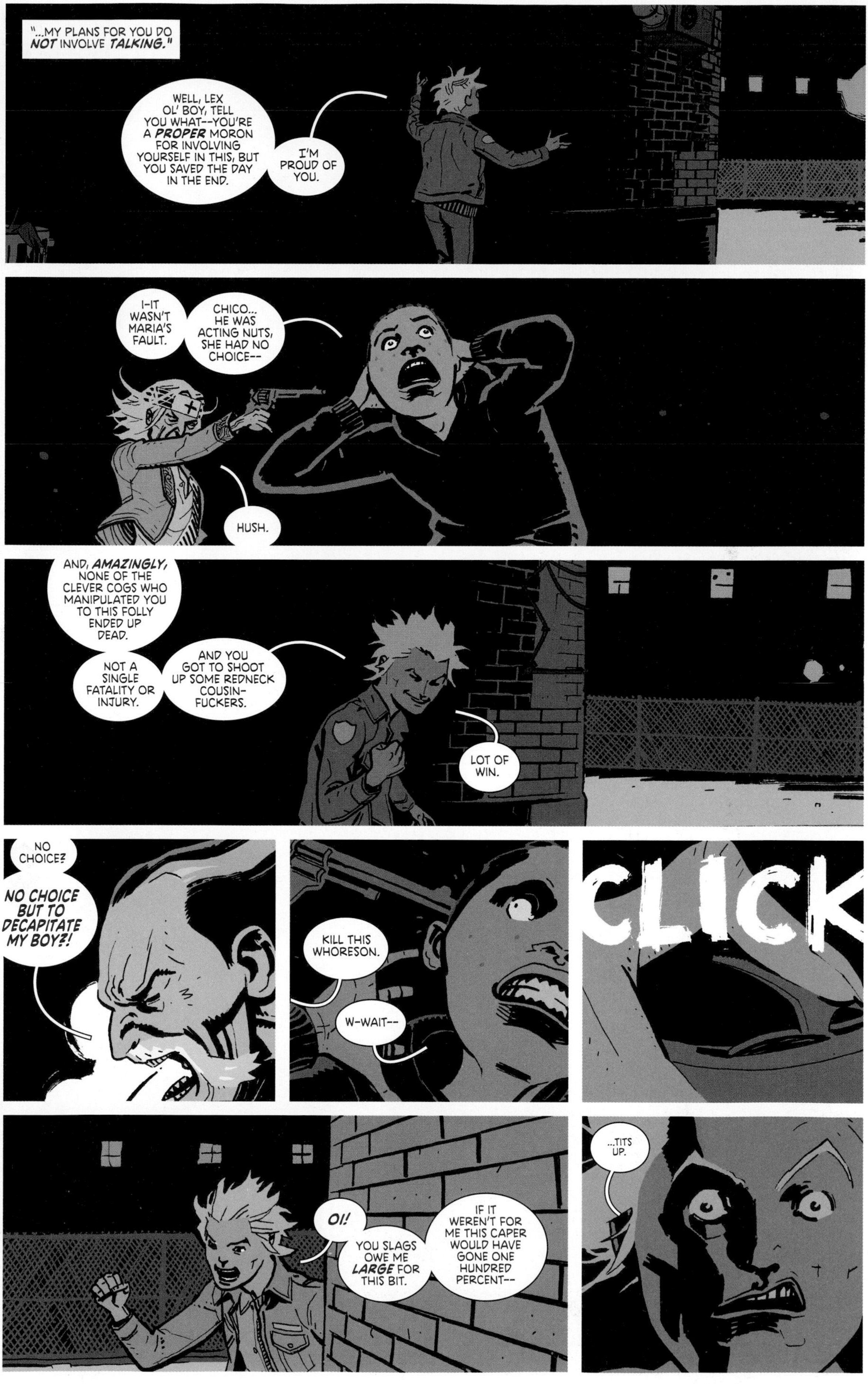
"...MY PLANS FOR YOU DO NOT INVOLVE TALKING."
WELL, LEX OL' BOY, TELL YOU WHAT--YOU'RE A PROPER MORON FOR INVOLVING YOURSELF IN THIS, BUT YOU SAVED THE DAY IN THE END.
I'M PROUD OF YOU.
I-IT WASN'T MARIA'S FAULT.
CHICO... HE WAS ACTING NUTS, SHE HAD NO CHOICE--
HUSH.
AND, AMAZINGLY, NONE OF THE CLEVER COGS WHO MANIPULATED YOU TO THIS FOLLY ENDED UP DEAD.
NOT A SINGLE FATALITY OR INJURY.
AND YOU GOT TO SHOOT UP SOME REDNECK COUSIN-FUCKERS.
LOT OF WIN.
NO CHOICE?
NO CHOICE BUT TO DECAPITATE MY BOY?!
KILL THIS WHORESON.
W-WAIT--
CLICK
OI!
YOU SLAGS OWE ME LARGE FOR THIS BIT.
IF IT WEREN'T FOR ME THIS CAPER WOULD HAVE GONE ONE HUNDRED PERCENT--
...TITS UP.

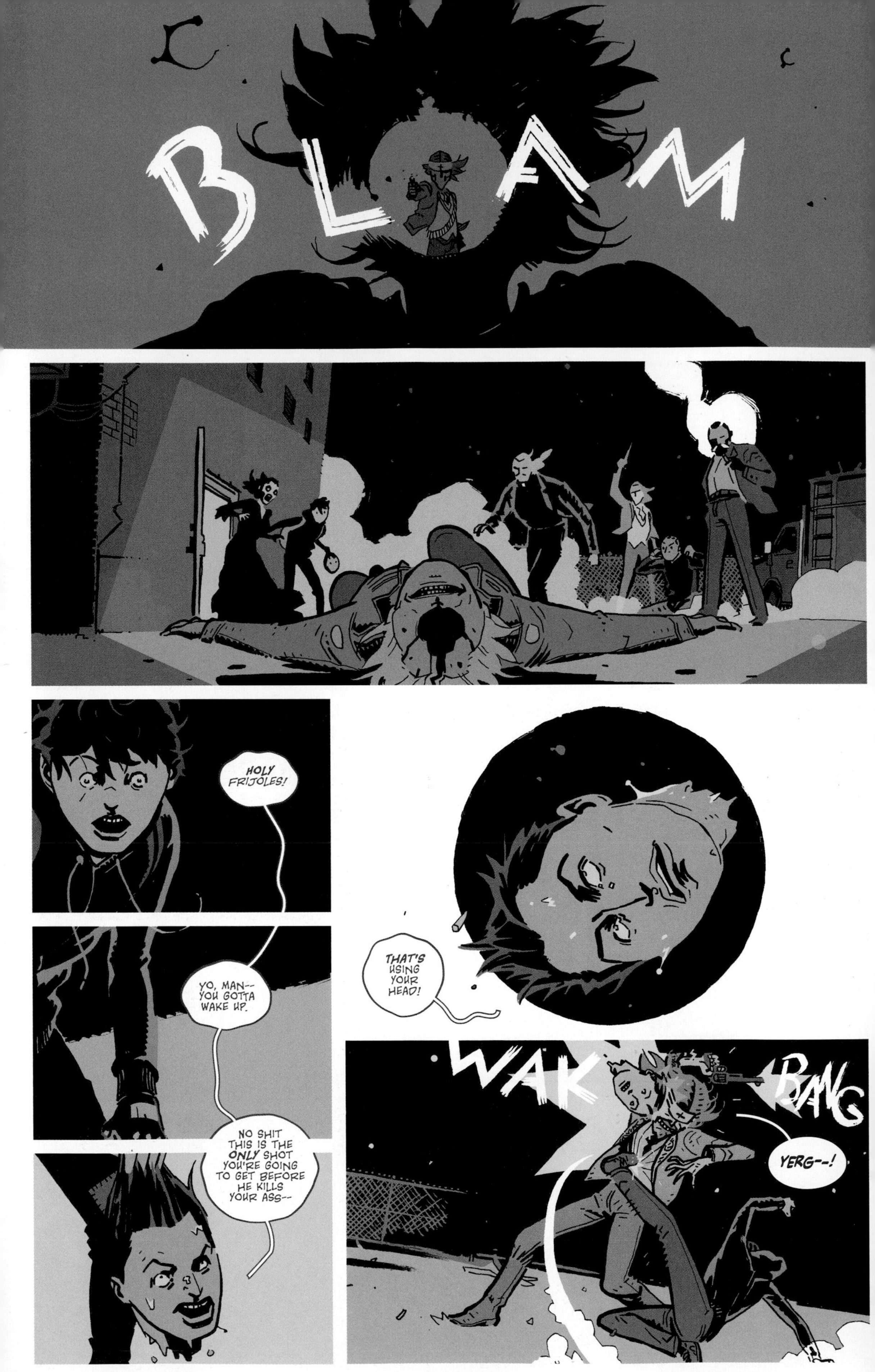
BLAM
HOLY FRIJOLES!
YO, MAN-- YOU GOTTA WAKE UP.
NO SHIT THIS IS THE ONLY SHOT YOU'RE GOING TO GET BEFORE HE KILLS YOUR ASS--
THAT'S USING YOUR HEAD!
WAK
BANG
YERG--!

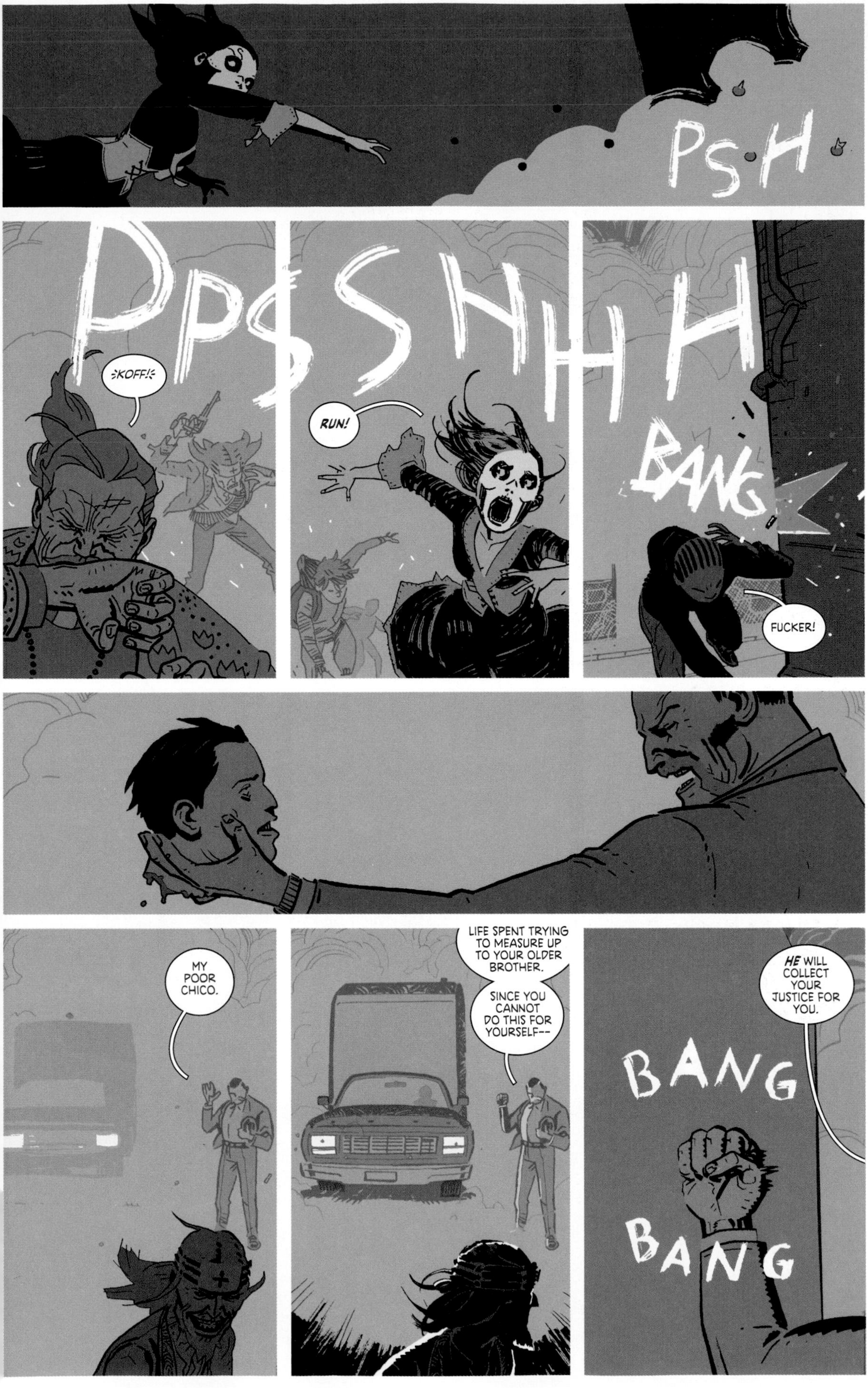
PSH
PPSSHHH
KOFF!
RUN!
BANG
FUCKER!
MY POOR CHICO.
LIFE SPENT TRYING TO MEASURE UP TO YOUR OLDER BROTHER.
SINCE YOU CANNOT DO THIS FOR YOURSELF--
HE WILL COLLECT YOUR JUSTICE FOR YOU.
BANG
BANG

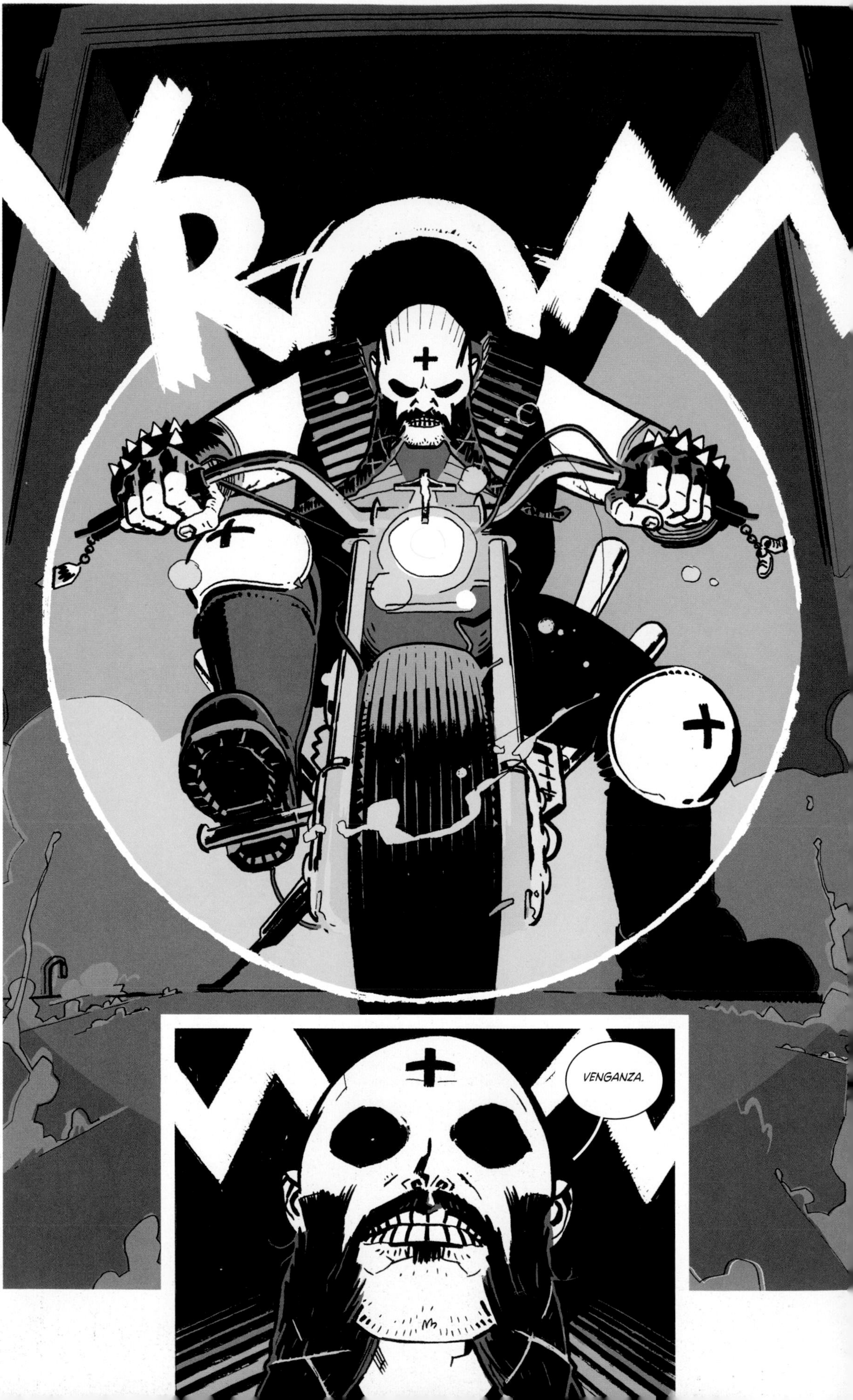
VROOM
VENGANZA.

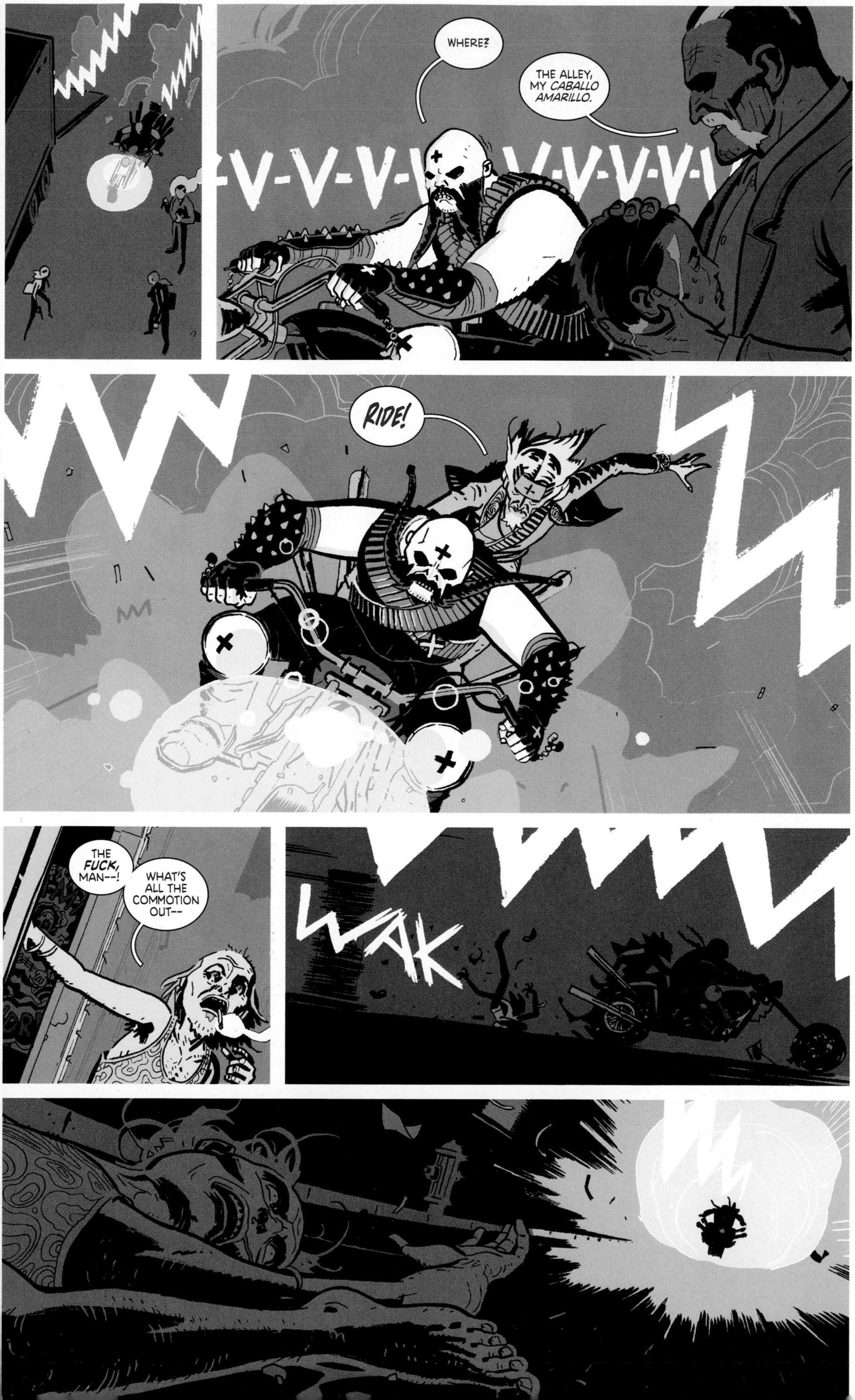

WHERE?
THE ALLEY, MY *CABALLO AMARILLO.*
V-V-V-V-V-V-V-V-V
RIDE!
THE *FUCK,* MAN--!
WHAT'S ALL THE COMMOTION OUT--
WAK

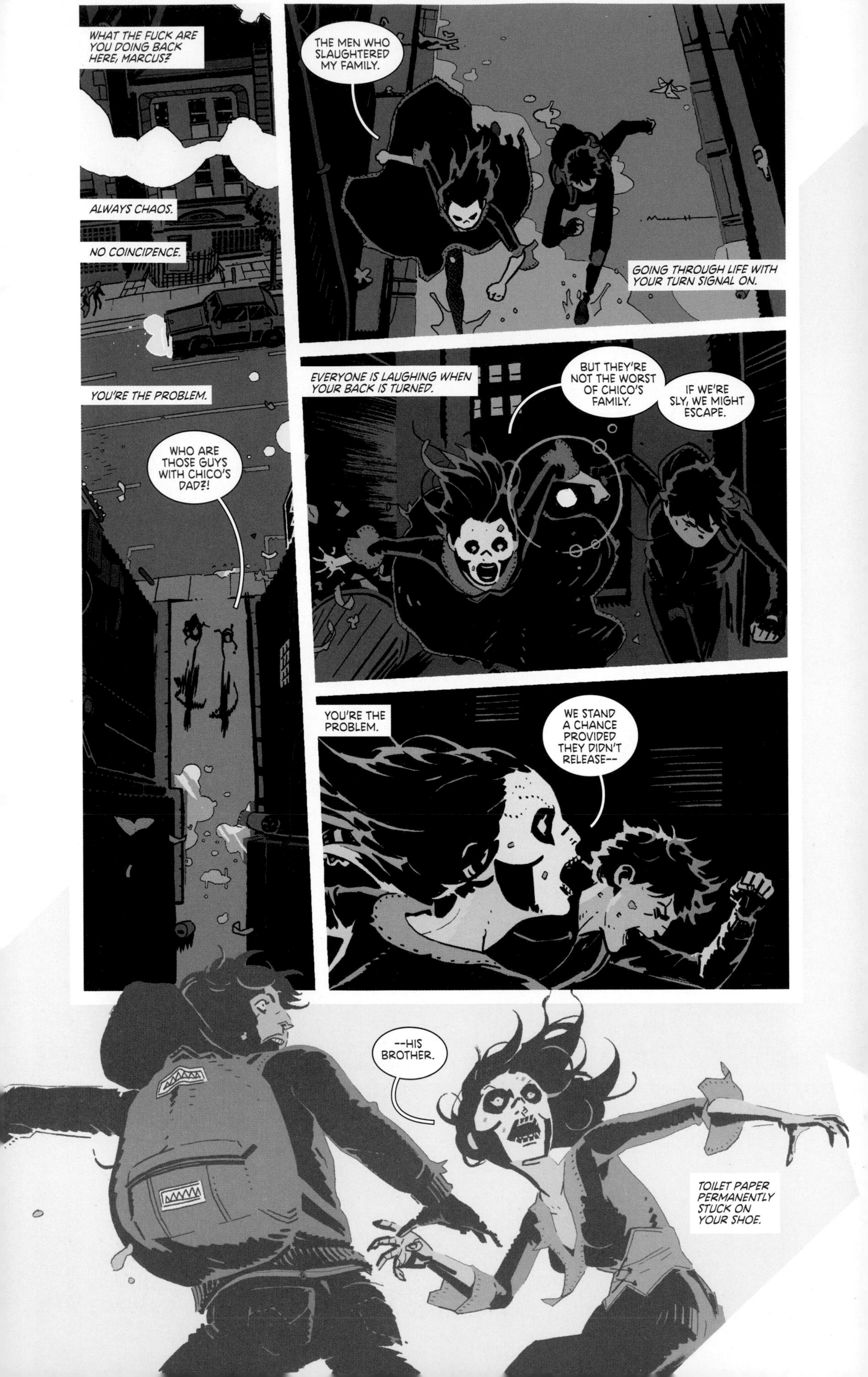
WHAT THE FUCK ARE YOU DOING BACK HERE, MARCUS?
THE MEN WHO SLAUGHTERED MY FAMILY.
ALWAYS CHAOS.
NO COINCIDENCE.
GOING THROUGH LIFE WITH YOUR TURN SIGNAL ON.
YOU'RE THE PROBLEM.
WHO ARE THOSE GUYS WITH CHICO'S DAD?!
EVERYONE IS LAUGHING WHEN YOUR BACK IS TURNED.
BUT THEY'RE NOT THE WORST OF CHICO'S FAMILY.
IF WE'RE SLY, WE MIGHT ESCAPE.
YOU'RE THE PROBLEM.
WE STAND A CHANCE PROVIDED THEY DIDN'T RELEASE--
--HIS BROTHER.
TOILET PAPER PERMANENTLY STUCK ON YOUR SHOE.

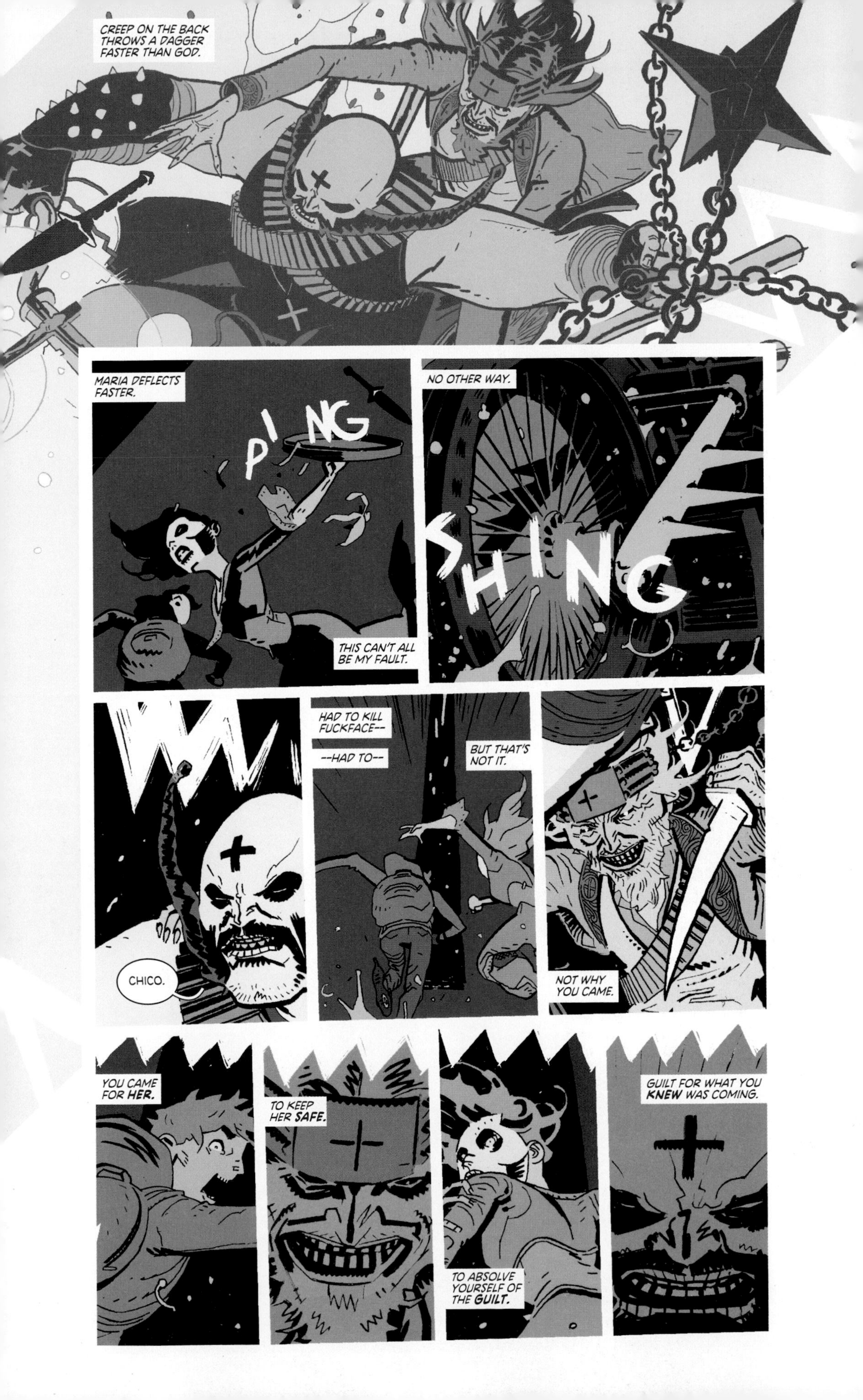
CREEP ON THE BACK THROWS A DAGGER FASTER THAN GOD.
MARIA DEFLECTS FASTER.
PING
THIS CAN'T ALL BE MY FAULT.
NO OTHER WAY.
SHING
CHICO.
HAD TO KILL FUCKFACE--
--HAD TO--
BUT THAT'S NOT IT.
NOT WHY YOU CAME.
YOU CAME FOR HER.
TO KEEP HER SAFE.
TO ABSOLVE YOURSELF OF THE GUILT.
GUILT FOR WHAT YOU KNEW WAS COMING.

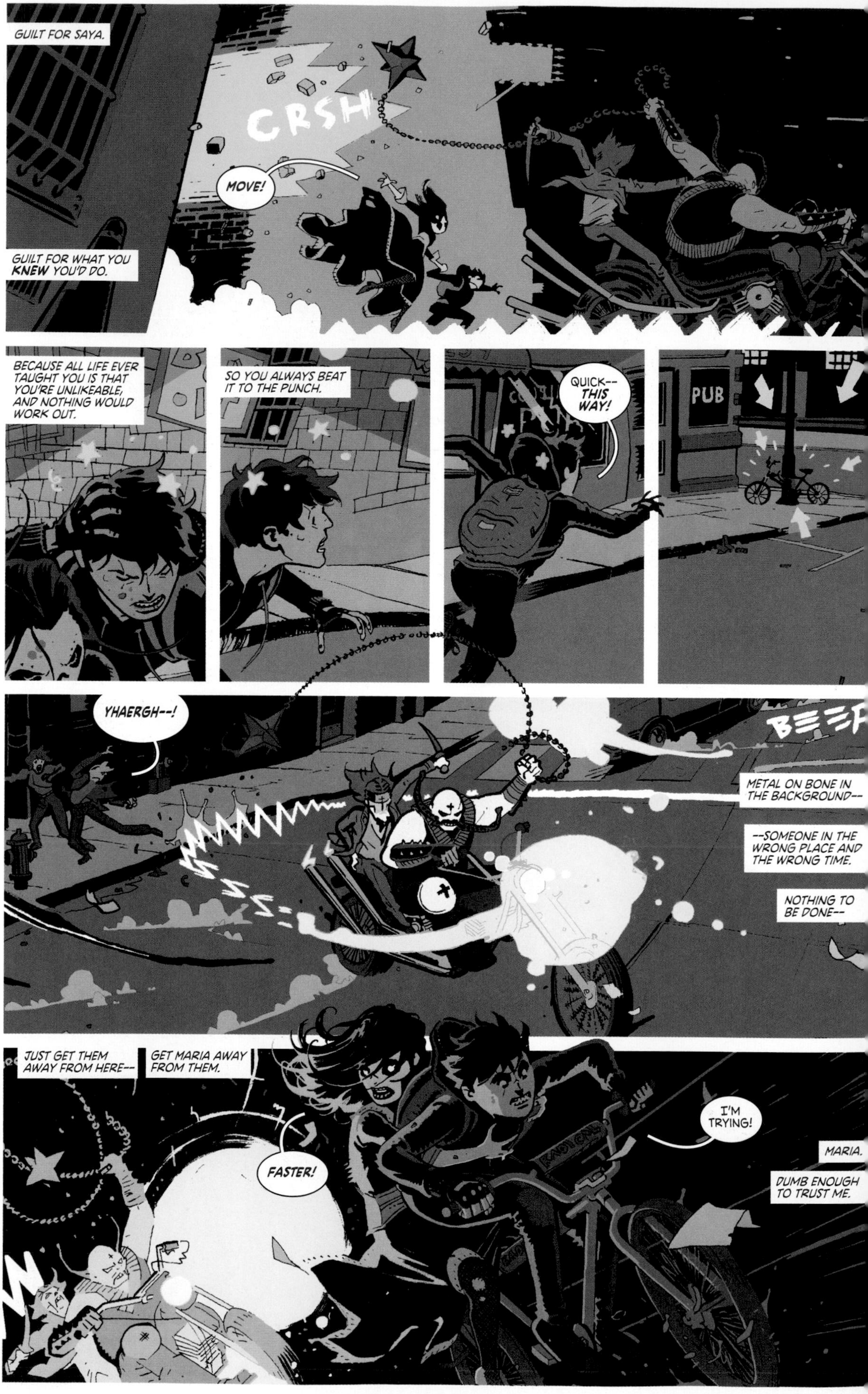

GUILT FOR SAYA.
CRSH
MOVE!
GUILT FOR WHAT YOU KNEW YOU'D DO.
BECAUSE ALL LIFE EVER TAUGHT YOU IS THAT YOU'RE UNLIKEABLE, AND NOTHING WOULD WORK OUT.
SO YOU ALWAYS BEAT IT TO THE PUNCH.
QUICK-- THIS WAY!
PUB
YHAERGH--!
BEEP
METAL ON BONE IN THE BACKGROUND--
--SOMEONE IN THE WRONG PLACE AND THE WRONG TIME.
NOTHING TO BE DONE--
JUST GET THEM AWAY FROM HERE--
GET MARIA AWAY FROM THEM.
FASTER!
I'M TRYING!
MARIA.
DUMB ENOUGH TO TRUST ME.

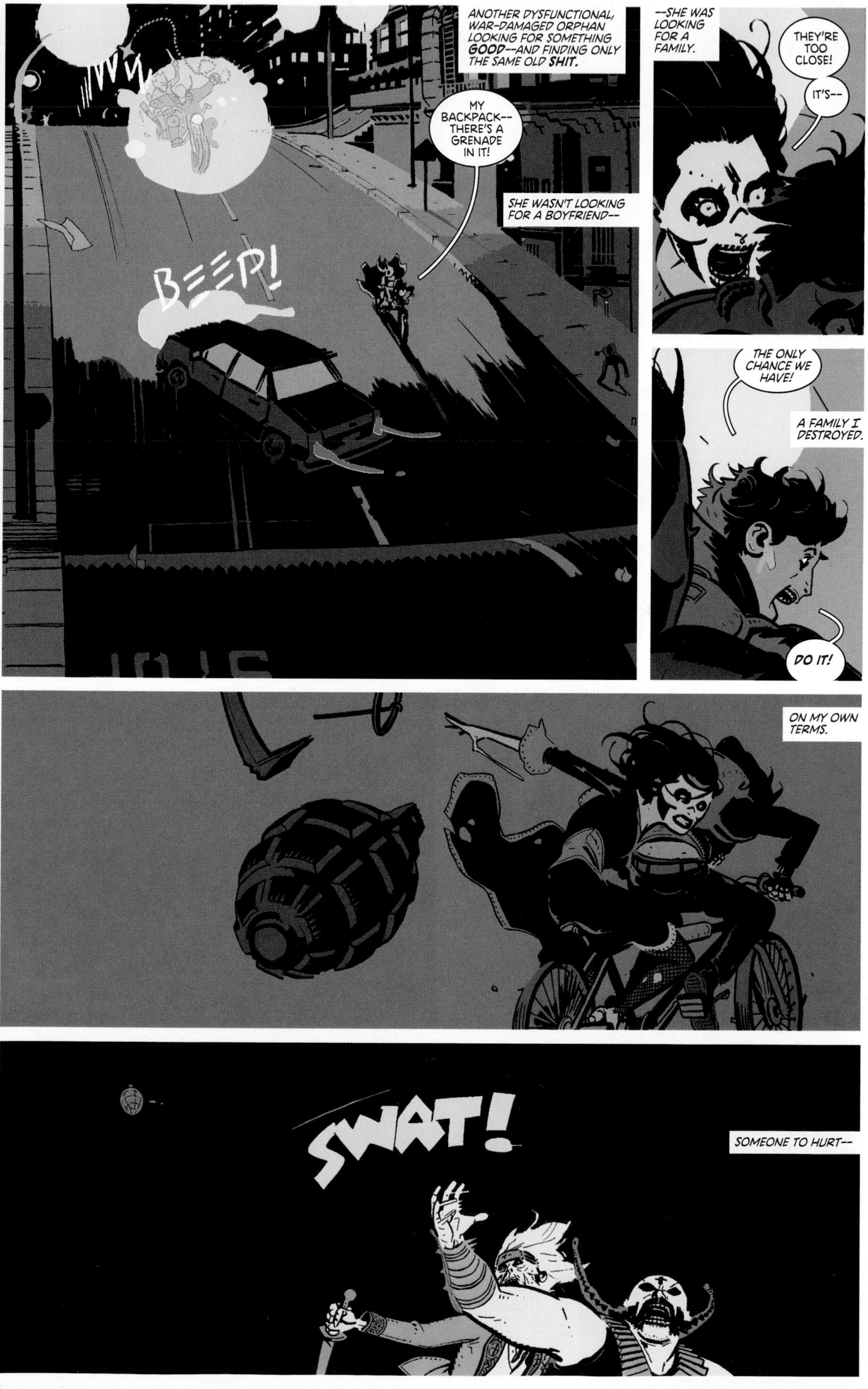
ANOTHER DYSFUNCTIONAL, WAR-DAMAGED ORPHAN LOOKING FOR SOMETHING GOOD--AND FINDING ONLY THE SAME OLD SHIT.
MY BACKPACK-- THERE'S A GRENADE IN IT!
SHE WASN'T LOOKING FOR A BOYFRIEND--
BEEP!
--SHE WAS LOOKING FOR A FAMILY.
THEY'RE TOO CLOSE!
IT'S--
THE ONLY CHANCE WE HAVE!
A FAMILY I DESTROYED.
DO IT!
ON MY OWN TERMS.
SWAT!
SOMEONE TO HURT--

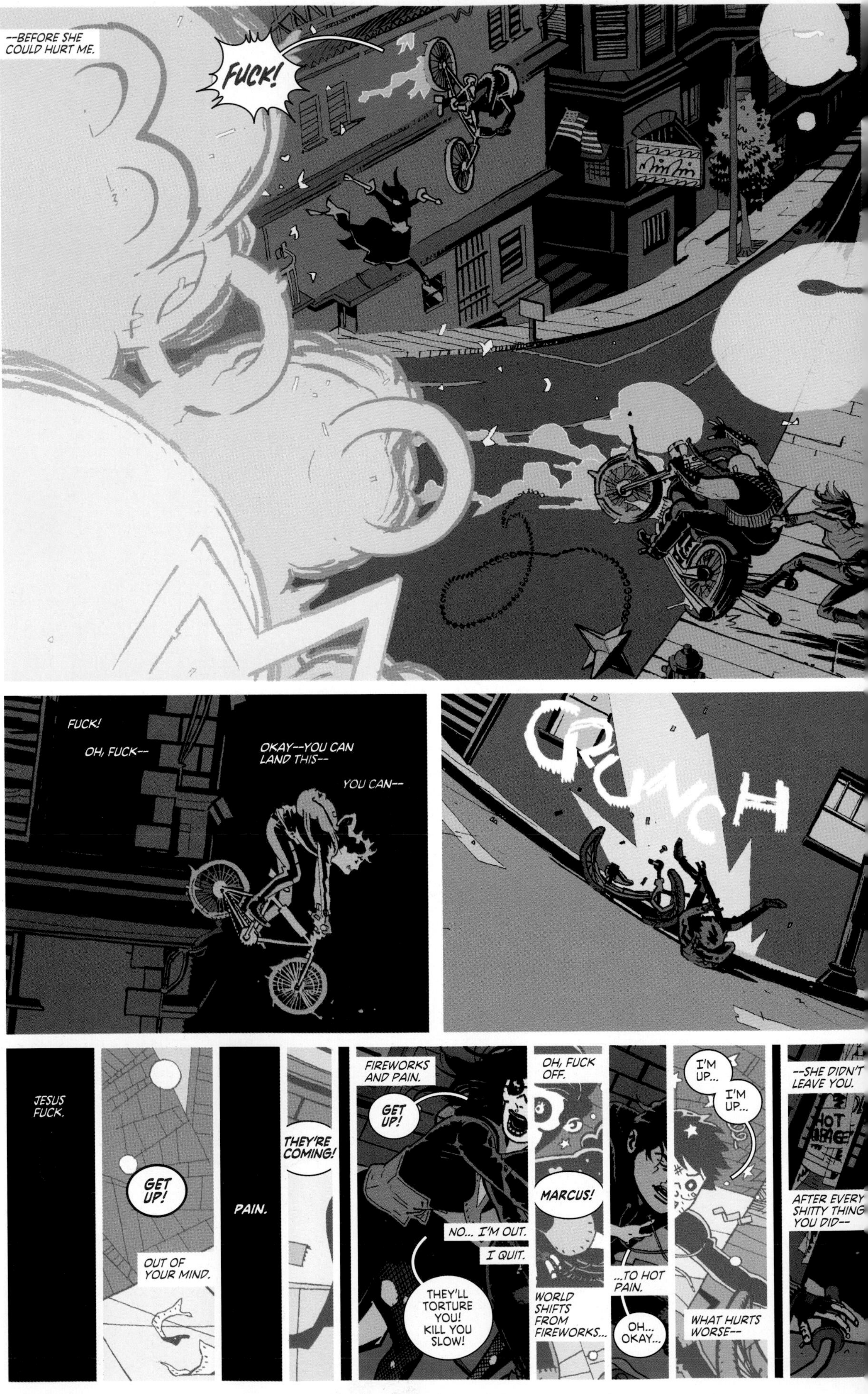
--BEFORE SHE COULD HURT ME.
FUCK!
FUCK!
OH, FUCK--
OKAY--YOU CAN LAND THIS--
YOU CAN--
CRUNCH
JESUS FUCK.
GET UP!
OUT OF YOUR MIND.
PAIN.
THEY'RE COMING!
FIREWORKS AND PAIN.
GET UP!
NO... I'M OUT.
I QUIT.
THEY'LL TORTURE YOU! KILL YOU SLOW!
OH, FUCK OFF.
MARCUS!
WORLD SHIFTS FROM FIREWORKS...
...TO HOT PAIN.
OH... OKAY...
I'M UP...
I'M UP...
WHAT HURTS WORSE--
--SHE DIDN'T LEAVE YOU.
AFTER EVERY SHITTY THING YOU DID--

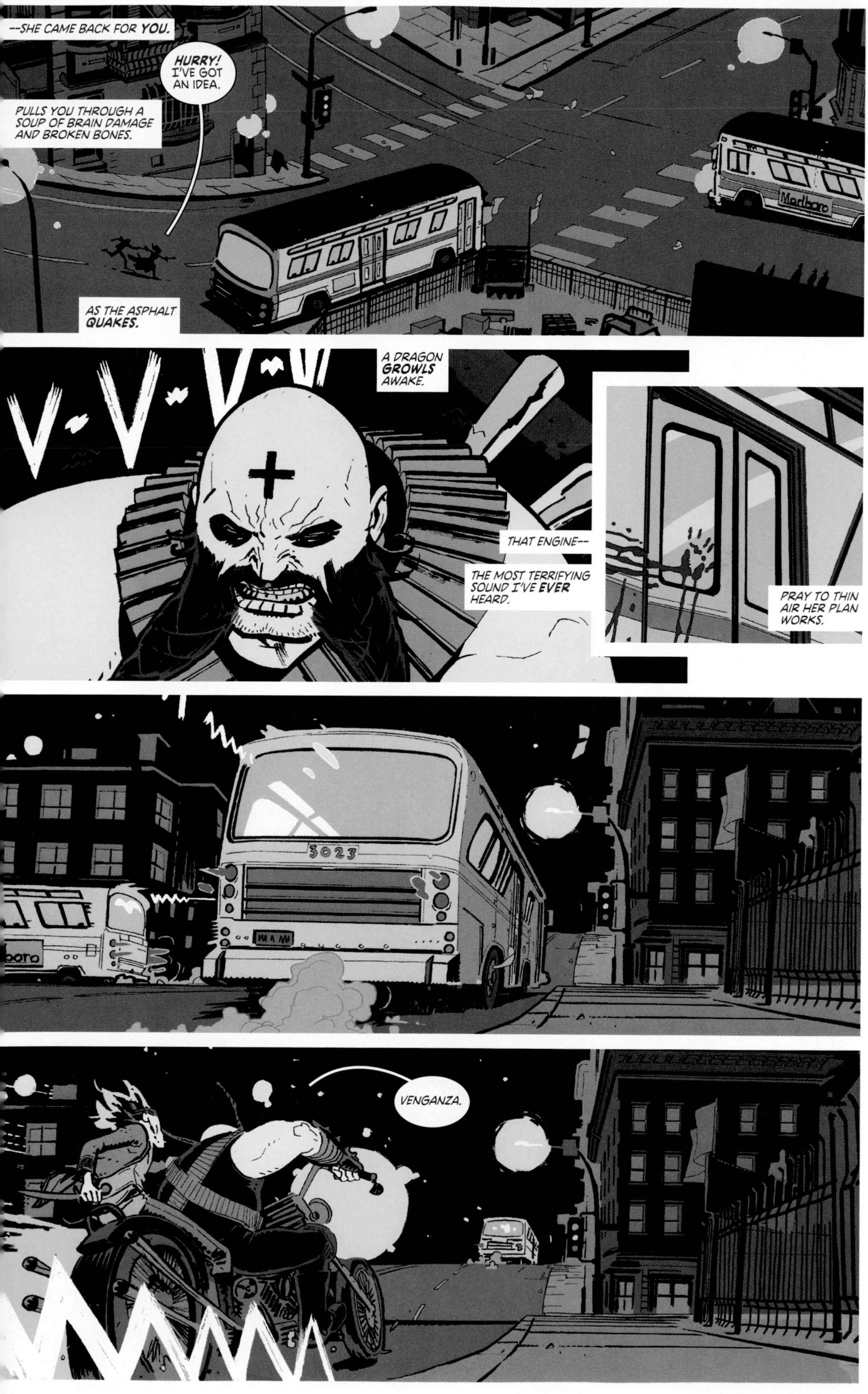
--SHE CAME BACK FOR YOU.
HURRY! I'VE GOT AN IDEA.
PULLS YOU THROUGH A SOUP OF BRAIN DAMAGE AND BROKEN BONES.
Marlboro
AS THE ASPHALT QUAKES.
A DRAGON GROWLS AWAKE.
THAT ENGINE--
THE MOST TERRIFYING SOUND I'VE EVER HEARD.
PRAY TO THIN AIR HER PLAN WORKS.
3023
VENGANZA.

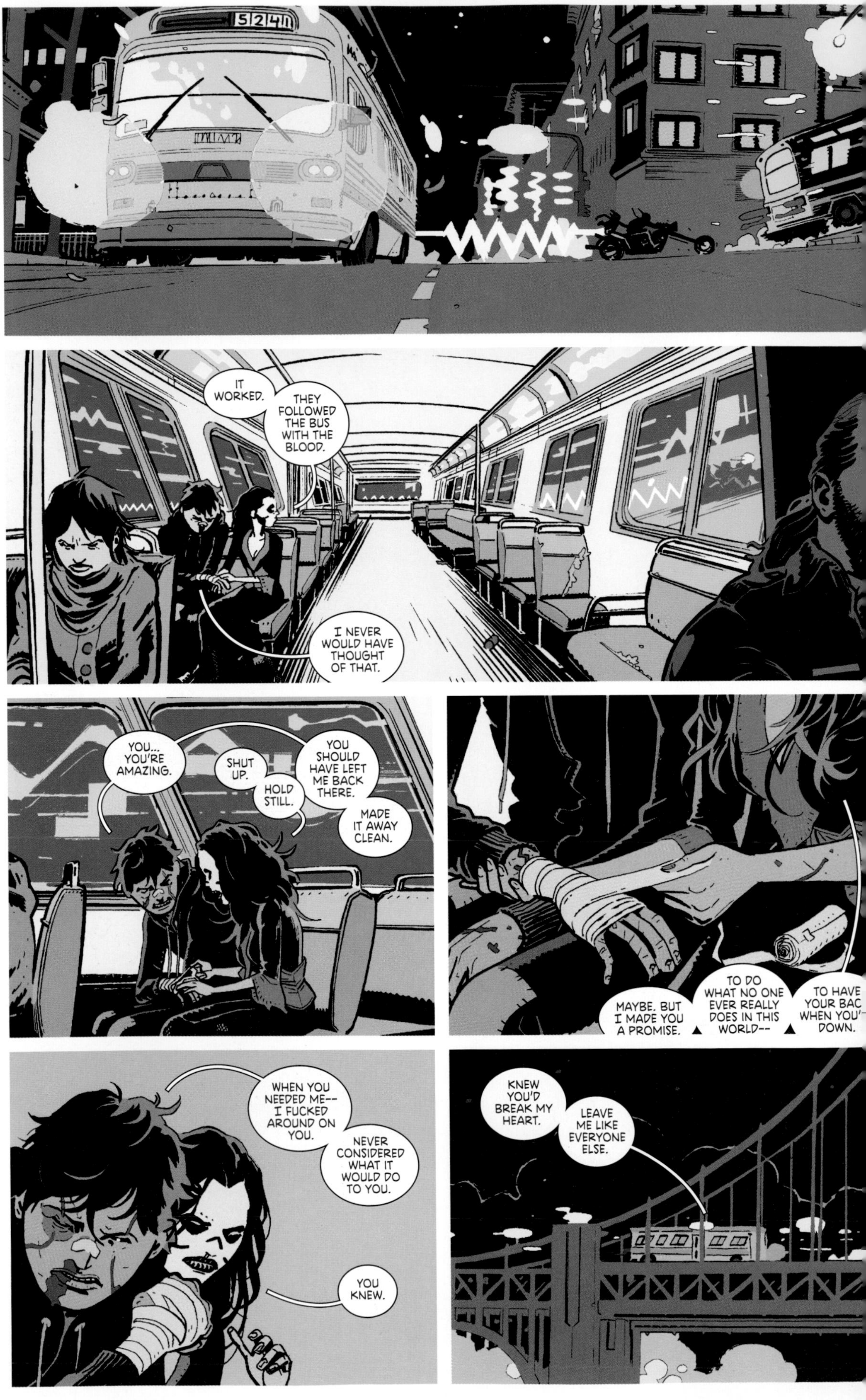
5240
IT WORKED.
THEY FOLLOWED THE BUS WITH THE BLOOD.
I NEVER WOULD HAVE THOUGHT OF THAT.
YOU... YOU'RE AMAZING.
SHUT UP.
HOLD STILL.
YOU SHOULD HAVE LEFT ME BACK THERE.
MADE IT AWAY CLEAN.
MAYBE. BUT I MADE YOU A PROMISE.
TO DO WHAT NO ONE EVER REALLY DOES IN THIS WORLD--
TO HAVE YOUR BAC WHEN YOU' DOWN.
WHEN YOU NEEDED ME-- I FUCKED AROUND ON YOU.
NEVER CONSIDERED WHAT IT WOULD DO TO YOU.
YOU KNEW.
KNEW YOU'D BREAK MY HEART.
LEAVE ME LIKE EVERYONE ELSE.

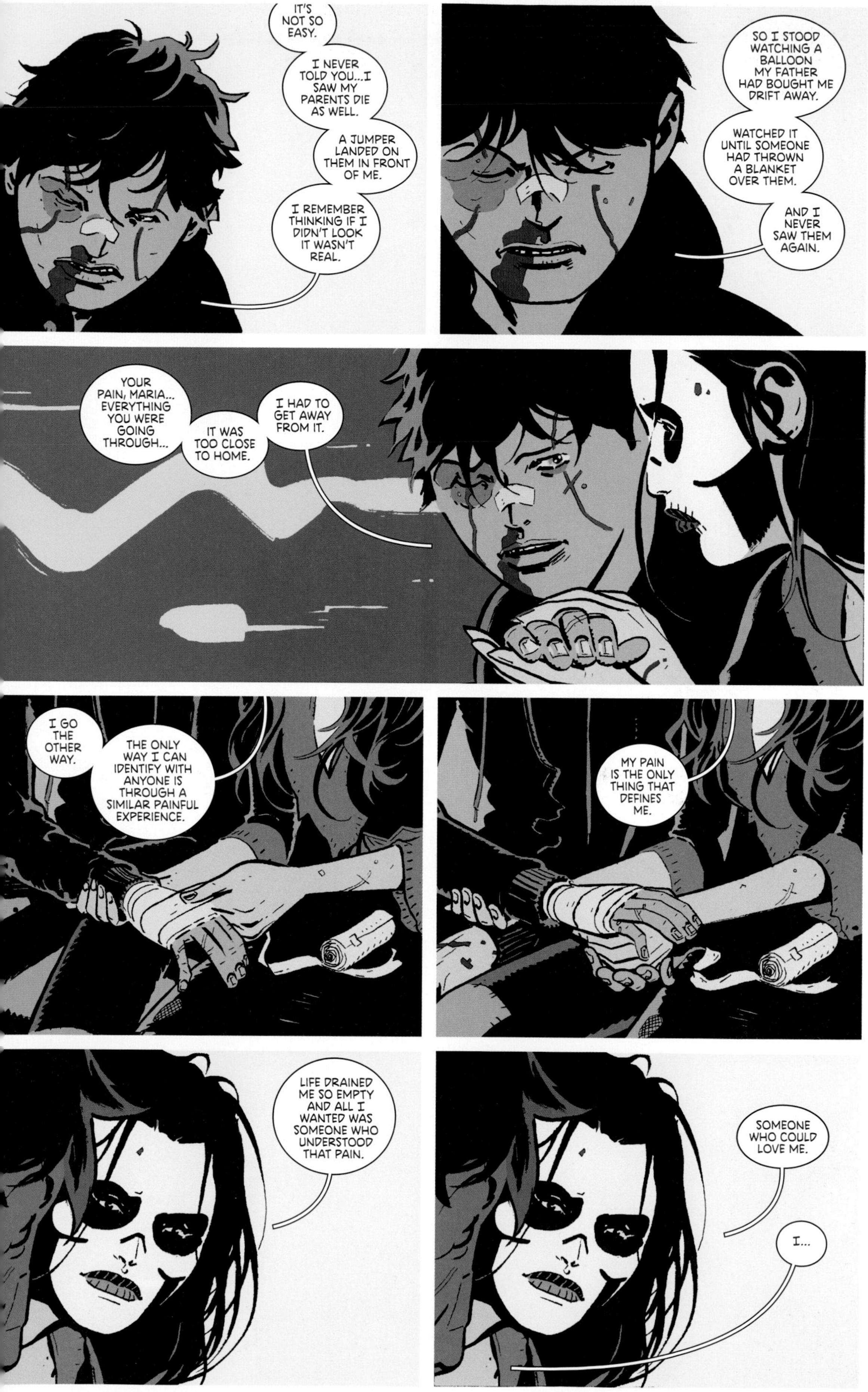
IT'S NOT SO EASY.
I NEVER TOLD YOU...I SAW MY PARENTS DIE AS WELL.
A JUMPER LANDED ON THEM IN FRONT OF ME.
I REMEMBER THINKING IF I DIDN'T LOOK IT WASN'T REAL.
SO I STOOD WATCHING A BALLOON MY FATHER HAD BOUGHT ME DRIFT AWAY.
WATCHED IT UNTIL SOMEONE HAD THROWN A BLANKET OVER THEM.
AND I NEVER SAW THEM AGAIN.
YOUR PAIN, MARIA... EVERYTHING YOU WERE GOING THROUGH...
IT WAS TOO CLOSE TO HOME.
I HAD TO GET AWAY FROM IT.
I GO THE OTHER WAY.
THE ONLY WAY I CAN IDENTIFY WITH ANYONE IS THROUGH A SIMILAR PAINFUL EXPERIENCE.
MY PAIN IS THE ONLY THING THAT DEFINES ME.
LIFE DRAINED ME SO EMPTY AND ALL I WANTED WAS SOMEONE WHO UNDERSTOOD THAT PAIN.
SOMEONE WHO COULD LOVE ME.
I...

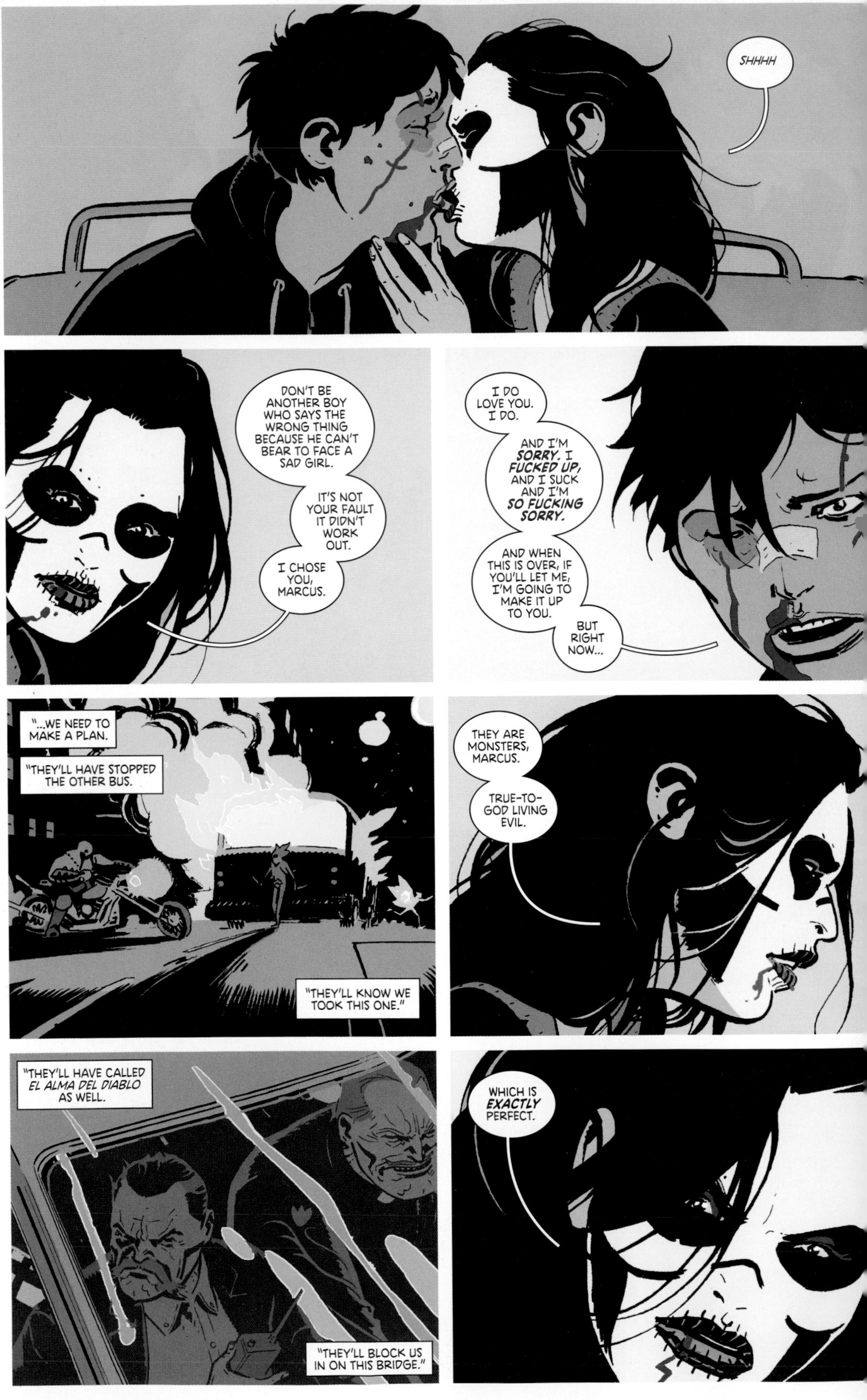
SHHHH
DON'T BE ANOTHER BOY WHO SAYS THE WRONG THING BECAUSE HE CAN'T BEAR TO FACE A SAD GIRL.
IT'S NOT YOUR FAULT IT DIDN'T WORK OUT.
I CHOSE YOU, MARCUS.
I DO LOVE YOU. I DO.
AND I'M SORRY. I FUCKED UP, AND I SUCK AND I'M SO FUCKING SORRY.
AND WHEN THIS IS OVER, IF YOU'LL LET ME, I'M GOING TO MAKE IT UP TO YOU.
BUT RIGHT NOW...
"...WE NEED TO MAKE A PLAN.
"THEY'LL HAVE STOPPED THE OTHER BUS.
"THEY'LL KNOW WE TOOK THIS ONE."
THEY ARE MONSTERS, MARCUS.
TRUE-TO-GOD LIVING EVIL.
"THEY'LL HAVE CALLED EL ALMA DEL DIABLO AS WELL.
"THEY'LL BLOCK US IN ON THIS BRIDGE."
WHICH IS EXACTLY PERFECT.

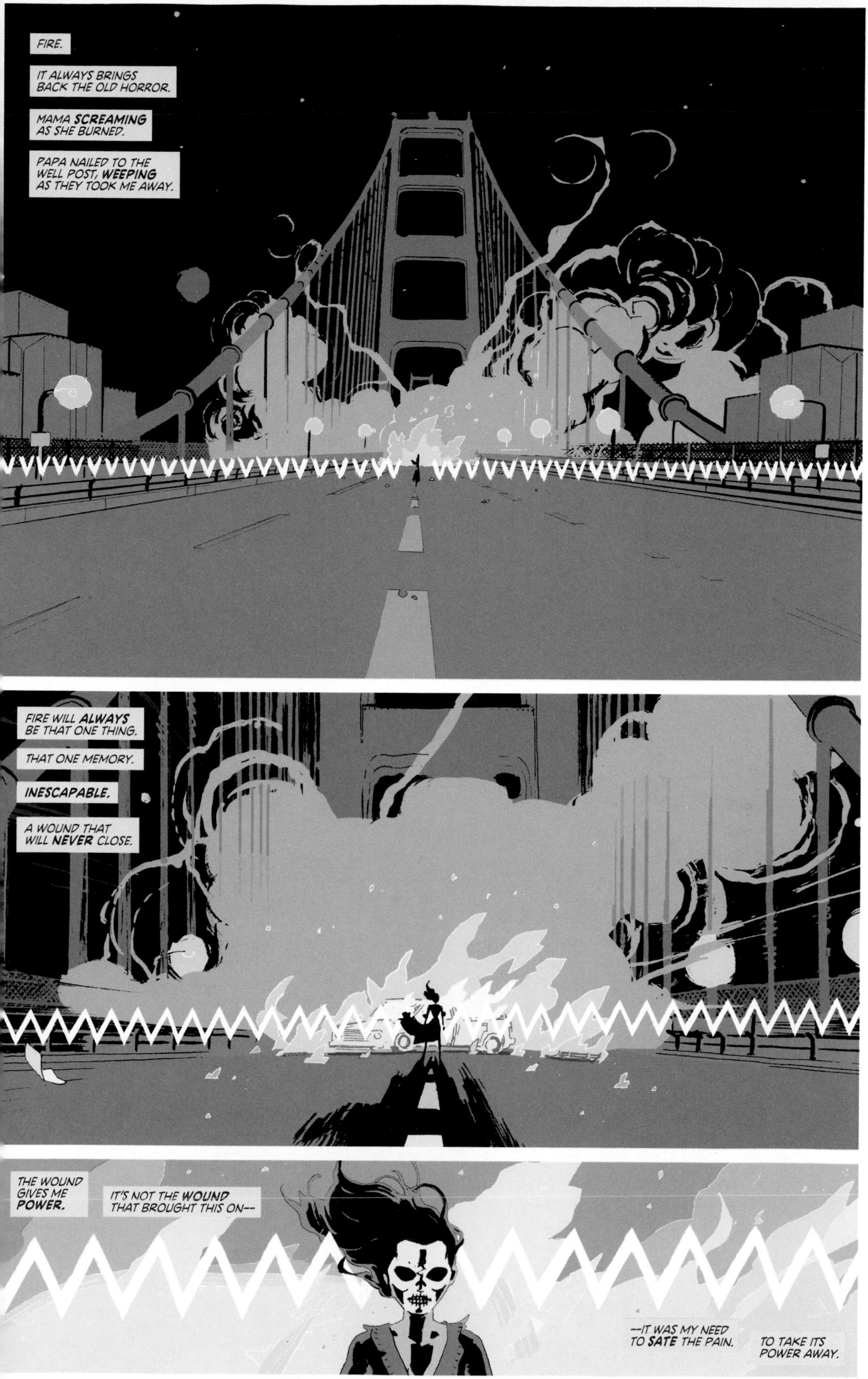
FIRE.
IT ALWAYS BRINGS BACK THE OLD HORROR.
MAMA **SCREAMING** AS SHE BURNED.
PAPA NAILED TO THE WELL POST, **WEEPING** AS THEY TOOK ME AWAY.
FIRE WILL **ALWAYS** BE THAT ONE THING.
THAT ONE MEMORY.
INESCAPABLE.
A WOUND THAT WILL **NEVER** CLOSE.
THE WOUND GIVES ME **POWER.**
IT'S NOT THE **WOUND** THAT BROUGHT THIS ON--
--IT WAS MY NEED TO **SATE** THE PAIN.
TO TAKE ITS POWER AWAY.

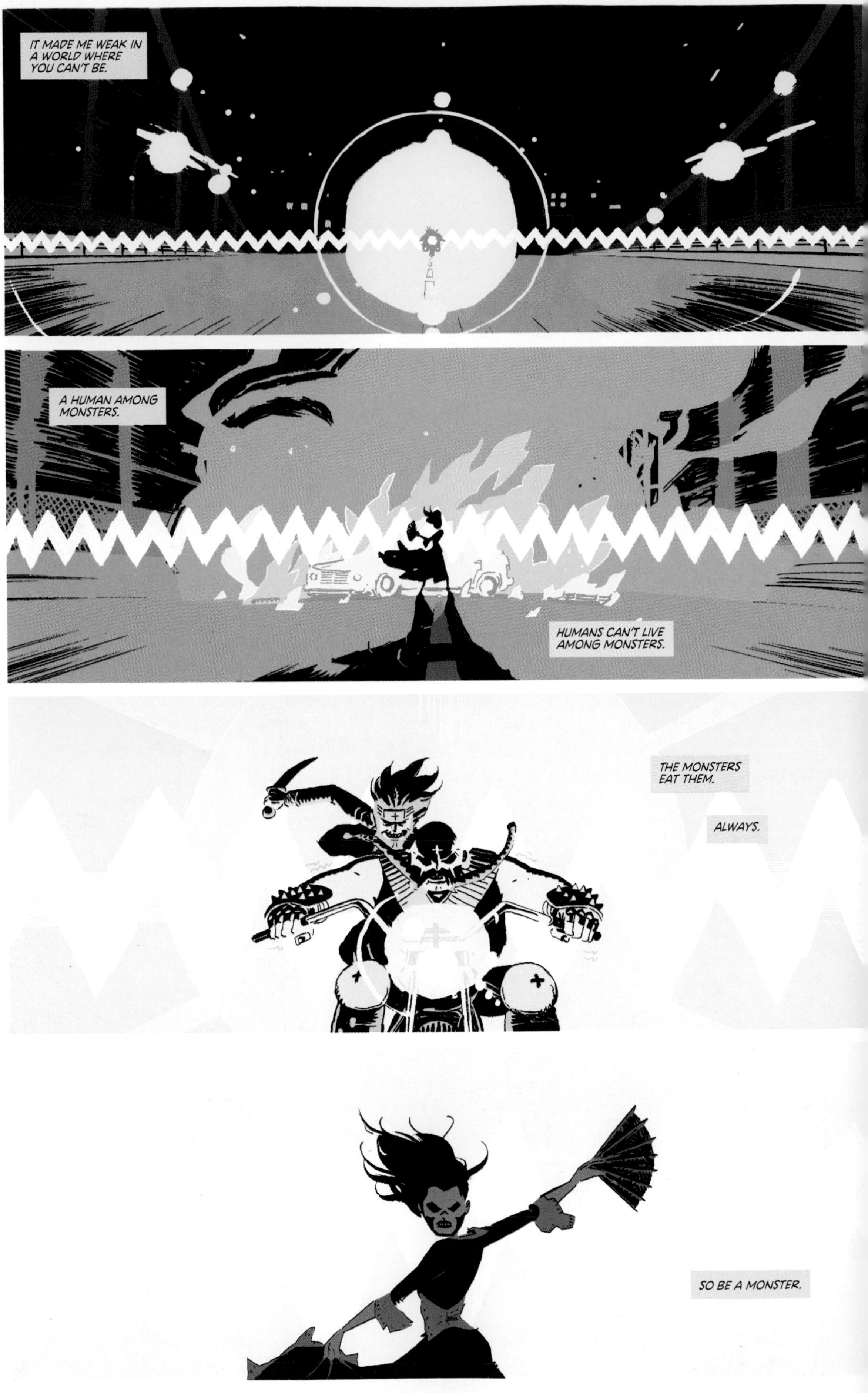
IT MADE ME WEAK IN A WORLD WHERE YOU CAN'T BE.
A HUMAN AMONG MONSTERS.
HUMANS CAN'T LIVE AMONG MONSTERS.
THE MONSTERS EAT THEM.
ALWAYS.
SO BE A MONSTER.

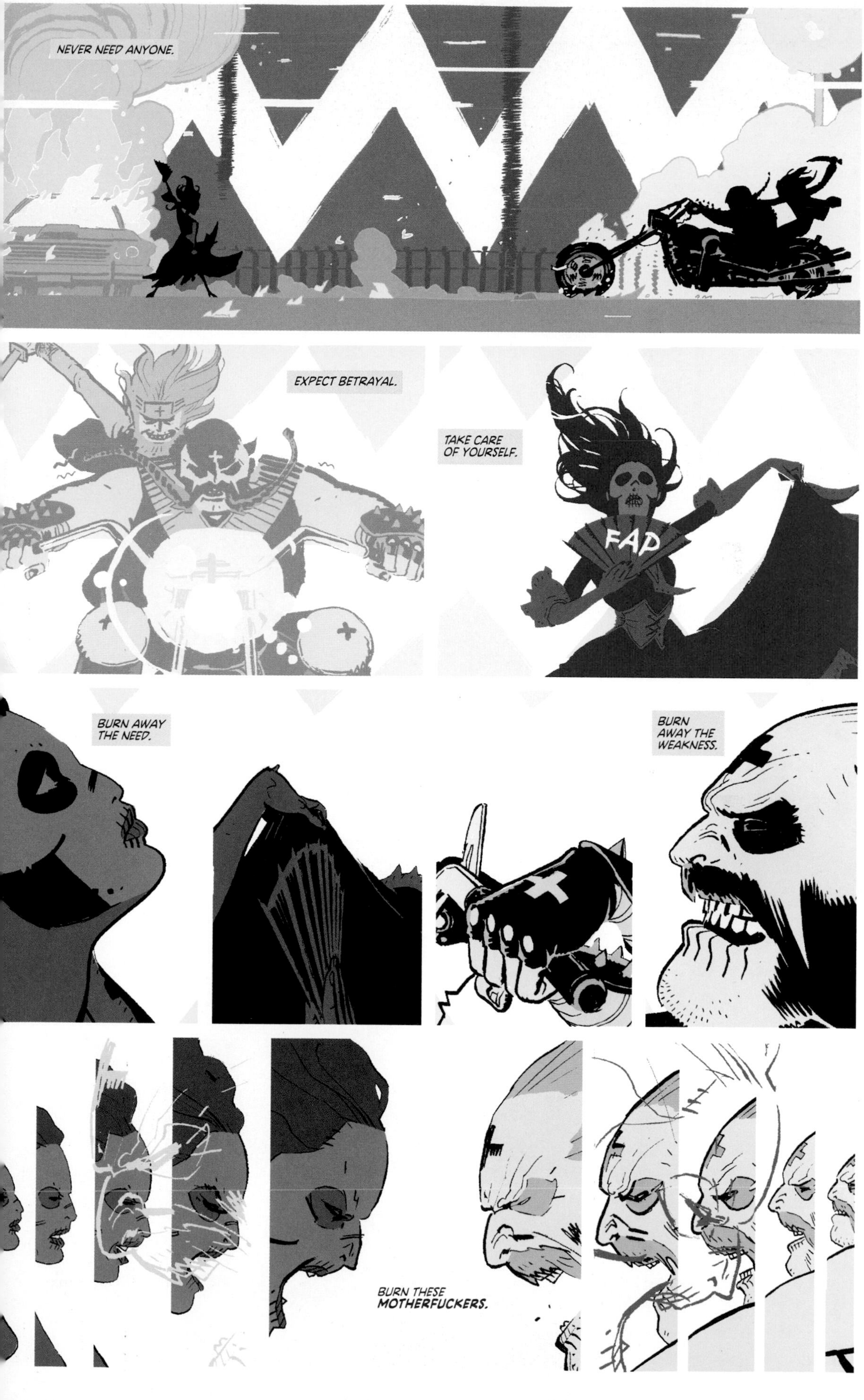
NEVER NEED ANYONE.
EXPECT BETRAYAL.
TAKE CARE OF YOURSELF.
FAP
BURN AWAY THE NEED.
BURN AWAY THE WEAKNESS.
BURN THESE MOTHERFUCKERS.

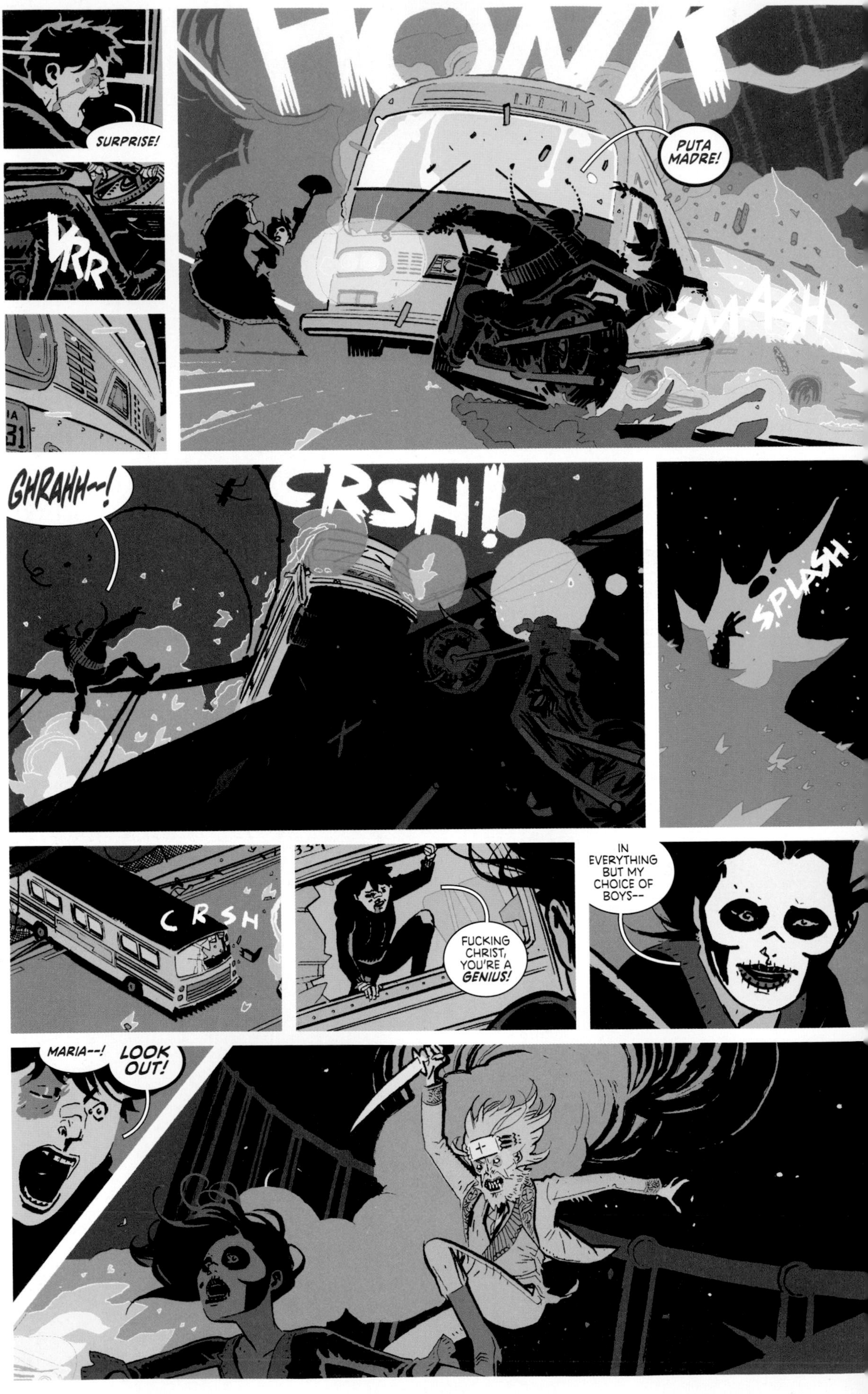
HONK
SURPRISE!
VRR
PUTA MADRE!
SMASH
GHRAHH--!
CRSH!
SPLASH
CRSH
FUCKING CHRIST, YOU'RE A GENIUS!
IN EVERYTHING BUT MY CHOICE OF BOYS--
MARIA--!
LOOK OUT!

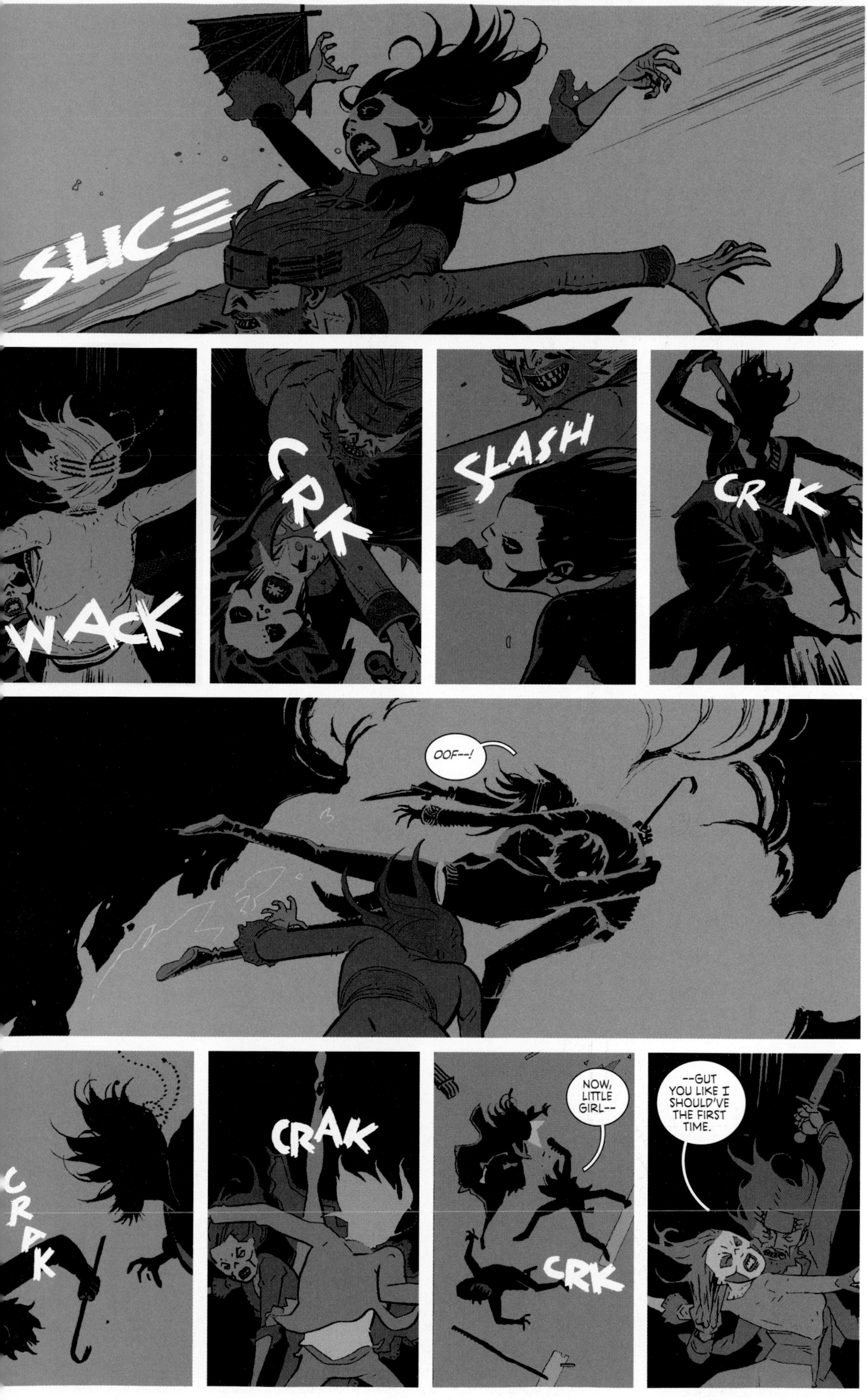
SLICE
WACK
CRK
SLASH
CR K
OOF--!
CRAK
CRAK
NOW, LITTLE GIRL--
CRK
--GUT YOU LIKE I SHOULD'VE THE FIRST TIME.

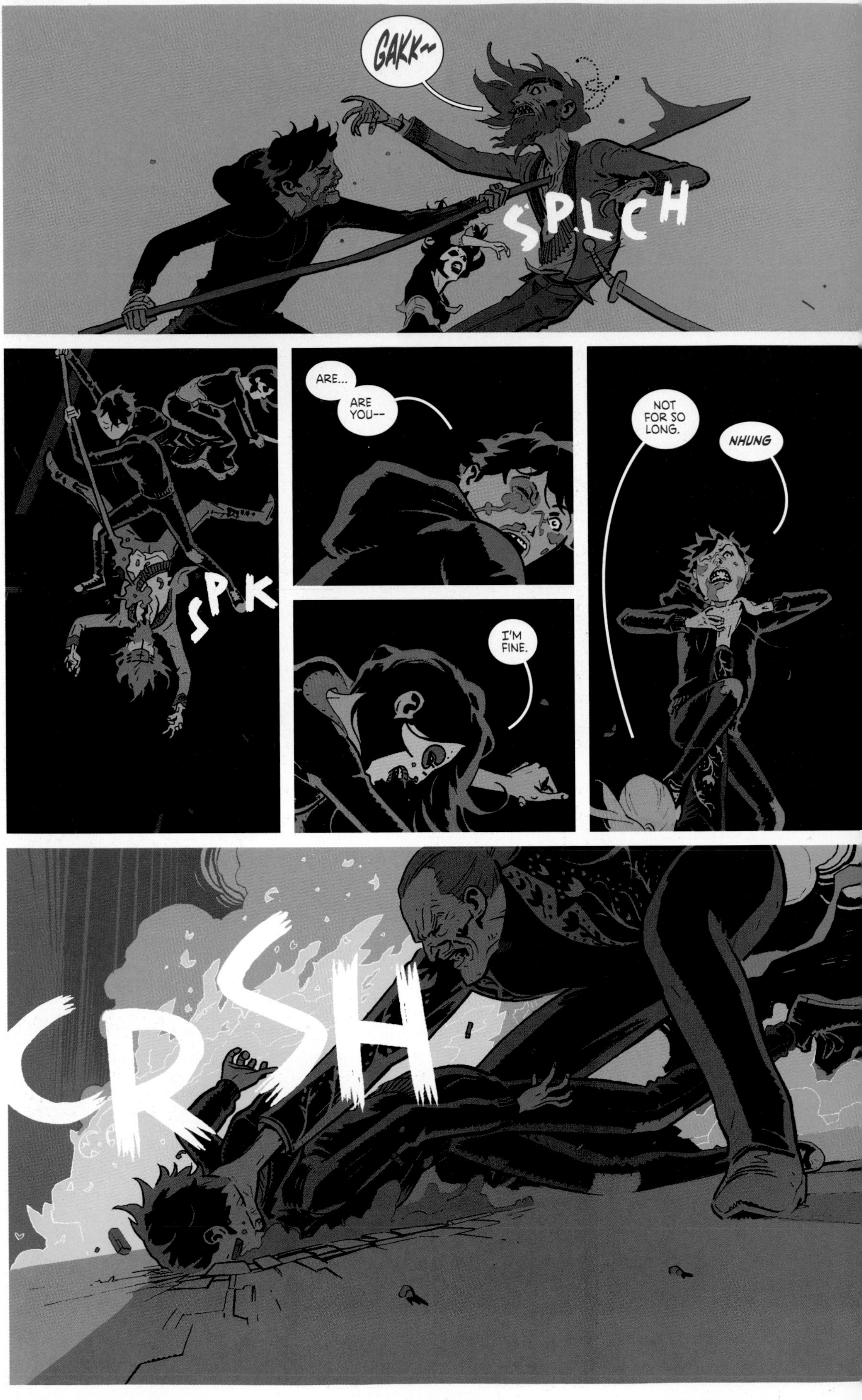
GAKK--
SPLCH
SPK
ARE...
ARE YOU--
I'M FINE.
NOT FOR SO LONG.
NHUNG
CRSH

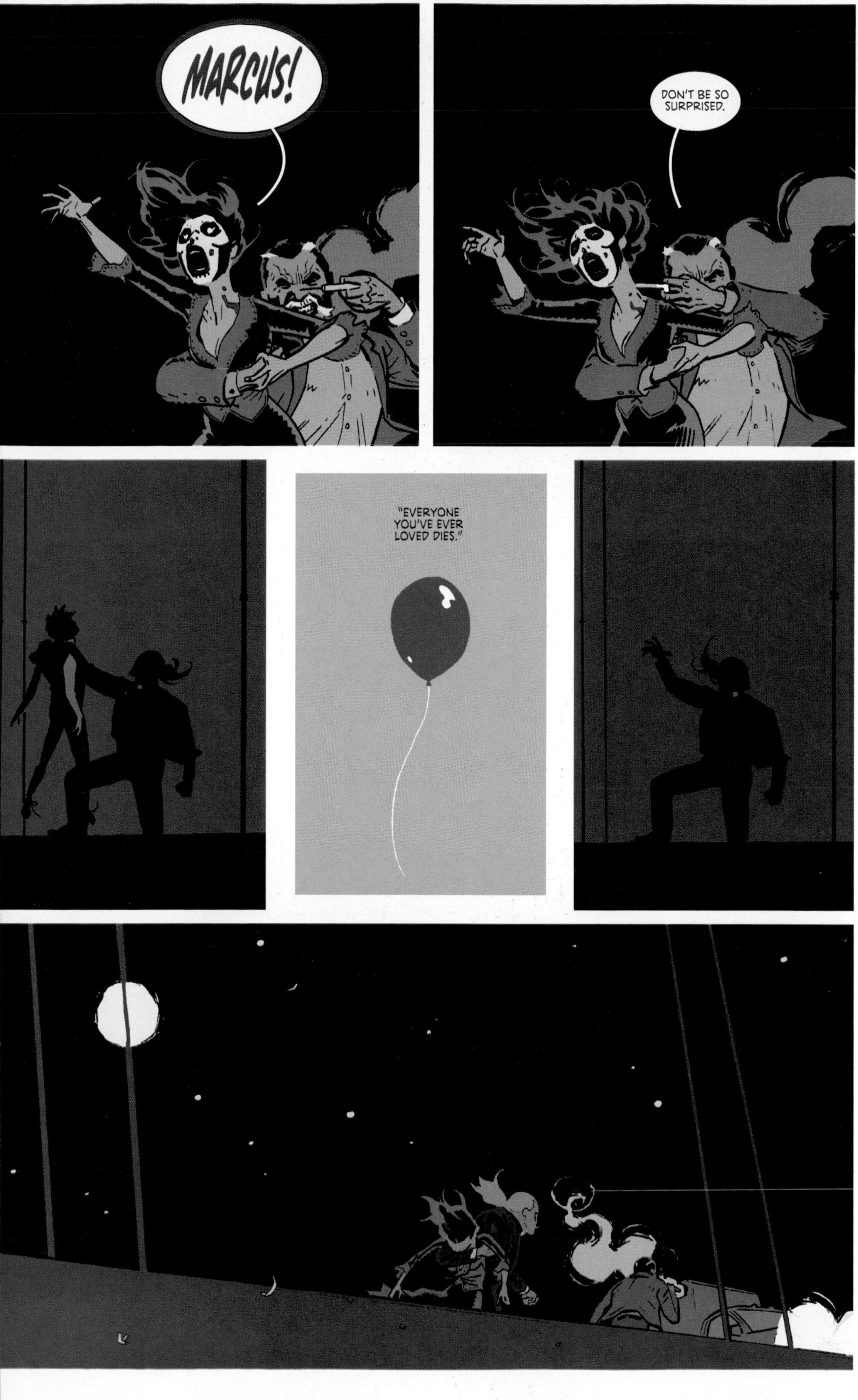
MARCUS!
DON'T BE SO SURPRISED.
"EVERYONE YOU'VE EVER LOVED DIES."

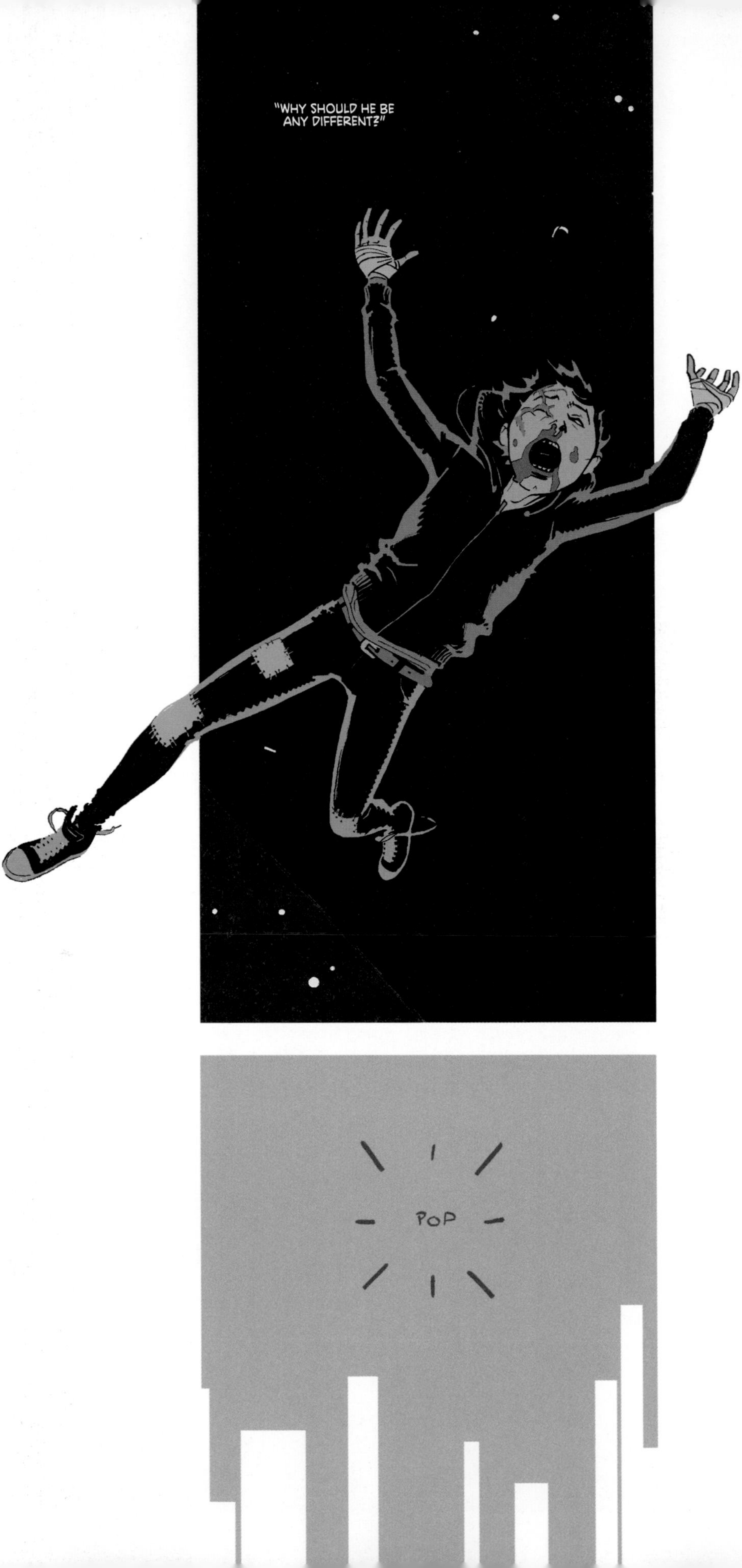
"WHY SHOULD HE BE ANY DIFFERENT?"
POP

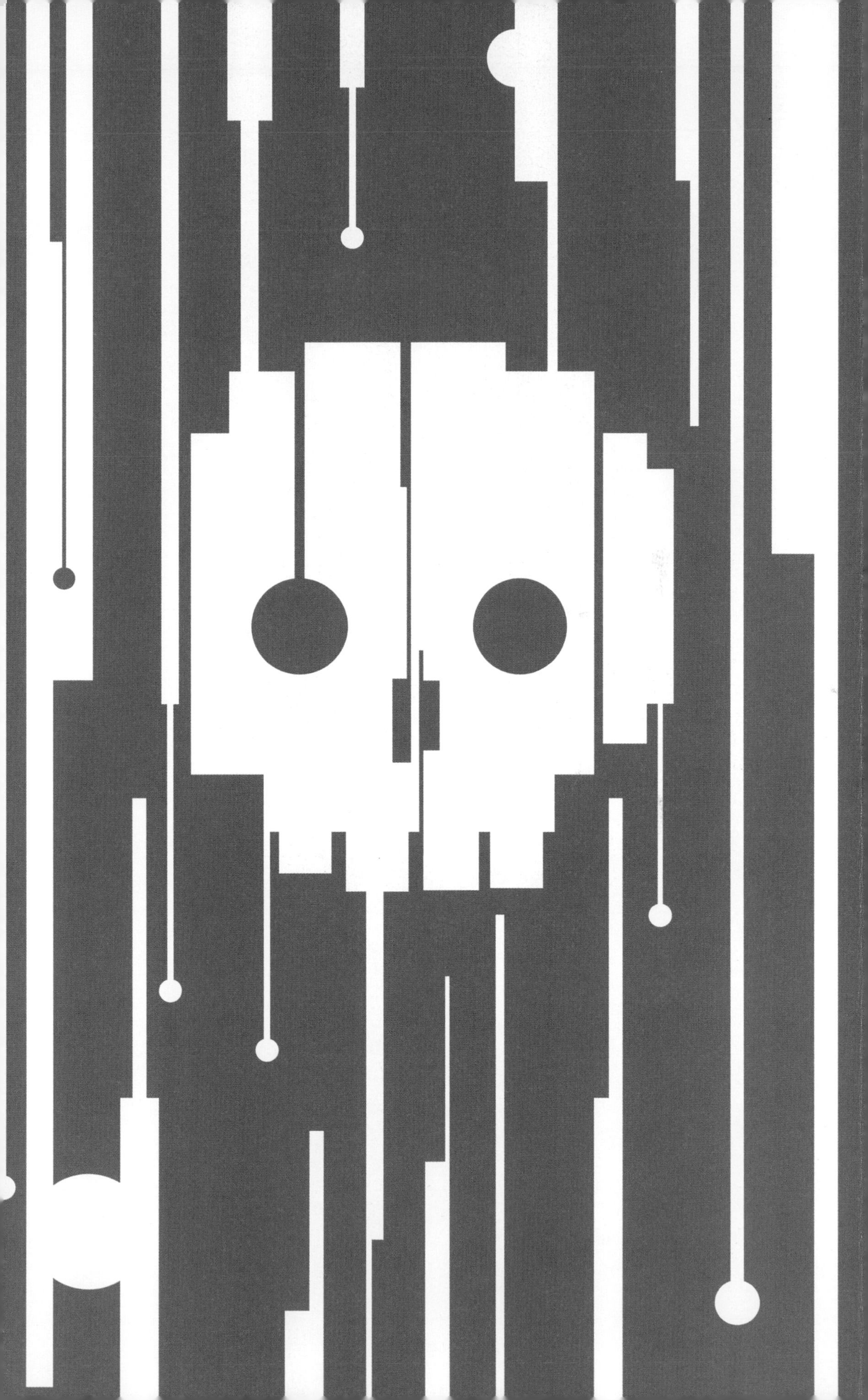

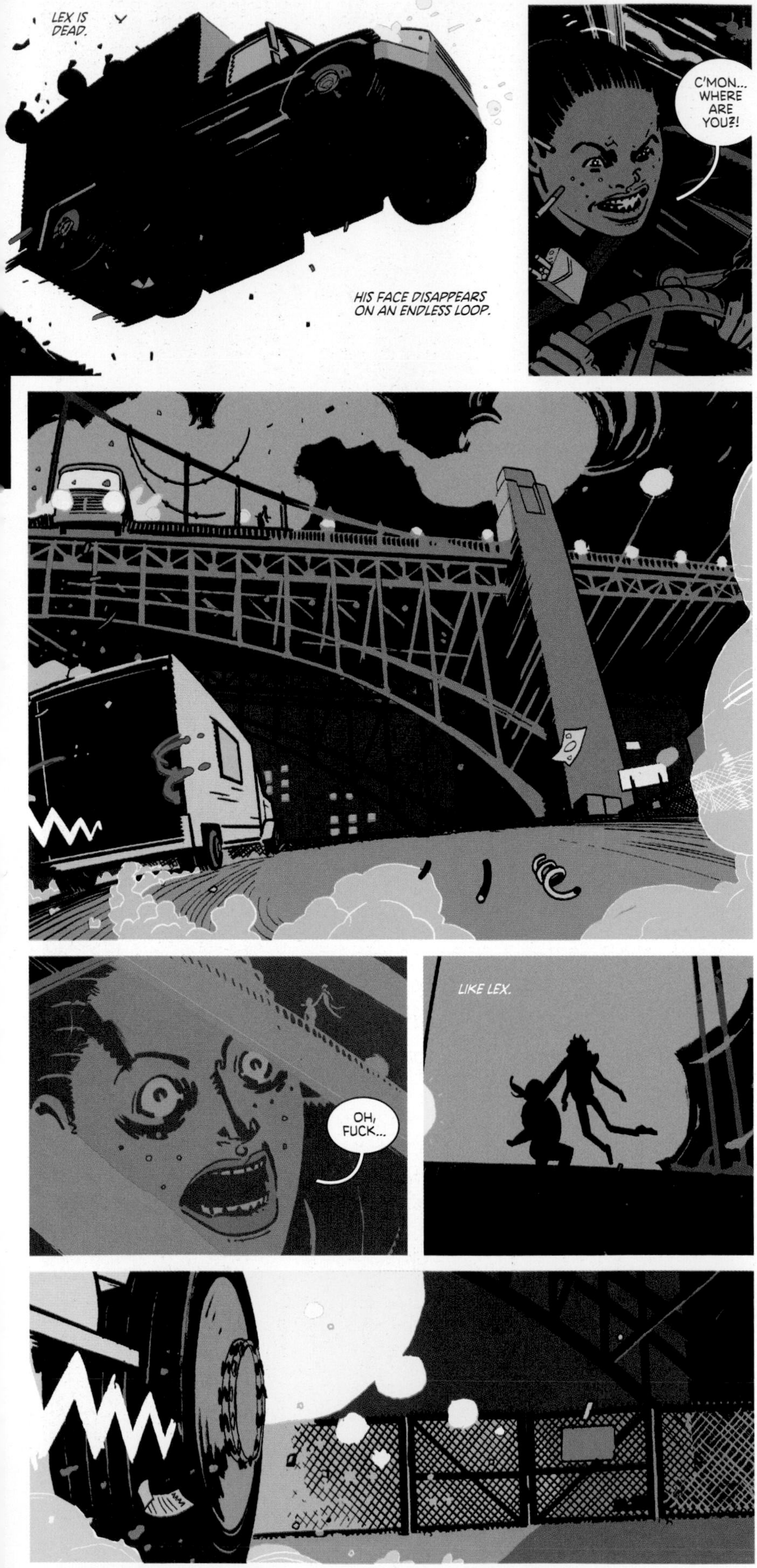
LEX IS DEAD.
HIS FACE DISAPPEARS ON AN ENDLESS LOOP.
C'MON... WHERE ARE YOU?!
OH, FUCK...
LIKE LEX.

HE DIES OVER AND OVER.

BECAUSE I FUCKED UP.

BECAUSE THOSE CARTEL FUCKERS GHOSTED ME.

IF I CAN'T FIND THEM--IF I CAN'T HELP MY FRIENDS--MARCUS AND MARIA ARE NEXT.

SHADOWS MOVING--FIGHTING--

I'M TOO LATE.

DIDN'T FIND THEM IN TIME.

FAILED AGAIN.

IT SHOULD HAVE BEEN ME.

DEAD IN SOME ALLEY.

MY FACE GONE.

AND IF LEX HADN'T TURNED THAT CORNER--

--IT WOULD HAVE BEEN.

IT **SHOULD** HAVE BEEN.

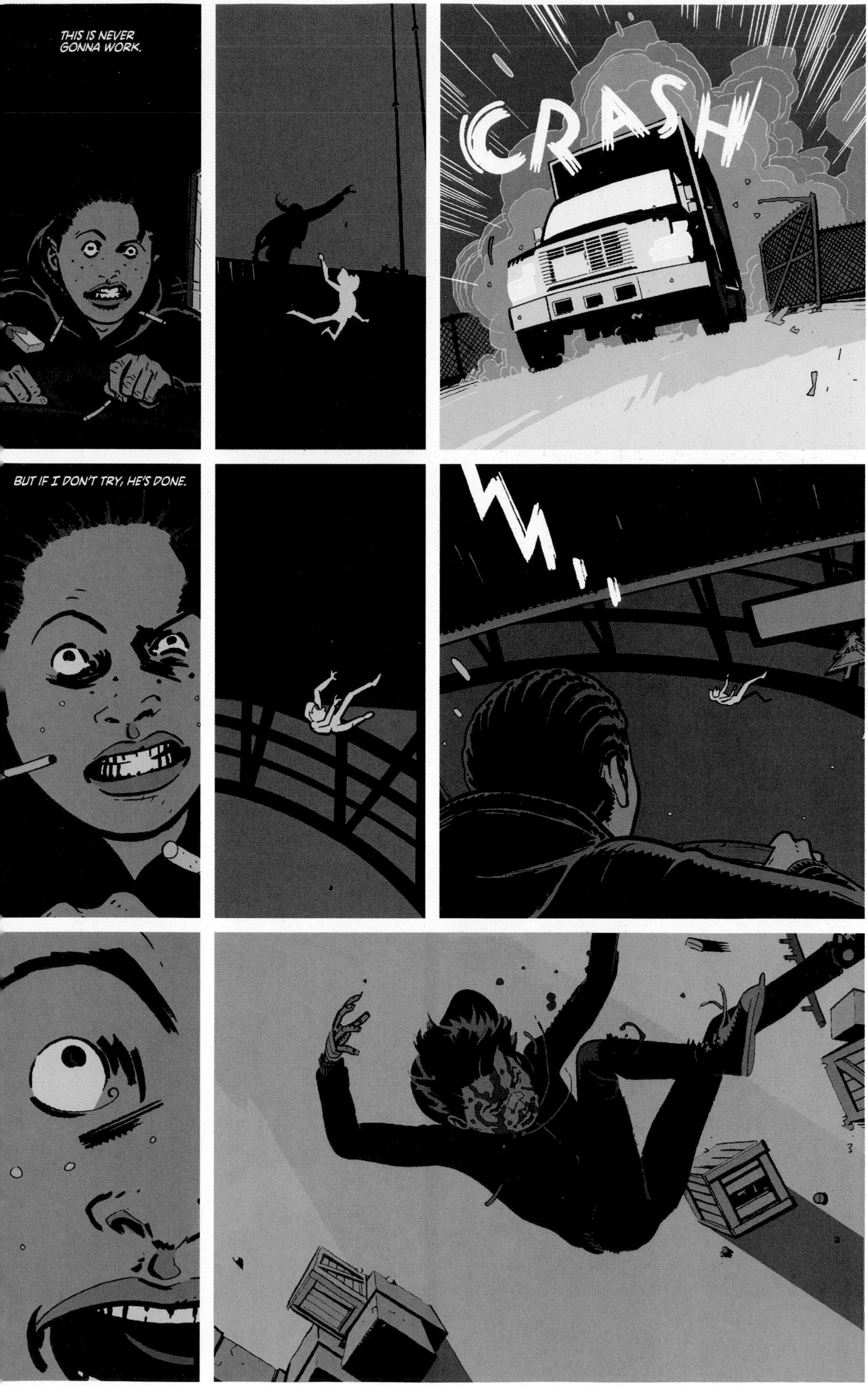
THIS IS NEVER GONNA WORK.
CRASH
BUT IF I DON'T TRY, HE'S DONE.

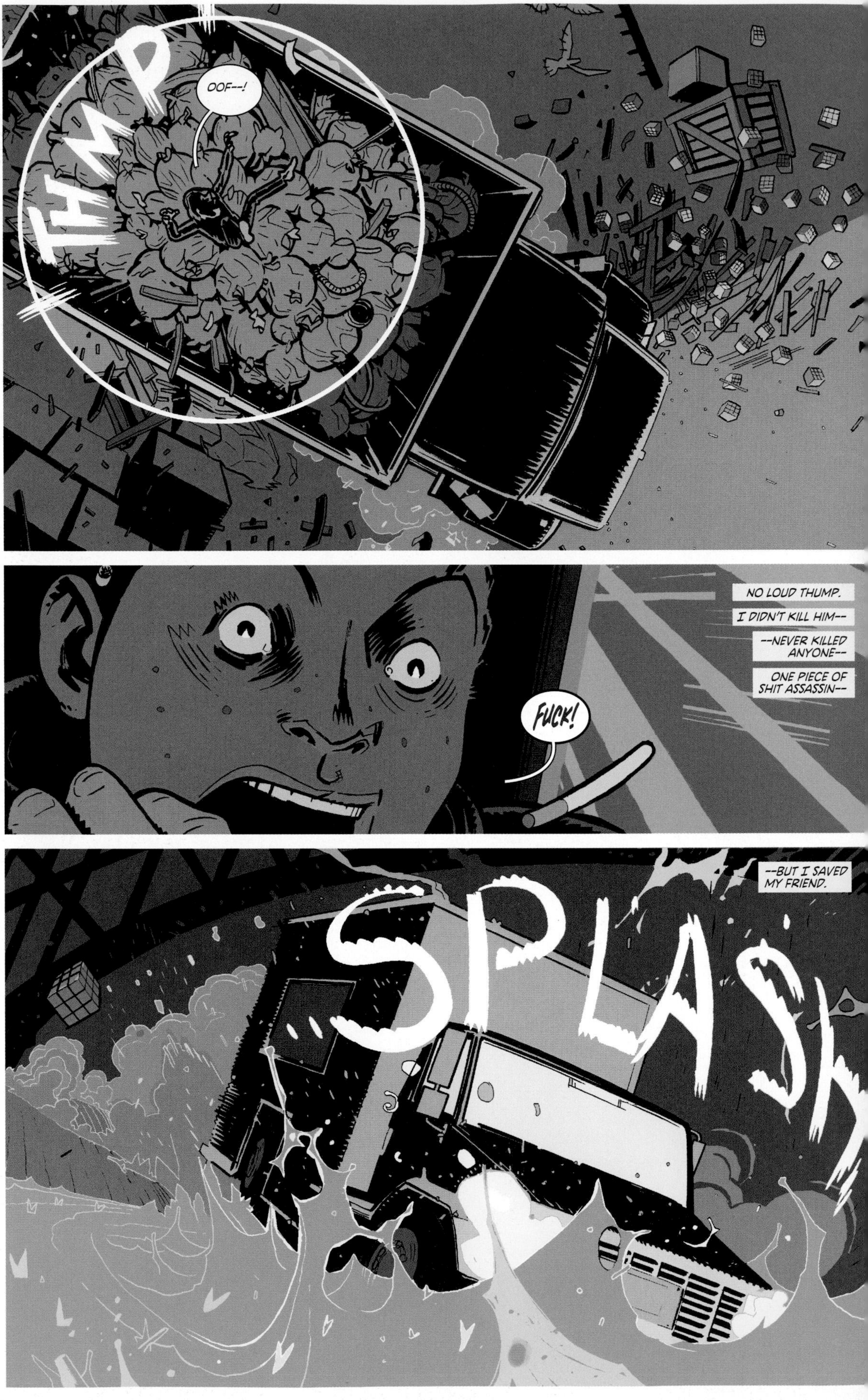
THMP
OOF--!
NO LOUD THUMP.
I DIDN'T KILL HIM--
--NEVER KILLED ANYONE--
ONE PIECE OF SHIT ASSASSIN--
FUCK!
--BUT I SAVED MY FRIEND.
SPLASH

WE ALL MAKE MISTAKES IN LIFE, MARIA.

IT'S NOT A QUESTION OF *IF*, ONLY *WHEN*.

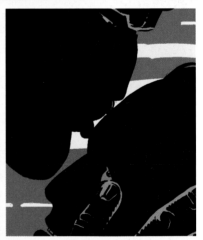

SO THE QUESTION BECOMES THE DEGREE OF THE *PUNISHMENT* SHOULD WE BE CAUGHT.

AND YOU, MY DEAR, HAVE BEEN CAUGHT.

IT WAS THE DAY I CAUGHT YOUR *THIEVING* FATHER THAT CHICO STAYED MY HAND FROM SENDING YOU TO HELL WITH THE REST OF YOUR FOUL RELATIONS.

MY *SWEET* BOY.

HE SHOWED YOU MERCY.

THIS IS HOW YOU REWARD HIM.

"AN EYE FOR AN EYE," THEY SAY.

BUT YOU HAVE TAKEN MY *SON*.

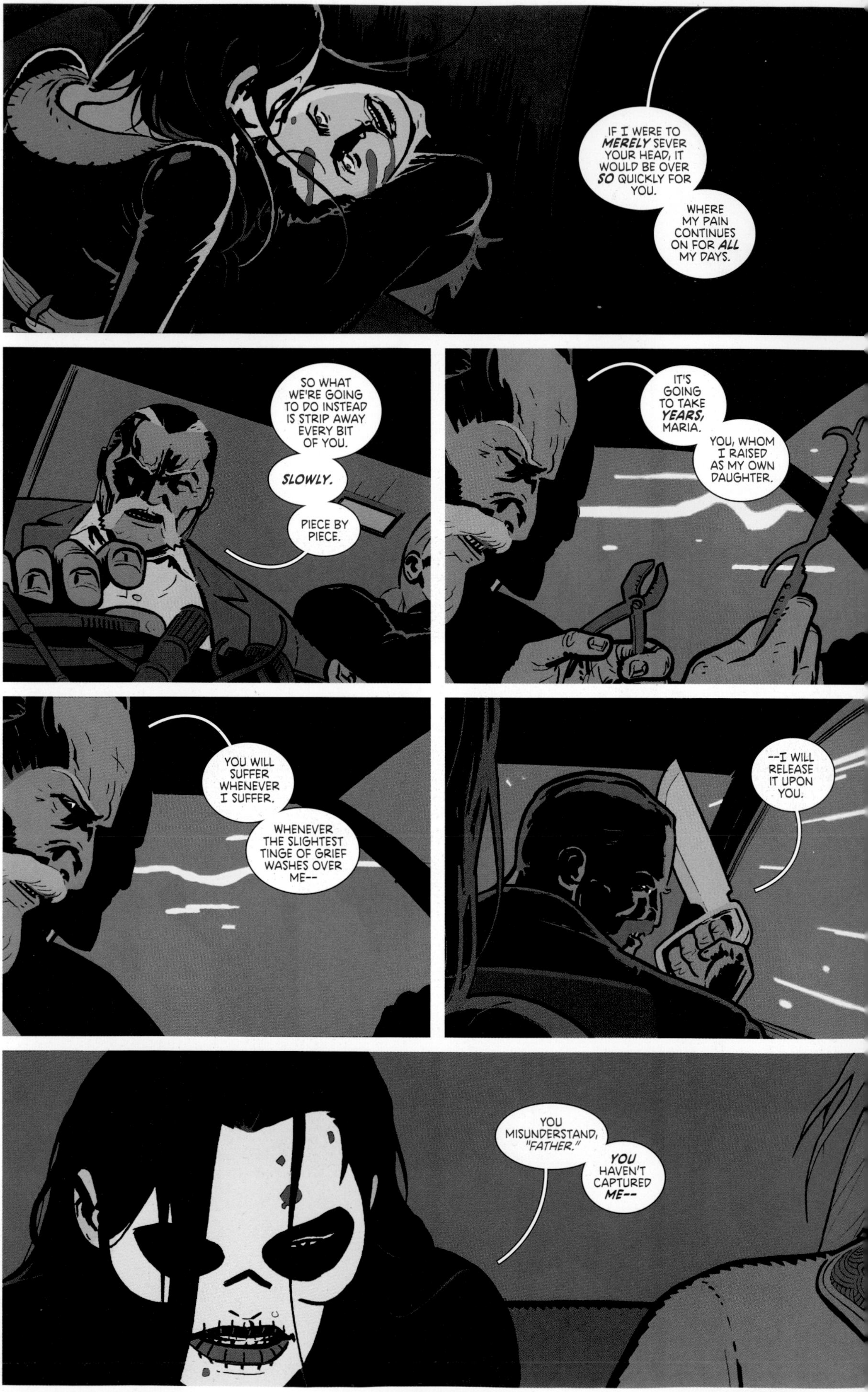
IF I WERE TO MERELY SEVER YOUR HEAD, IT WOULD BE OVER SO QUICKLY FOR YOU.
WHERE MY PAIN CONTINUES ON FOR ALL MY DAYS.
SO WHAT WE'RE GOING TO DO INSTEAD IS STRIP AWAY EVERY BIT OF YOU.
SLOWLY.
PIECE BY PIECE.
IT'S GOING TO TAKE YEARS, MARIA.
YOU, WHOM I RAISED AS MY OWN DAUGHTER.
YOU WILL SUFFER WHENEVER I SUFFER.
WHENEVER THE SLIGHTEST TINGE OF GRIEF WASHES OVER ME--
--I WILL RELEASE IT UPON YOU.
YOU MISUNDERSTAND, "FATHER."
YOU HAVEN'T CAPTURED ME--

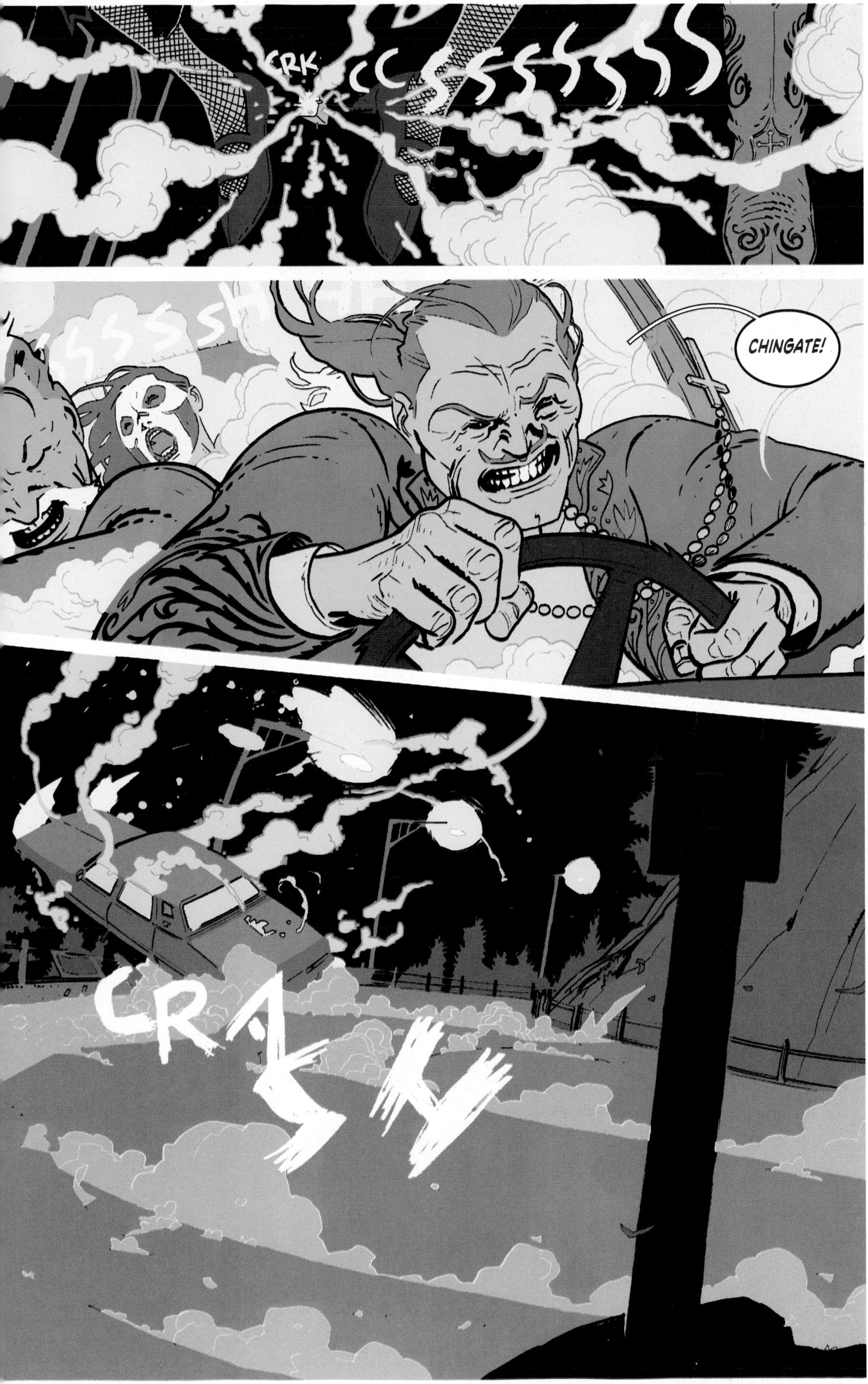
CRK
CCSSSSSSS
SSSSSSH
CHINGATE!
CRASH

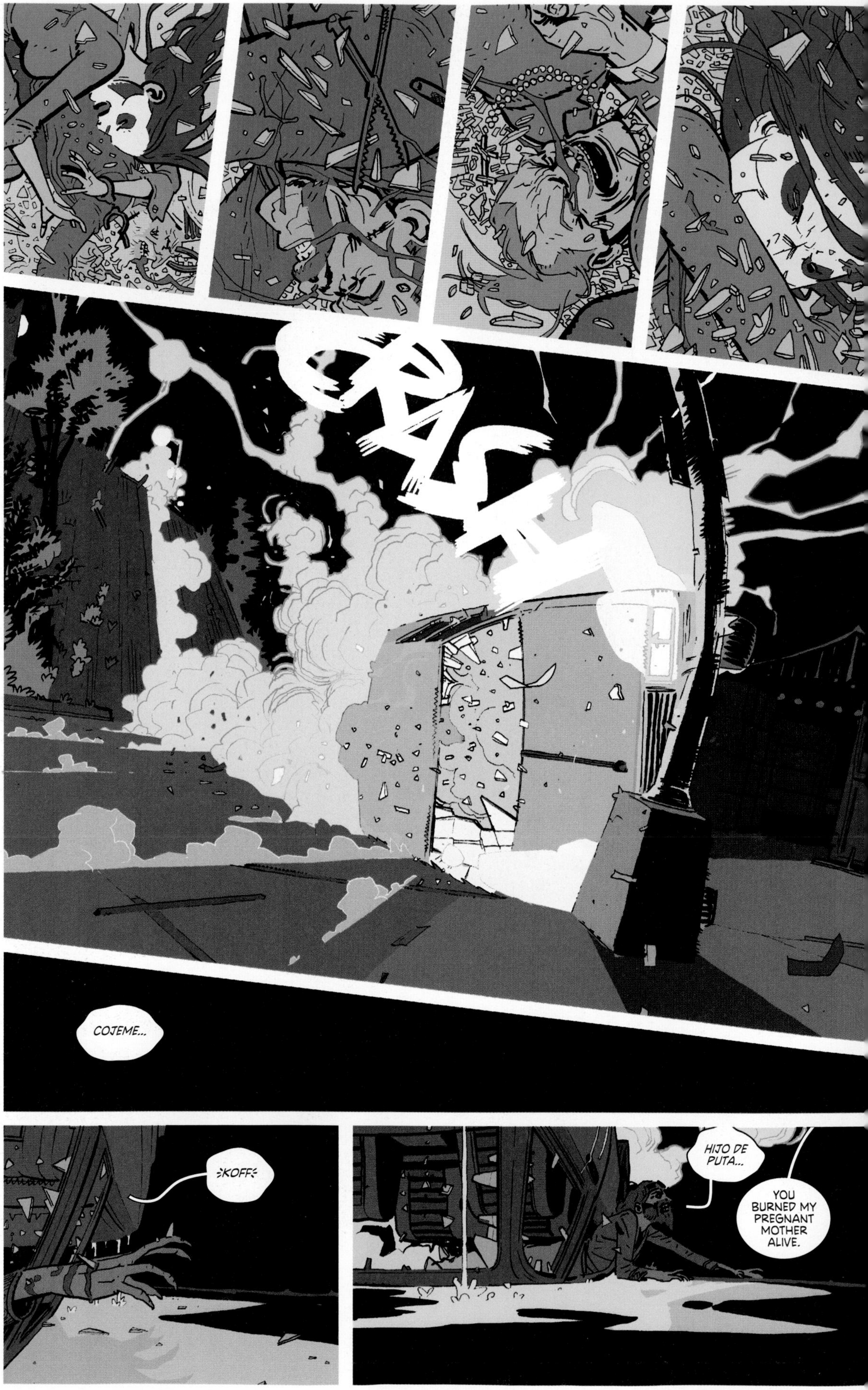
CRASH
COJEME...
KOFF
HIJO DE PUTA...
YOU BURNED MY PREGNANT MOTHER ALIVE.

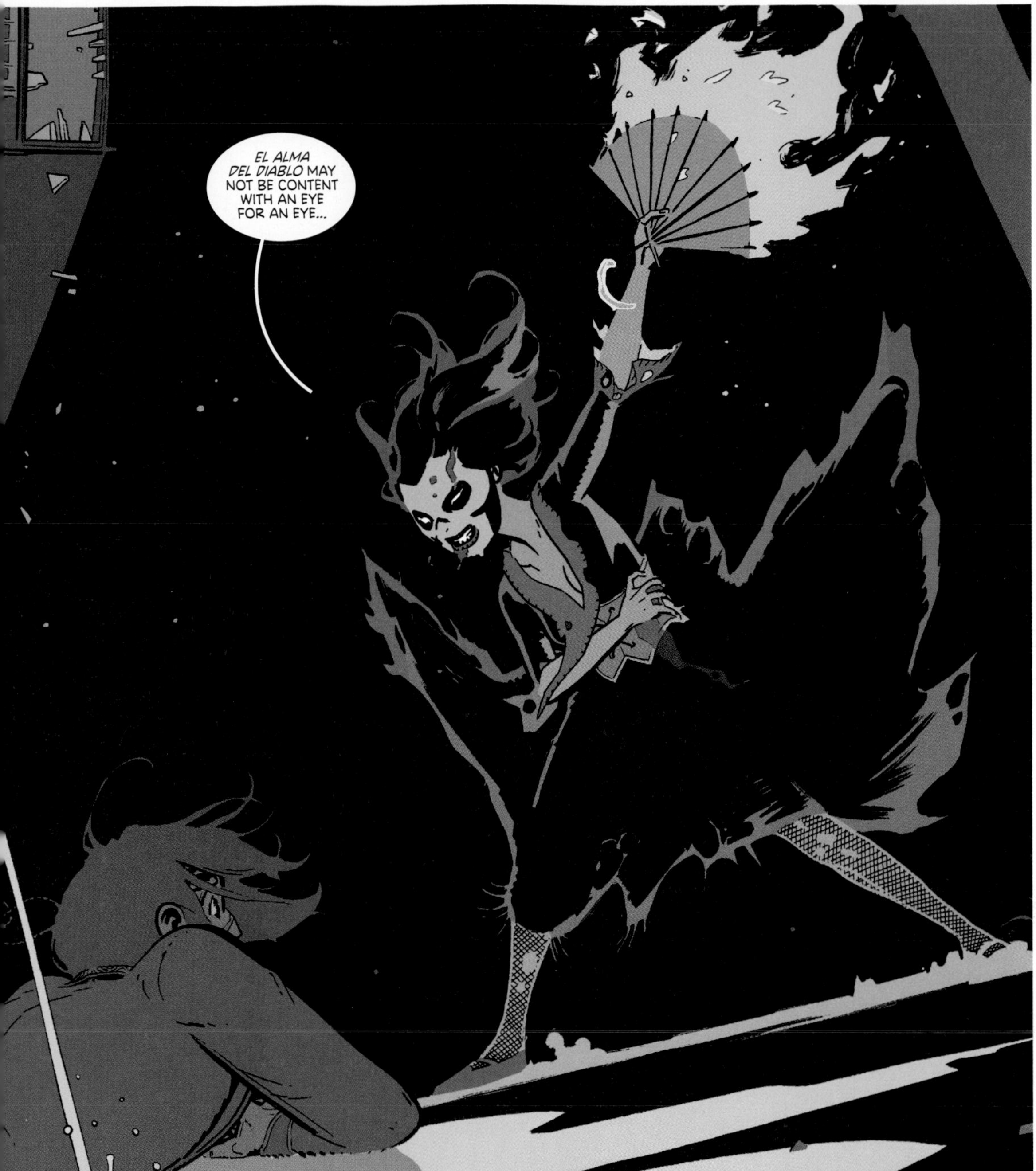
EL ALMA DEL DIABLO MAY NOT BE CONTENT WITH AN EYE FOR AN EYE...

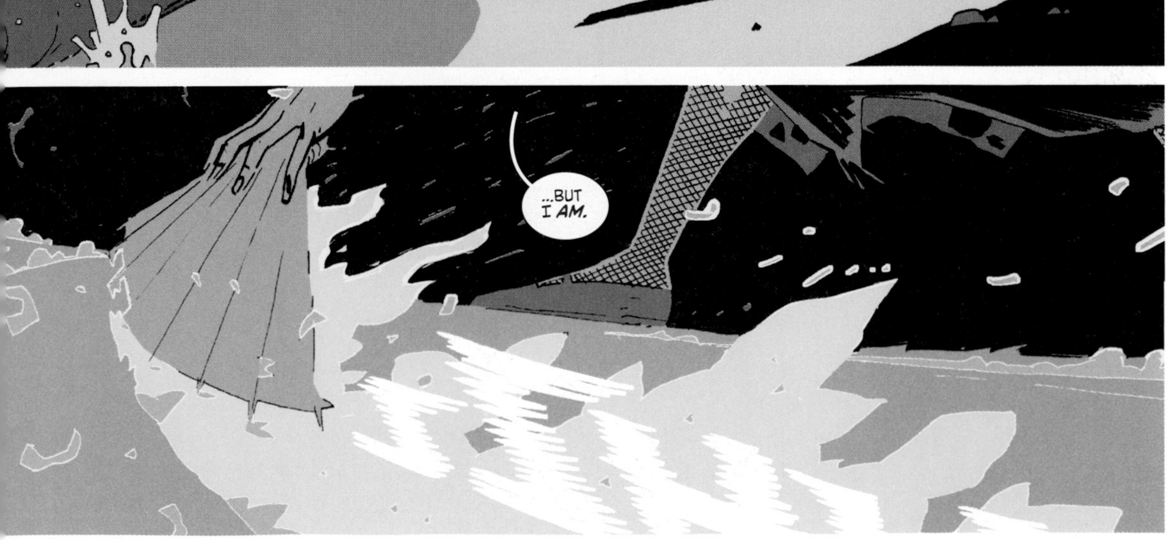
...BUT I AM.

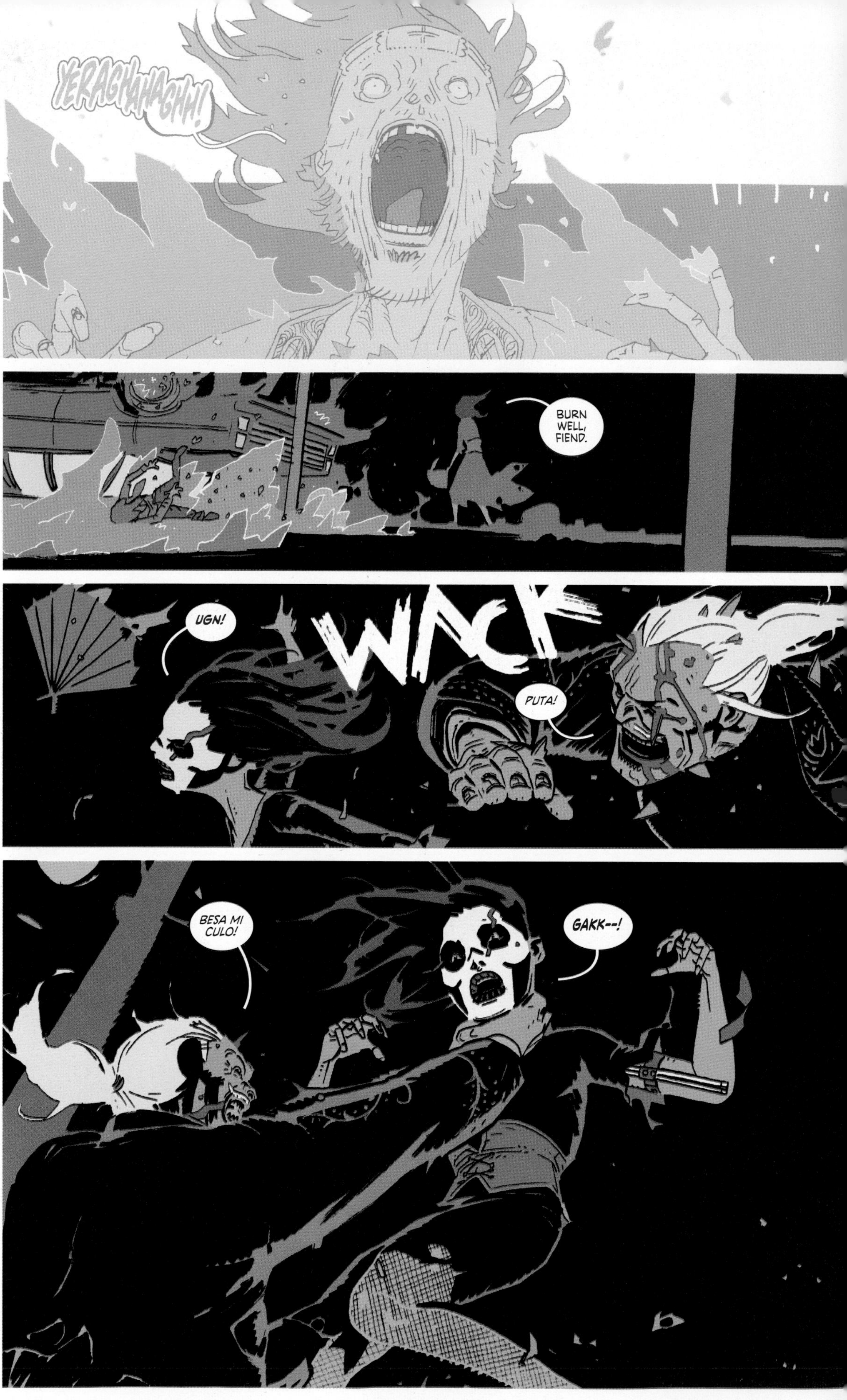
YERAGHAHAGHH!
BURN WELL, FIEND.
UGN!
WACK
PUTA!
BESA MI CULO!
GAKK--!

YOUR MOTHER DIED LIKE A DOG-- *AS WILL YOU.*

GAAK--

NO.

SHNK

MY MOTHER DIED AS A VICTIM.

IN HER KITCHEN.

SHLK

SHLK

SPSCH

COOKING POZOLE FOR HER FAMILY.

FIR

FIR

HURK--!

MURDERED BY GUTLESS COWARDS.

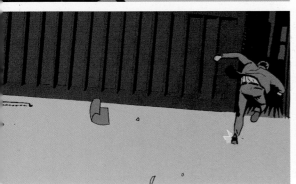

BECAUSE A DESPERATE FATHER STOLE TO FEED HIS FAMILY!

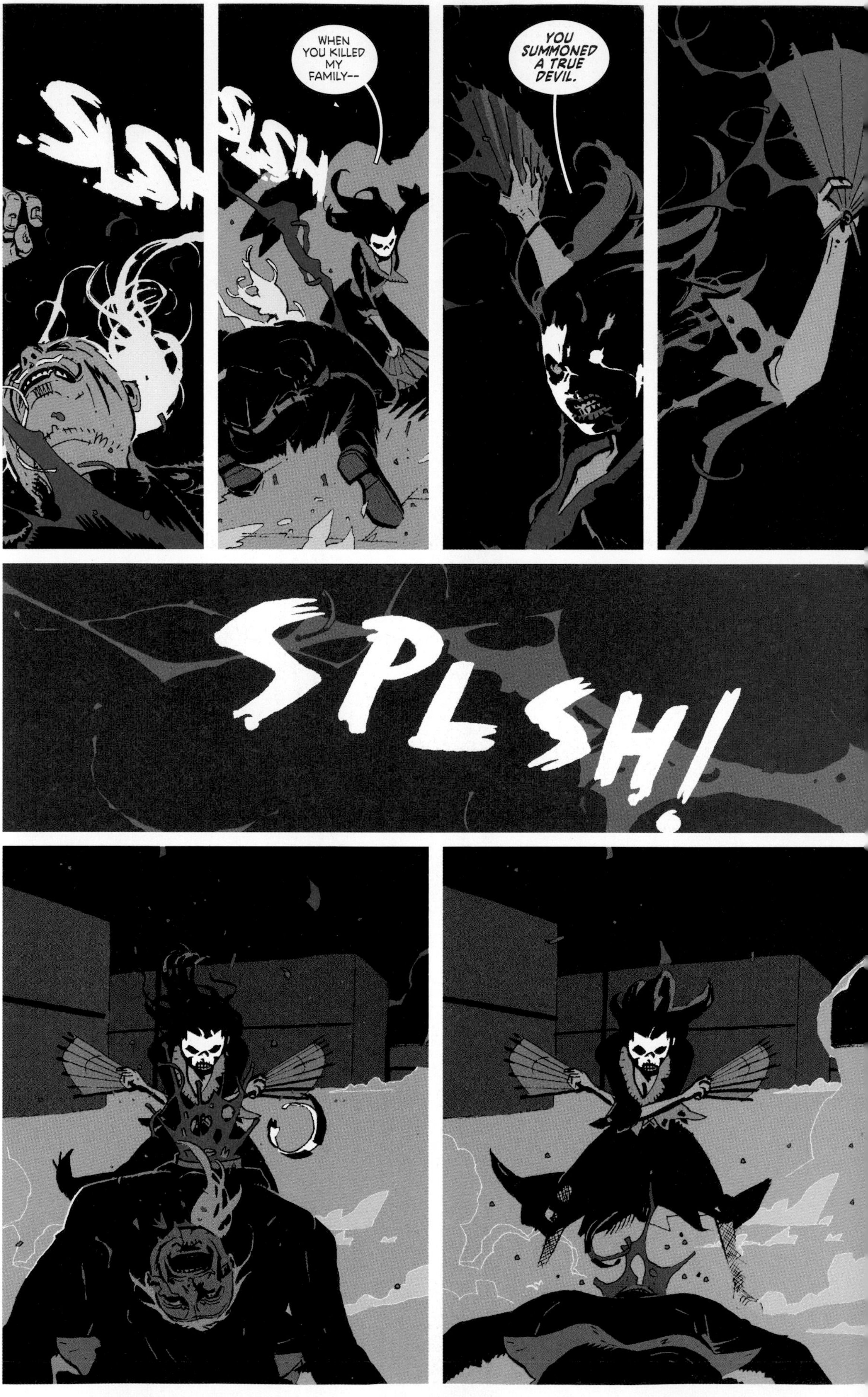
SPLSH
WHEN YOU KILLED MY FAMILY--
YOU SUMMONED A TRUE DEVIL.
SPLSH!

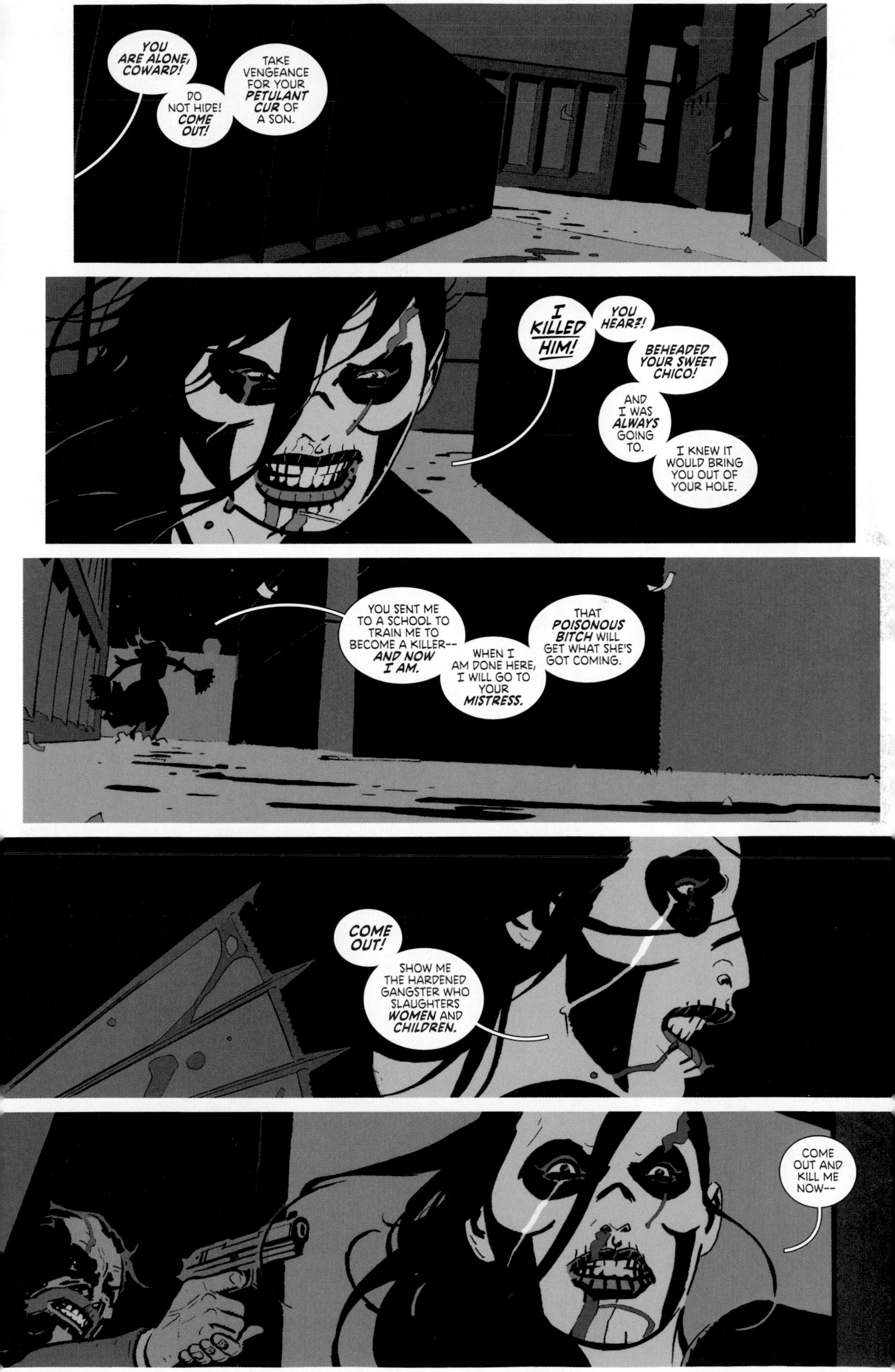
YOU ARE ALONE, COWARD!
DO NOT HIDE! COME OUT!
TAKE VENGEANCE FOR YOUR PETULANT CUR OF A SON.
I KILLED HIM!
YOU HEAR?!
BEHEADED YOUR SWEET CHICO!
AND I WAS ALWAYS GOING TO.
I KNEW IT WOULD BRING YOU OUT OF YOUR HOLE.
YOU SENT ME TO A SCHOOL TO TRAIN ME TO BECOME A KILLER-- AND NOW I AM.
WHEN I AM DONE HERE, I WILL GO TO YOUR MISTRESS.
THAT POISONOUS BITCH WILL GET WHAT SHE'S GOT COMING.
COME OUT!
SHOW ME THE HARDENED GANGSTER WHO SLAUGHTERS WOMEN AND CHILDREN.
COME OUT AND KILL ME NOW--

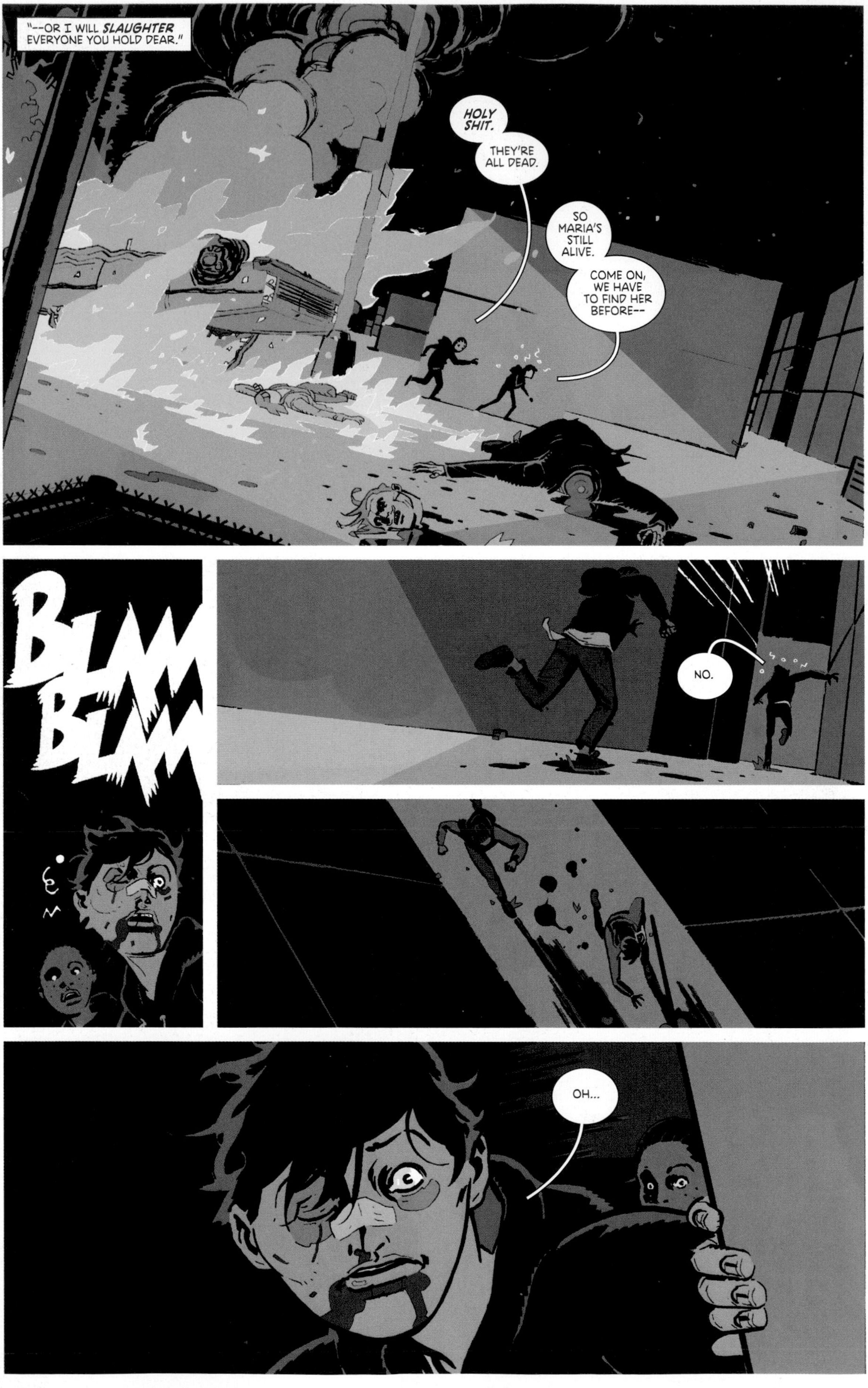
"--OR I WILL SLAUGHTER EVERYONE YOU HOLD DEAR."
HOLY SHIT.
THEY'RE ALL DEAD.
SO MARIA'S STILL ALIVE.
COME ON, WE HAVE TO FIND HER BEFORE--
BLAM BLAM
NO.
OH...

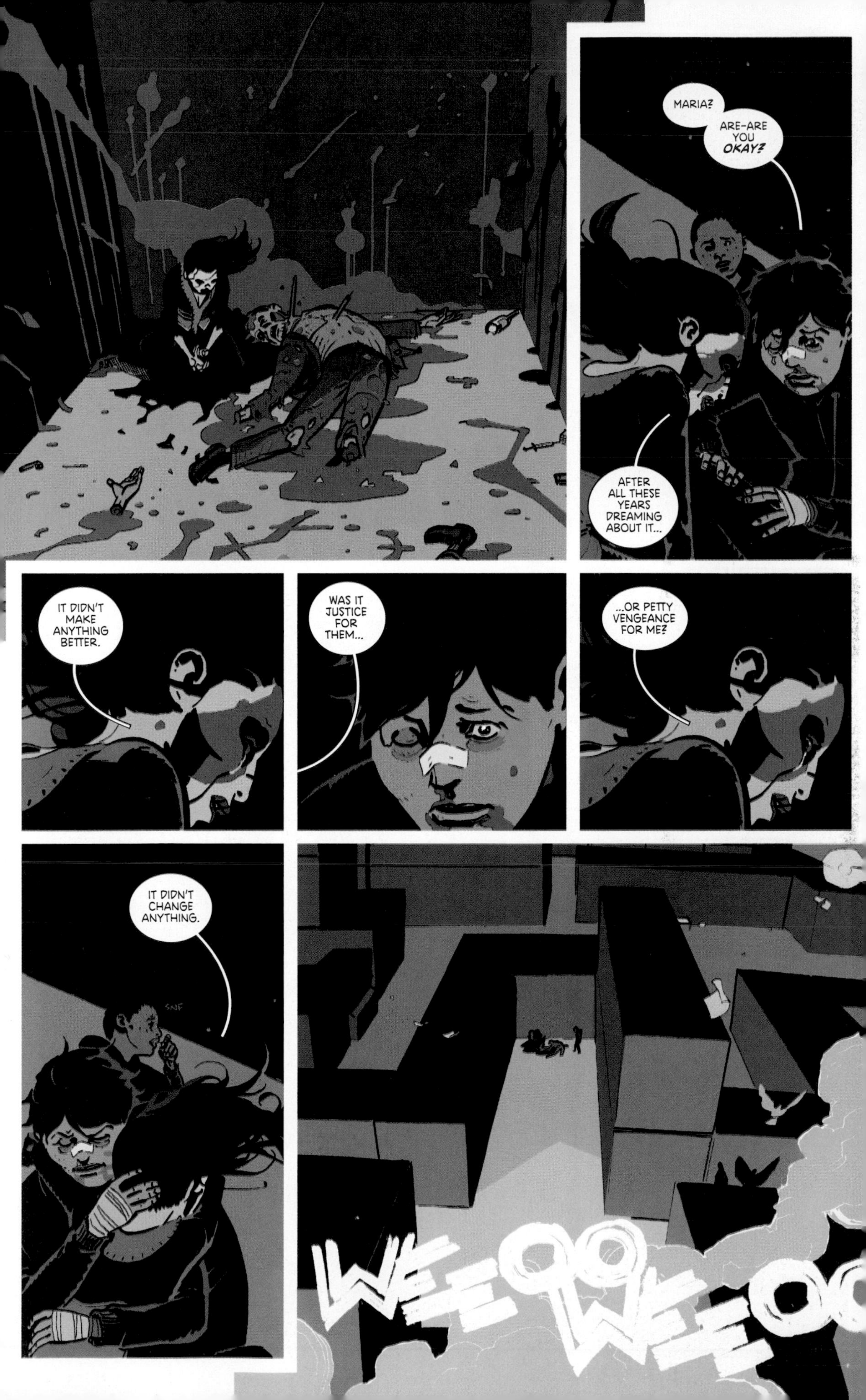
MARIA?
ARE-ARE YOU OKAY?
AFTER ALL THESE YEARS DREAMING ABOUT IT...
IT DIDN'T MAKE ANYTHING BETTER.
WAS IT JUSTICE FOR THEM...
...OR PETTY VENGEANCE FOR ME?
IT DIDN'T CHANGE ANYTHING.
SNF
WEEOO WEEOO

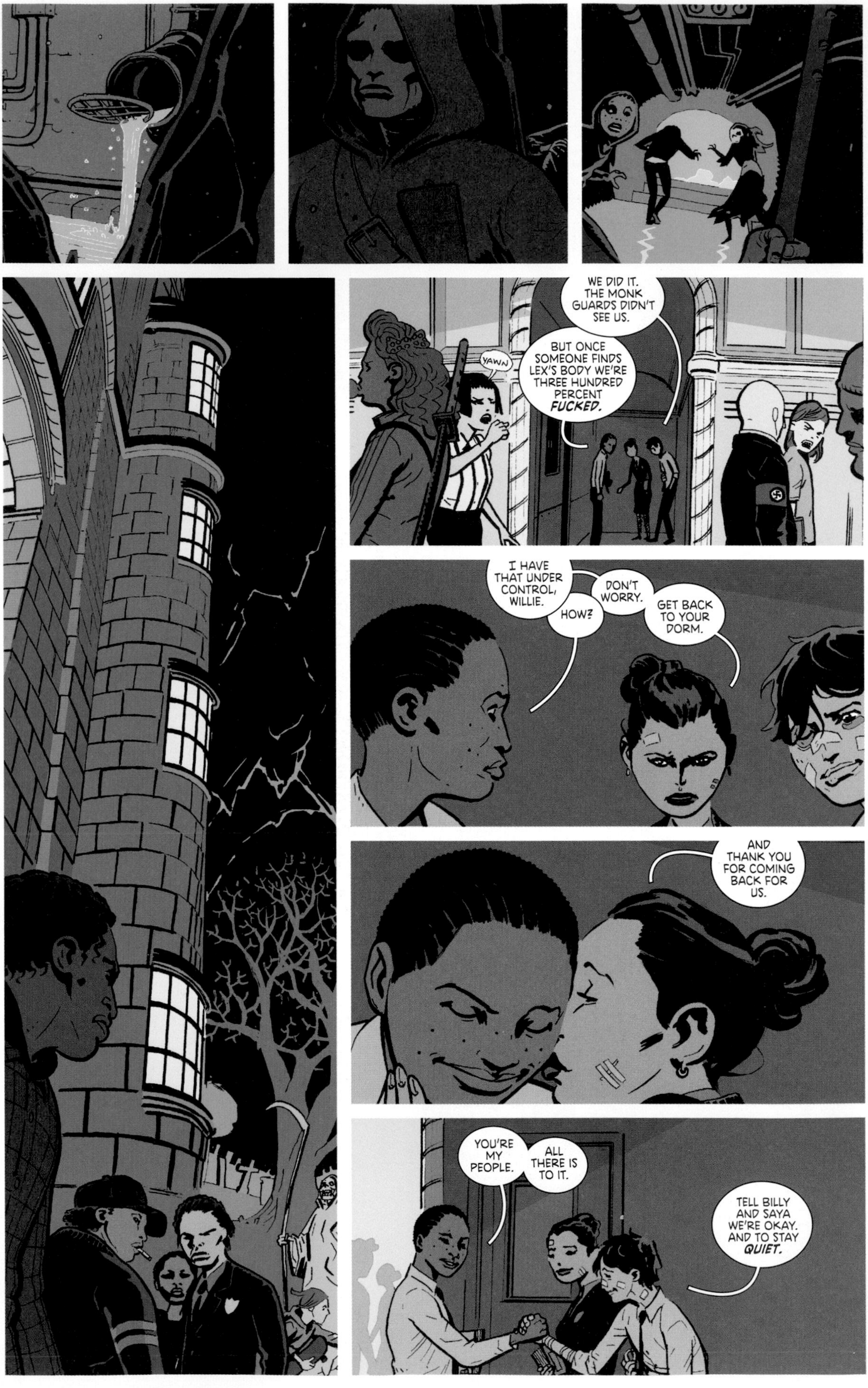
WE DID IT. THE MONK GUARDS DIDN'T SEE US.
YAWN
BUT ONCE SOMEONE FINDS LEX'S BODY WE'RE THREE HUNDRED PERCENT FUCKED.
I HAVE THAT UNDER CONTROL, WILLIE.
HOW?
DON'T WORRY.
GET BACK TO YOUR DORM.
AND THANK YOU FOR COMING BACK FOR US.
YOU'RE MY PEOPLE.
ALL THERE IS TO IT.
TELL BILLY AND SAYA WE'RE OKAY. AND TO STAY QUIET.

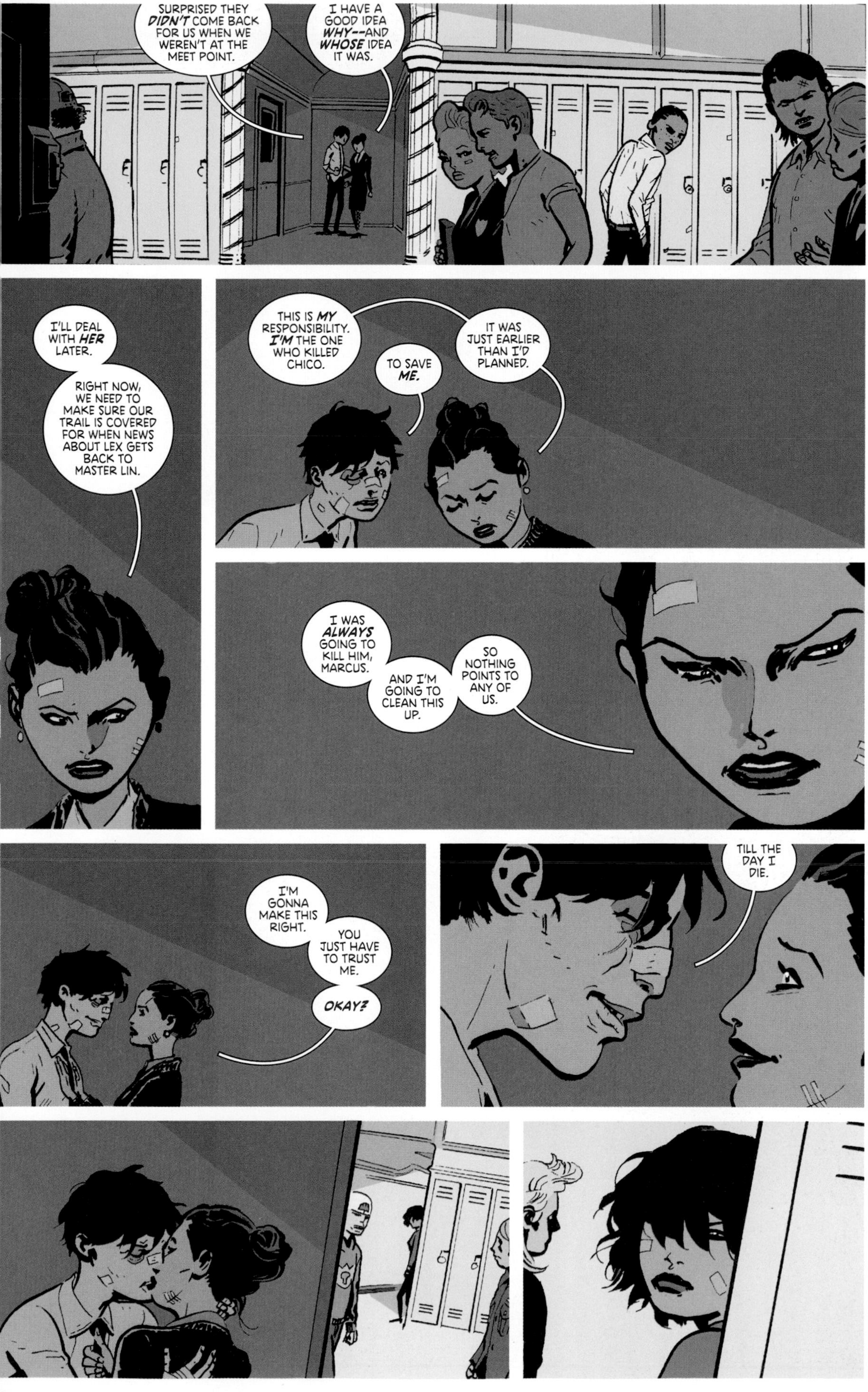
SURPRISED THEY DIDN'T COME BACK FOR US WHEN WE WEREN'T AT THE MEET POINT.
I HAVE A GOOD IDEA WHY--AND WHOSE IDEA IT WAS.
I'LL DEAL WITH HER LATER.
RIGHT NOW, WE NEED TO MAKE SURE OUR TRAIL IS COVERED FOR WHEN NEWS ABOUT LEX GETS BACK TO MASTER LIN.
THIS IS MY RESPONSIBILITY. I'M THE ONE WHO KILLED CHICO.
TO SAVE ME.
IT WAS JUST EARLIER THAN I'D PLANNED.
I WAS ALWAYS GOING TO KILL HIM, MARCUS.
AND I'M GOING TO CLEAN THIS UP.
SO NOTHING POINTS TO ANY OF US.
I'M GONNA MAKE THIS RIGHT.
YOU JUST HAVE TO TRUST ME.
OKAY?
TILL THE DAY I DIE.

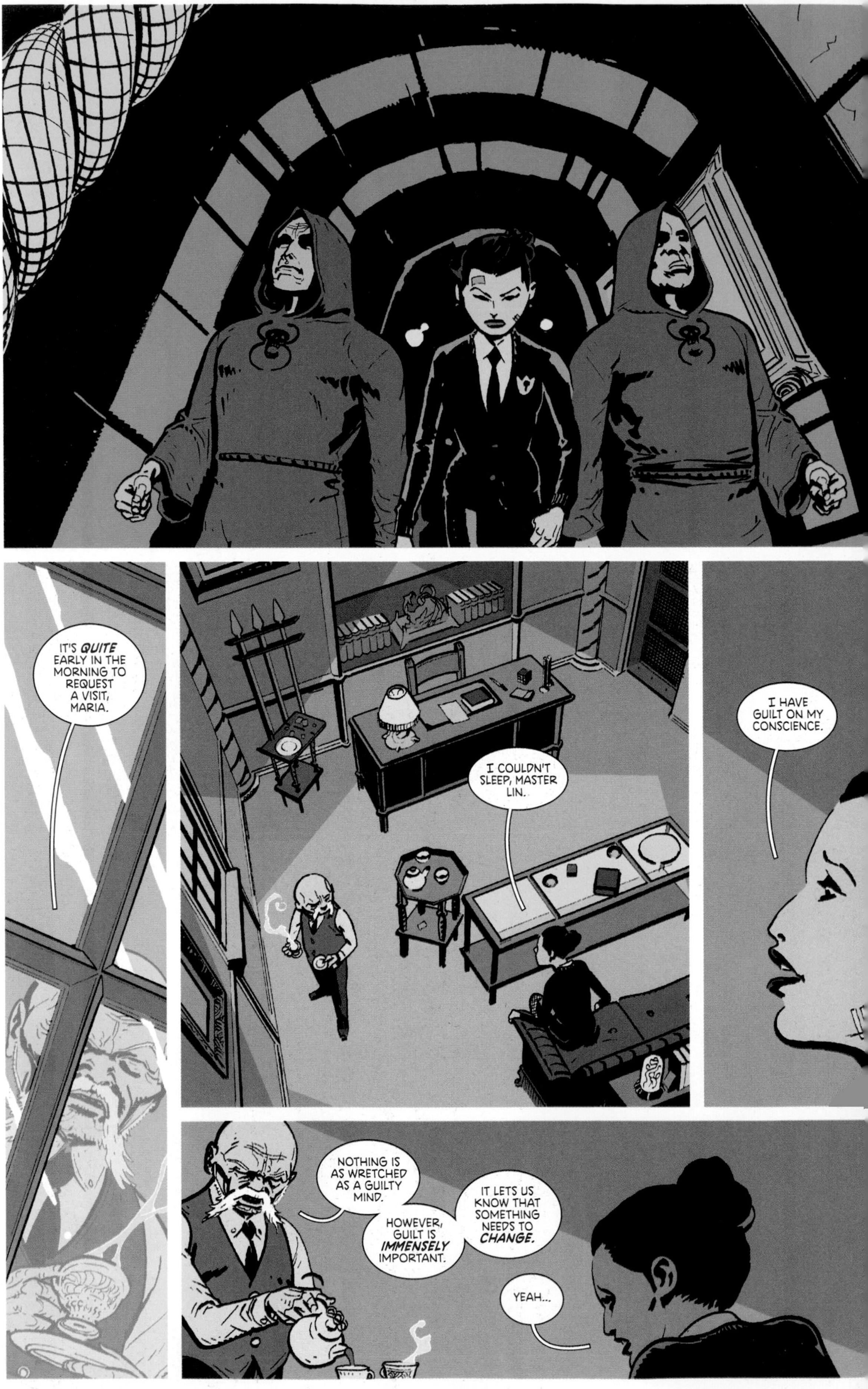

IT'S *QUITE* EARLY IN THE MORNING TO REQUEST A VISIT, MARIA.
I COULDN'T SLEEP, MASTER LIN.
I HAVE GUILT ON MY CONSCIENCE.
NOTHING IS AS WRETCHED AS A GUILTY MIND.
HOWEVER, GUILT IS *IMMENSELY* IMPORTANT.
IT LETS US KNOW THAT SOMETHING NEEDS TO *CHANGE.*
YEAH...

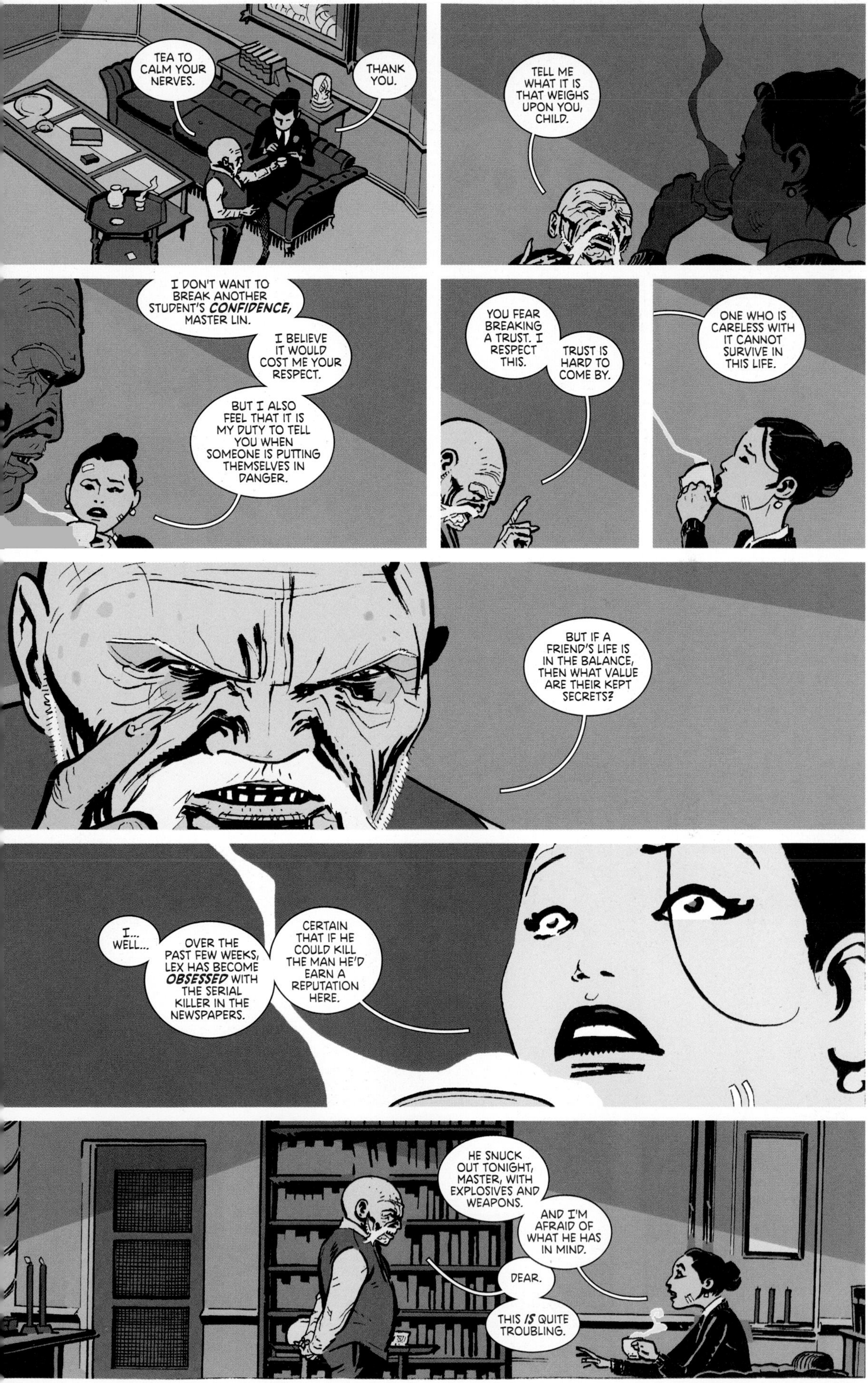
TEA TO CALM YOUR NERVES.
THANK YOU.
TELL ME WHAT IT IS THAT WEIGHS UPON YOU, CHILD.
I DON'T WANT TO BREAK ANOTHER STUDENT'S CONFIDENCE, MASTER LIN.
I BELIEVE IT WOULD COST ME YOUR RESPECT.
BUT I ALSO FEEL THAT IT IS MY DUTY TO TELL YOU WHEN SOMEONE IS PUTTING THEMSELVES IN DANGER.
YOU FEAR BREAKING A TRUST. I RESPECT THIS.
TRUST IS HARD TO COME BY.
ONE WHO IS CARELESS WITH IT CANNOT SURVIVE IN THIS LIFE.
BUT IF A FRIEND'S LIFE IS IN THE BALANCE, THEN WHAT VALUE ARE THEIR KEPT SECRETS?
I... WELL...
OVER THE PAST FEW WEEKS, LEX HAS BECOME OBSESSED WITH THE SERIAL KILLER IN THE NEWSPAPERS.
CERTAIN THAT IF HE COULD KILL THE MAN HE'D EARN A REPUTATION HERE.
HE SNUCK OUT TONIGHT, MASTER, WITH EXPLOSIVES AND WEAPONS.
AND I'M AFRAID OF WHAT HE HAS IN MIND.
DEAR.
THIS IS QUITE TROUBLING.

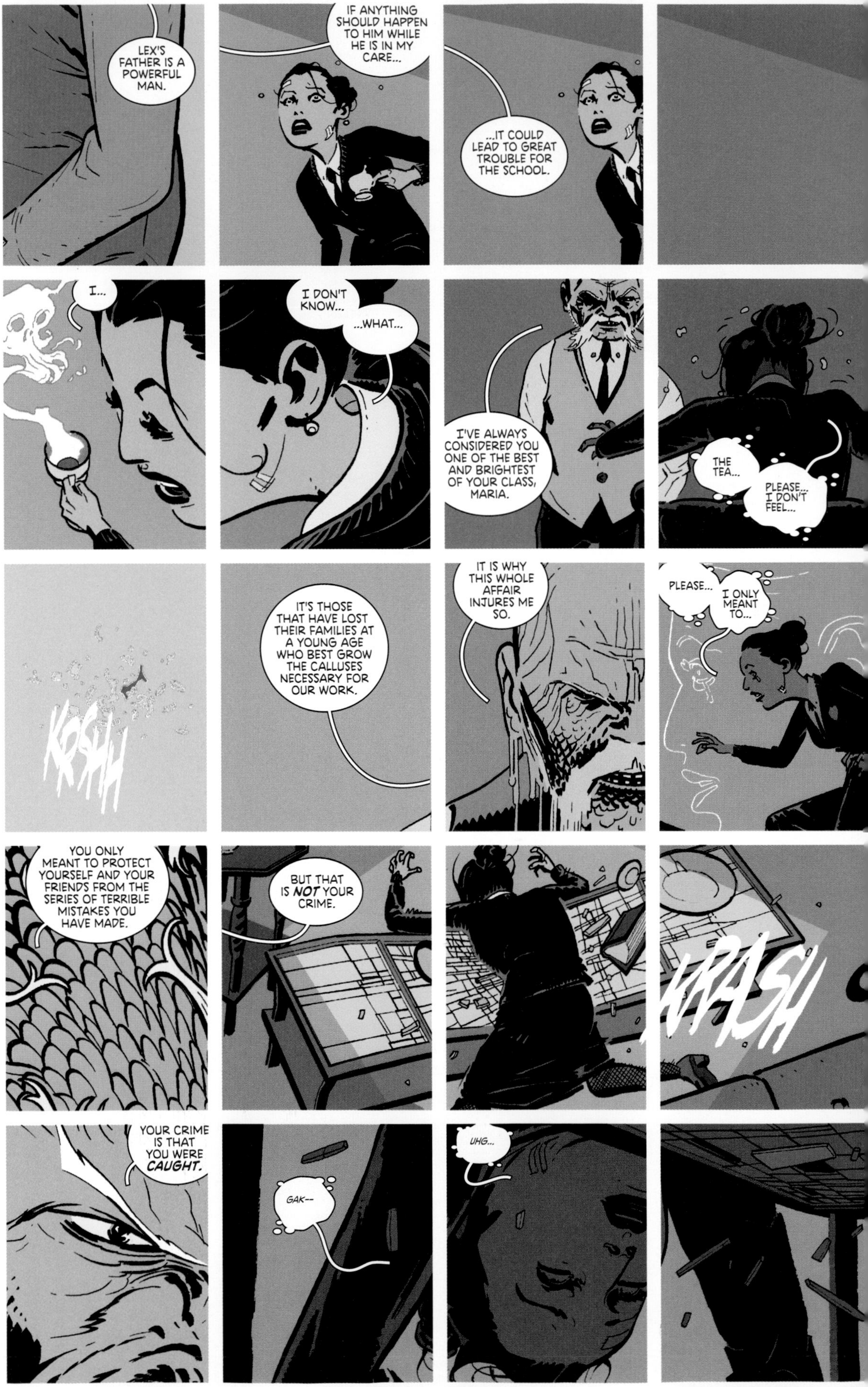
LEX'S FATHER IS A POWERFUL MAN.
IF ANYTHING SHOULD HAPPEN TO HIM WHILE HE IS IN MY CARE...
...IT COULD LEAD TO GREAT TROUBLE FOR THE SCHOOL.
I...
I DON'T KNOW...
...WHAT...
I'VE ALWAYS CONSIDERED YOU ONE OF THE BEST AND BRIGHTEST OF YOUR CLASS, MARIA.
THE TEA...
PLEASE... I DON'T FEEL...
KRSHH
IT'S THOSE THAT HAVE LOST THEIR FAMILIES AT A YOUNG AGE WHO BEST GROW THE CALLUSES NECESSARY FOR OUR WORK.
IT IS WHY THIS WHOLE AFFAIR INJURES ME SO.
PLEASE...
I ONLY MEANT TO...
YOU ONLY MEANT TO PROTECT YOURSELF AND YOUR FRIENDS FROM THE SERIES OF TERRIBLE MISTAKES YOU HAVE MADE.
BUT THAT IS **NOT** YOUR CRIME.
KRASH
YOUR CRIME IS THAT YOU WERE ***CAUGHT.***
GAK--
UHG...

"YOU DID NOT COVER YOUR TRACKS, MARIA.

"EARNED A FAILING MARK.

"NOT ONLY IN CHICO'S *EXECUTION METHOD*-- BUT HIS *DISPOSAL.*

"YOU AND YOUR CLASSMATES HAVE YET TO TAKE MY THREATS *SERIOUSLY.*

"BUT I ASSURE YOU, THEY ARE *QUITE* GRAVE.

"UNFORTUNATELY FOR YOU, MARIA..."

"...THAT THIS LESSON YOU LEARNED FAR TOO LATE."

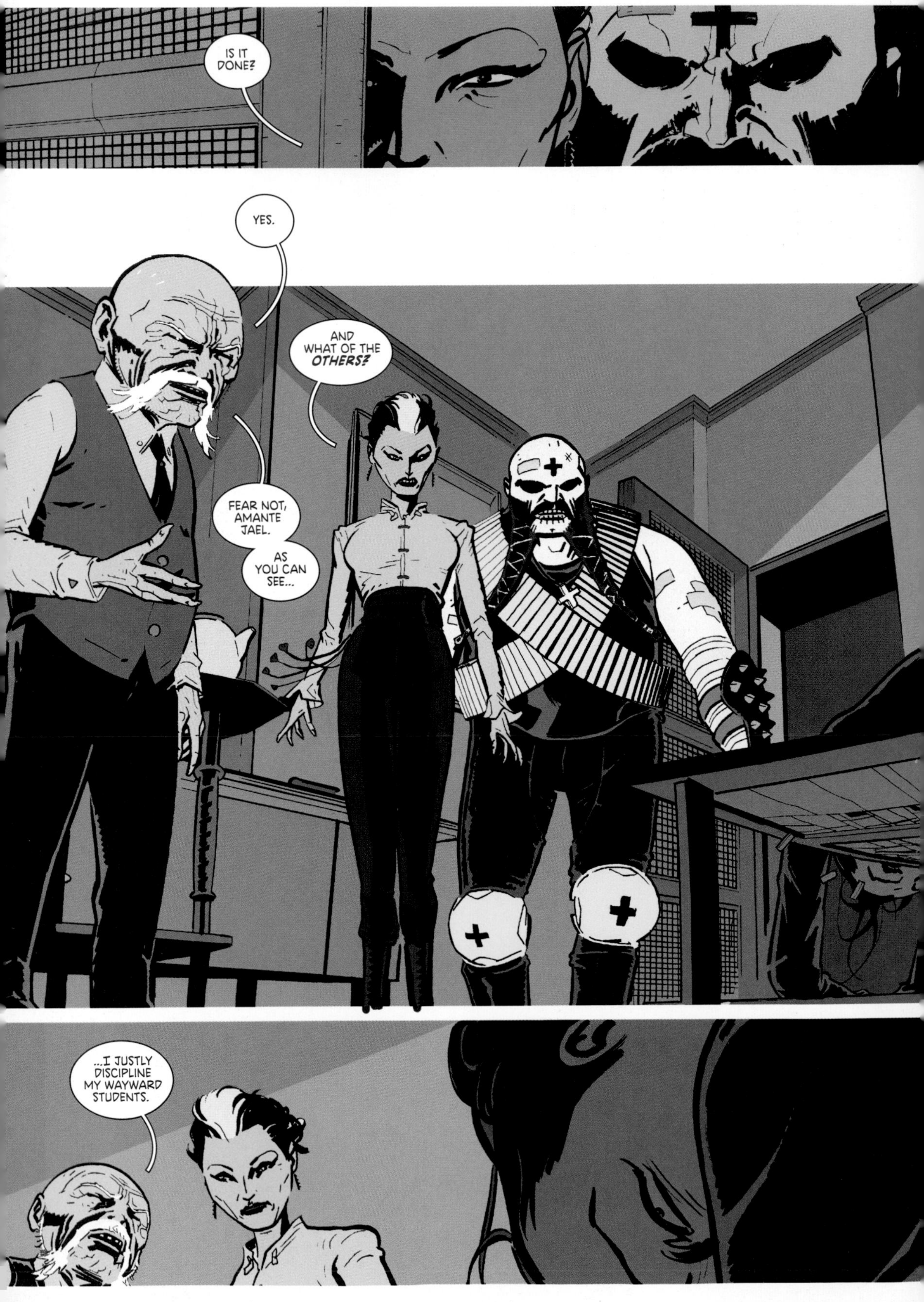
IS IT DONE?
YES.
AND WHAT OF THE *OTHERS?*
FEAR NOT, AMANTE JAEL.
AS YOU CAN SEE...
...I JUSTLY DISCIPLINE MY WAYWARD STUDENTS.

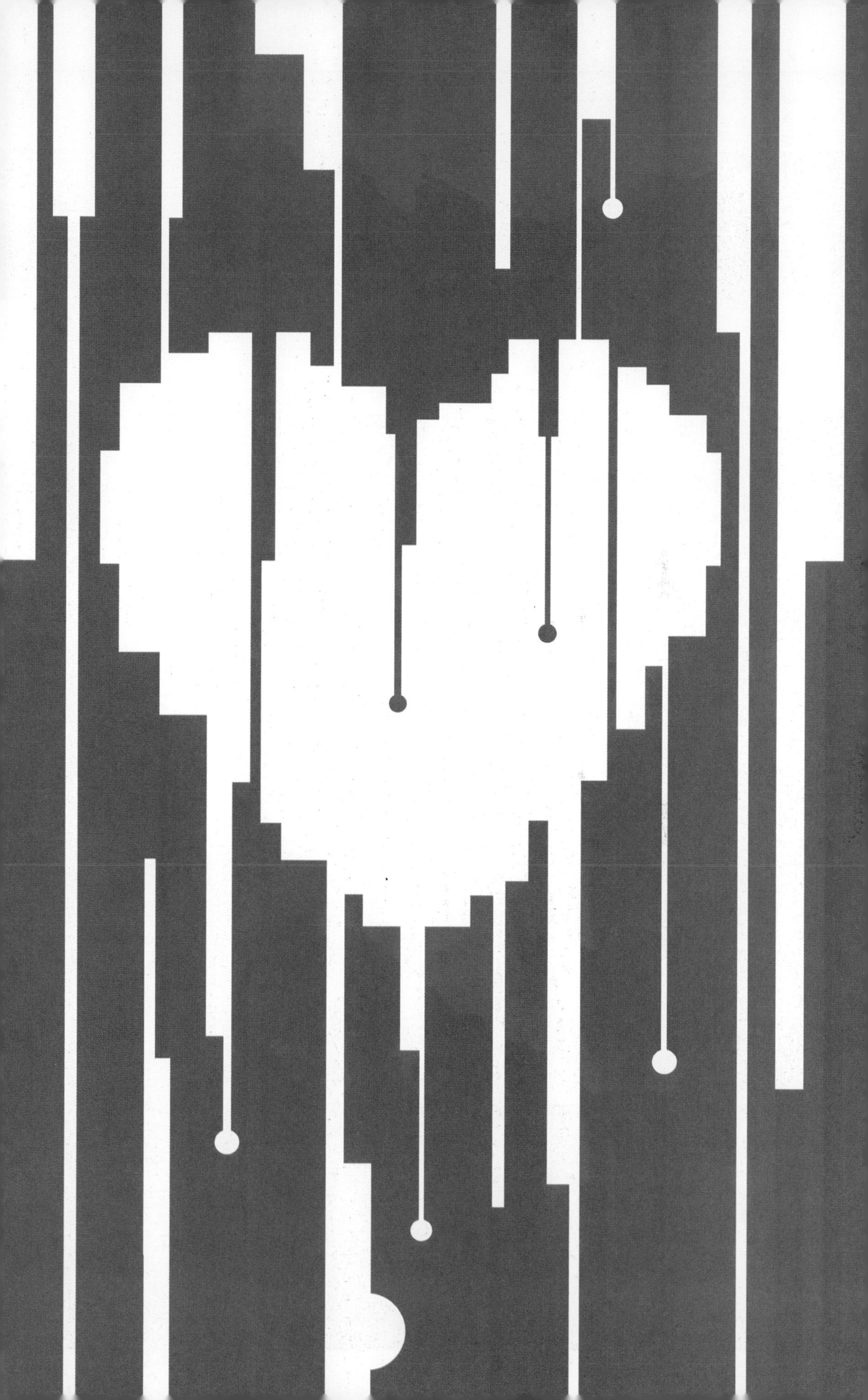

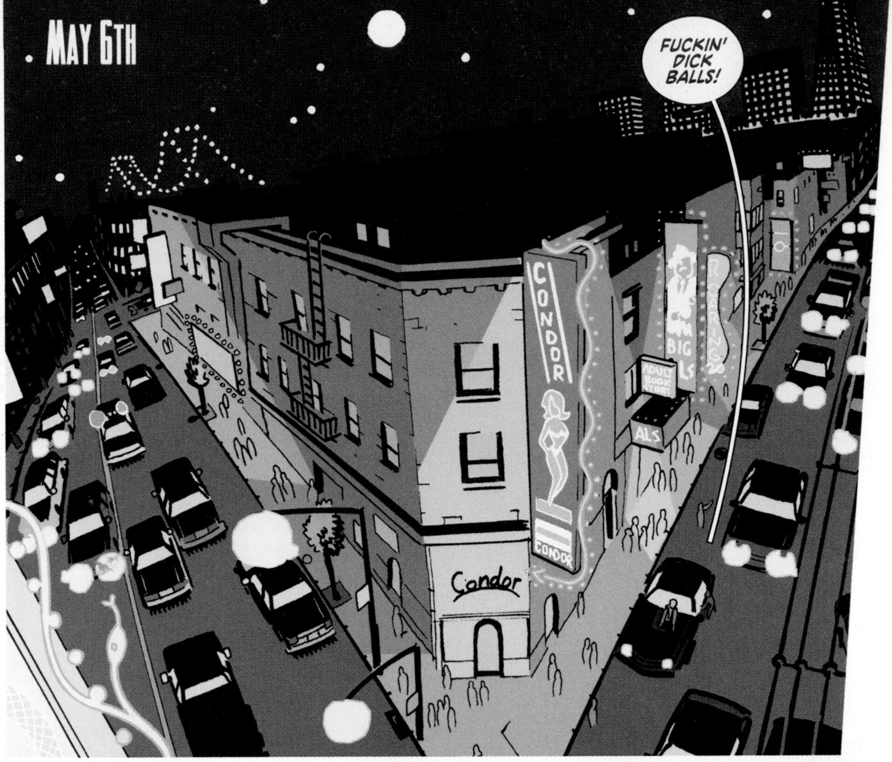
MAY 6TH
FUCKIN' DICK BALLS!
CONDOR
Condor
ALS

I HAVEN'T SAID AN HONEST THING IN WEEKS. NOTHING. WHAT AM I TRYING TO DO? WHAT AM I TRYING TO SAY? QUOTING SOME DEPECHE MODE; SUE ME.

THINGS ARE BADLY FUCKED AND I CAN'T KEEP IT TOGETHER.

IT'S BEEN TWO MONTHS SINCE MARIA RAN OFF.

DISAPPEARED IN THE NIGHT.

THERE ISN'T A MORAL AT THE END OF **EVERY** STORY.

MOSTLY JUST HEARTBREAK AND CONFUSION.

LEX TOOK THE FALL FOR THE TROUBLE WE CAUSED.

WE ALL LIED, BLAMED HIM.

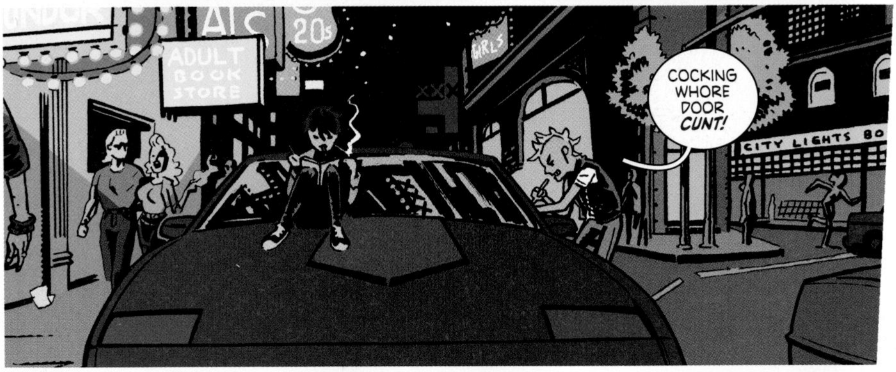
ADULT BOOK STORE
ALS
20s
GIRLS
COCKING WHORE DOOR **CUNT!**
CITY LIGHTS BO

THERE IS NO SUCH THING AS LOVE. I'M DONE HUNTING FOR IT.

EVERYONE'S A LIAR. EVERYONE'S SELFISH.

I ALWAYS KNEW MARIA WAS DAMAGED.

ALWAYS KNEW THIS IS WHERE WE WERE HEADING. KNEW EVERYTHING SHE SAID WAS A LIE.

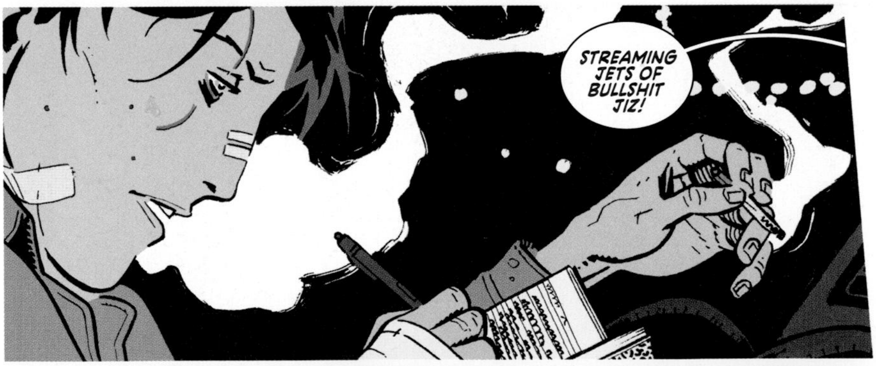
STREAMING JETS OF BULLSHIT JIZ!

MAYBE THAT'S HOW SHE KEPT ME AROUND. LYING AWAY ALL OF MY CONCERNS.

I MUST'VE NEEDED LIES SOMETHING FIERCE BECAUSE I BOUGHT IT ALL.

EVERYONE GETS TIRED OF EVERYONE ELSE. EVERYONE WILL CHEAT.

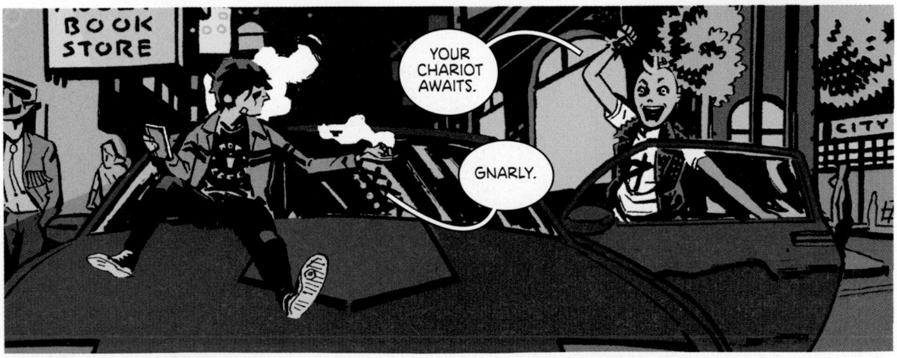
BOOK STORE
YOUR CHARIOT AWAITS.
GNARLY.
CITY

NEED NEW DISTRACTIONS TO KEEP ME FROM BEING AWARE OF IT.

DURING CHANGE LIFE IS UNCOMFORTABLE. BUT ONLY TO THE DEGREE THAT YOU HOLD ONTO THE PAST.

LIKE THE PHANTOM LIMB THAT STILL ITCHES AFTER IT'S BEEN SEVERED.

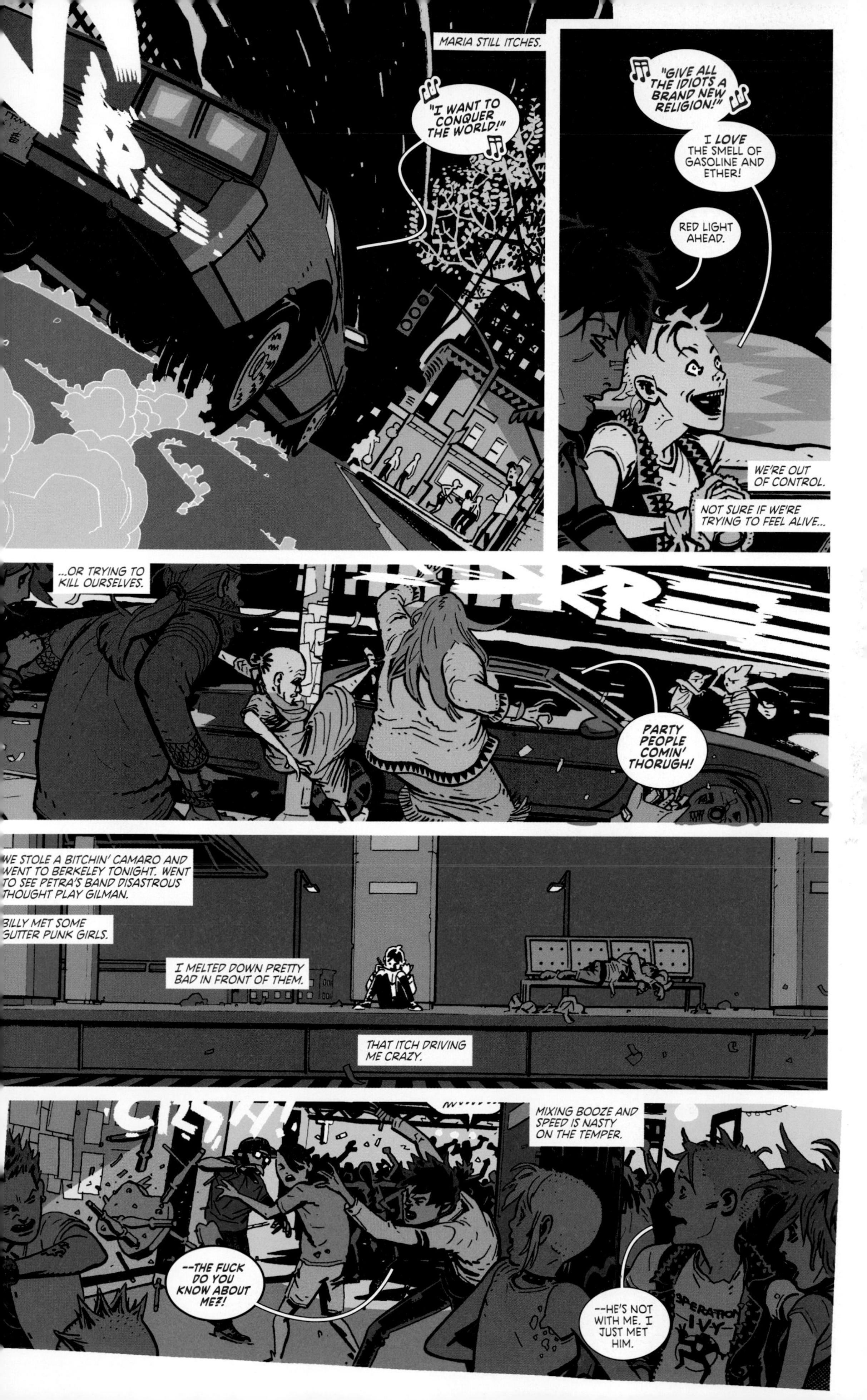

MARIA STILL ITCHES.
"I WANT TO CONQUER THE WORLD!"
"GIVE ALL THE IDIOTS A BRAND NEW RELIGION!"
I LOVE THE SMELL OF GASOLINE AND ETHER!
RED LIGHT AHEAD.
WE'RE OUT OF CONTROL.
NOT SURE IF WE'RE TRYING TO FEEL ALIVE...
...OR TRYING TO KILL OURSELVES.
PARTY PEOPLE COMIN' THORUGH!
WE STOLE A BITCHIN' CAMARO AND WENT TO BERKELEY TONIGHT. WENT TO SEE PETRA'S BAND DISASTROUS THOUGHT PLAY GILMAN.
BILLY MET SOME GUTTER PUNK GIRLS.
I MELTED DOWN PRETTY BAD IN FRONT OF THEM.
THAT ITCH DRIVING ME CRAZY.
MIXING BOOZE AND SPEED IS NASTY ON THE TEMPER.
--THE FUCK DO YOU KNOW ABOUT ME?!
--HE'S NOT WITH ME. I JUST MET HIM.

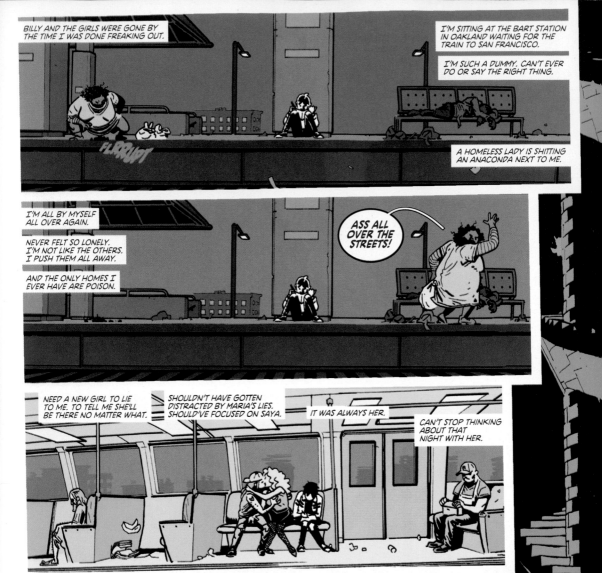

BILLY AND THE GIRLS WERE GONE BY THE TIME I WAS DONE FREAKING OUT.

I'M SITTING AT THE BART STATION IN OAKLAND WAITING FOR THE TRAIN TO SAN FRANCISCO.

I'M SUCH A DUMMY. CAN'T EVER DO OR SAY THE RIGHT THING.

FLRRRWT

A HOMELESS LADY IS SHITTING AN ANACONDA NEXT TO ME.

I'M ALL BY MYSELF ALL OVER AGAIN.

NEVER FELT SO LONELY. I'M NOT LIKE THE OTHERS. I PUSH THEM ALL AWAY.

AND THE ONLY HOMES I EVER HAVE ARE POISON.

ASS ALL OVER THE STREETS!

NEED A NEW GIRL TO LIE TO ME. TO TELL ME SHE'LL BE THERE NO MATTER WHAT.

SHOULDN'T HAVE GOTTEN DISTRACTED BY MARIA'S LIES. SHOULD'VE FOCUSED ON SAYA.

IT WAS ALWAYS HER.

CAN'T STOP THINKING ABOUT THAT NIGHT WITH HER.

SAYA IS SO BEAUTIFUL IN SO MANY WAYS, YET HORROR-STRICKEN- TERRIBLE IN SO MANY OTHERS.

I THINK SHE'S LOST HER HEART.

IT'S SHATTERED AND DRY.

IT LEAVES SPLINTERS IN THOSE WHO CARE FOR HER.

MAYBE WE COULD SAVE EACH OTHER.

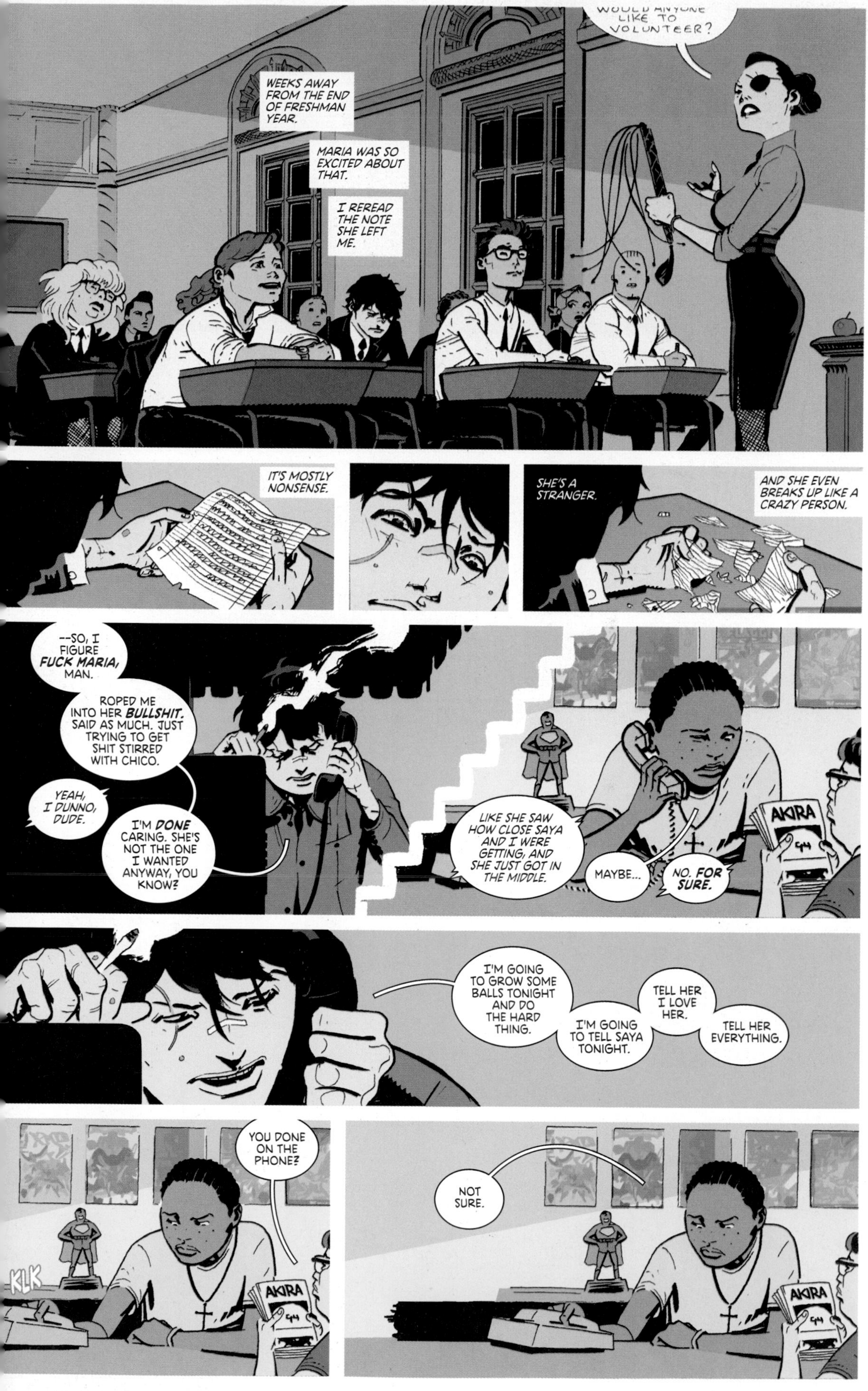
WOULD ANYONE LIKE TO VOLUNTEER?
WEEKS AWAY FROM THE END OF FRESHMAN YEAR.
MARIA WAS SO EXCITED ABOUT THAT.
I REREAD THE NOTE SHE LEFT ME.
IT'S MOSTLY NONSENSE.
SHE'S A STRANGER.
AND SHE EVEN BREAKS UP LIKE A CRAZY PERSON.
--SO, I FIGURE FUCK MARIA, MAN.
ROPED ME INTO HER BULLSHIT. SAID AS MUCH. JUST TRYING TO GET SHIT STIRRED WITH CHICO.
YEAH, I DUNNO, DUDE.
I'M DONE CARING. SHE'S NOT THE ONE I WANTED ANYWAY, YOU KNOW?
LIKE SHE SAW HOW CLOSE SAYA AND I WERE GETTING, AND SHE JUST GOT IN THE MIDDLE.
MAYBE...
NO. FOR SURE.
AKIRA
I'M GOING TO GROW SOME BALLS TONIGHT AND DO THE HARD THING.
I'M GOING TO TELL SAYA TONIGHT.
TELL HER I LOVE HER.
TELL HER EVERYTHING.
KLIK
YOU DONE ON THE PHONE?
AKIRA
NOT SURE.
AKIRA

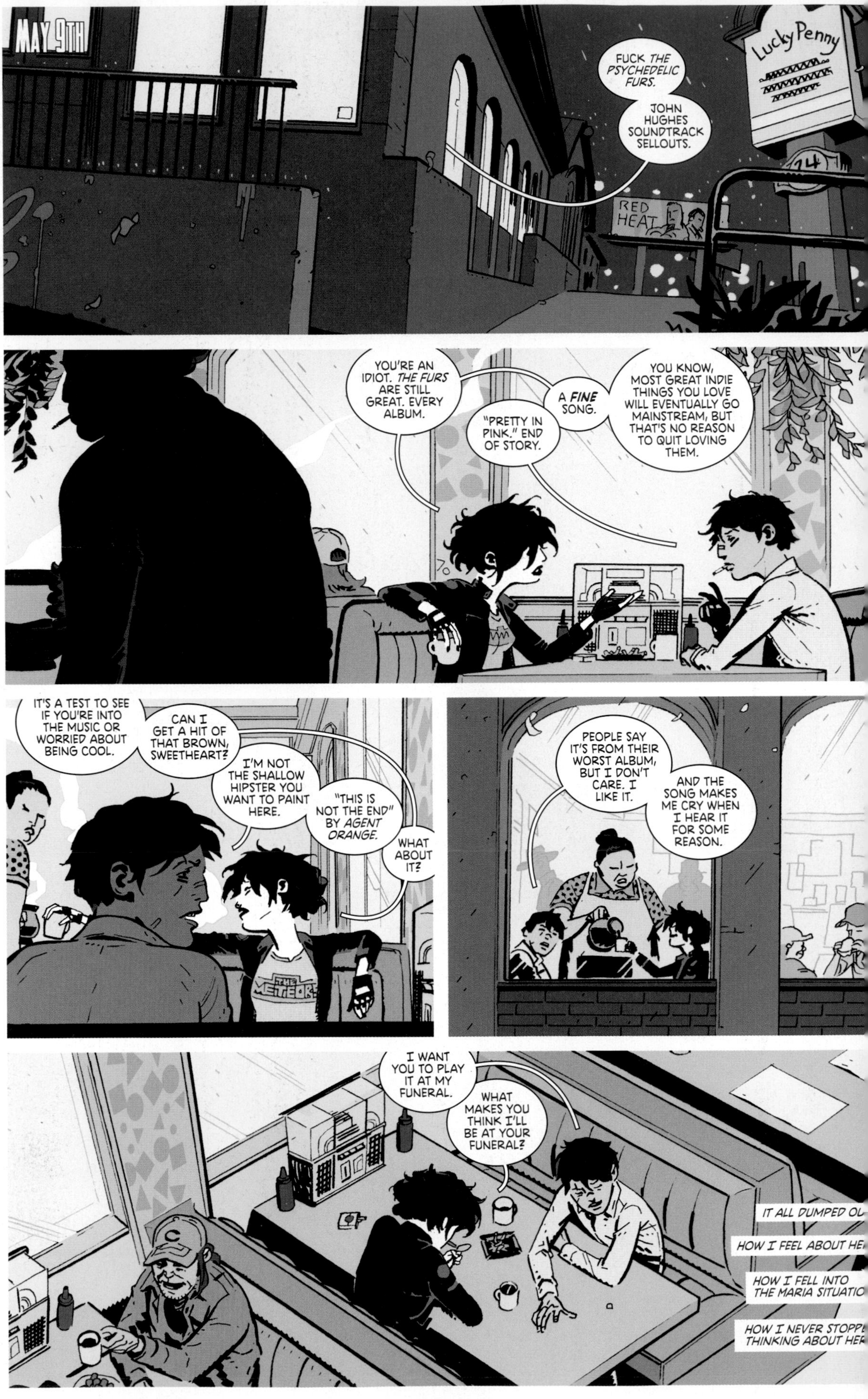
MAY 9TH
FUCK THE PSYCHEDELIC FURS.
JOHN HUGHES SOUNDTRACK SELLOUTS.
Lucky Penny
RED HEAT
YOU'RE AN IDIOT. THE FURS ARE STILL GREAT. EVERY ALBUM.
"PRETTY IN PINK." END OF STORY.
A FINE SONG.
YOU KNOW, MOST GREAT INDIE THINGS YOU LOVE WILL EVENTUALLY GO MAINSTREAM, BUT THAT'S NO REASON TO QUIT LOVING THEM.
IT'S A TEST TO SEE IF YOU'RE INTO THE MUSIC OR WORRIED ABOUT BEING COOL.
CAN I GET A HIT OF THAT BROWN, SWEETHEART?
I'M NOT THE SHALLOW HIPSTER YOU WANT TO PAINT HERE.
"THIS IS NOT THE END" BY AGENT ORANGE.
WHAT ABOUT IT?
THE METEORS
PEOPLE SAY IT'S FROM THEIR WORST ALBUM, BUT I DON'T CARE. I LIKE IT.
AND THE SONG MAKES ME CRY WHEN I HEAR IT FOR SOME REASON.
I WANT YOU TO PLAY IT AT MY FUNERAL.
WHAT MAKES YOU THINK I'LL BE AT YOUR FUNERAL?

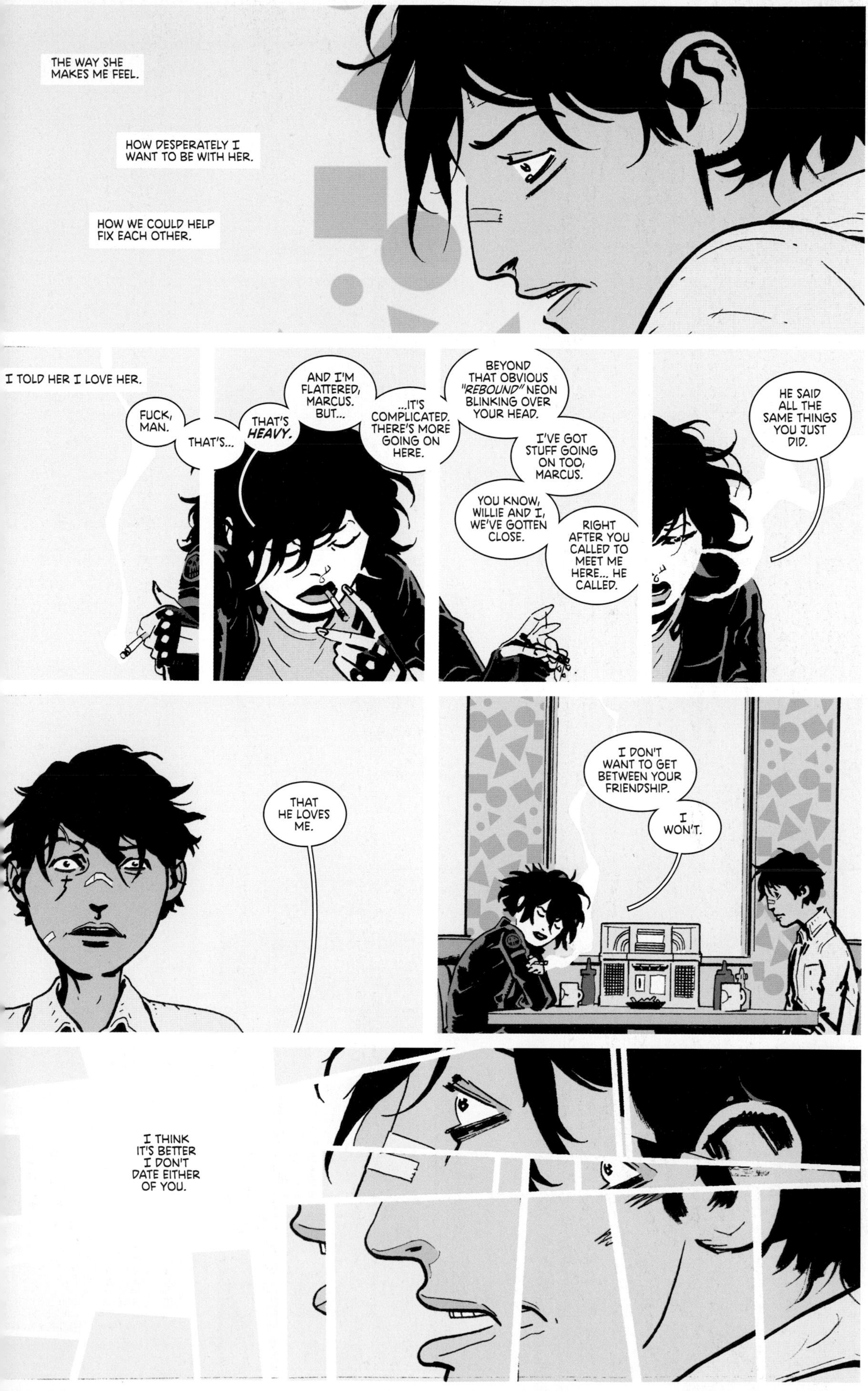
THE WAY SHE MAKES ME FEEL.
HOW DESPERATELY I WANT TO BE WITH HER.
HOW WE COULD HELP FIX EACH OTHER.
I TOLD HER I LOVE HER.
FUCK, MAN.
THAT'S...
THAT'S HEAVY.
AND I'M FLATTERED, MARCUS. BUT...
...IT'S COMPLICATED. THERE'S MORE GOING ON HERE.
BEYOND THAT OBVIOUS "REBOUND" NEON BLINKING OVER YOUR HEAD.
I'VE GOT STUFF GOING ON TOO, MARCUS.
YOU KNOW, WILLIE AND I, WE'VE GOTTEN CLOSE.
RIGHT AFTER YOU CALLED TO MEET ME HERE... HE CALLED.
HE SAID ALL THE SAME THINGS YOU JUST DID.
THAT HE LOVES ME.
I DON'T WANT TO GET BETWEEN YOUR FRIENDSHIP.
I WON'T.
I THINK IT'S BETTER I DON'T DATE EITHER OF YOU.

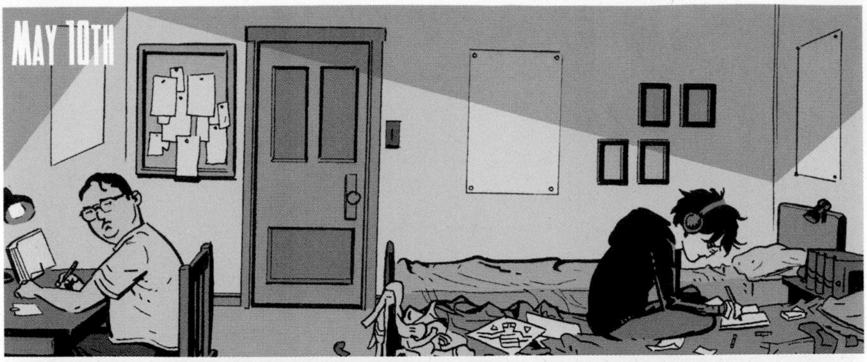
MAY 10TH

LIKE A DRUG. THE WITHDRAWALS HURT WORSE THAN THE REJECTION, WORSE THAN WILLIE'S BETRAYAL.

WHAT DID I EXPECT?

SHE'D THROW HER ARMS AROUND ME, TELL ME SHE FEELS THE SAME WAY?

I WAS SICK OF MARIA, RIGHT? I CHEATED ON HER WITH SAYA FOR A REASON. WAS SAYA A REBOUND PLAY?

DO I SUFFER "THE GRASS IS ALWAYS GREENER" SYNDROME?

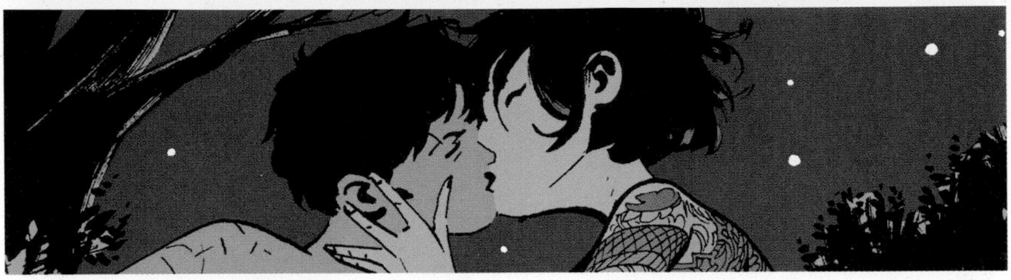

PINING FOR MY CHANCE AT SAYA.

SAYA WHO KISSED ME.

SAYA WHO SLEPT WITH ME.

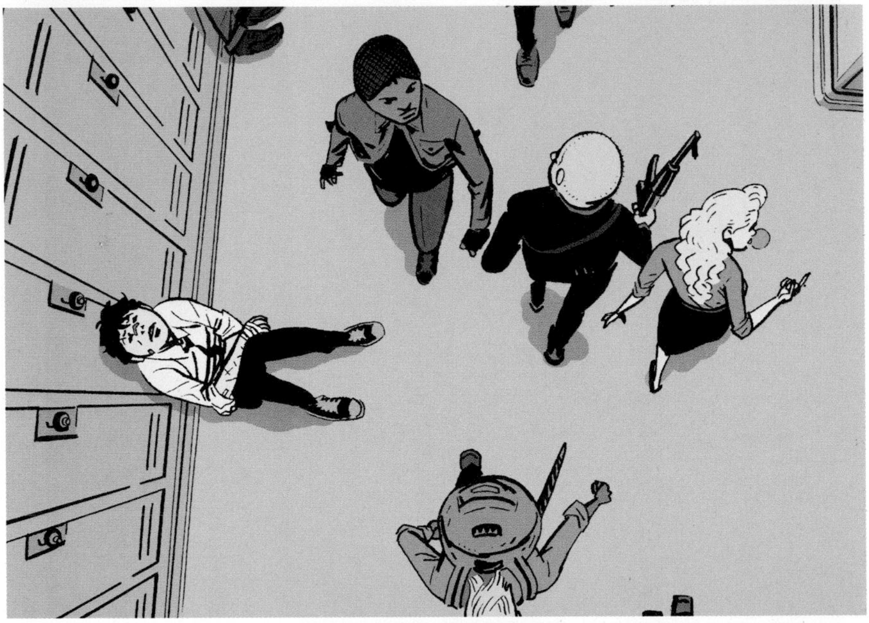

DID I LOVE EITHER OF THEM?

MAYBE WHEN YOU'RE 15 EVERY GIRL YOU'RE INTO FEELS LIKE LOVE.

IT'S JUST A GAME TO THE GIRLS.

AND WILLIE. MY "BEST FRIEND."

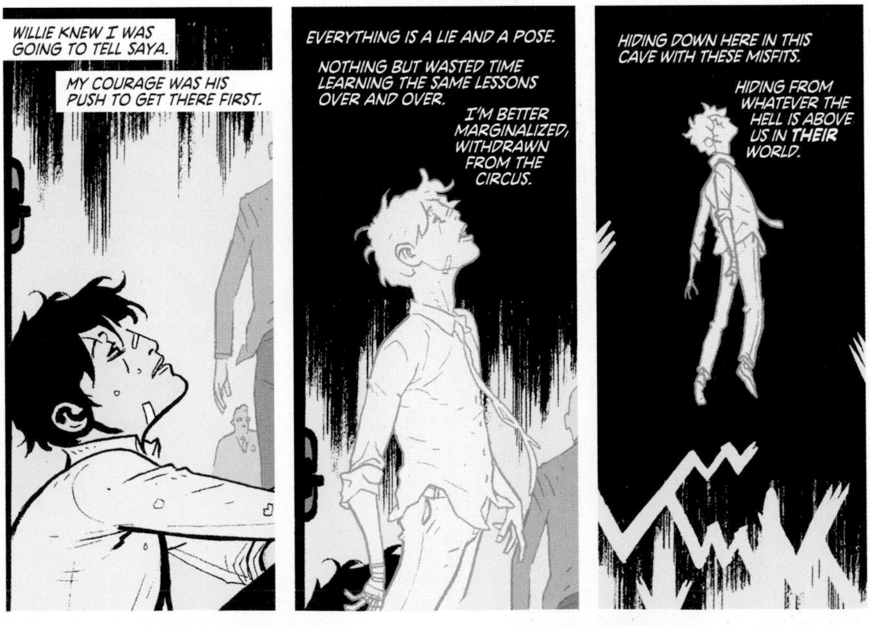
WILLIE KNEW I WAS GOING TO TELL SAYA.
MY COURAGE WAS HIS PUSH TO GET THERE FIRST.
EVERYTHING IS A LIE AND A POSE.
NOTHING BUT WASTED TIME LEARNING THE SAME LESSONS OVER AND OVER.
I'M BETTER MARGINALIZED, WITHDRAWN FROM THE CIRCUS.
HIDING DOWN HERE IN THIS CAVE WITH THESE MISFITS.
HIDING FROM WHATEVER THE HELL IS ABOVE US IN **THEIR** WORLD.

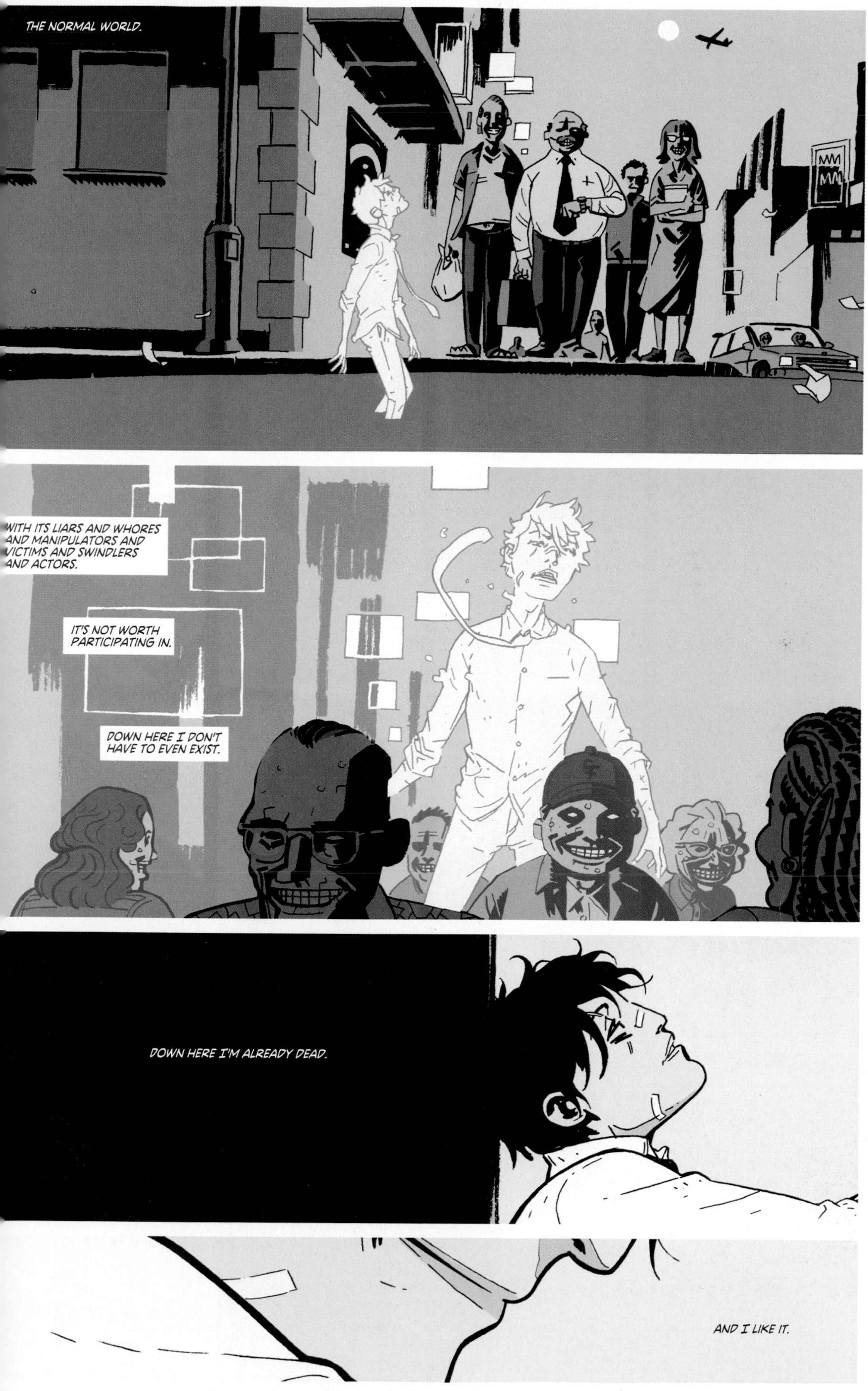
THE NORMAL WORLD.
WITH ITS LIARS AND WHORES AND MANIPULATORS AND VICTIMS AND SWINDLERS AND ACTORS.
IT'S NOT WORTH PARTICIPATING IN.
DOWN HERE I DON'T HAVE TO EVEN EXIST.
DOWN HERE I'M ALREADY DEAD.
AND I LIKE IT.

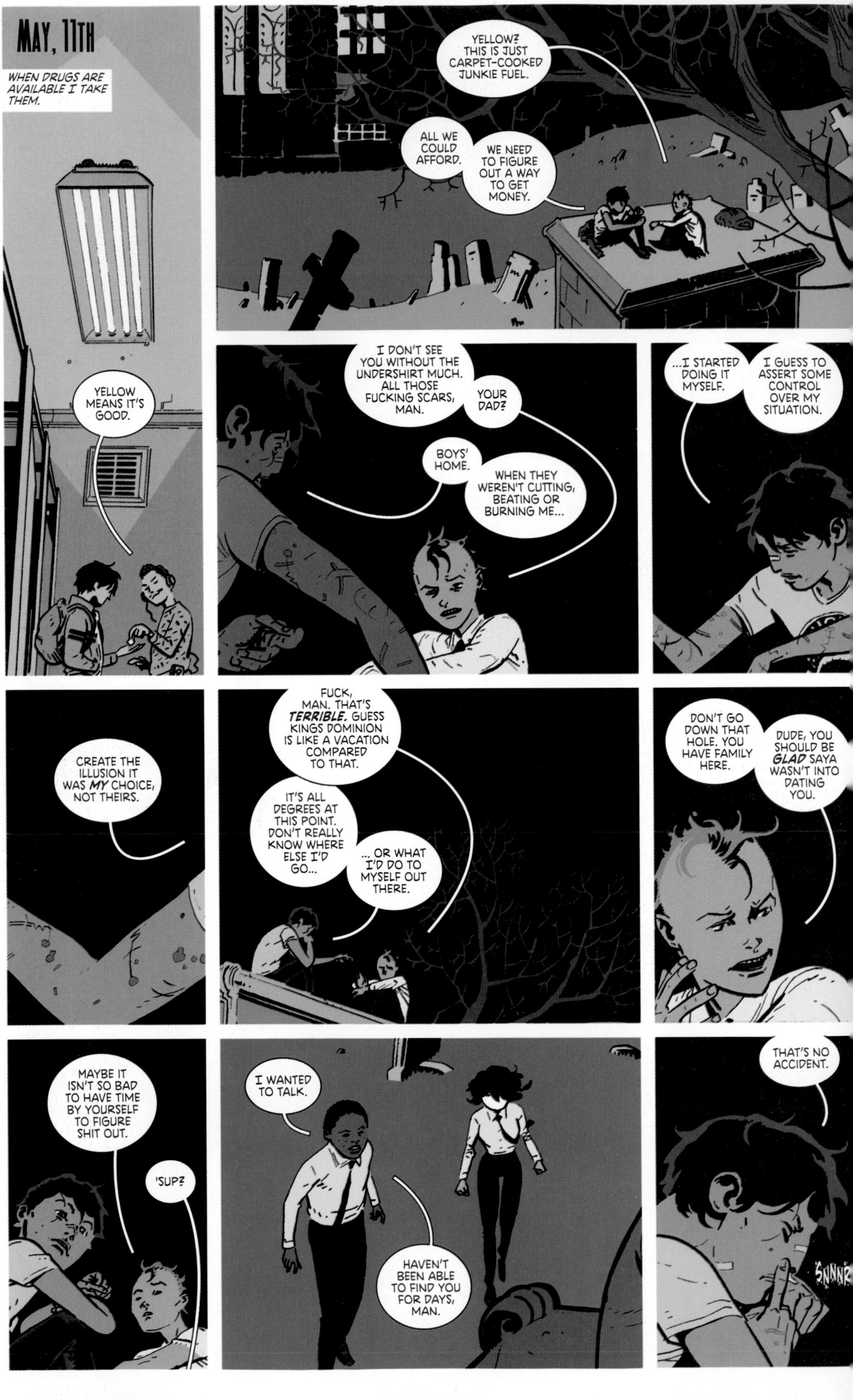
MAY, 11TH
WHEN DRUGS ARE AVAILABLE I TAKE THEM.
YELLOW MEANS IT'S GOOD.
YELLOW? THIS IS JUST CARPET-COOKED JUNKIE FUEL.
ALL WE COULD AFFORD.
WE NEED TO FIGURE OUT A WAY TO GET MONEY.
I DON'T SEE YOU WITHOUT THE UNDERSHIRT MUCH. ALL THOSE FUCKING SCARS, MAN.
YOUR DAD?
BOYS' HOME.
WHEN THEY WEREN'T CUTTING, BEATING OR BURNING ME...
...I STARTED DOING IT MYSELF.
I GUESS TO ASSERT SOME CONTROL OVER MY SITUATION.
CREATE THE ILLUSION IT WAS MY CHOICE, NOT THEIRS.
FUCK, MAN. THAT'S TERRIBLE. GUESS KINGS DOMINION IS LIKE A VACATION COMPARED TO THAT.
IT'S ALL DEGREES AT THIS POINT. DON'T REALLY KNOW WHERE ELSE I'D GO...
... OR WHAT I'D DO TO MYSELF OUT THERE.
DON'T GO DOWN THAT HOLE. YOU HAVE FAMILY HERE.
DUDE, YOU SHOULD BE GLAD SAYA WASN'T INTO DATING YOU.
MAYBE IT ISN'T SO BAD TO HAVE TIME BY YOURSELF TO FIGURE SHIT OUT.
'SUP?
I WANTED TO TALK.
HAVEN'T BEEN ABLE TO FIND YOU FOR DAYS, MAN.
THAT'S NO ACCIDENT.
SNNNR

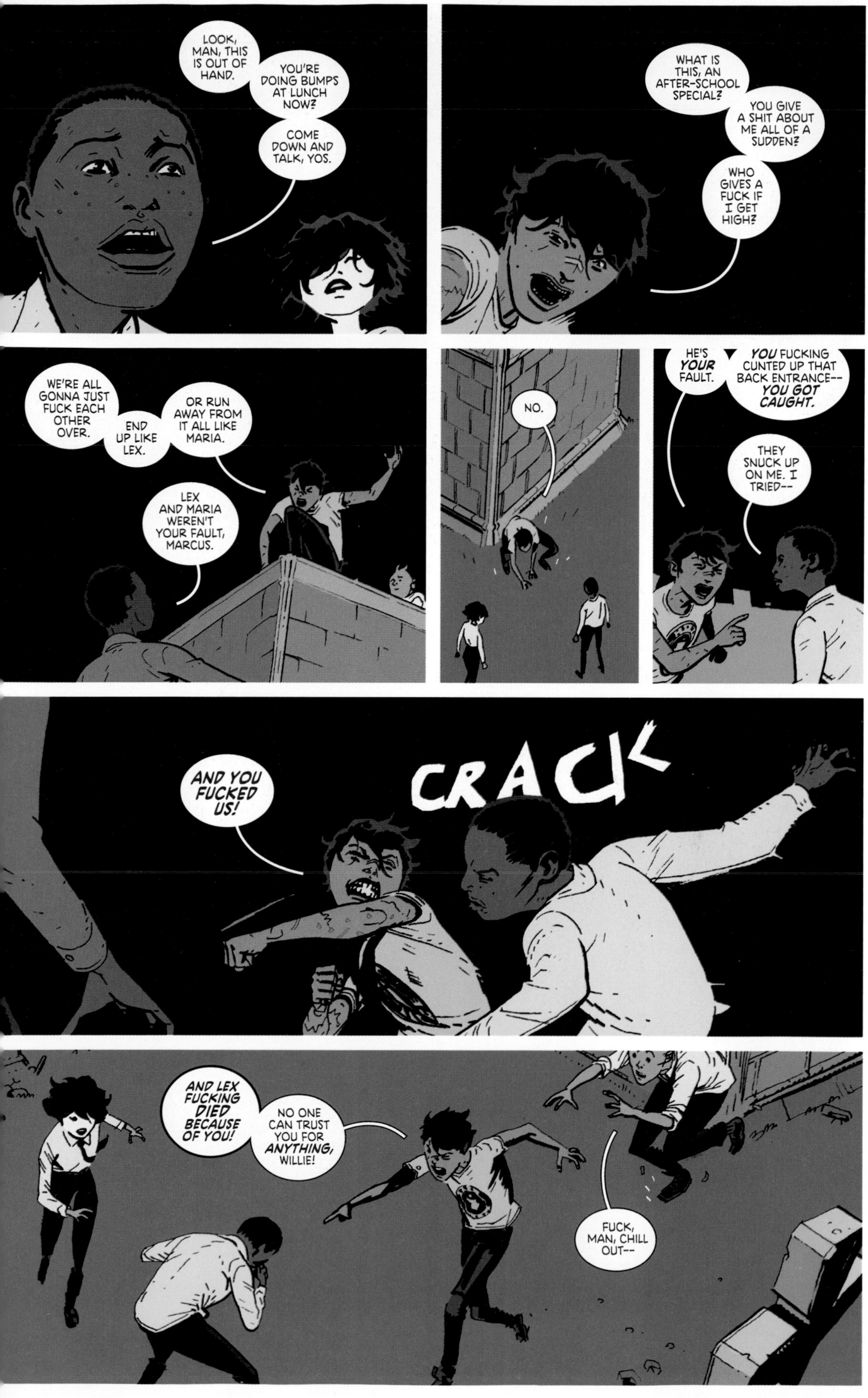
LOOK, MAN, THIS IS OUT OF HAND.
YOU'RE DOING BUMPS AT LUNCH NOW?
COME DOWN AND TALK, YOS.
WHAT IS THIS, AN AFTER-SCHOOL SPECIAL?
YOU GIVE A SHIT ABOUT ME ALL OF A SUDDEN?
WHO GIVES A FUCK IF I GET HIGH?
WE'RE ALL GONNA JUST FUCK EACH OTHER OVER.
END UP LIKE LEX.
OR RUN AWAY FROM IT ALL LIKE MARIA.
LEX AND MARIA WEREN'T YOUR FAULT, MARCUS.
NO.
HE'S *YOUR* FAULT.
YOU FUCKING CUNTED UP THAT BACK ENTRANCE-- *YOU GOT CAUGHT.*
THEY SNUCK UP ON ME. I TRIED--
AND YOU FUCKED US!
CRACK
AND LEX FUCKING DIED BECAUSE OF YOU!
NO ONE CAN TRUST YOU FOR *ANYTHING,* WILLIE!
FUCK, MAN, CHILL OUT--

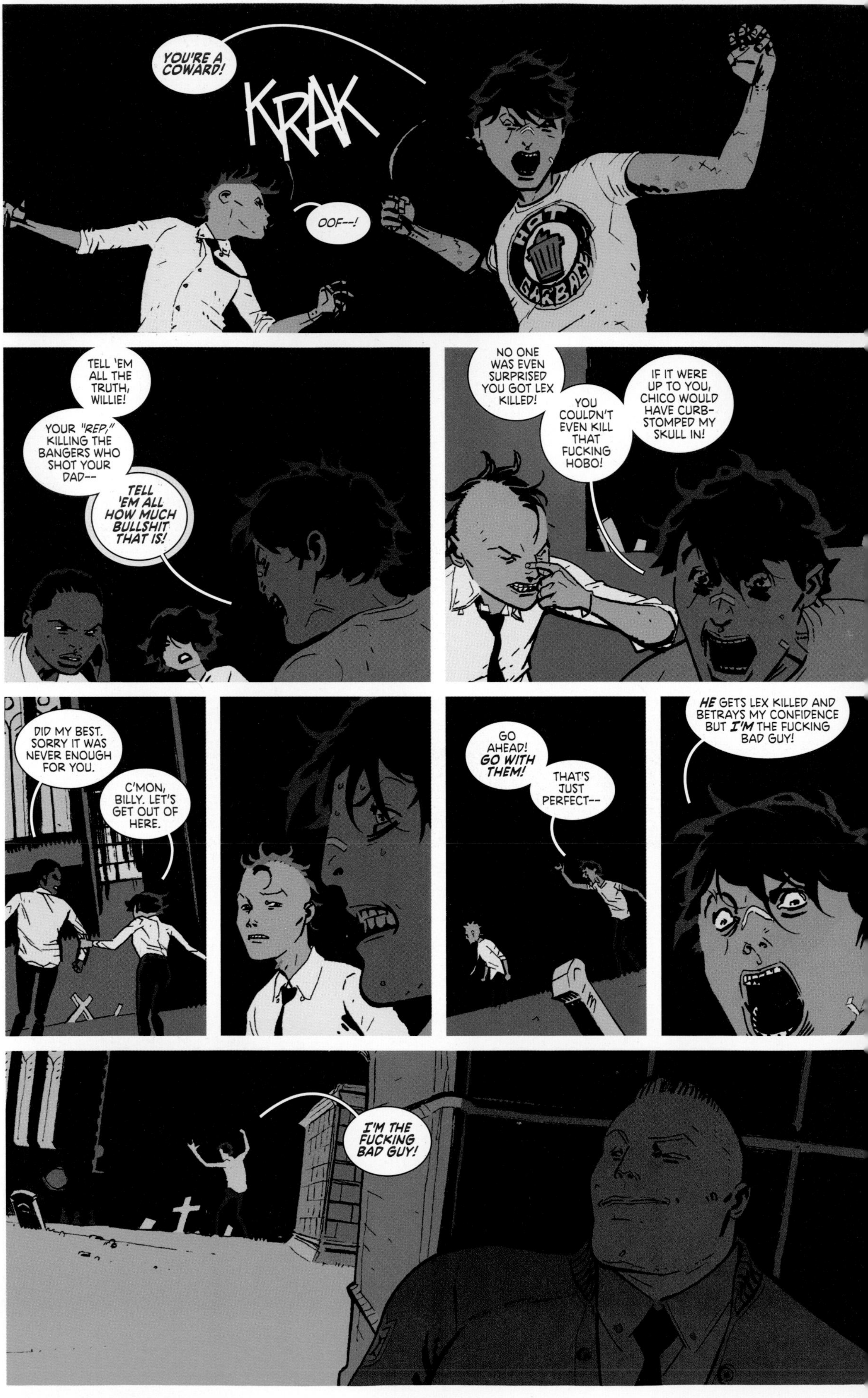
YOU'RE A COWARD!
KRAK
OOF--!
TELL 'EM ALL THE TRUTH, WILLIE!
YOUR "REP," KILLING THE BANGERS WHO SHOT YOUR DAD--
TELL 'EM ALL HOW MUCH BULLSHIT THAT IS!
NO ONE WAS EVEN SURPRISED YOU GOT LEX KILLED!
YOU COULDN'T EVEN KILL THAT FUCKING HOBO!
IF IT WERE UP TO YOU, CHICO WOULD HAVE CURB-STOMPED MY SKULL IN!
DID MY BEST. SORRY IT WAS NEVER ENOUGH FOR YOU.
C'MON, BILLY. LET'S GET OUT OF HERE.
GO AHEAD! GO WITH THEM!
THAT'S JUST PERFECT--
HE GETS LEX KILLED AND BETRAYS MY CONFIDENCE BUT I'M THE FUCKING BAD GUY!
I'M THE FUCKING BAD GUY!

THE SAME DREAM EVERY NIGHT.

THE OLD HOUSE.

MY DAD HAD A FRAMED PICTURE OF A SURFER ON A GIANT WAVE IN HIS DEN.

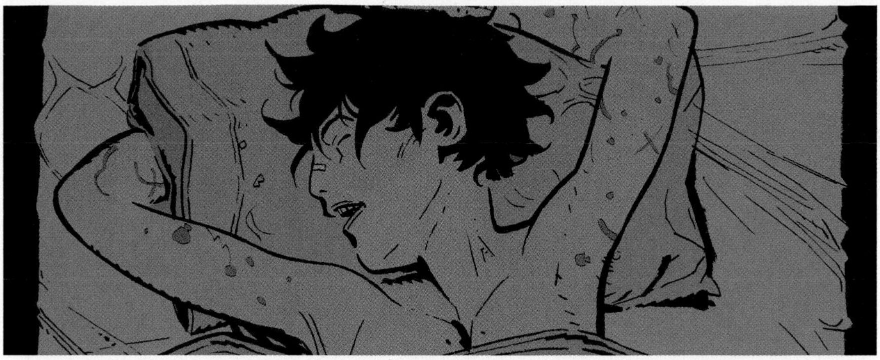

THE WAVE ALWAYS LOOKED SO HUGE.

MY PAPA TOLD ME THAT WAS LIFE.

THIS GIANT THING TRYING TO GET YOU THAT YOU HAD TO FIND PLEASURE IN RIDING.

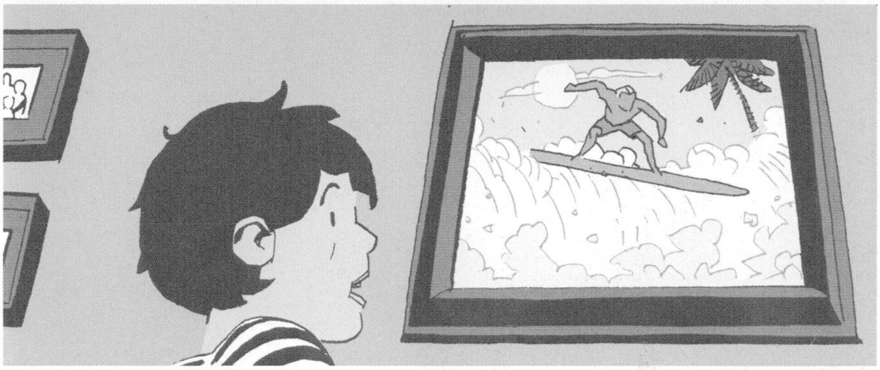

MY PAPA USED TO SURF.

USED TO DRIVE ME ON THE BACK OF HIS DIRT BIKE TO THE BEACH.

I WOULD SIT AND WATCH HIM.

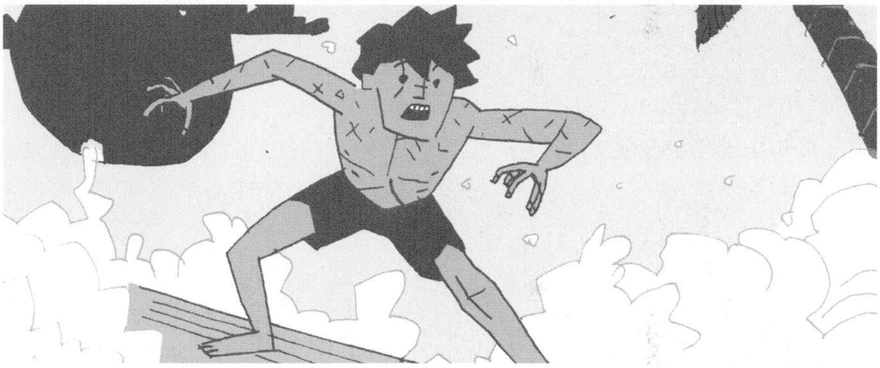

I THINK A LOT ABOUT THAT PAINTING AND OUR OLD HOUSE.

I THINK A LOT ABOUT THAT WAVE.

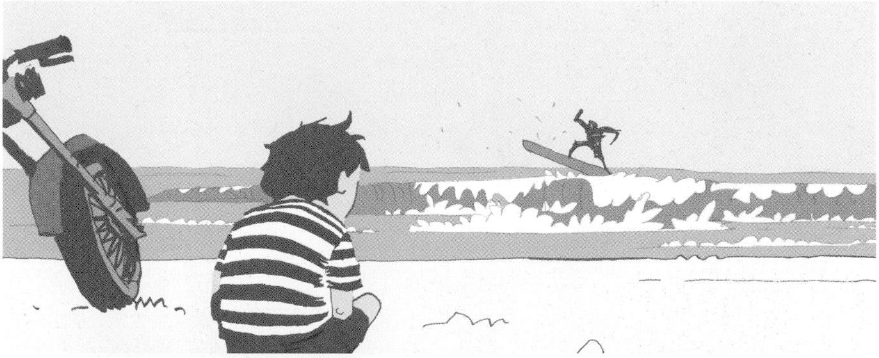

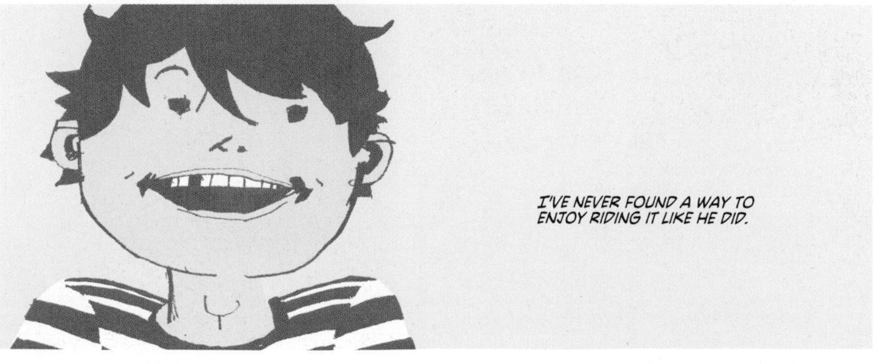
I'VE NEVER FOUND A WAY TO ENJOY RIDING IT LIKE HE DID.

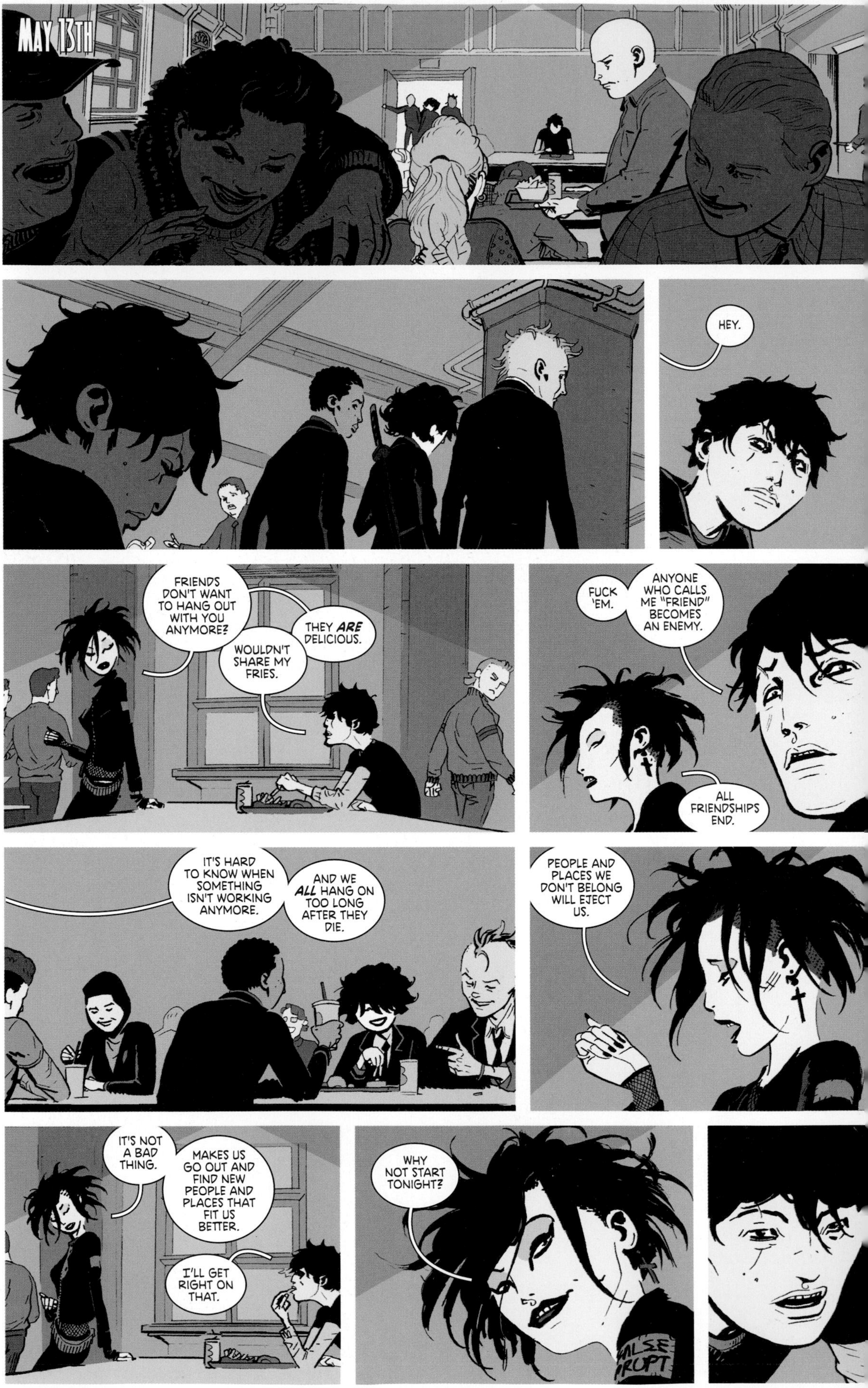
MAY 13TH
HEY.
FRIENDS DON'T WANT TO HANG OUT WITH YOU ANYMORE?
WOULDN'T SHARE MY FRIES.
THEY *ARE* DELICIOUS.
FUCK 'EM.
ANYONE WHO CALLS ME "FRIEND" BECOMES AN ENEMY.
ALL FRIENDSHIPS END.
IT'S HARD TO KNOW WHEN SOMETHING ISN'T WORKING ANYMORE.
AND WE *ALL* HANG ON TOO LONG AFTER THEY DIE.
PEOPLE AND PLACES WE DON'T BELONG WILL EJECT US.
IT'S NOT A BAD THING.
MAKES US GO OUT AND FIND NEW PEOPLE AND PLACES THAT FIT US BETTER.
I'LL GET RIGHT ON THAT.
WHY NOT START TONIGHT?

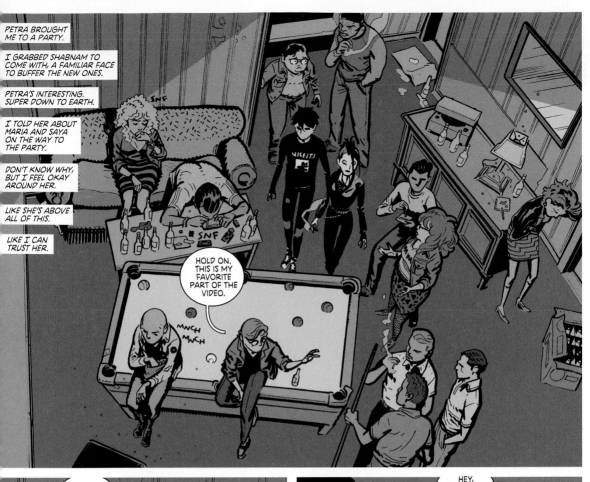

PETRA BROUGHT ME TO A PARTY.

I GRABBED SHABNAM TO COME WITH, A FAMILIAR FACE TO BUFFER THE NEW ONES.

PETRA'S INTERESTING. SUPER DOWN TO EARTH.

I TOLD HER ABOUT MARIA AND SAYA ON THE WAY TO THE PARTY.

DON'T KNOW WHY, BUT I FEEL OKAY AROUND HER.

LIKE SHE'S ABOVE ALL OF THIS.

LIKE I CAN TRUST HER.

SNF

SNF

MNCH MNCH

HOLD ON. THIS IS MY FAVORITE PART OF THE VIDEO.

FU-CK.

NOBODY SKATES POOL LIKE LUCERO. GNARLY FLOW, TOTALLY FLUID.

ZORLAC TEAM HAS MORE HEART.

HEY, SHABNAM.

DUDE, THAT'S THE GIRL I WAS TELLING YOU ABOUT.

KELLY. SHE'S SUPER HOT, RIGHT?

I WANTED TO SCORE POINTS WITH THE NEW GROUP.

I TOLD SHABNAM IF HE DRANK ALL THE BONG WATER SHE'D BE IMPRESSED.

OH, JESUS CHRIST!

IT FELT GOOD TO MAKE THEM LAUGH AT HIM.

EVERYONE KICKS THE DOG.

HAHA HAHA HA

HAHA HA

BLORF

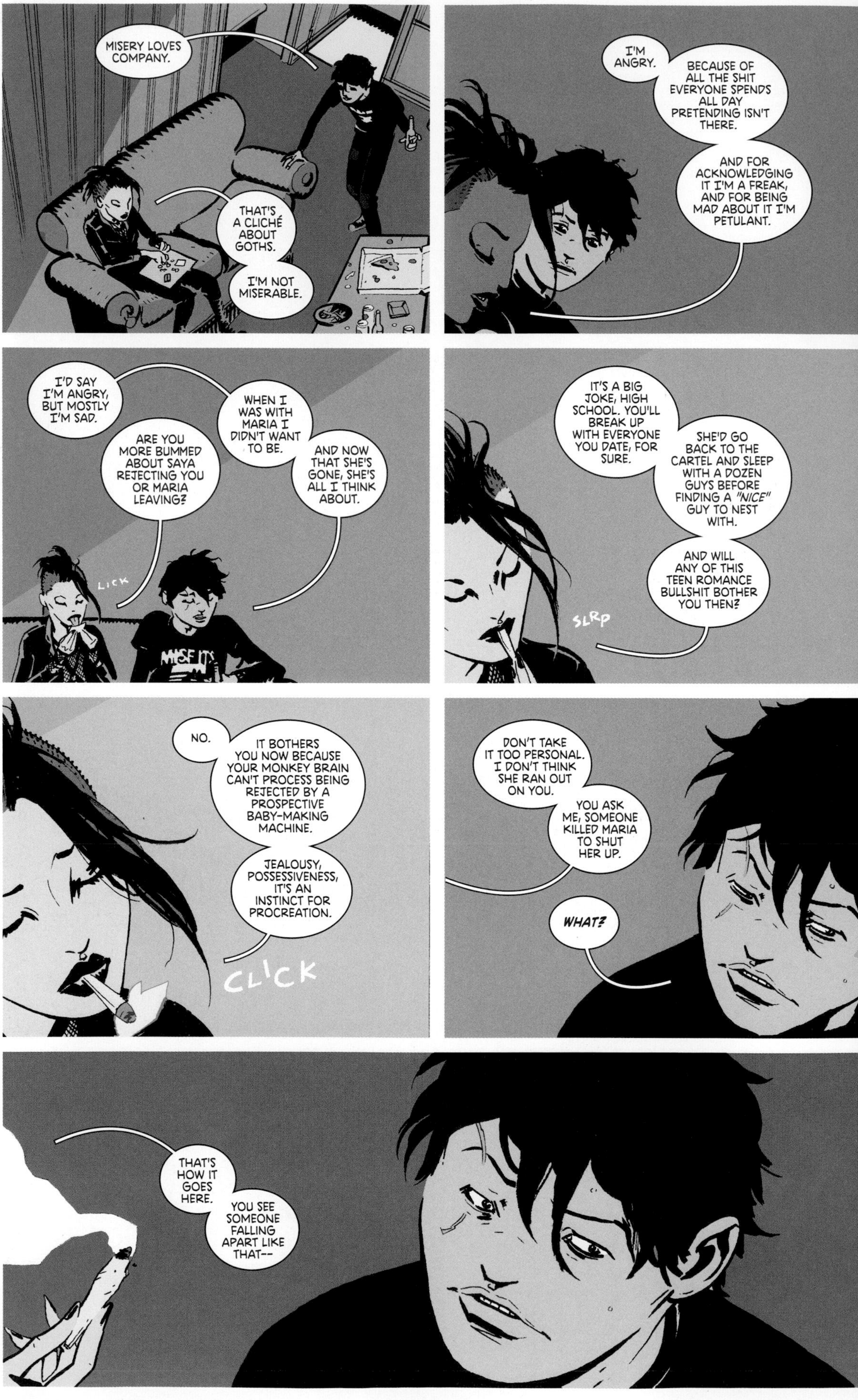
MISERY LOVES COMPANY.
THAT'S A CLICHÉ ABOUT GOTHS.
I'M NOT MISERABLE.
I'M ANGRY.
BECAUSE OF ALL THE SHIT EVERYONE SPENDS ALL DAY PRETENDING ISN'T THERE.
AND FOR ACKNOWLEDGING IT I'M A FREAK, AND FOR BEING MAD ABOUT IT I'M PETULANT.
I'D SAY I'M ANGRY, BUT MOSTLY I'M SAD.
WHEN I WAS WITH MARIA I DIDN'T WANT TO BE.
AND NOW THAT SHE'S GONE, SHE'S ALL I THINK ABOUT.
ARE YOU MORE BUMMED ABOUT SAYA REJECTING YOU OR MARIA LEAVING?
LICK
IT'S A BIG JOKE, HIGH SCHOOL. YOU'LL BREAK UP WITH EVERYONE YOU DATE, FOR SURE.
SHE'D GO BACK TO THE CARTEL AND SLEEP WITH A DOZEN GUYS BEFORE FINDING A "NICE" GUY TO NEST WITH.
AND WILL ANY OF THIS TEEN ROMANCE BULLSHIT BOTHER YOU THEN?
SLRP
NO.
IT BOTHERS YOU NOW BECAUSE YOUR MONKEY BRAIN CAN'T PROCESS BEING REJECTED BY A PROSPECTIVE BABY-MAKING MACHINE.
JEALOUSY, POSSESSIVENESS, IT'S AN INSTINCT FOR PROCREATION.
CLICK
DON'T TAKE IT TOO PERSONAL. I DON'T THINK SHE RAN OUT ON YOU.
YOU ASK ME, SOMEONE KILLED MARIA TO SHUT HER UP.
WHAT?
THAT'S HOW IT GOES HERE.
YOU SEE SOMEONE FALLING APART LIKE THAT--

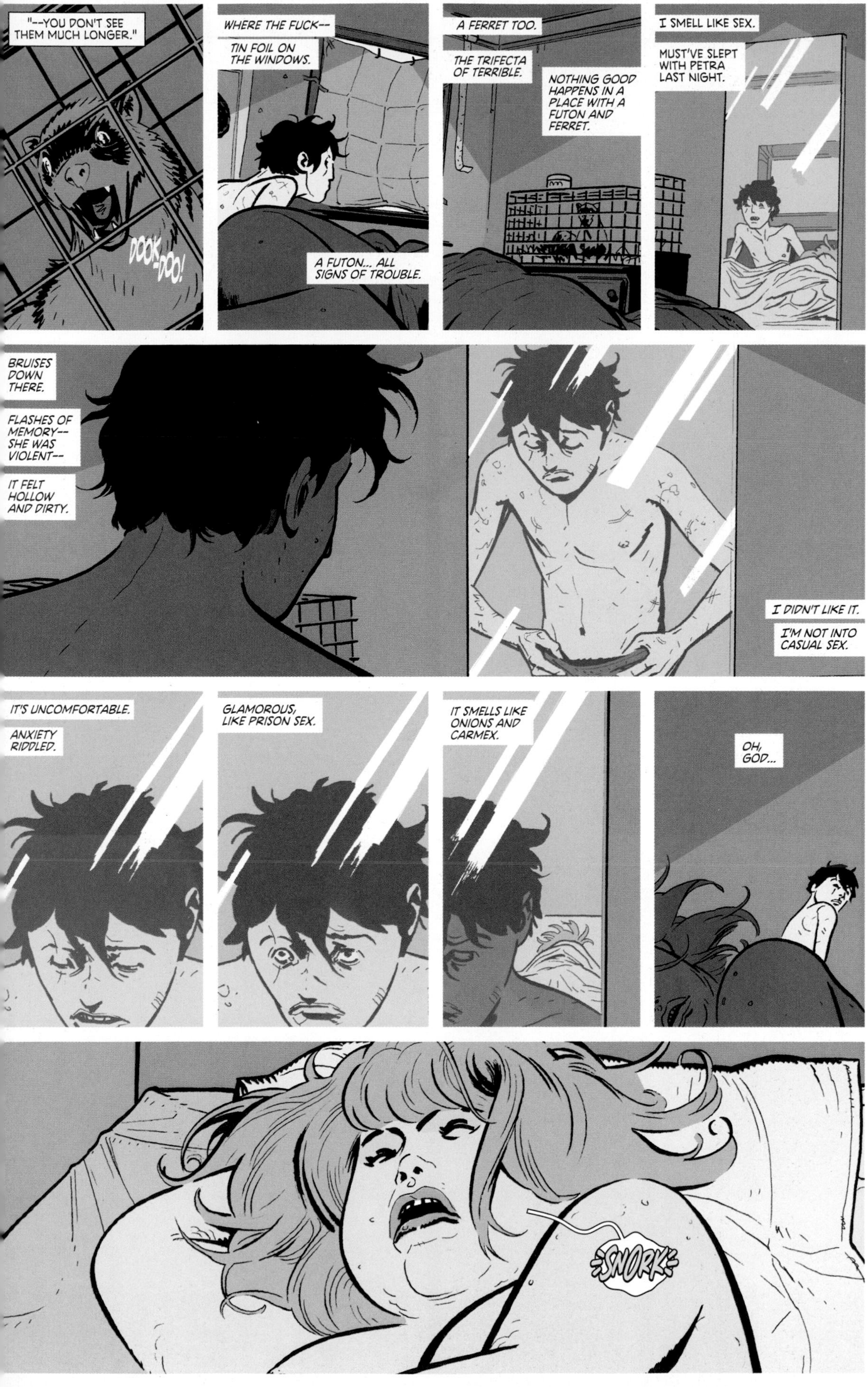
"--YOU DON'T SEE THEM MUCH LONGER."
DOOK-DOO!
WHERE THE FUCK--
TIN FOIL ON THE WINDOWS.
A FUTON... ALL SIGNS OF TROUBLE.
A FERRET TOO.
THE TRIFECTA OF TERRIBLE.
NOTHING GOOD HAPPENS IN A PLACE WITH A FUTON AND FERRET.
I SMELL LIKE SEX.
MUST'VE SLEPT WITH PETRA LAST NIGHT.
BRUISES DOWN THERE.
FLASHES OF MEMORY-- SHE WAS VIOLENT--
IT FELT HOLLOW AND DIRTY.
I DIDN'T LIKE IT.
I'M NOT INTO CASUAL SEX.
IT'S UNCOMFORTABLE.
ANXIETY RIDDLED.
GLAMOROUS, LIKE PRISON SEX.
IT SMELLS LIKE ONIONS AND CARMEX.
OH, GOD...
SNORK

A DARK HOLE.

*FALLING DEEPER
EVERY DAY.*

I NEED TO MAKE A CHANGE.

BUT DON'T I ALWAYS?

*EACH DAY IS
WORSE THAN
THE ONE
BEFORE IT.*

*NEED TO GET
COMFORTABLE
BEING ALONE.*

MY DICK IS SORE.

*BUT I KNOW
THE TRUTH NOW.*

*THE COLD
HARD
BULLSHIT.*

PETRA IS RIGHT.

*SOMEONE
KILLED MARIA.*

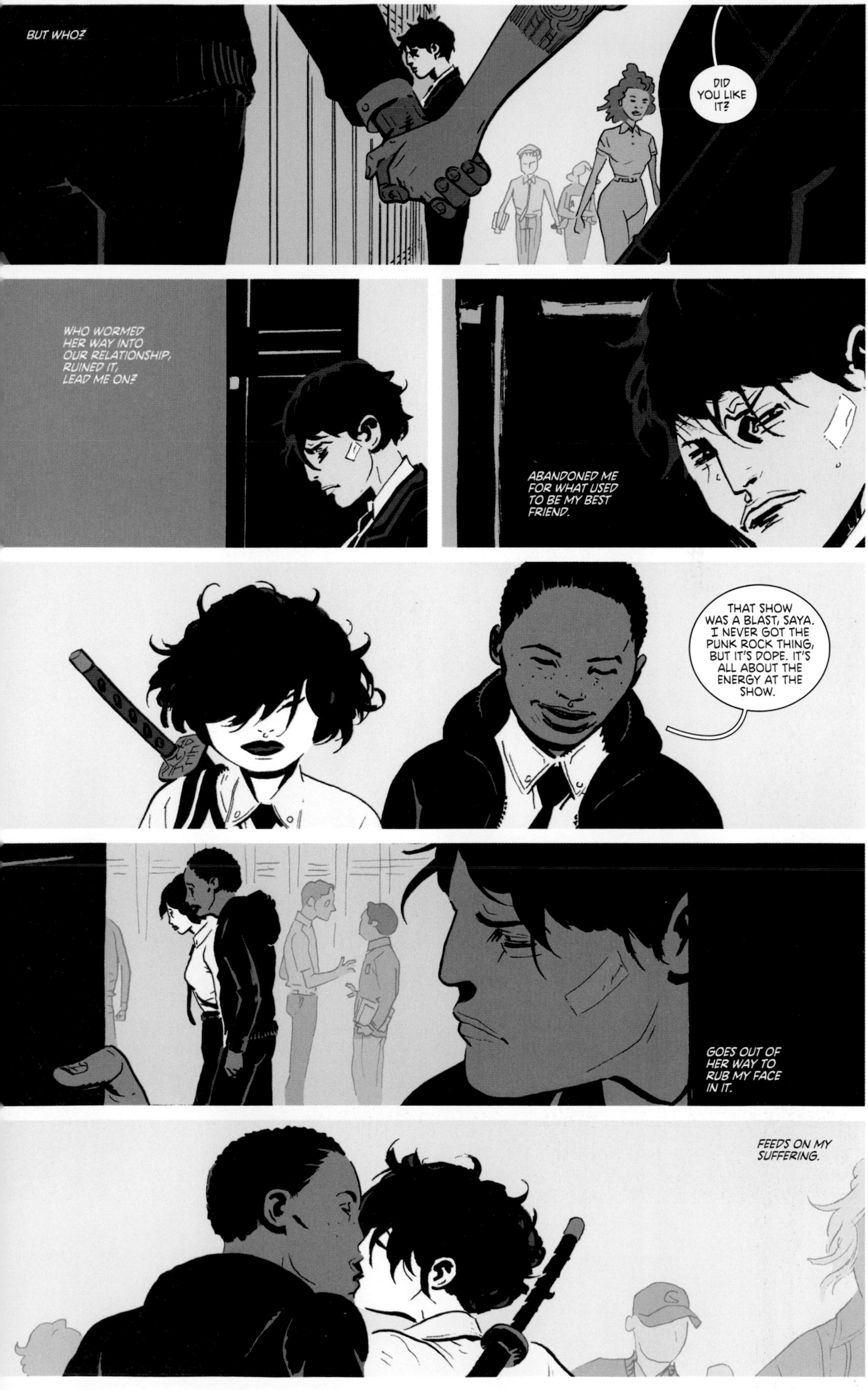
BUT WHO?
DID YOU LIKE IT?
WHO WORMED HER WAY INTO OUR RELATIONSHIP, RUINED IT, LEAD ME ON?
ABANDONED ME FOR WHAT USED TO BE MY BEST FRIEND.
THAT SHOW WAS A BLAST, SAYA. I NEVER GOT THE PUNK ROCK THING, BUT IT'S DOPE. IT'S ALL ABOUT THE ENERGY AT THE SHOW.
GOES OUT OF HER WAY TO RUB MY FACE IN IT.
FEEDS ON MY SUFFERING.

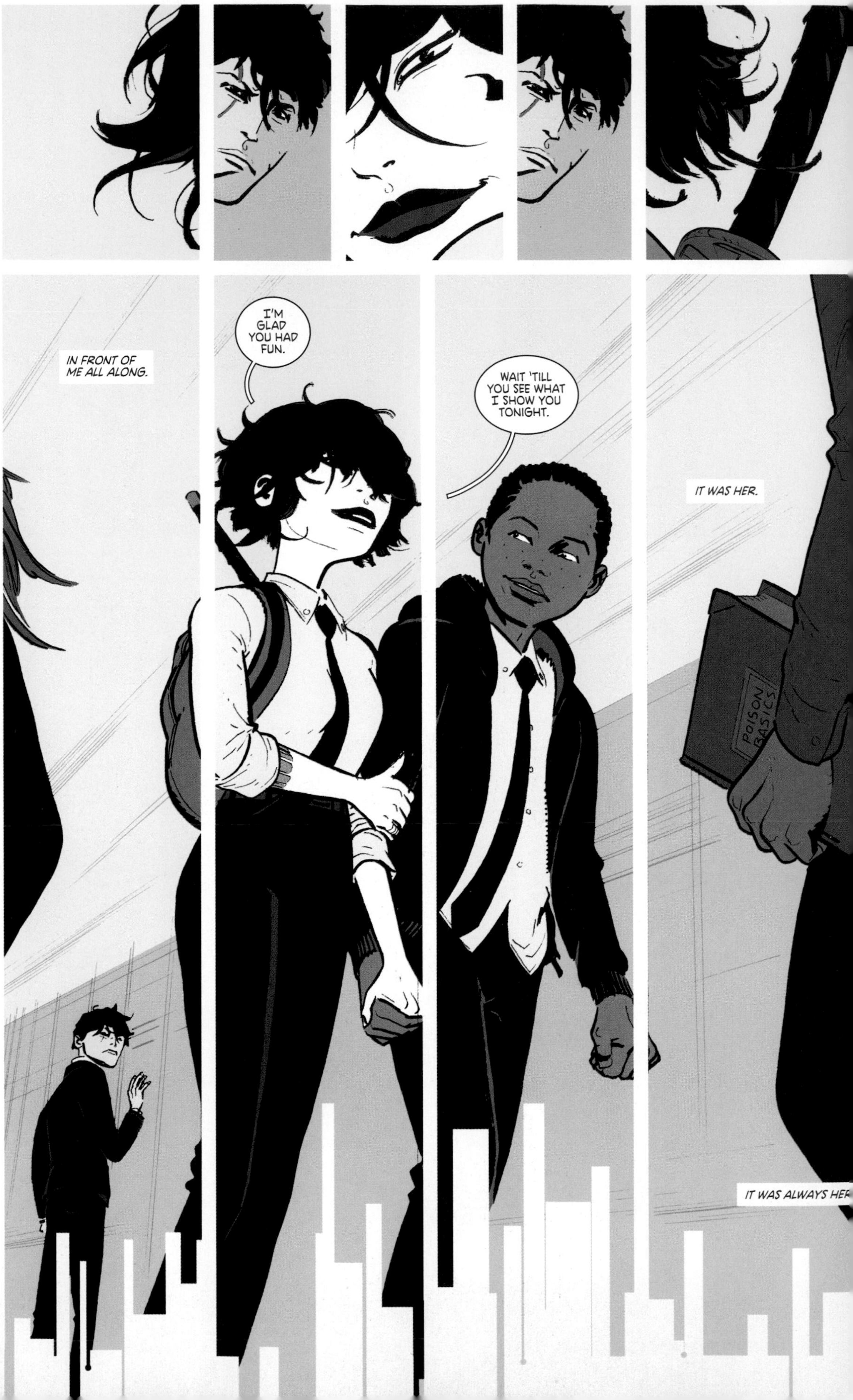
IN FRONT OF ME ALL ALONG.
I'M GLAD YOU HAD FUN.
WAIT 'TILL YOU SEE WHAT I SHOW YOU TONIGHT.
IT WAS HER.
POISON BASICS
IT WAS ALWAYS HER

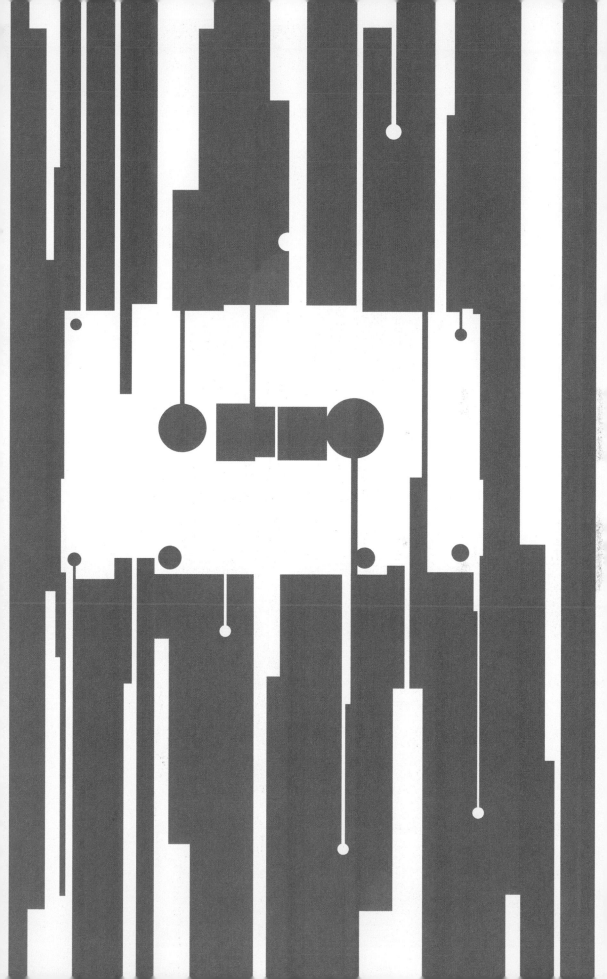

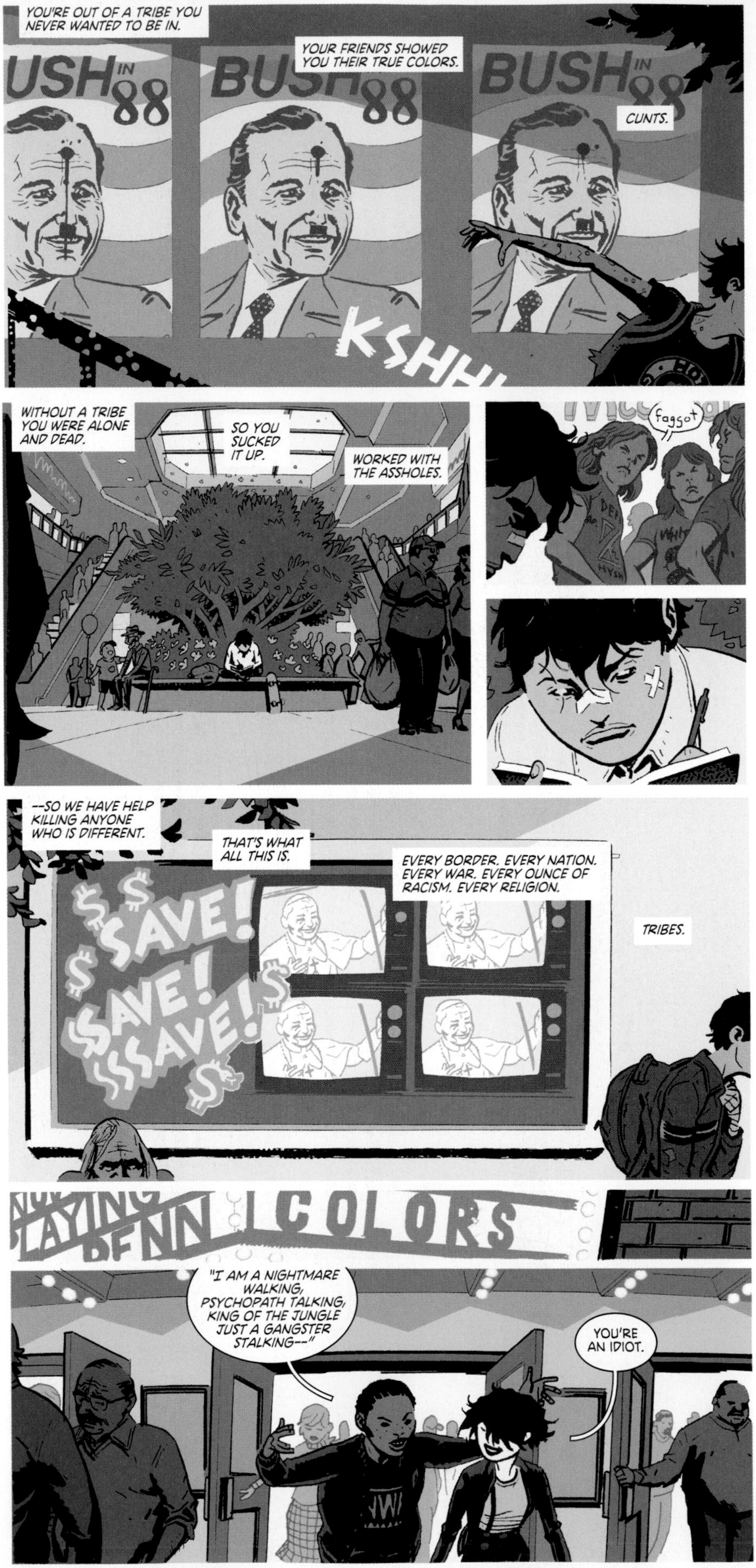
YOU'RE OUT OF A TRIBE YOU NEVER WANTED TO BE IN.
BUSH IN 88
YOUR FRIENDS SHOWED YOU THEIR TRUE COLORS.
CUNTS.
KSHH
WITHOUT A TRIBE YOU WERE ALONE AND DEAD.
SO YOU SUCKED IT UP.
WORKED WITH THE ASSHOLES.
faggot
--SO WE HAVE HELP KILLING ANYONE WHO IS DIFFERENT.
THAT'S WHAT ALL THIS IS.
EVERY BORDER. EVERY NATION. EVERY WAR. EVERY OUNCE OF RACISM. EVERY RELIGION.
TRIBES.
SAVE! SAVE! SAVE!
COLORS
"I AM A NIGHTMARE WALKING, PSYCHOPATH TALKING, KING OF THE JUNGLE JUST A GANGSTER STALKING--"
YOU'RE AN IDIOT.

SPINELESS POLITICIANS LOOKING OUT FOR NUMBER ONE.

HYPNOTICALLY FINGER-FUCKING AN ANCIENT INSTINCT TO SECURE TRIBAL ALLIANCES.

I GET IT. IN THE HARSH WILDERNESS OF OUR EVOLUTION YOU NEEDED THE TRIBE FOR SURVIVAL.

AND WE NEVER LOST THAT INSTINCT.

GANGS OF CAPITULATING ASSHOLES.

EVERY ACTION A POSE TO SECURE ACCEPTANCE.

MONKEYS TRYING TO TRICK OTHER MONKEYS INTO LOVING US SO WE DON'T STARVE IN THE WOODS, SO WE CAN SECURE A MATE--

THE ILLUSION OF SAFETY INSIDE A MOB.

I DON'T NEED A CLAN. DON'T NEED A FAMILY.

I'M BETTER OFF ON MY OWN. ON GUARD.

NO LONGER SURROUNDED BY PEOPLE WHO DON'T HAVE MY BEST INTEREST AT HEART.

BUT I'M JUST LIKE THEM.

AFRAID AND ALONE, INSTINCTS SCREAMING FOR ME TO JOIN A GANG.

TRYING TO FIT IN WITH THEM FUCKED MY SOUL.

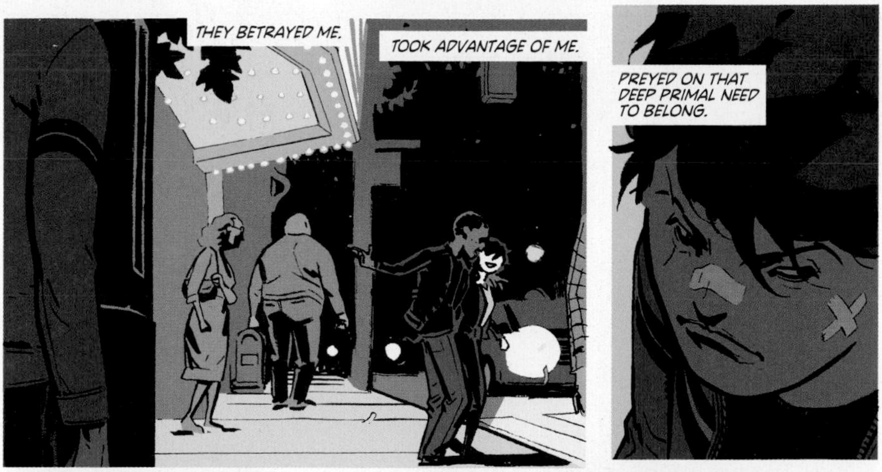
THEY BETRAYED ME.
TOOK ADVANTAGE OF ME.
PREYED ON THAT DEEP PRIMAL NEED TO BELONG.

WALK AWAY.

GROW STRONGER THROUGH SELF-RELIANCE.

DEAL WITH THEM ANOTHER DAY.

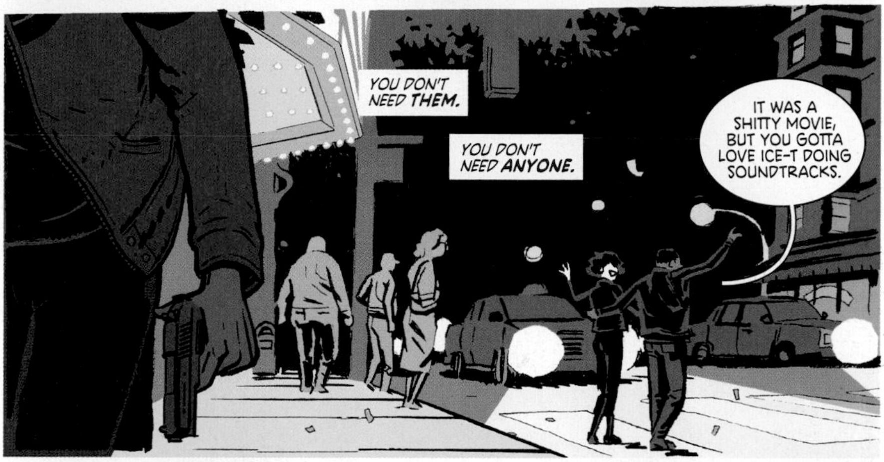
YOU DON'T NEED THEM.
YOU DON'T NEED ANYONE.
IT WAS A SHITTY MOVIE, BUT YOU GOTTA LOVE ICE-T DOING SOUNDTRACKS.

CAN'T TRUST ANYONE.

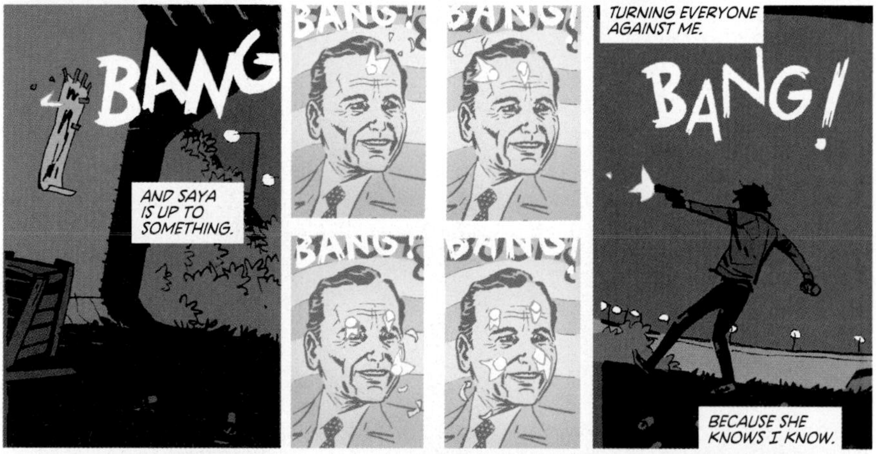
BANG
AND SAYA IS UP TO SOMETHING.
TURNING EVERYONE AGAINST ME.
BANG!
BECAUSE SHE KNOWS I KNOW.

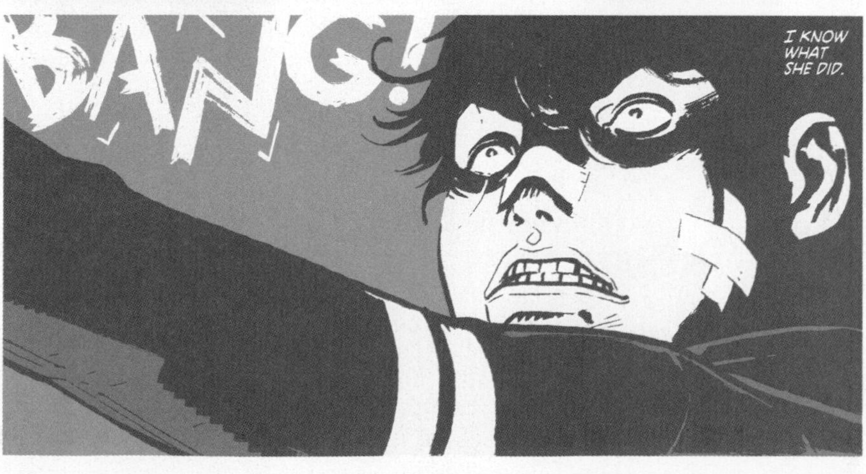
BANG!
I KNOW WHAT SHE DID.

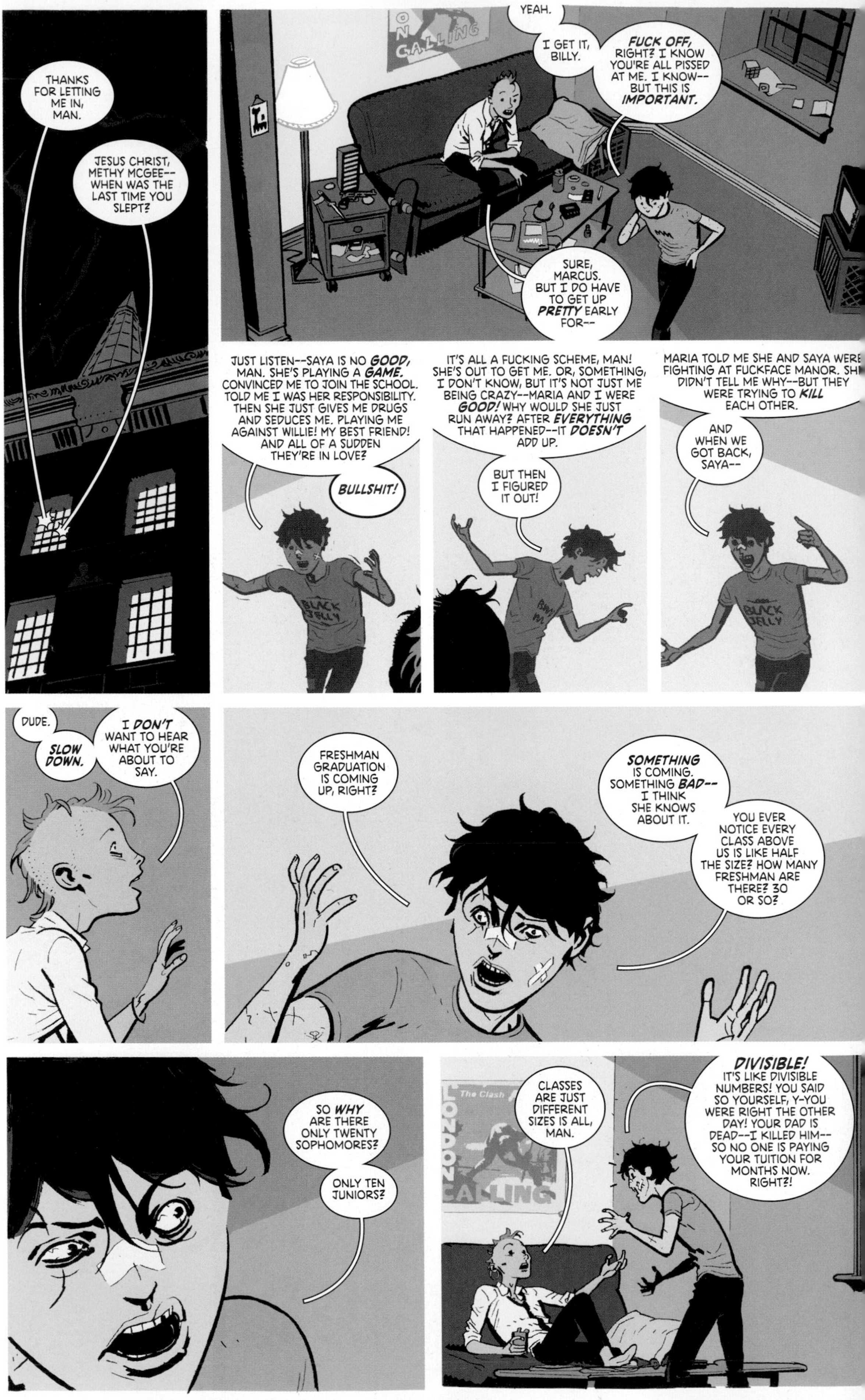
THANKS FOR LETTING ME IN, MAN.
JESUS CHRIST, METHY MCGEE-- WHEN WAS THE LAST TIME YOU SLEPT?
ON CALLING
YEAH.
I GET IT, BILLY.
FUCK OFF, RIGHT? I KNOW YOU'RE ALL PISSED AT ME. I KNOW-- BUT THIS IS IMPORTANT.
SURE, MARCUS. BUT I DO HAVE TO GET UP PRETTY EARLY FOR--
JUST LISTEN--SAYA IS NO GOOD, MAN. SHE'S PLAYING A GAME. CONVINCED ME TO JOIN THE SCHOOL. TOLD ME I WAS HER RESPONSIBILITY. THEN SHE JUST GIVES ME DRUGS AND SEDUCES ME. PLAYING ME AGAINST WILLIE! MY BEST FRIEND! AND ALL OF A SUDDEN THEY'RE IN LOVE?
BULLSHIT!
BLACK JELLY
IT'S ALL A FUCKING SCHEME, MAN! SHE'S OUT TO GET ME. OR, SOMETHING, I DON'T KNOW, BUT IT'S NOT JUST ME BEING CRAZY--MARIA AND I WERE GOOD! WHY WOULD SHE JUST RUN AWAY? AFTER EVERYTHING THAT HAPPENED--IT DOESN'T ADD UP.
BUT THEN I FIGURED IT OUT!
MARIA TOLD ME SHE AND SAYA WERE FIGHTING AT FUCKFACE MANOR. SHE DIDN'T TELL ME WHY--BUT THEY WERE TRYING TO KILL EACH OTHER.
AND WHEN WE GOT BACK, SAYA--
BLACK JELLY
DUDE.
SLOW DOWN.
I DON'T WANT TO HEAR WHAT YOU'RE ABOUT TO SAY.
FRESHMAN GRADUATION IS COMING UP, RIGHT?
SOMETHING IS COMING. SOMETHING BAD-- I THINK SHE KNOWS ABOUT IT.
YOU EVER NOTICE EVERY CLASS ABOVE US IS LIKE HALF THE SIZE? HOW MANY FRESHMAN ARE THERE? 30 OR SO?
SO WHY ARE THERE ONLY TWENTY SOPHOMORES?
ONLY TEN JUNIORS?
The Clash
LONDON CALLING
CLASSES ARE JUST DIFFERENT SIZES IS ALL, MAN.
DIVISIBLE! IT'S LIKE DIVISIBLE NUMBERS! YOU SAID SO YOURSELF, Y-YOU WERE RIGHT THE OTHER DAY! YOUR DAD IS DEAD--I KILLED HIM-- SO NO ONE IS PAYING YOUR TUITION FOR MONTHS NOW. RIGHT?!

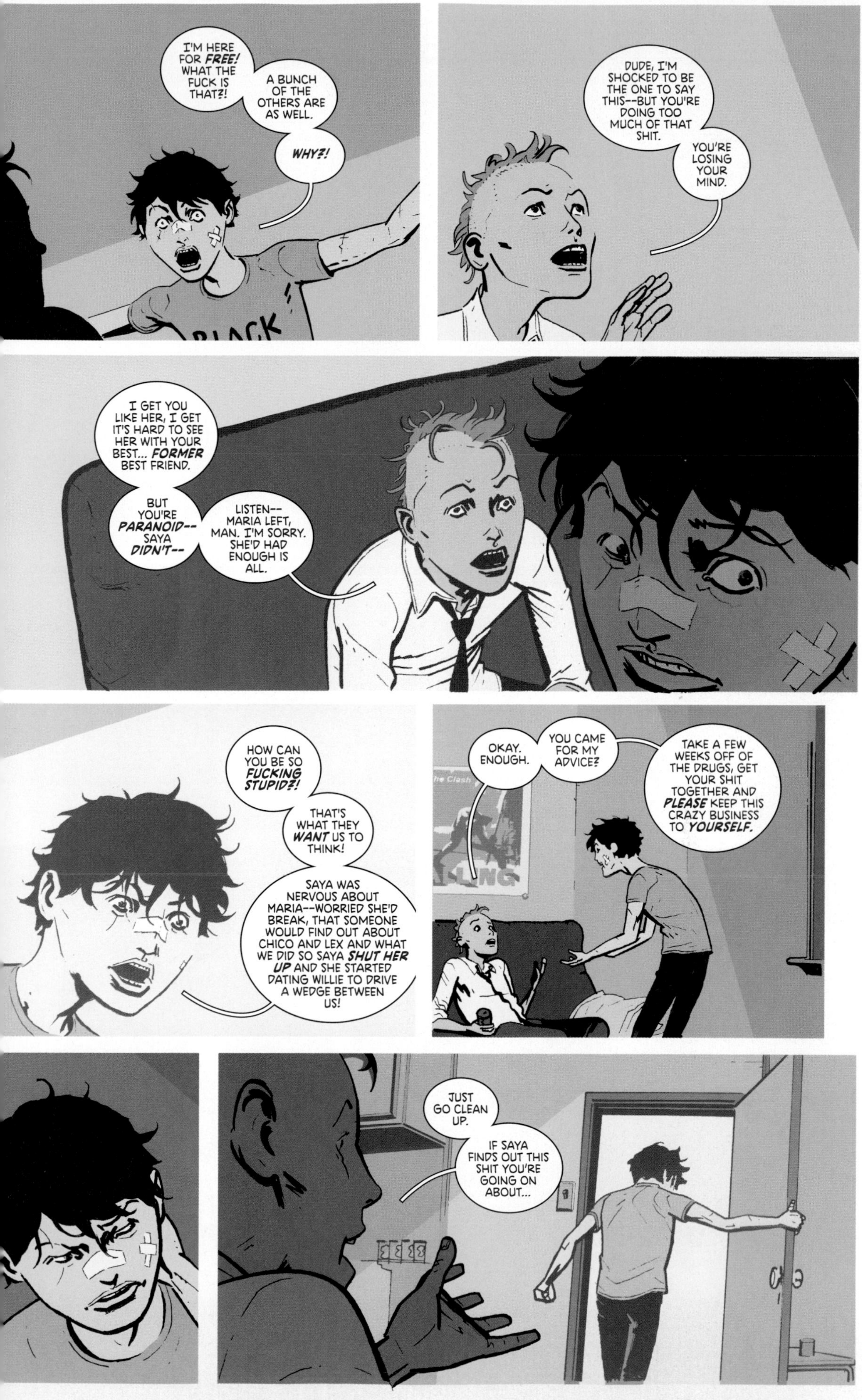
I'M HERE FOR FREE! WHAT THE FUCK IS THAT?!
A BUNCH OF THE OTHERS ARE AS WELL.
WHY?!
DUDE, I'M SHOCKED TO BE THE ONE TO SAY THIS--BUT YOU'RE DOING TOO MUCH OF THAT SHIT.
YOU'RE LOSING YOUR MIND.
I GET YOU LIKE HER, I GET IT'S HARD TO SEE HER WITH YOUR BEST... FORMER BEST FRIEND.
BUT YOU'RE PARANOID-- SAYA DIDN'T--
LISTEN-- MARIA LEFT, MAN. I'M SORRY. SHE'D HAD ENOUGH IS ALL.
HOW CAN YOU BE SO FUCKING STUPID?!
THAT'S WHAT THEY WANT US TO THINK!
SAYA WAS NERVOUS ABOUT MARIA--WORRIED SHE'D BREAK, THAT SOMEONE WOULD FIND OUT ABOUT CHICO AND LEX AND WHAT WE DID SO SAYA SHUT HER UP AND SHE STARTED DATING WILLIE TO DRIVE A WEDGE BETWEEN US!
OKAY. ENOUGH.
YOU CAME FOR MY ADVICE?
TAKE A FEW WEEKS OFF OF THE DRUGS, GET YOUR SHIT TOGETHER AND PLEASE KEEP THIS CRAZY BUSINESS TO YOURSELF.
JUST GO CLEAN UP.
IF SAYA FINDS OUT THIS SHIT YOU'RE GOING ON ABOUT...

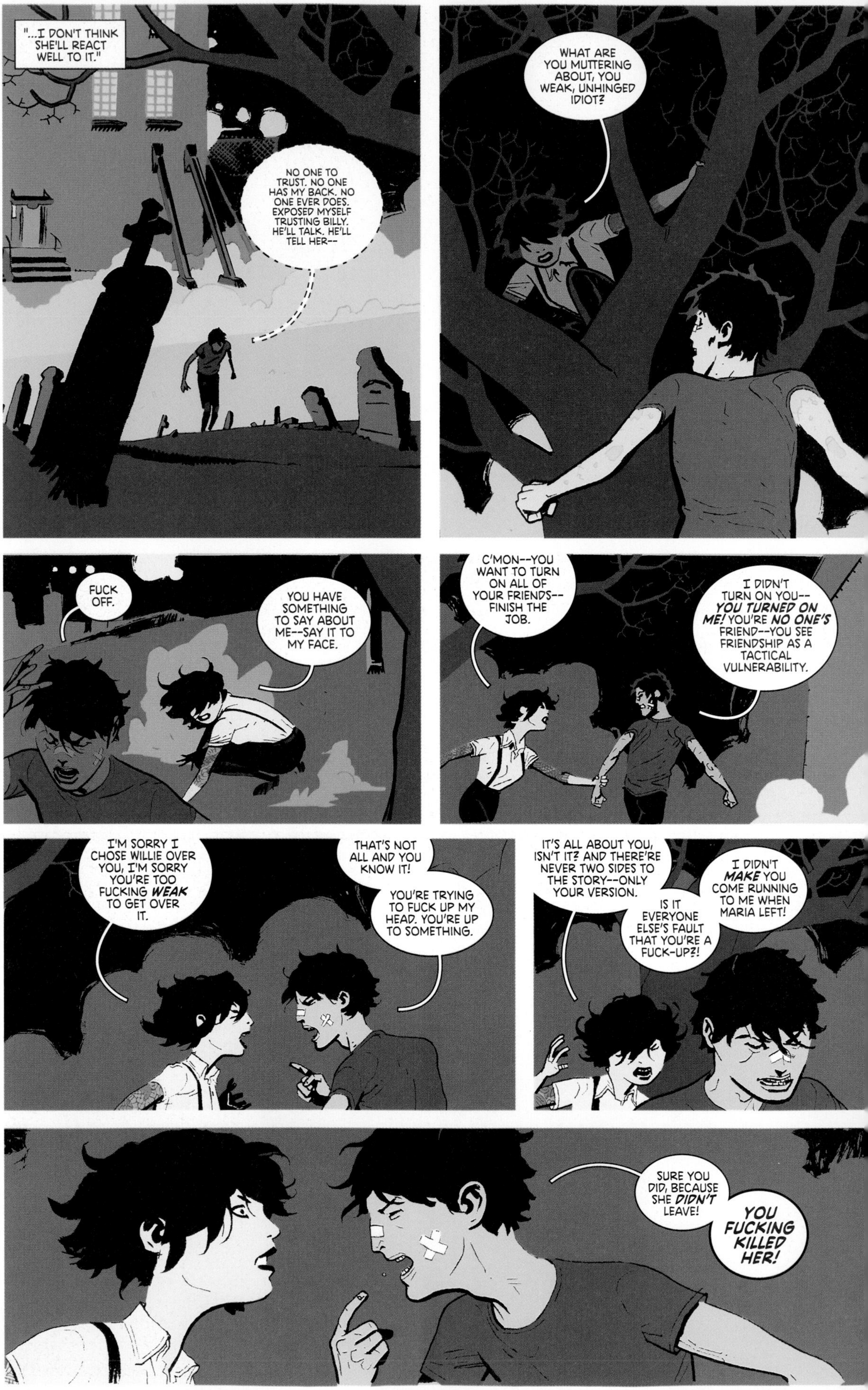

"...I DON'T THINK SHE'LL REACT WELL TO IT."
NO ONE TO TRUST. NO ONE HAS MY BACK. NO ONE EVER DOES. EXPOSED MYSELF TRUSTING BILLY. HE'LL TALK. HE'LL TELL HER--
WHAT ARE YOU MUTTERING ABOUT, YOU WEAK, UNHINGED IDIOT?
FUCK OFF.
YOU HAVE SOMETHING TO SAY ABOUT ME--SAY IT TO MY FACE.
C'MON--YOU WANT TO TURN ON ALL OF YOUR FRIENDS--FINISH THE JOB.
I DIDN'T TURN ON YOU--YOU TURNED ON ME! YOU'RE NO ONE'S FRIEND--YOU SEE FRIENDSHIP AS A TACTICAL VULNERABILITY.
I'M SORRY I CHOSE WILLIE OVER YOU, I'M SORRY YOU'RE TOO FUCKING WEAK TO GET OVER IT.
THAT'S NOT ALL AND YOU KNOW IT!
YOU'RE TRYING TO FUCK UP MY HEAD. YOU'RE UP TO SOMETHING.
IT'S ALL ABOUT YOU, ISN'T IT? AND THERE'RE NEVER TWO SIDES TO THE STORY--ONLY YOUR VERSION.
IS IT EVERYONE ELSE'S FAULT THAT YOU'RE A FUCK-UP?!
I DIDN'T MAKE YOU COME RUNNING TO ME WHEN MARIA LEFT!
SURE YOU DID, BECAUSE SHE DIDN'T LEAVE!
YOU FUCKING KILLED HER!

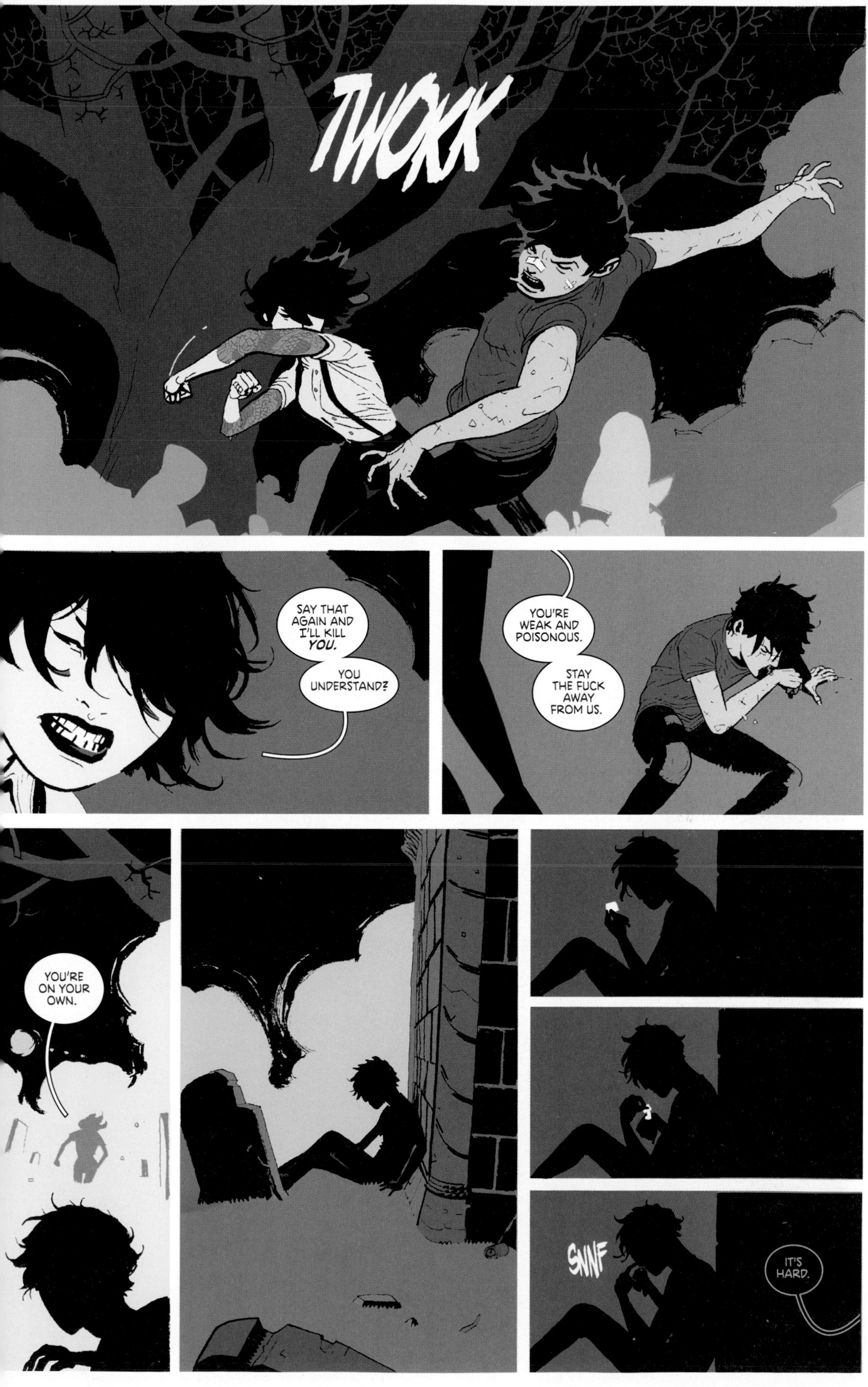
TWOKK
SAY THAT AGAIN AND I'LL KILL *YOU.*
YOU UNDERSTAND?
YOU'RE WEAK AND POISONOUS.
STAY THE FUCK AWAY FROM US.
YOU'RE ON YOUR OWN.
SNIF
IT'S HARD.

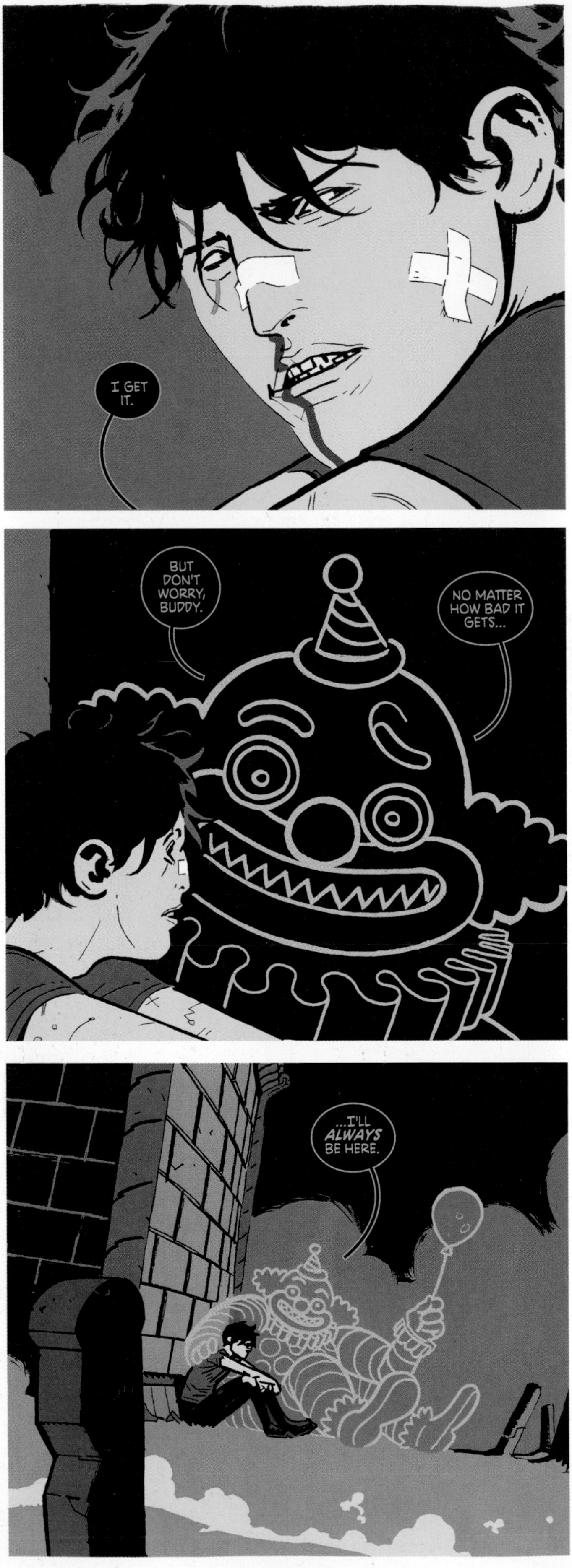
I GET IT.
BUT DON'T WORRY, BUDDY.
NO MATTER HOW BAD IT GETS...
...I'LL *ALWAYS* BE HERE.

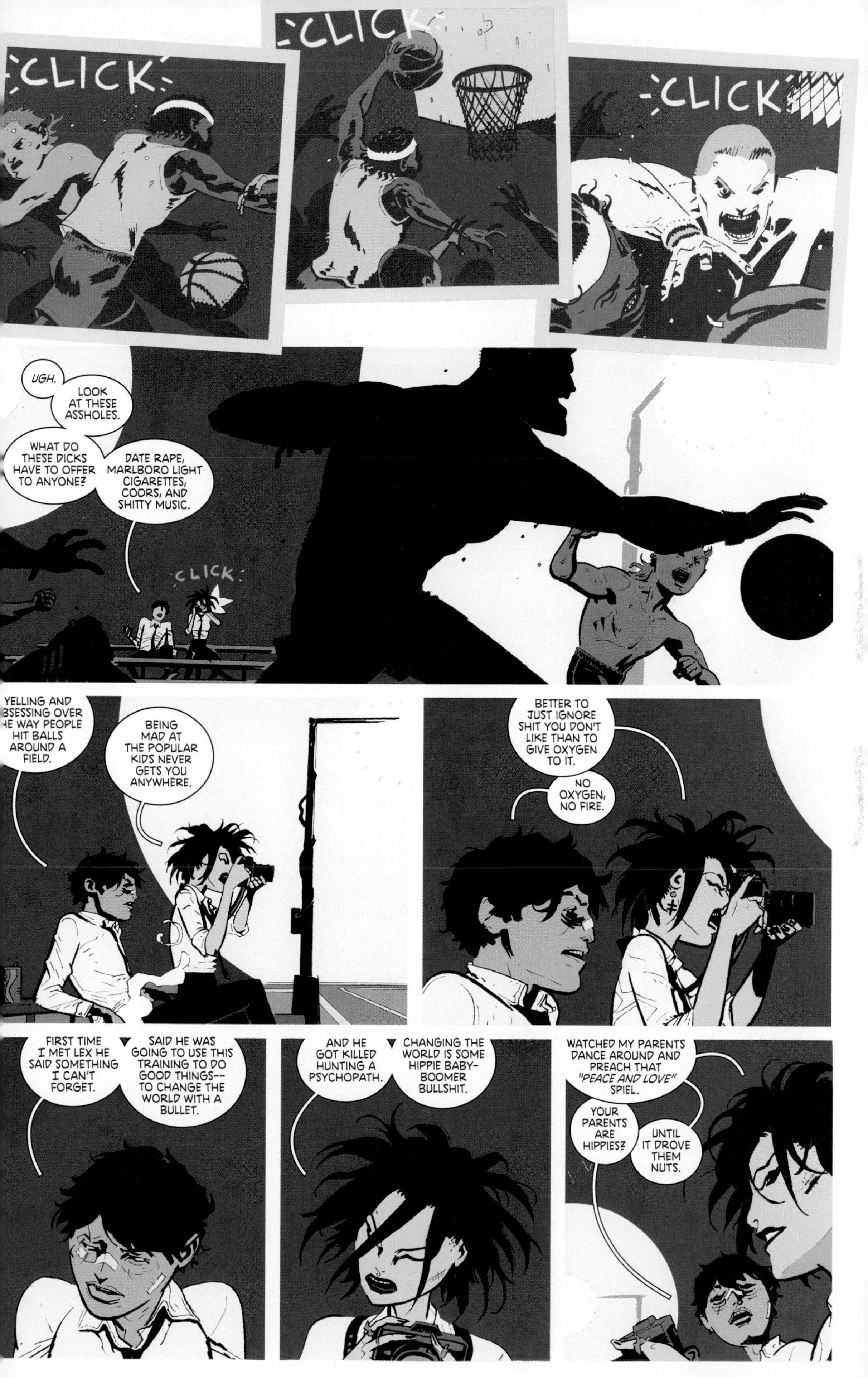
CLICK
CLICK
CLICK
UGH.
LOOK AT THESE ASSHOLES.
WHAT DO THESE DICKS HAVE TO OFFER TO ANYONE?
DATE RAPE, MARLBORO LIGHT CIGARETTES, COORS, AND SHITTY MUSIC.
CLICK
YELLING AND BSESSING OVER HE WAY PEOPLE HIT BALLS AROUND A FIELD.
BEING MAD AT THE POPULAR KIDS NEVER GETS YOU ANYWHERE.
BETTER TO JUST IGNORE SHIT YOU DON'T LIKE THAN TO GIVE OXYGEN TO IT.
NO OXYGEN, NO FIRE.
FIRST TIME I MET LEX HE SAID SOMETHING I CAN'T FORGET.
SAID HE WAS GOING TO USE THIS TRAINING TO DO GOOD THINGS-- TO CHANGE THE WORLD WITH A BULLET.
AND HE GOT KILLED HUNTING A PSYCHOPATH.
CHANGING THE WORLD IS SOME HIPPIE BABY-BOOMER BULLSHIT.
WATCHED MY PARENTS DANCE AROUND AND PREACH THAT *"PEACE AND LOVE"* SPIEL.
YOUR PARENTS ARE HIPPIES?
UNTIL IT DROVE THEM NUTS.

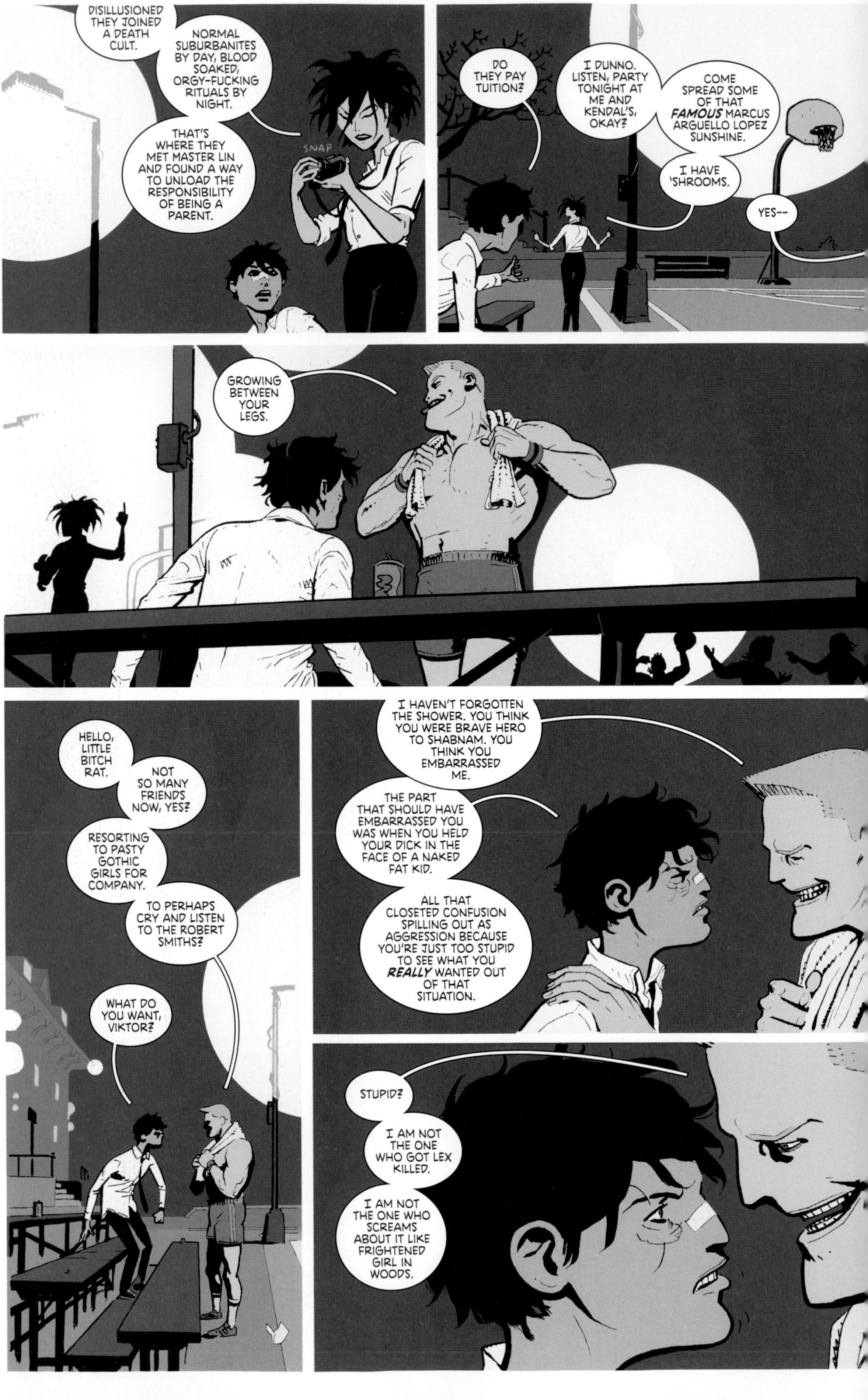

DISILLUSIONED THEY JOINED A DEATH CULT.
NORMAL SUBURBANITES BY DAY, BLOOD SOAKED, ORGY-FUCKING RITUALS BY NIGHT.
THAT'S WHERE THEY MET MASTER LIN AND FOUND A WAY TO UNLOAD THE RESPONSIBILITY OF BEING A PARENT.
SNAP
DO THEY PAY TUITION?
I DUNNO. LISTEN, PARTY TONIGHT AT ME AND KENDAL'S, OKAY?
COME SPREAD SOME OF THAT FAMOUS MARCUS ARGUELLO LOPEZ SUNSHINE.
I HAVE 'SHROOMS.
YES--
GROWING BETWEEN YOUR LEGS.
HELLO, LITTLE BITCH RAT.
NOT SO MANY FRIENDS NOW, YES?
RESORTING TO PASTY GOTHIC GIRLS FOR COMPANY.
TO PERHAPS CRY AND LISTEN TO THE ROBERT SMITHS?
WHAT DO YOU WANT, VIKTOR?
I HAVEN'T FORGOTTEN THE SHOWER. YOU THINK YOU WERE BRAVE HERO TO SHABNAM. YOU THINK YOU EMBARRASSED ME.
THE PART THAT SHOULD HAVE EMBARRASSED YOU WAS WHEN YOU HELD YOUR DICK IN THE FACE OF A NAKED FAT KID.
ALL THAT CLOSETED CONFUSION SPILLING OUT AS AGGRESSION BECAUSE YOU'RE JUST TOO STUPID TO SEE WHAT YOU REALLY WANTED OUT OF THAT SITUATION.
STUPID?
I AM NOT THE ONE WHO GOT LEX KILLED.
I AM NOT THE ONE WHO SCREAMS ABOUT IT LIKE FRIGHTENED GIRL IN WOODS.

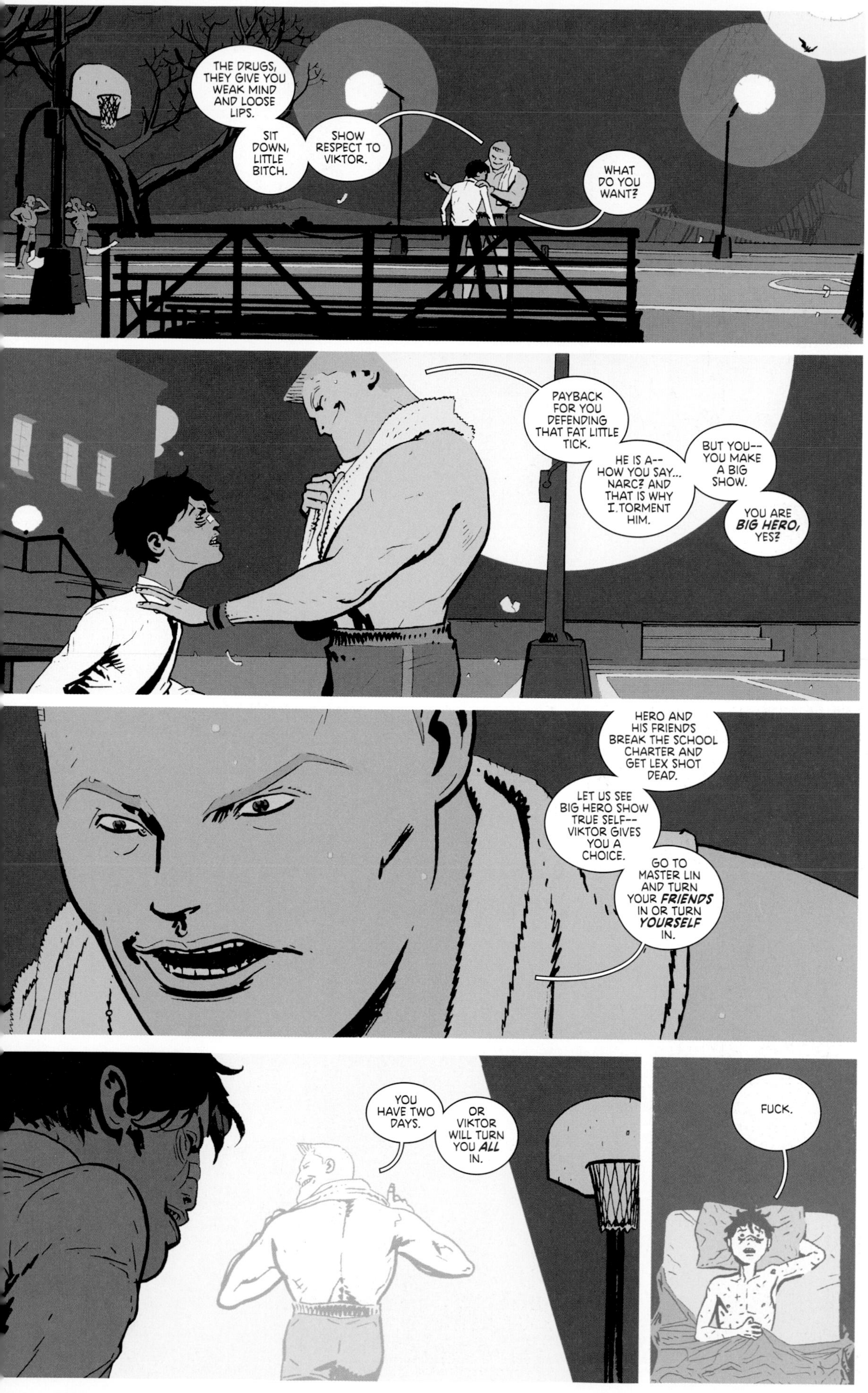
THE DRUGS, THEY GIVE YOU WEAK MIND AND LOOSE LIPS.
SIT DOWN, LITTLE BITCH.
SHOW RESPECT TO VIKTOR.
WHAT DO YOU WANT?
PAYBACK FOR YOU DEFENDING THAT FAT LITTLE TICK.
HE IS A-- HOW YOU SAY... NARC? AND THAT IS WHY I TORMENT HIM.
BUT YOU-- YOU MAKE A BIG SHOW.
YOU ARE BIG HERO, YES?
HERO AND HIS FRIENDS BREAK THE SCHOOL CHARTER AND GET LEX SHOT DEAD.
LET US SEE BIG HERO SHOW TRUE SELF-- VIKTOR GIVES YOU A CHOICE.
GO TO MASTER LIN AND TURN YOUR FRIENDS IN OR TURN YOURSELF IN.
YOU HAVE TWO DAYS.
OR VIKTOR WILL TURN YOU ALL IN.
FUCK.

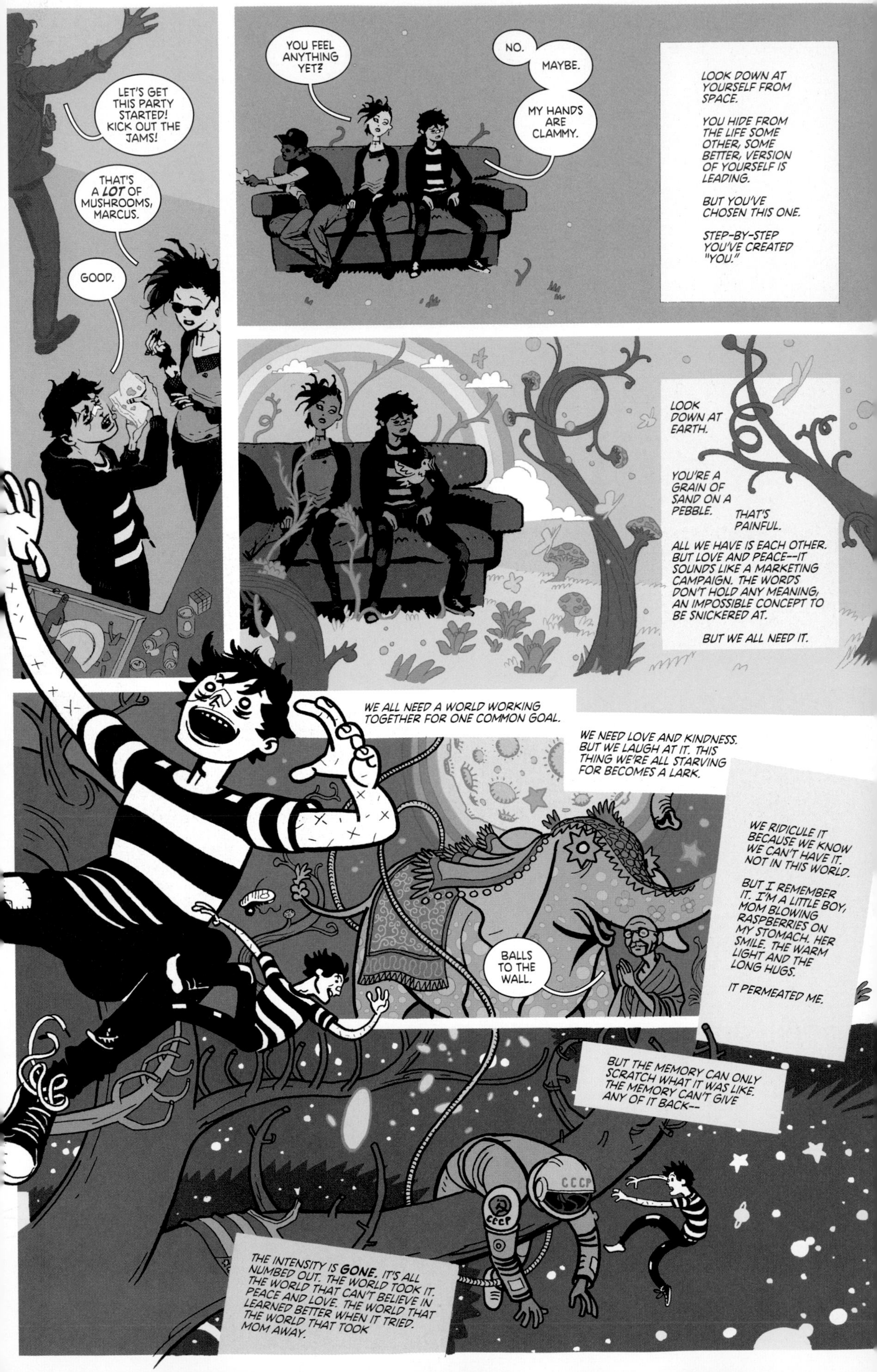
LET'S GET THIS PARTY STARTED! KICK OUT THE JAMS!
THAT'S A LOT OF MUSHROOMS, MARCUS.
GOOD.
YOU FEEL ANYTHING YET?
NO.
MAYBE.
MY HANDS ARE CLAMMY.
LOOK DOWN AT YOURSELF FROM SPACE.
YOU HIDE FROM THE LIFE SOME OTHER, SOME BETTER, VERSION OF YOURSELF IS LEADING.
BUT YOU'VE CHOSEN THIS ONE.
STEP-BY-STEP YOU'VE CREATED "YOU."
LOOK DOWN AT EARTH.
YOU'RE A GRAIN OF SAND ON A PEBBLE.
THAT'S PAINFUL.
ALL WE HAVE IS EACH OTHER. BUT LOVE AND PEACE--IT SOUNDS LIKE A MARKETING CAMPAIGN. THE WORDS DON'T HOLD ANY MEANING, AN IMPOSSIBLE CONCEPT TO BE SNICKERED AT.
BUT WE ALL NEED IT.
WE ALL NEED A WORLD WORKING TOGETHER FOR ONE COMMON GOAL.
WE NEED LOVE AND KINDNESS. BUT WE LAUGH AT IT. THIS THING WE'RE ALL STARVING FOR BECOMES A LARK.
WE RIDICULE IT BECAUSE WE KNOW WE CAN'T HAVE IT. NOT IN THIS WORLD.
BUT I REMEMBER IT. I'M A LITTLE BOY, MOM BLOWING RASPBERRIES ON MY STOMACH. HER SMILE. THE WARM LIGHT AND THE LONG HUGS.
IT PERMEATED ME.
BALLS TO THE WALL.
BUT THE MEMORY CAN ONLY SCRATCH WHAT IT WAS LIKE. THE MEMORY CAN'T GIVE ANY OF IT BACK--
CCCP
CCCP
THE INTENSITY IS GONE. IT'S ALL NUMBED OUT. THE WORLD TOOK IT. THE WORLD THAT CAN'T BELIEVE IN PEACE AND LOVE. THE WORLD THAT LEARNED BETTER WHEN IT TRIED. THE WORLD THAT TOOK MOM AWAY.

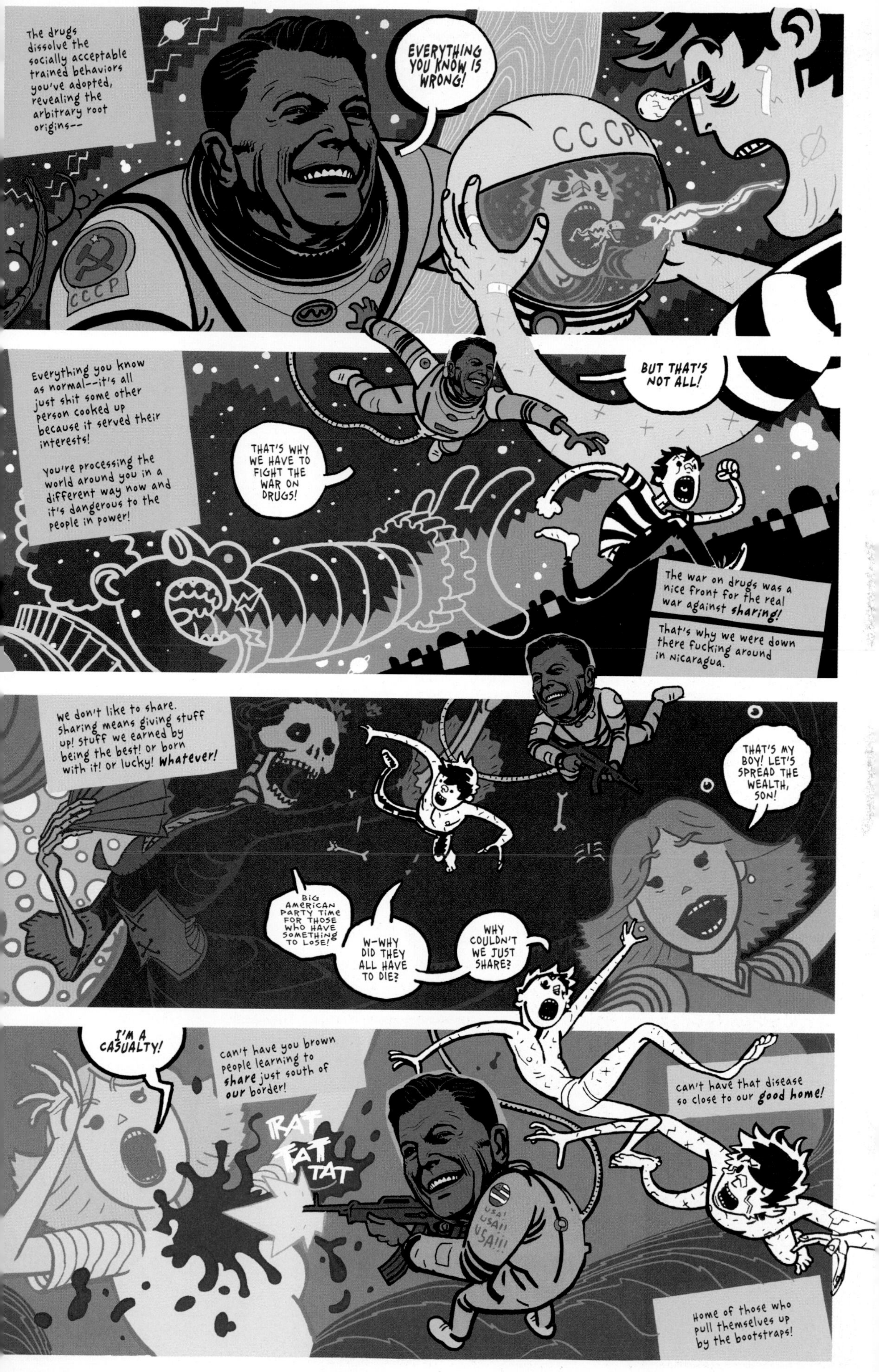

The drugs dissolve the socially acceptable trained behaviors you've adopted, revealing the arbitrary root origins--
EVERYTHING YOU KNOW IS WRONG!
CCCP
CCCP
CCCP
Everything you know as normal--it's all just shit some other person cooked up because it served their interests!
You're processing the world around you in a different way now and it's dangerous to the people in power!
BUT THAT'S NOT ALL!
THAT'S WHY WE HAVE TO FIGHT THE WAR ON DRUGS!
The war on drugs was a nice front for the real war against sharing!
That's why we were down there fucking around in Nicaragua.
We don't like to share. Sharing means giving stuff up! Stuff we earned by being the best! Or born with it! Or lucky! Whatever!
THAT'S MY BOY! LET'S SPREAD THE WEALTH, SON!
BIG AMERICAN PARTY TIME FOR THOSE WHO HAVE SOMETHING TO LOSE!
W-WHY DID THEY ALL HAVE TO DIE?
WHY COULDN'T WE JUST SHARE?
I'M A CASUALTY!
Can't have you brown people learning to share just south of our border!
Can't have that disease so close to our good home!
RAT TAT TAT
USA! USA!! USA!!!
Home of those who pull themselves up by the bootstraps!

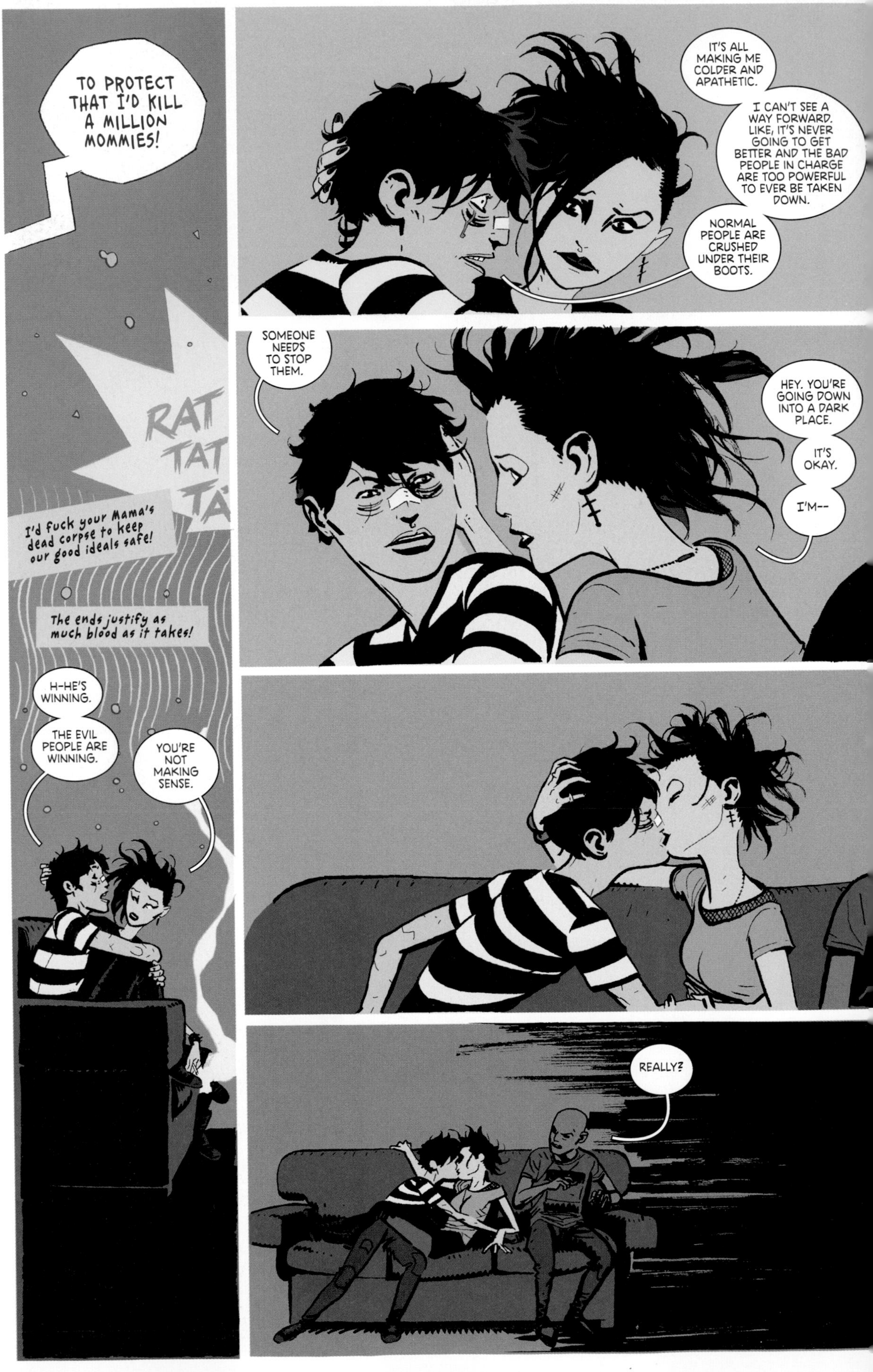

TO PROTECT THAT I'D KILL A MILLION MOMMIES!
RAT TAT TA
I'd fuck your Mama's dead corpse to keep our good ideals safe!
The ends justify as much blood as it takes!
H-HE'S WINNING.
THE EVIL PEOPLE ARE WINNING.
YOU'RE NOT MAKING SENSE.
IT'S ALL MAKING ME COLDER AND APATHETIC.
I CAN'T SEE A WAY FORWARD. LIKE, IT'S NEVER GOING TO GET BETTER AND THE BAD PEOPLE IN CHARGE ARE TOO POWERFUL TO EVER BE TAKEN DOWN.
NORMAL PEOPLE ARE CRUSHED UNDER THEIR BOOTS.
SOMEONE NEEDS TO STOP THEM.
HEY. YOU'RE GOING DOWN INTO A DARK PLACE.
IT'S OKAY.
I'M--
REALLY?

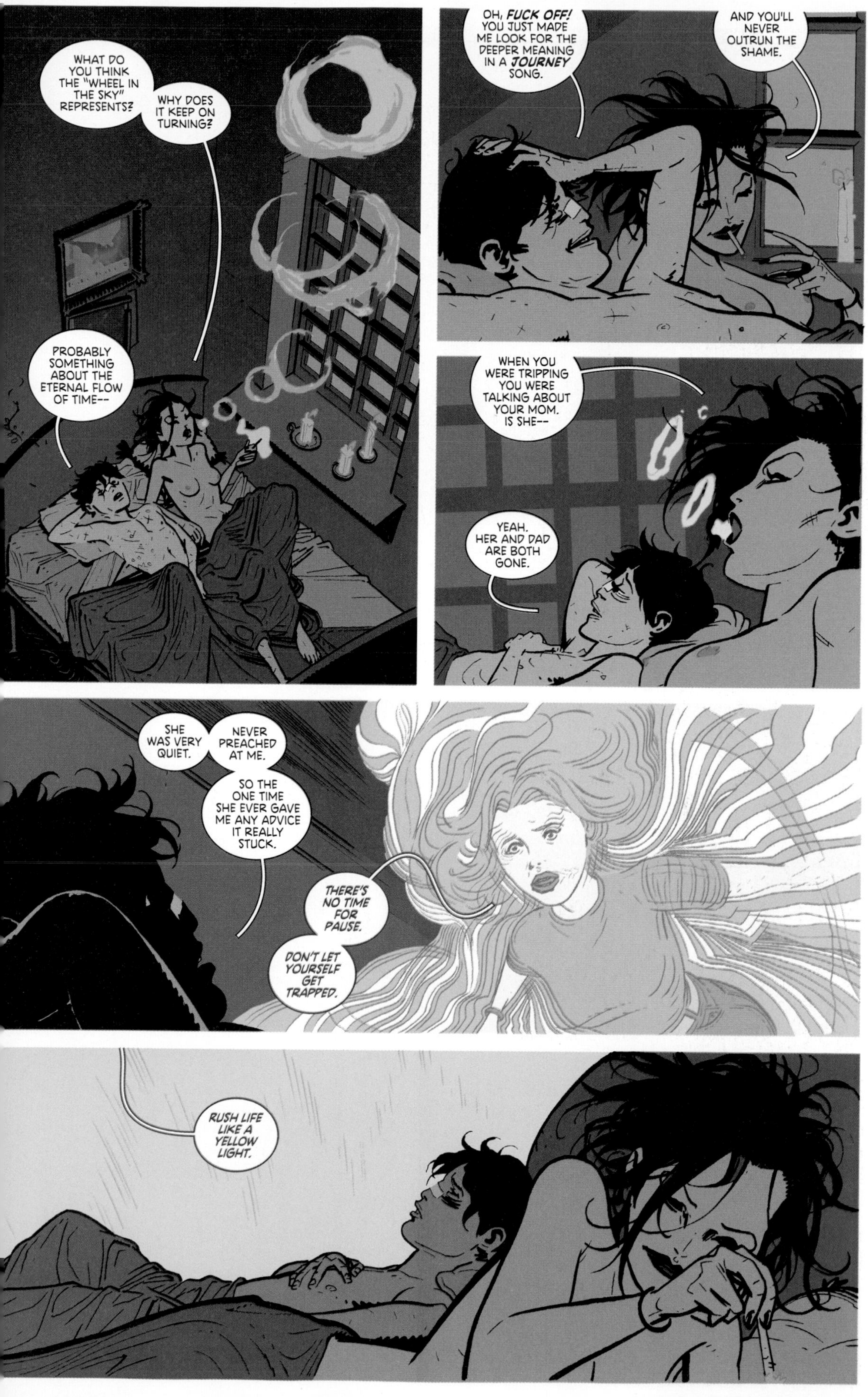

WHAT DO YOU THINK THE "WHEEL IN THE SKY" REPRESENTS?
WHY DOES IT KEEP ON TURNING?
PROBABLY SOMETHING ABOUT THE ETERNAL FLOW OF TIME--
OH, FUCK OFF! YOU JUST MADE ME LOOK FOR THE DEEPER MEANING IN A JOURNEY SONG.
AND YOU'LL NEVER OUTRUN THE SHAME.
WHEN YOU WERE TRIPPING YOU WERE TALKING ABOUT YOUR MOM. IS SHE--
YEAH. HER AND DAD ARE BOTH GONE.
SHE WAS VERY QUIET.
NEVER PREACHED AT ME.
SO THE ONE TIME SHE EVER GAVE ME ANY ADVICE IT REALLY STUCK.
THERE'S NO TIME FOR PAUSE.
DON'T LET YOURSELF GET TRAPPED.
RUSH LIFE LIKE A YELLOW LIGHT.

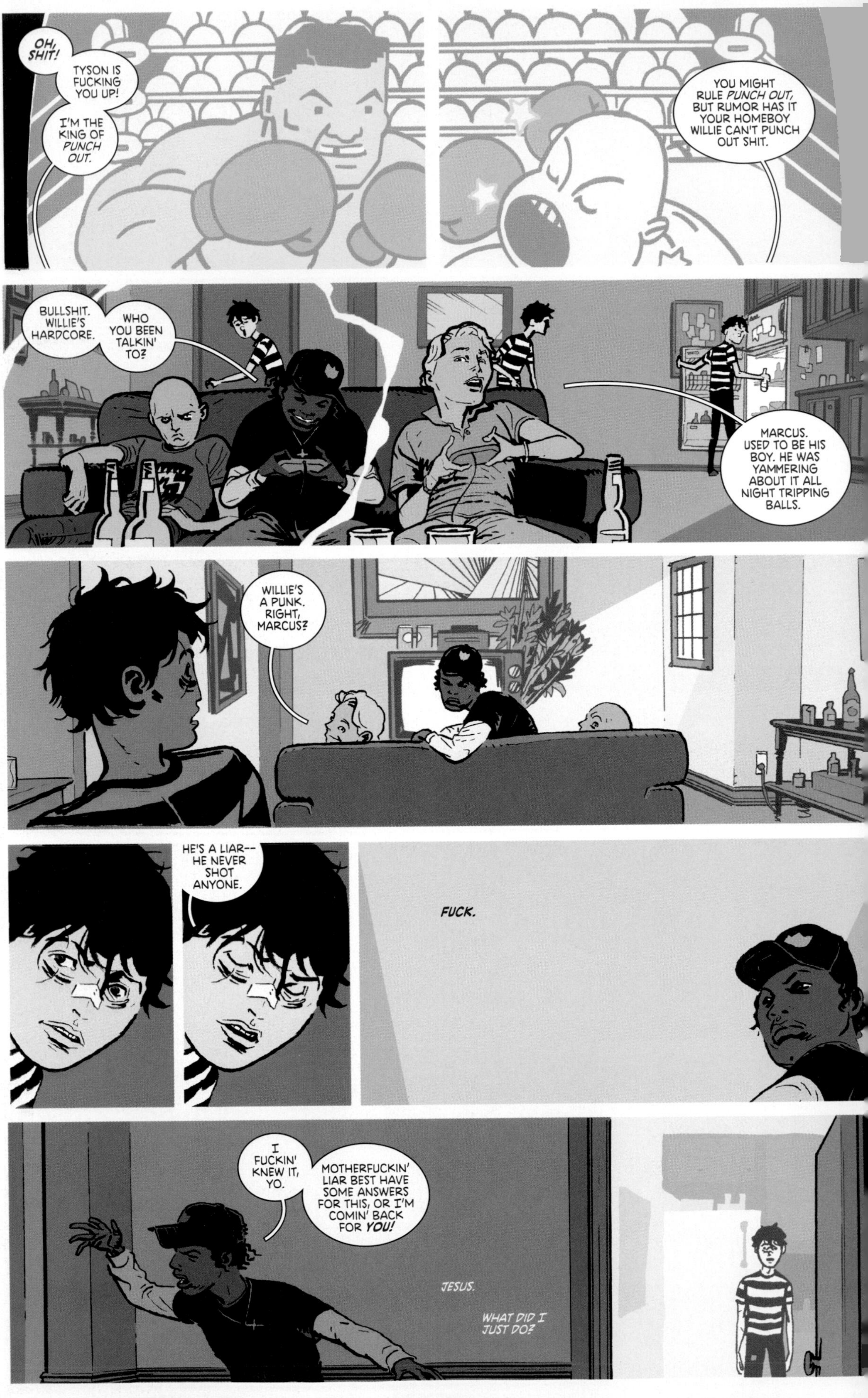
OH, SHIT!
TYSON IS FUCKING YOU UP!
I'M THE KING OF PUNCH OUT.
YOU MIGHT RULE PUNCH OUT, BUT RUMOR HAS IT YOUR HOMEBOY WILLIE CAN'T PUNCH OUT SHIT.
BULLSHIT. WILLIE'S HARDCORE.
WHO YOU BEEN TALKIN' TO?
MARCUS. USED TO BE HIS BOY. HE WAS YAMMERING ABOUT IT ALL NIGHT TRIPPING BALLS.
WILLIE'S A PUNK. RIGHT, MARCUS?
HE'S A LIAR-- HE NEVER SHOT ANYONE.
FUCK.
I FUCKIN' KNEW IT, YO.
MOTHERFUCKIN' LIAR BEST HAVE SOME ANSWERS FOR THIS, OR I'M COMIN' BACK FOR YOU!
JESUS.
WHAT DID I JUST DO?

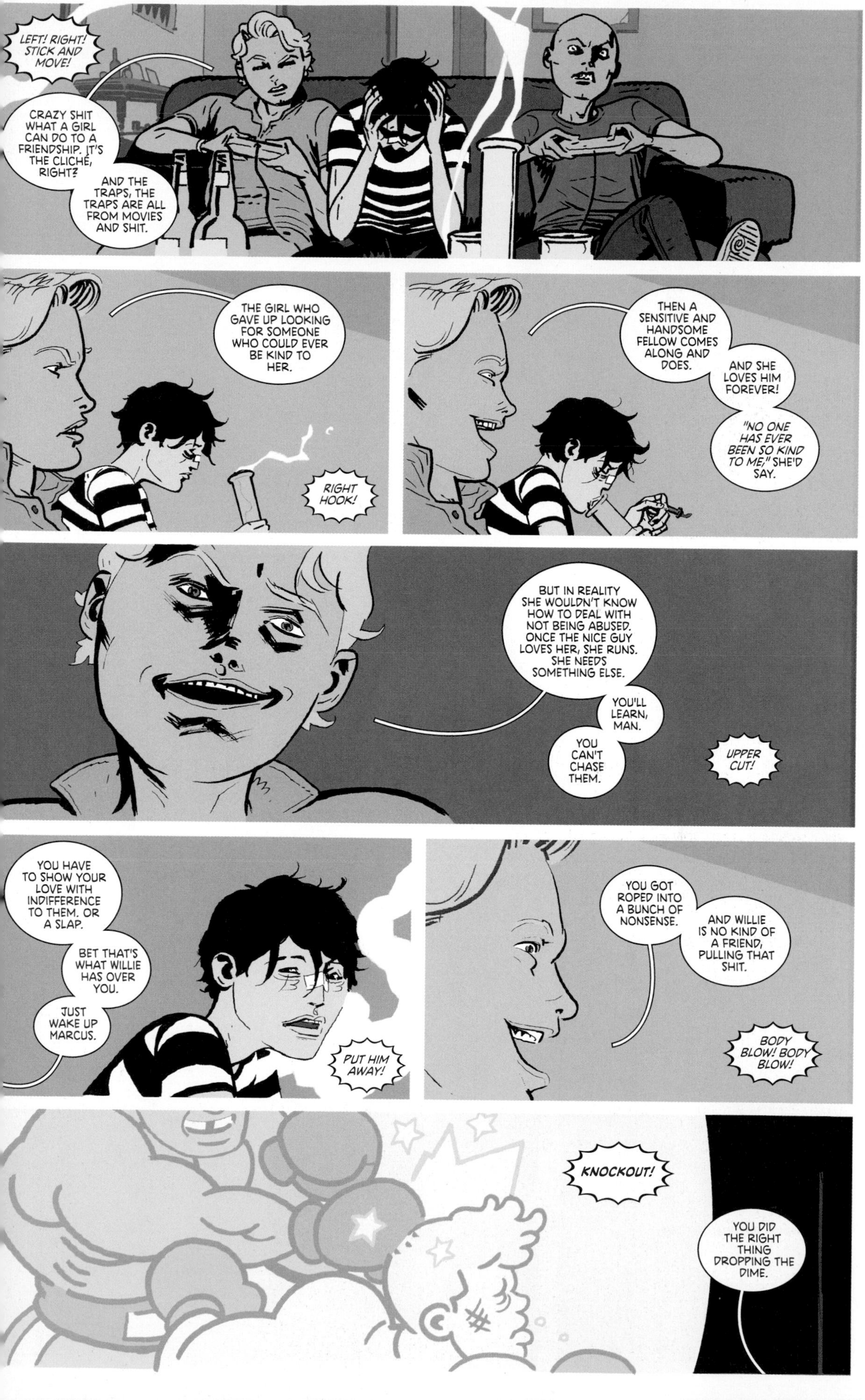
LEFT! RIGHT! STICK AND MOVE!
CRAZY SHIT WHAT A GIRL CAN DO TO A FRIENDSHIP. IT'S THE CLICHÉ, RIGHT?
AND THE TRAPS, THE TRAPS ARE ALL FROM MOVIES AND SHIT.
THE GIRL WHO GAVE UP LOOKING FOR SOMEONE WHO COULD EVER BE KIND TO HER.
RIGHT HOOK!
THEN A SENSITIVE AND HANDSOME FELLOW COMES ALONG AND DOES.
AND SHE LOVES HIM FOREVER!
"NO ONE HAS EVER BEEN SO KIND TO ME," SHE'D SAY.
BUT IN REALITY SHE WOULDN'T KNOW HOW TO DEAL WITH NOT BEING ABUSED. ONCE THE NICE GUY LOVES HER, SHE RUNS. SHE NEEDS SOMETHING ELSE.
YOU'LL LEARN, MAN.
YOU CAN'T CHASE THEM.
UPPER CUT!
YOU HAVE TO SHOW YOUR LOVE WITH INDIFFERENCE TO THEM. OR A SLAP.
BET THAT'S WHAT WILLIE HAS OVER YOU.
JUST WAKE UP MARCUS.
PUT HIM AWAY!
YOU GOT ROPED INTO A BUNCH OF NONSENSE.
AND WILLIE IS NO KIND OF A FRIEND, PULLING THAT SHIT.
BODY BLOW! BODY BLOW!
KNOCKOUT!
YOU DID THE RIGHT THING DROPPING THE DIME.

NO SLEEP. HEAD SWIMMING WITH TRACERS AND LEFTOVERS FROM THE BAG OF MUSHROOMS.

AND GUILT.

THE KIND THAT LOCKS YOUR ENTIRE BODY UP. FEELS LIKE TERROR.

WILLIE DIDN'T DESERVE THAT.

I HAVE TO WARN HIM.

REVEALING YOURSELF WILL HURT YOU.

WE ALL WANT TO TRUST, WE ALL WANT TO DISCLOSE, TO BE UNDERSTOOD--

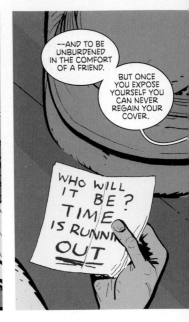

--AND TO BE UNBURDENED IN THE COMFORT OF A FRIEND.

BUT ONCE YOU EXPOSE YOURSELF YOU CAN NEVER REGAIN YOUR COVER.

WHO WILL IT BE? TIME IS RUNNI OUT

EXPOSURE IS THE ENEMY.

RISK ONLY THE MANDATORY.

FRIENDS DO *NOT* LAST.

NEITHER WILL YOU IF YOU TRUST YOUR LIFE TO THEM.

THEY WILL BE THE ONES WHO KILL YOU.

AAIIEEEEE!

MOTHER FUCK...

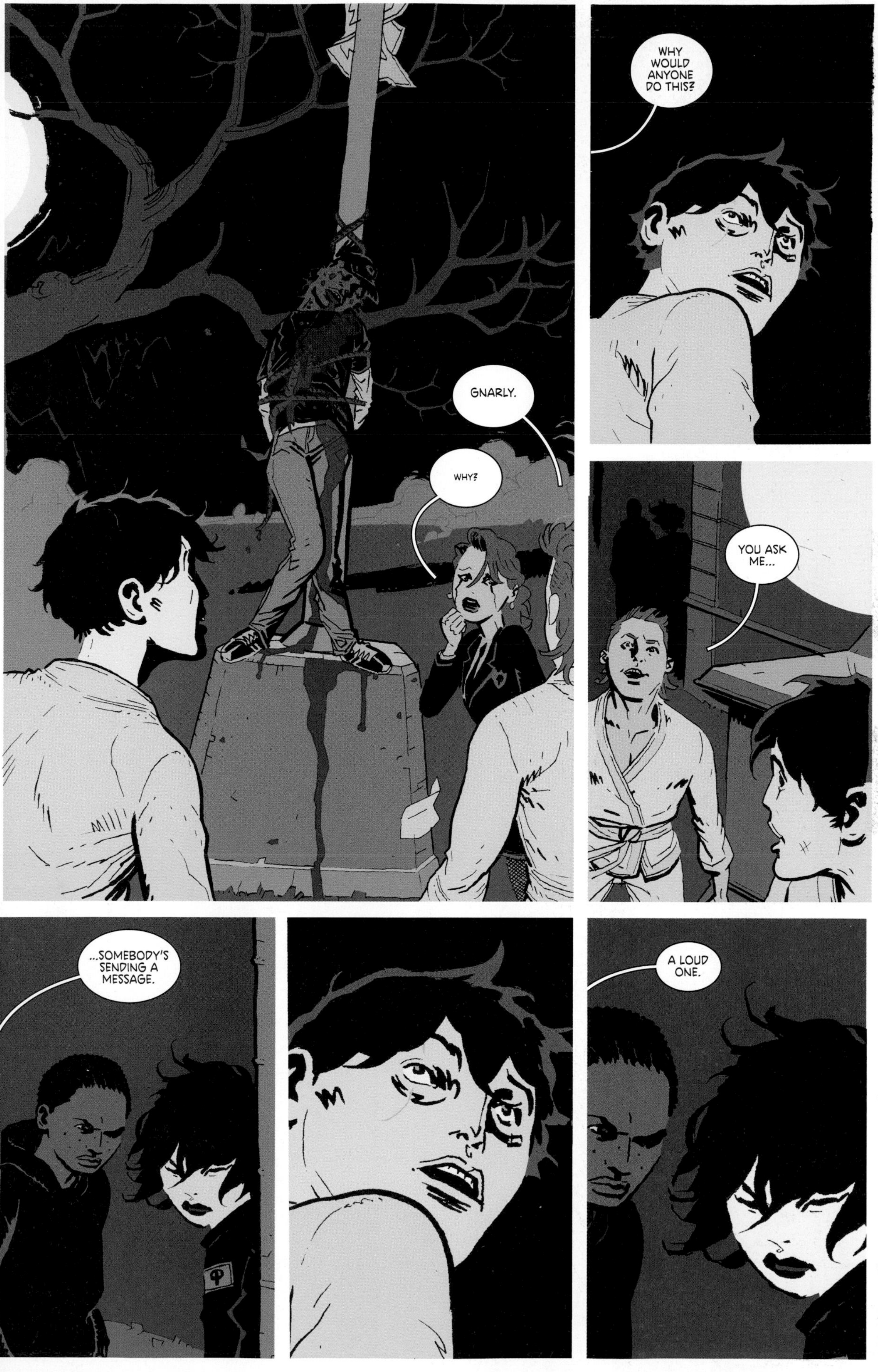
GNARLY.
WHY?
WHY WOULD ANYONE DO THIS?
YOU ASK ME...
...SOMEBODY'S SENDING A MESSAGE.
A LOUD ONE.

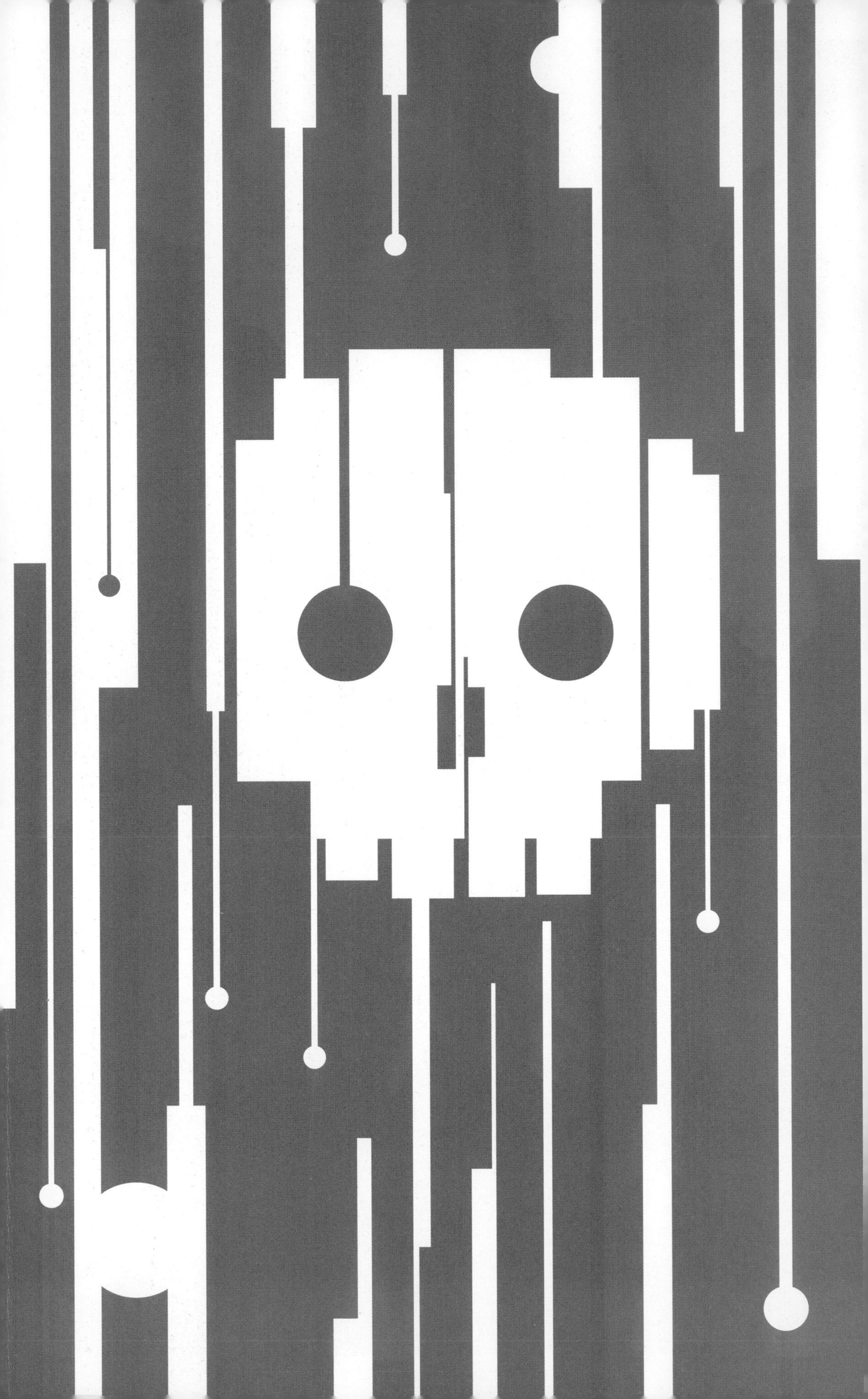

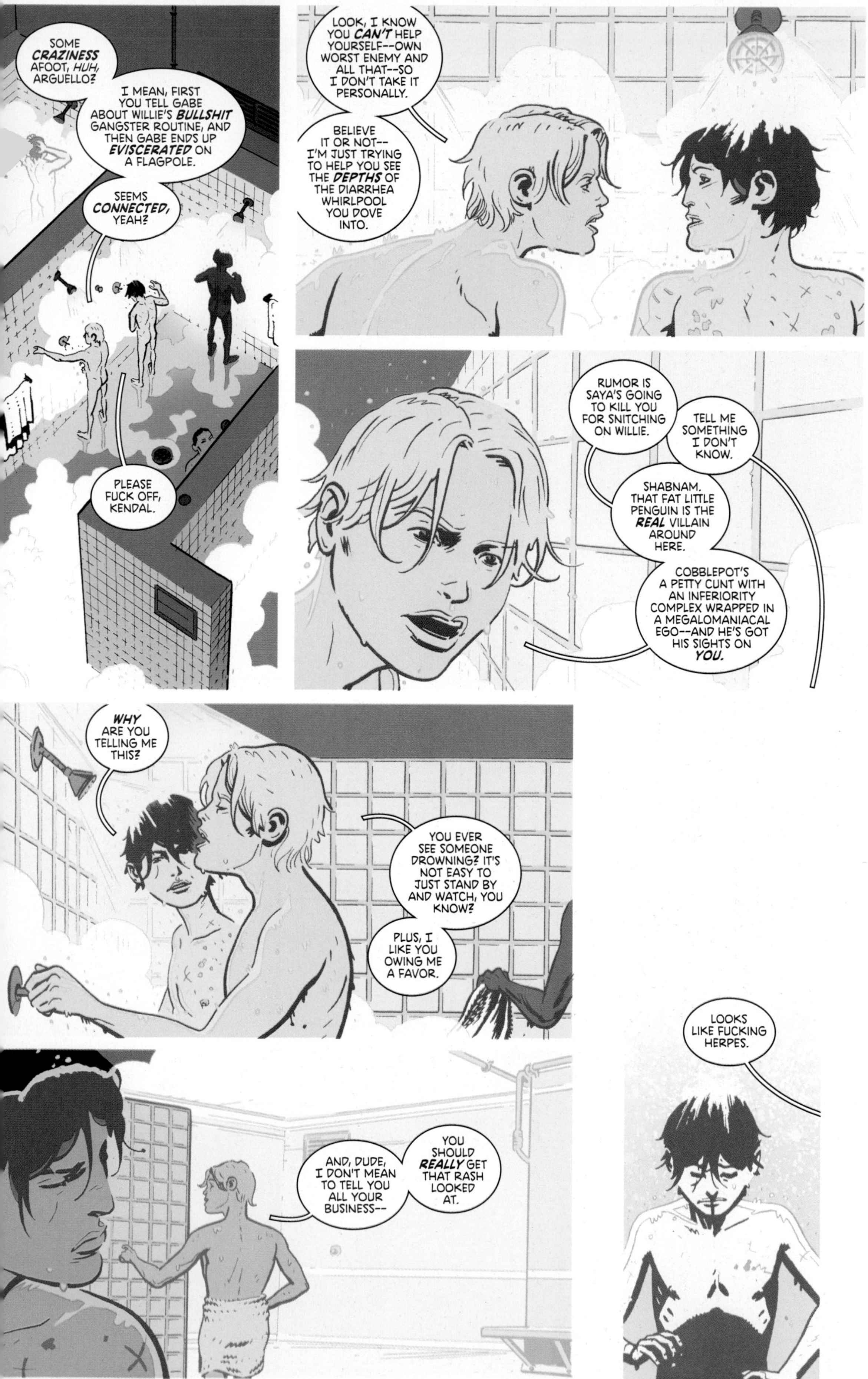
SOME CRAZINESS AFOOT, HUH, ARGUELLO?
I MEAN, FIRST YOU TELL GABE ABOUT WILLIE'S BULLSHIT GANGSTER ROUTINE, AND THEN GABE ENDS UP EVISCERATED ON A FLAGPOLE.
SEEMS CONNECTED, YEAH?
PLEASE FUCK OFF, KENDAL.
LOOK, I KNOW YOU CAN'T HELP YOURSELF--OWN WORST ENEMY AND ALL THAT--SO I DON'T TAKE IT PERSONALLY.
BELIEVE IT OR NOT-- I'M JUST TRYING TO HELP YOU SEE THE DEPTHS OF THE DIARRHEA WHIRLPOOL YOU DOVE INTO.
RUMOR IS SAYA'S GOING TO KILL YOU FOR SNITCHING ON WILLIE.
TELL ME SOMETHING I DON'T KNOW.
SHABNAM. THAT FAT LITTLE PENGUIN IS THE REAL VILLAIN AROUND HERE.
COBBLEPOT'S A PETTY CUNT WITH AN INFERIORITY COMPLEX WRAPPED IN A MEGALOMANIACAL EGO--AND HE'S GOT HIS SIGHTS ON YOU.
WHY ARE YOU TELLING ME THIS?
YOU EVER SEE SOMEONE DROWNING? IT'S NOT EASY TO JUST STAND BY AND WATCH, YOU KNOW?
PLUS, I LIKE YOU OWING ME A FAVOR.
AND, DUDE, I DON'T MEAN TO TELL YOU ALL YOUR BUSINESS--
YOU SHOULD REALLY GET THAT RASH LOOKED AT.
LOOKS LIKE FUCKING HERPES.

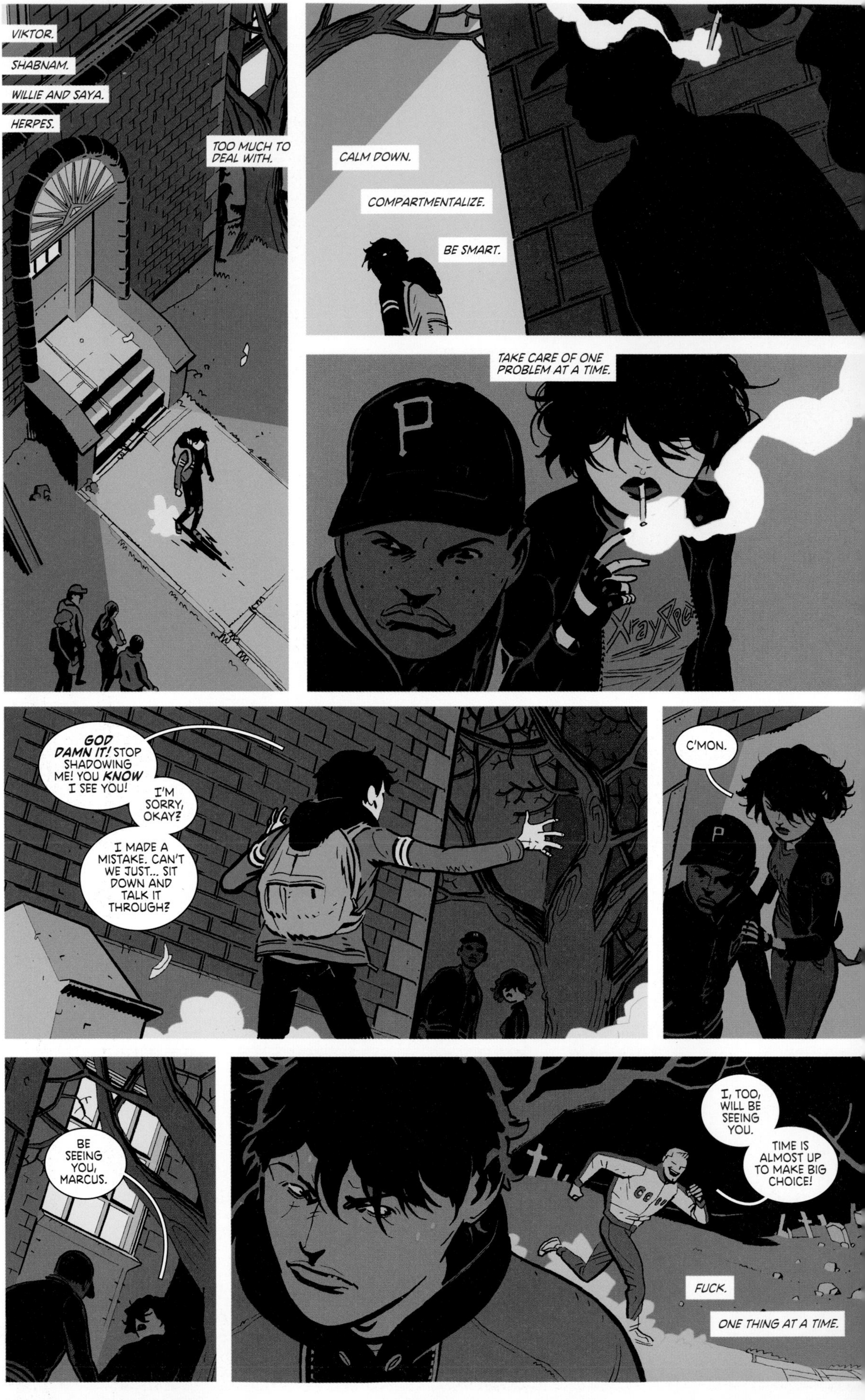
VIKTOR.
SHABNAM.
WILLIE AND SAYA.
HERPES.
TOO MUCH TO DEAL WITH.
CALM DOWN.
COMPARTMENTALIZE.
BE SMART.
TAKE CARE OF ONE PROBLEM AT A TIME.
GOD DAMN IT! STOP SHADOWING ME! YOU KNOW I SEE YOU!
I'M SORRY, OKAY?
I MADE A MISTAKE. CAN'T WE JUST... SIT DOWN AND TALK IT THROUGH?
C'MON.
BE SEEING YOU, MARCUS.
I, TOO, WILL BE SEEING YOU.
TIME IS ALMOST UP TO MAKE BIG CHOICE!
FUCK.
ONE THING AT A TIME.

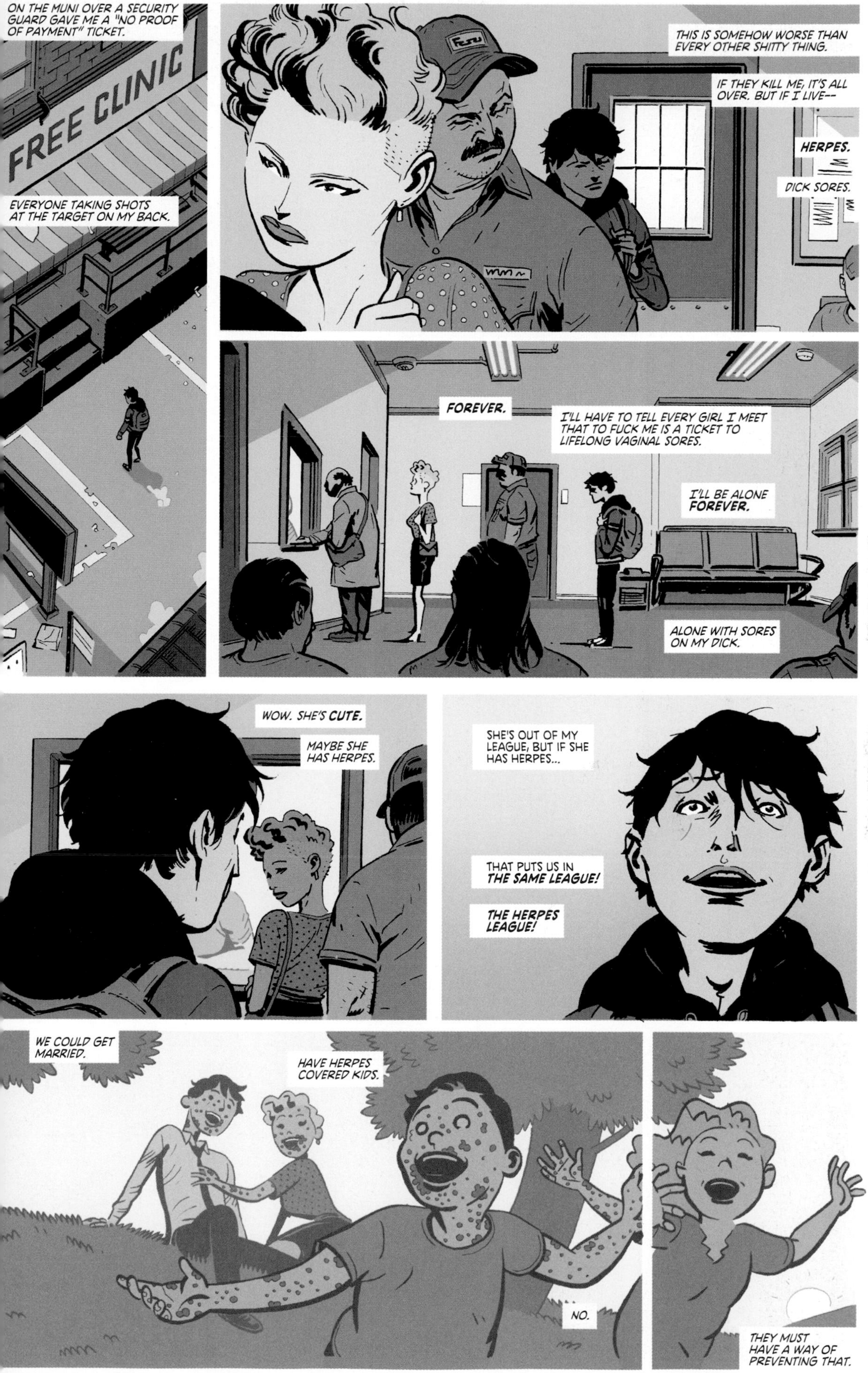
ON THE MUNI OVER A SECURITY GUARD GAVE ME A "NO PROOF OF PAYMENT" TICKET.
FREE CLINIC
EVERYONE TAKING SHOTS AT THE TARGET ON MY BACK.
THIS IS SOMEHOW WORSE THAN EVERY OTHER SHITTY THING.
IF THEY KILL ME, IT'S ALL OVER. BUT IF I LIVE--
HERPES.
DICK SORES.
FOREVER.
I'LL HAVE TO TELL EVERY GIRL I MEET THAT TO FUCK ME IS A TICKET TO LIFELONG VAGINAL SORES.
I'LL BE ALONE FOREVER.
ALONE WITH SORES ON MY DICK.
WOW. SHE'S CUTE.
MAYBE SHE HAS HERPES.
SHE'S OUT OF MY LEAGUE, BUT IF SHE HAS HERPES...
THAT PUTS US IN THE SAME LEAGUE!
THE HERPES LEAGUE!
WE COULD GET MARRIED.
HAVE HERPES COVERED KIDS.
NO.
THEY MUST HAVE A WAY OF PREVENTING THAT.

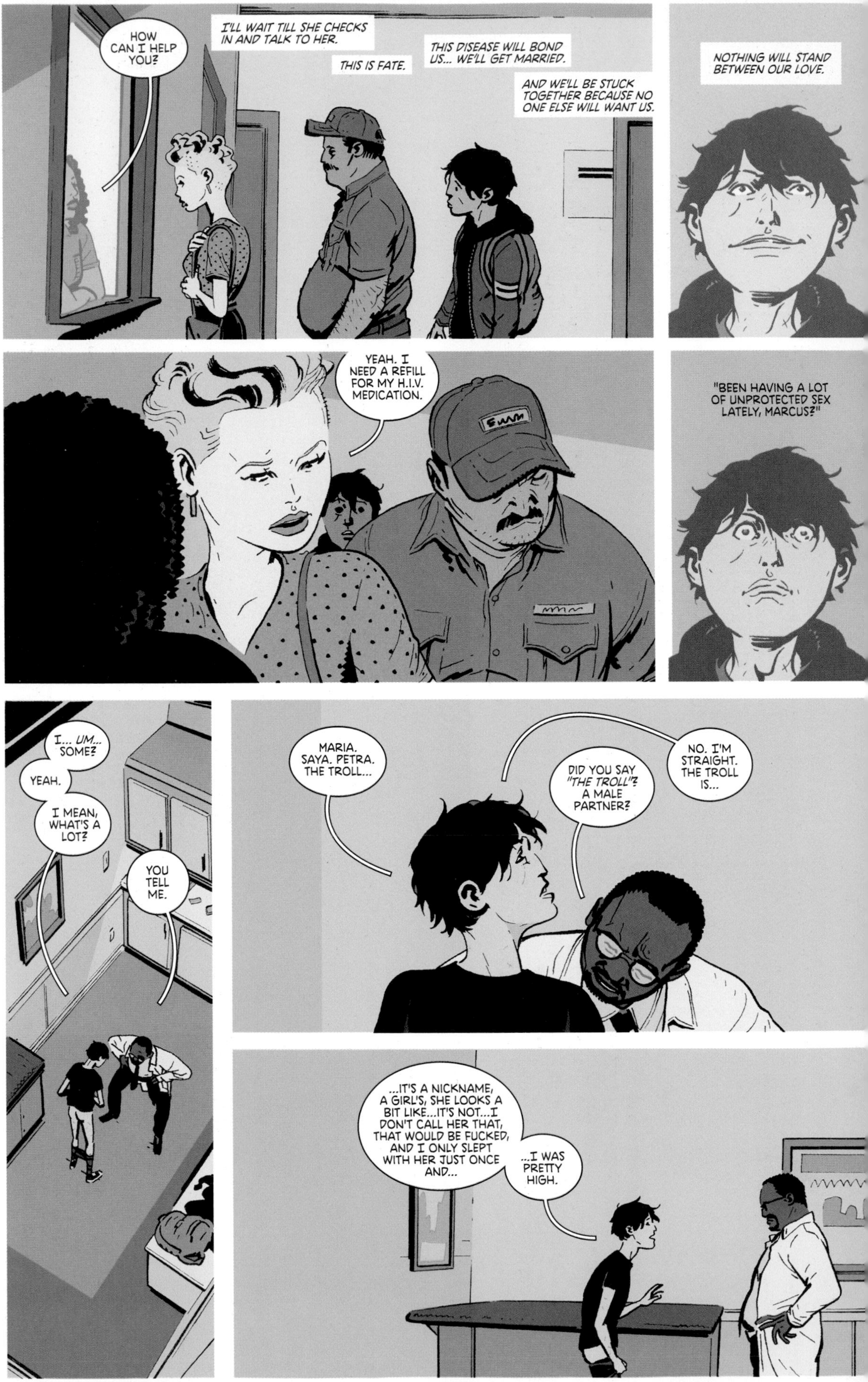
HOW CAN I HELP YOU?
I'LL WAIT TILL SHE CHECKS IN AND TALK TO HER.
THIS IS FATE.
THIS DISEASE WILL BOND US... WE'LL GET MARRIED.
AND WE'LL BE STUCK TOGETHER BECAUSE NO ONE ELSE WILL WANT US.
NOTHING WILL STAND BETWEEN OUR LOVE.
YEAH. I NEED A REFILL FOR MY H.I.V. MEDICATION.
"BEEN HAVING A LOT OF UNPROTECTED SEX LATELY, MARCUS?"
I... UM... SOME?
YEAH.
I MEAN, WHAT'S A LOT?
YOU TELL ME.
MARIA. SAYA. PETRA. THE TROLL...
DID YOU SAY "THE TROLL"? A MALE PARTNER?
NO. I'M STRAIGHT. THE TROLL IS...
...IT'S A NICKNAME, A GIRL'S, SHE LOOKS A BIT LIKE...IT'S NOT...I DON'T CALL HER THAT, THAT WOULD BE FUCKED, AND I ONLY SLEPT WITH HER JUST ONCE AND...
...I WAS PRETTY HIGH.

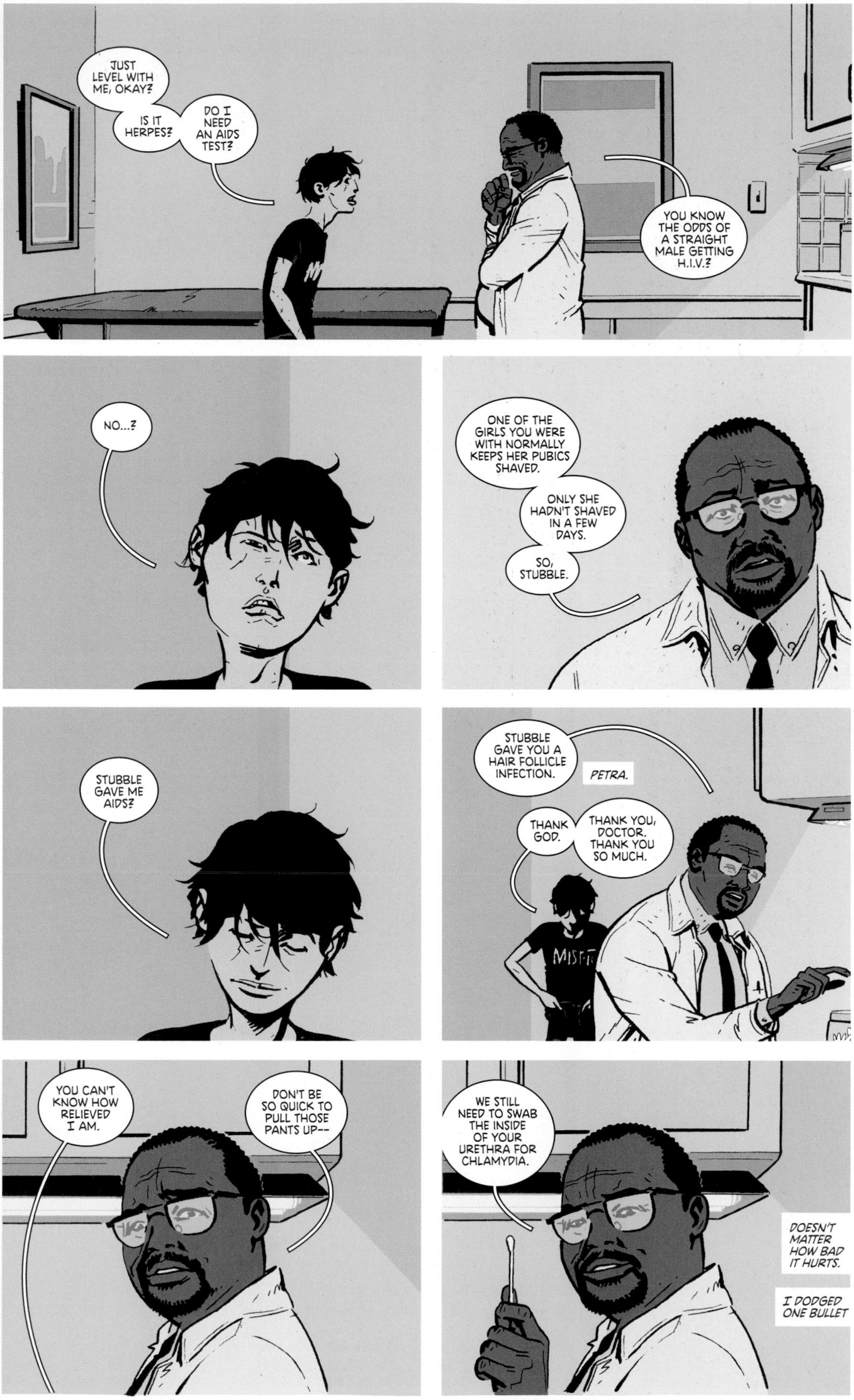
JUST LEVEL WITH ME, OKAY?
IS IT HERPES?
DO I NEED AN AIDS TEST?
YOU KNOW THE ODDS OF A STRAIGHT MALE GETTING H.I.V.?
NO...?
ONE OF THE GIRLS YOU WERE WITH NORMALLY KEEPS HER PUBICS SHAVED.
ONLY SHE HADN'T SHAVED IN A FEW DAYS.
SO, STUBBLE.
STUBBLE GAVE ME AIDS?
STUBBLE GAVE YOU A HAIR FOLLICLE INFECTION.
PETRA.
THANK GOD.
THANK YOU, DOCTOR. THANK YOU SO MUCH.
YOU CAN'T KNOW HOW RELIEVED I AM.
DON'T BE SO QUICK TO PULL THOSE PANTS UP--
WE STILL NEED TO SWAB THE INSIDE OF YOUR URETHRA FOR CHLAMYDIA.
DOESN'T MATTER HOW BAD IT HURTS.
I DODGED ONE BULLET

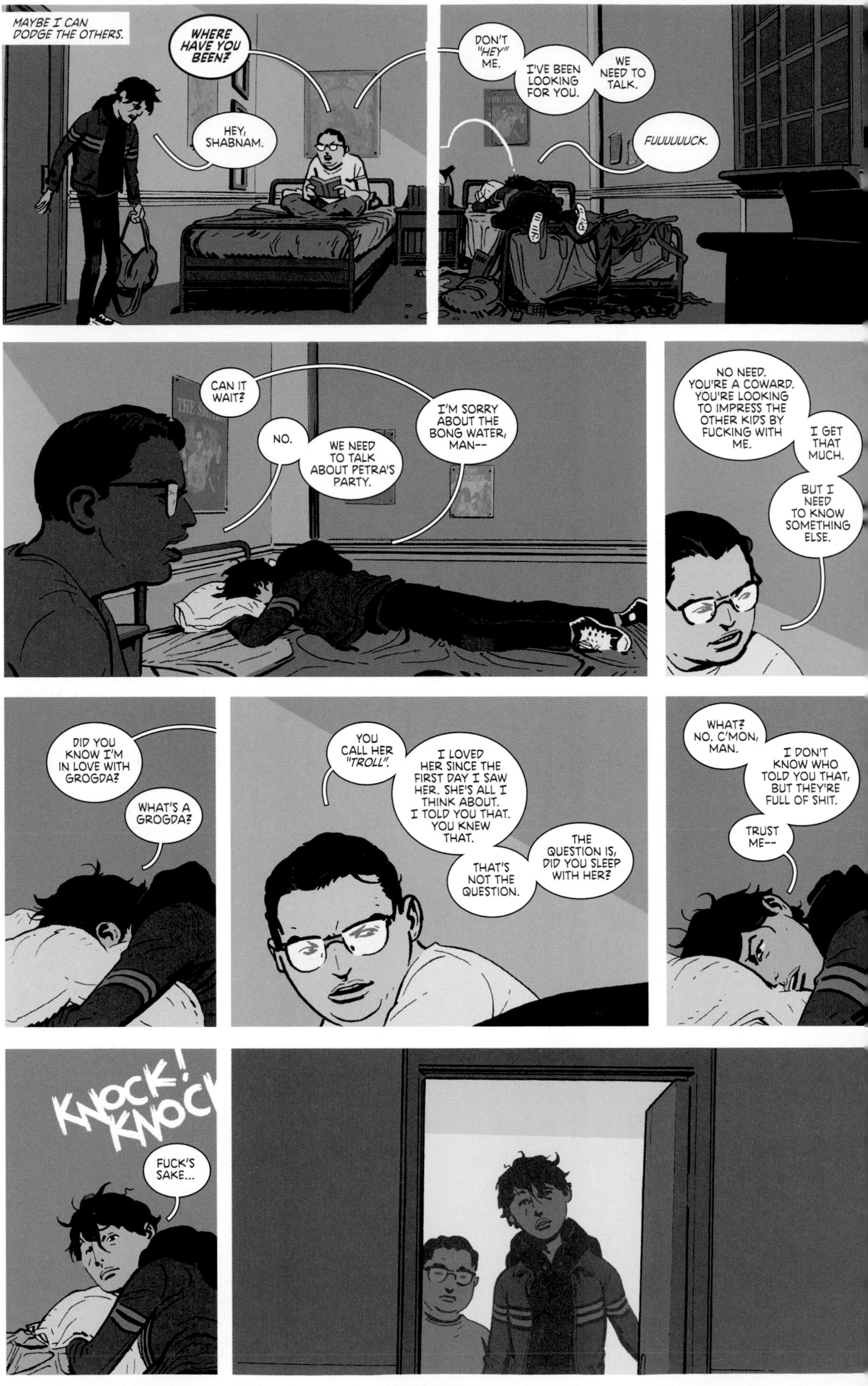
MAYBE I CAN DODGE THE OTHERS.
WHERE HAVE YOU BEEN?
HEY, SHABNAM.
DON'T "HEY" ME.
I'VE BEEN LOOKING FOR YOU.
WE NEED TO TALK.
FUUUUUUCK.
CAN IT WAIT?
NO.
WE NEED TO TALK ABOUT PETRA'S PARTY.
I'M SORRY ABOUT THE BONG WATER, MAN--
NO NEED. YOU'RE A COWARD. YOU'RE LOOKING TO IMPRESS THE OTHER KIDS BY FUCKING WITH ME.
I GET THAT MUCH.
BUT I NEED TO KNOW SOMETHING ELSE.
DID YOU KNOW I'M IN LOVE WITH GROGDA?
WHAT'S A GROGDA?
YOU CALL HER "TROLL".
I LOVED HER SINCE THE FIRST DAY I SAW HER. SHE'S ALL I THINK ABOUT. I TOLD YOU THAT. YOU KNEW THAT.
THAT'S NOT THE QUESTION.
THE QUESTION IS, DID YOU SLEEP WITH HER?
WHAT? NO. C'MON, MAN.
I DON'T KNOW WHO TOLD YOU THAT, BUT THEY'RE FULL OF SHIT.
TRUST ME--
KNOCK! KNOCK
FUCK'S SAKE...

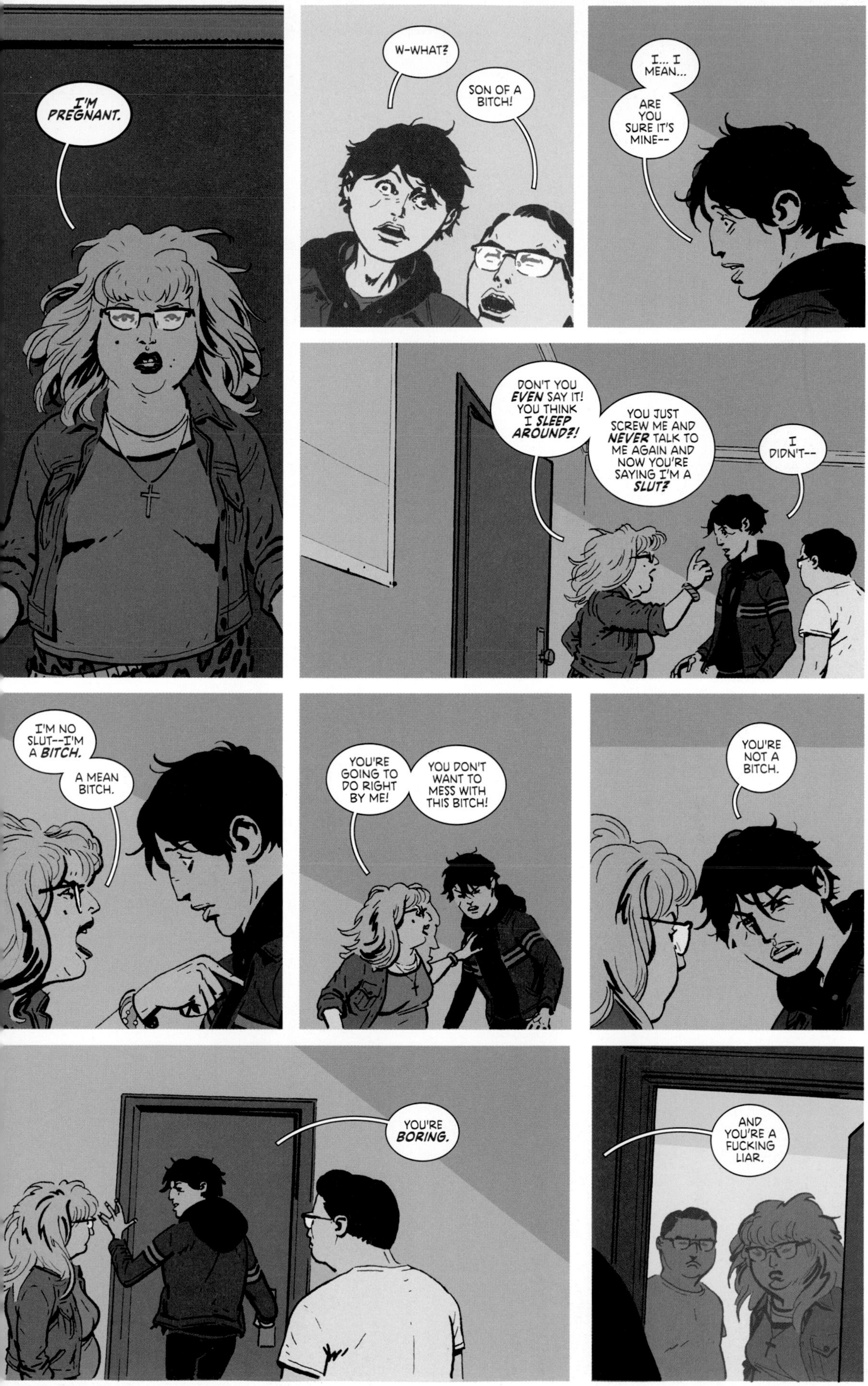
I'M PREGNANT.
W-WHAT?
SON OF A BITCH!
I... I MEAN...
ARE YOU SURE IT'S MINE--
DON'T YOU EVEN SAY IT! YOU THINK I SLEEP AROUND?!
YOU JUST SCREW ME AND NEVER TALK TO ME AGAIN AND NOW YOU'RE SAYING I'M A SLUT?
I DIDN'T--
I'M NO SLUT--I'M A BITCH.
A MEAN BITCH.
YOU'RE GOING TO DO RIGHT BY ME!
YOU DON'T WANT TO MESS WITH THIS BITCH!
YOU'RE NOT A BITCH.
YOU'RE BORING.
AND YOU'RE A FUCKING LIAR.

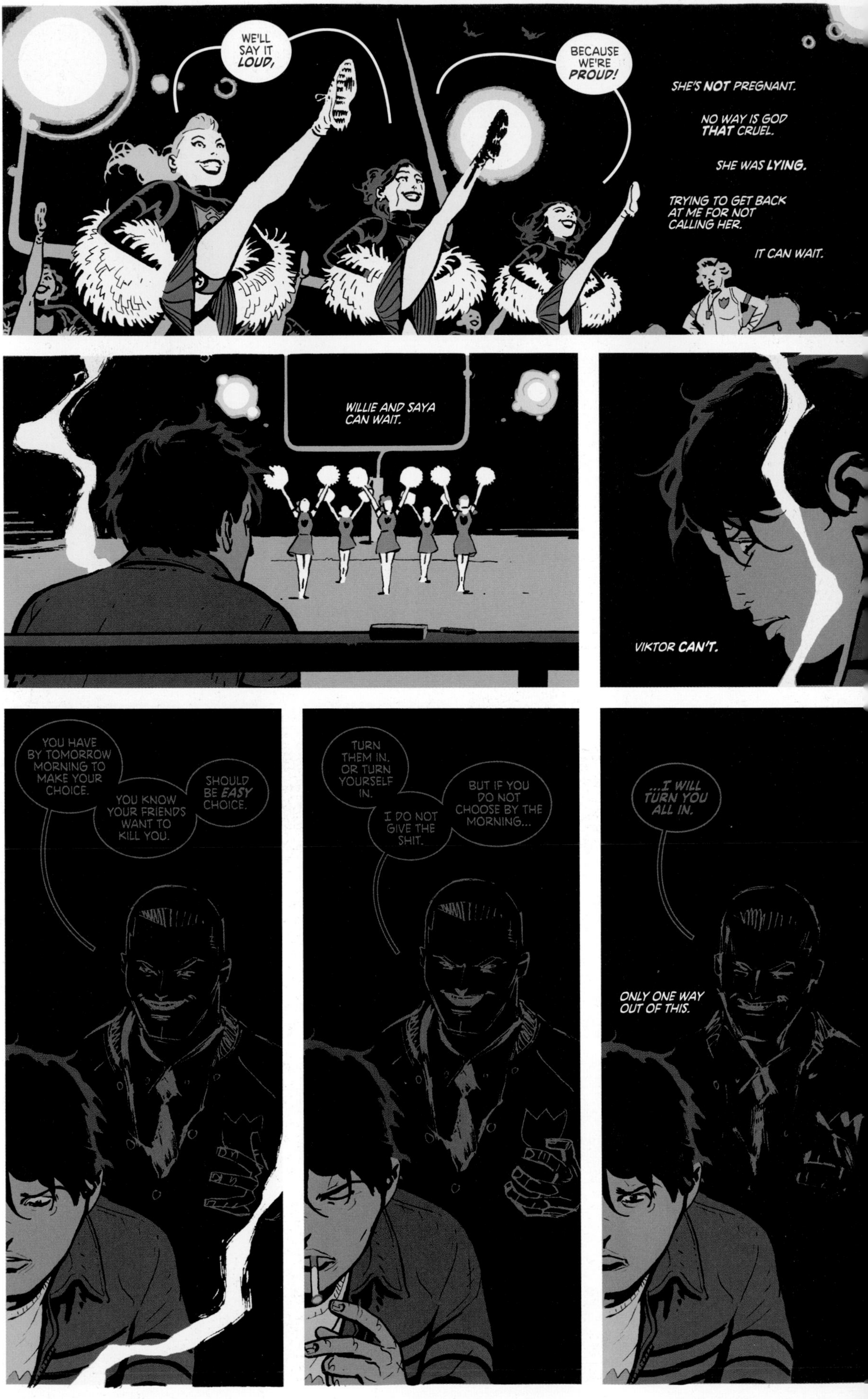

WE'LL SAY IT LOUD,
BECAUSE WE'RE PROUD!
SHE'S NOT PREGNANT.
NO WAY IS GOD THAT CRUEL.
SHE WAS LYING.
TRYING TO GET BACK AT ME FOR NOT CALLING HER.
IT CAN WAIT.
WILLIE AND SAYA CAN WAIT.
VIKTOR CAN'T.
YOU HAVE BY TOMORROW MORNING TO MAKE YOUR CHOICE.
YOU KNOW YOUR FRIENDS WANT TO KILL YOU.
SHOULD BE EASY CHOICE.
TURN THEM IN. OR TURN YOURSELF IN.
I DO NOT GIVE THE SHIT.
BUT IF YOU DO NOT CHOOSE BY THE MORNING...
...I WILL TURN YOU ALL IN.
ONLY ONE WAY OUT OF THIS.

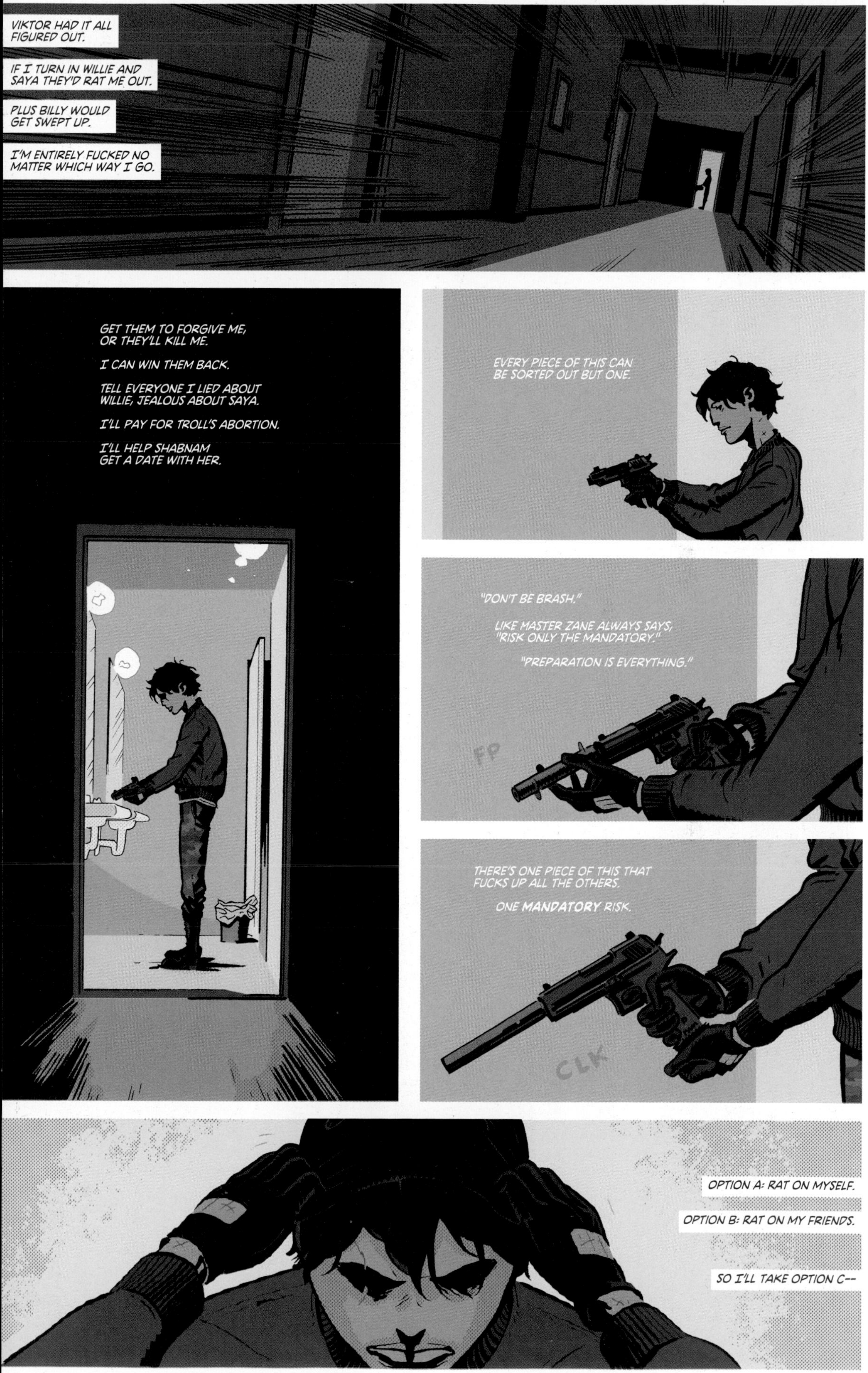
VIKTOR HAD IT ALL FIGURED OUT.
IF I TURN IN WILLIE AND SAYA THEY'D RAT ME OUT.
PLUS BILLY WOULD GET SWEPT UP.
I'M ENTIRELY FUCKED NO MATTER WHICH WAY I GO.
GET THEM TO FORGIVE ME, OR THEY'LL KILL ME.
I CAN WIN THEM BACK.
TELL EVERYONE I LIED ABOUT WILLIE, JEALOUS ABOUT SAYA.
I'LL PAY FOR TROLL'S ABORTION.
I'LL HELP SHABNAM GET A DATE WITH HER.
EVERY PIECE OF THIS CAN BE SORTED OUT BUT ONE.
"DON'T BE BRASH."
LIKE MASTER ZANE ALWAYS SAYS, "RISK ONLY THE MANDATORY."
"PREPARATION IS EVERYTHING."
FP
THERE'S ONE PIECE OF THIS THAT FUCKS UP ALL THE OTHERS.
ONE MANDATORY RISK.
CLK
OPTION A: RAT ON MYSELF.
OPTION B: RAT ON MY FRIENDS.
SO I'LL TAKE OPTION C--

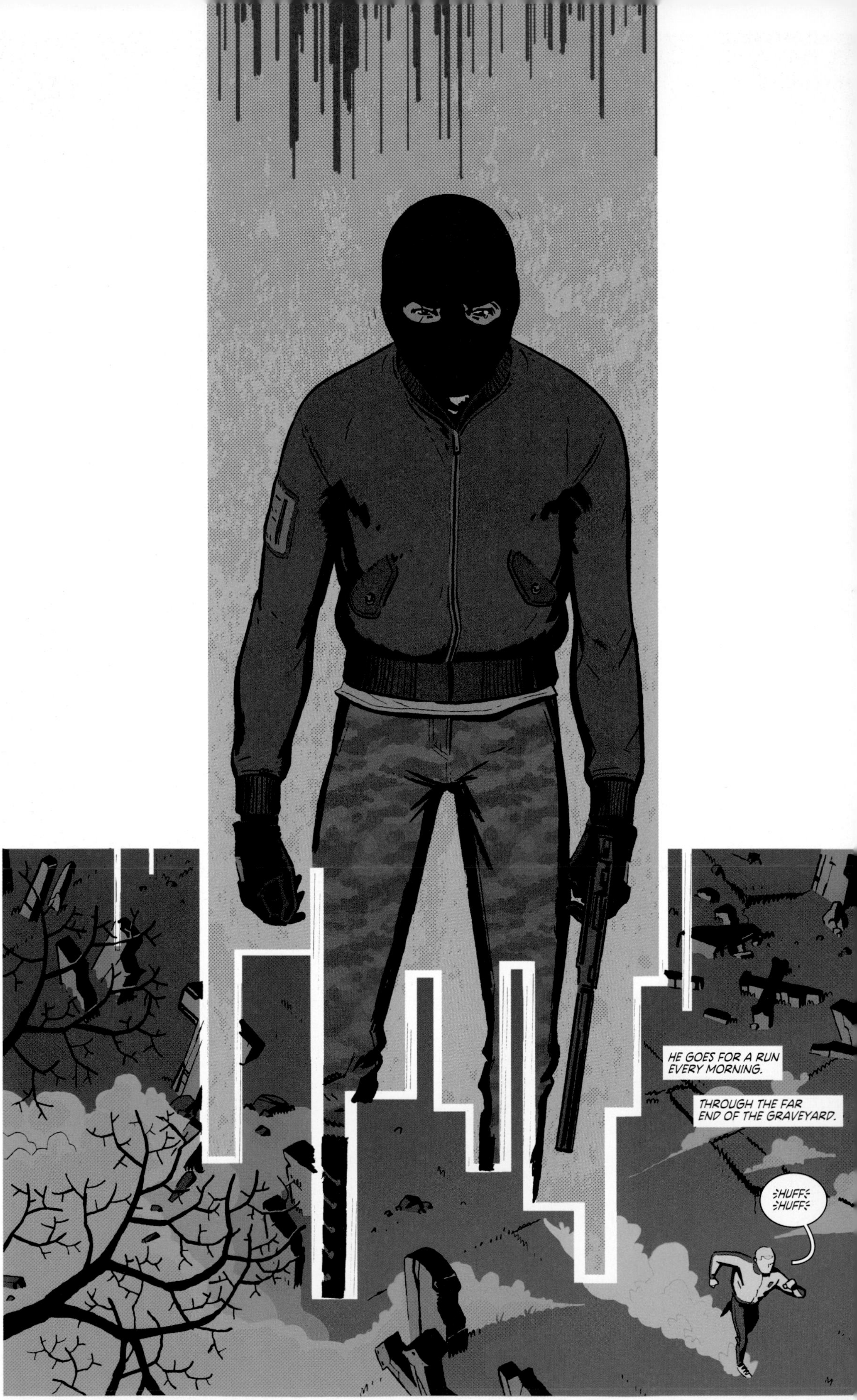
HE GOES FOR A RUN EVERY MORNING.
THROUGH THE FAR END OF THE GRAVEYARD.
HUFF HUFF

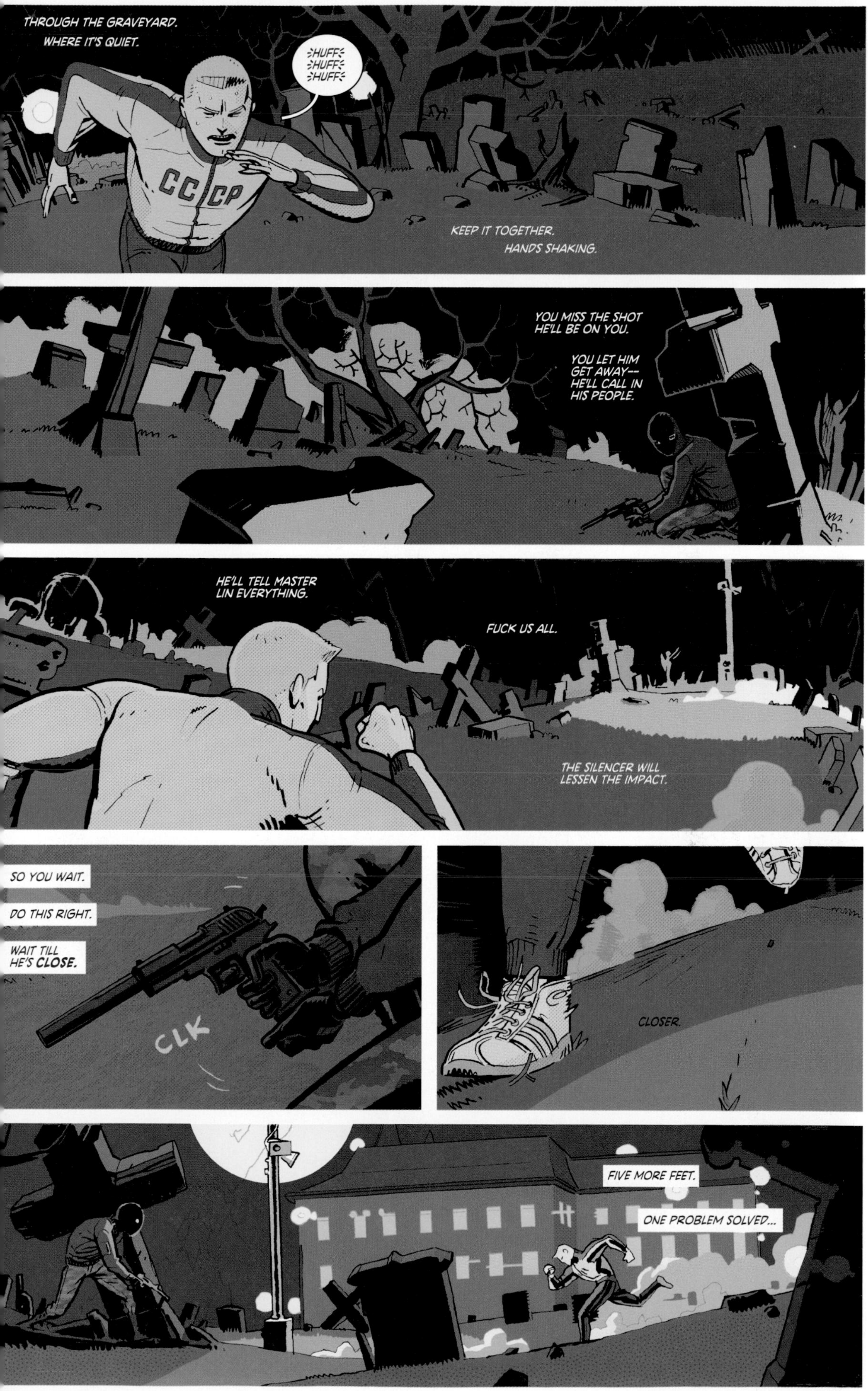
THROUGH THE GRAVEYARD.
WHERE IT'S QUIET.
HUFF HUFF HUFF
KEEP IT TOGETHER.
HANDS SHAKING.
YOU MISS THE SHOT HE'LL BE ON YOU.
YOU LET HIM GET AWAY-- HE'LL CALL IN HIS PEOPLE.
HE'LL TELL MASTER LIN EVERYTHING.
FUCK US ALL.
THE SILENCER WILL LESSEN THE IMPACT.
SO YOU WAIT.
DO THIS RIGHT.
WAIT TILL HE'S CLOSE.
CLK
CLOSER.
FIVE MORE FEET.
ONE PROBLEM SOLVED...

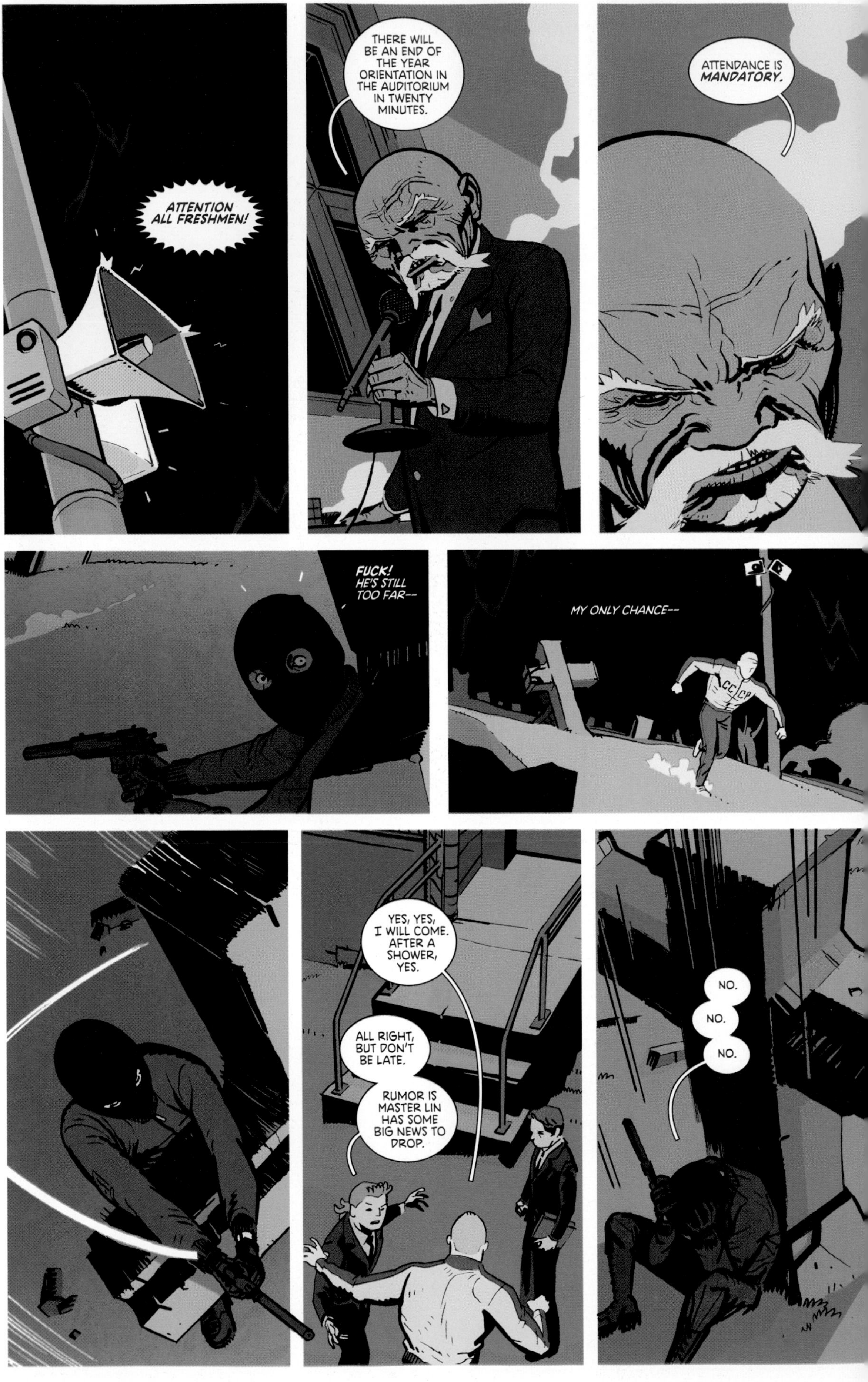

ATTENTION ALL FRESHMEN!
THERE WILL BE AN END OF THE YEAR ORIENTATION IN THE AUDITORIUM IN TWENTY MINUTES.
ATTENDANCE IS MANDATORY.
FUCK! HE'S STILL TOO FAR--
MY ONLY CHANCE--
YES, YES, I WILL COME. AFTER A SHOWER, YES.
ALL RIGHT, BUT DON'T BE LATE.
RUMOR IS MASTER LIN HAS SOME BIG NEWS TO DROP.
NO.
NO.
NO.

DON'T TAKE TOO LONG, VIKTOR.

TODAY'S ASSEMBLY IS QUITE IMPORTANT.

HATE TO SEE MASTER LIN HOLD YOU BACK.

AND MASTER LIN WOULD HATE TO SMELL *STINK* OF MY EXERCISE.

BUT THANK YOU FOR ADVICE.

AND FUCK TO YOU, "*MASTER ZANE.*"

STUPID NAME.

LIKE VIDEO GAME CHARACTER.

OR SMURF.

SCREEK

F'SH

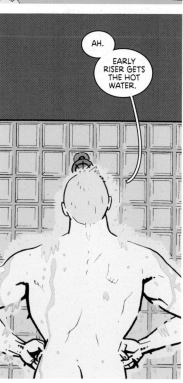

AH.

EARLY RISER GETS THE HOT WATER.

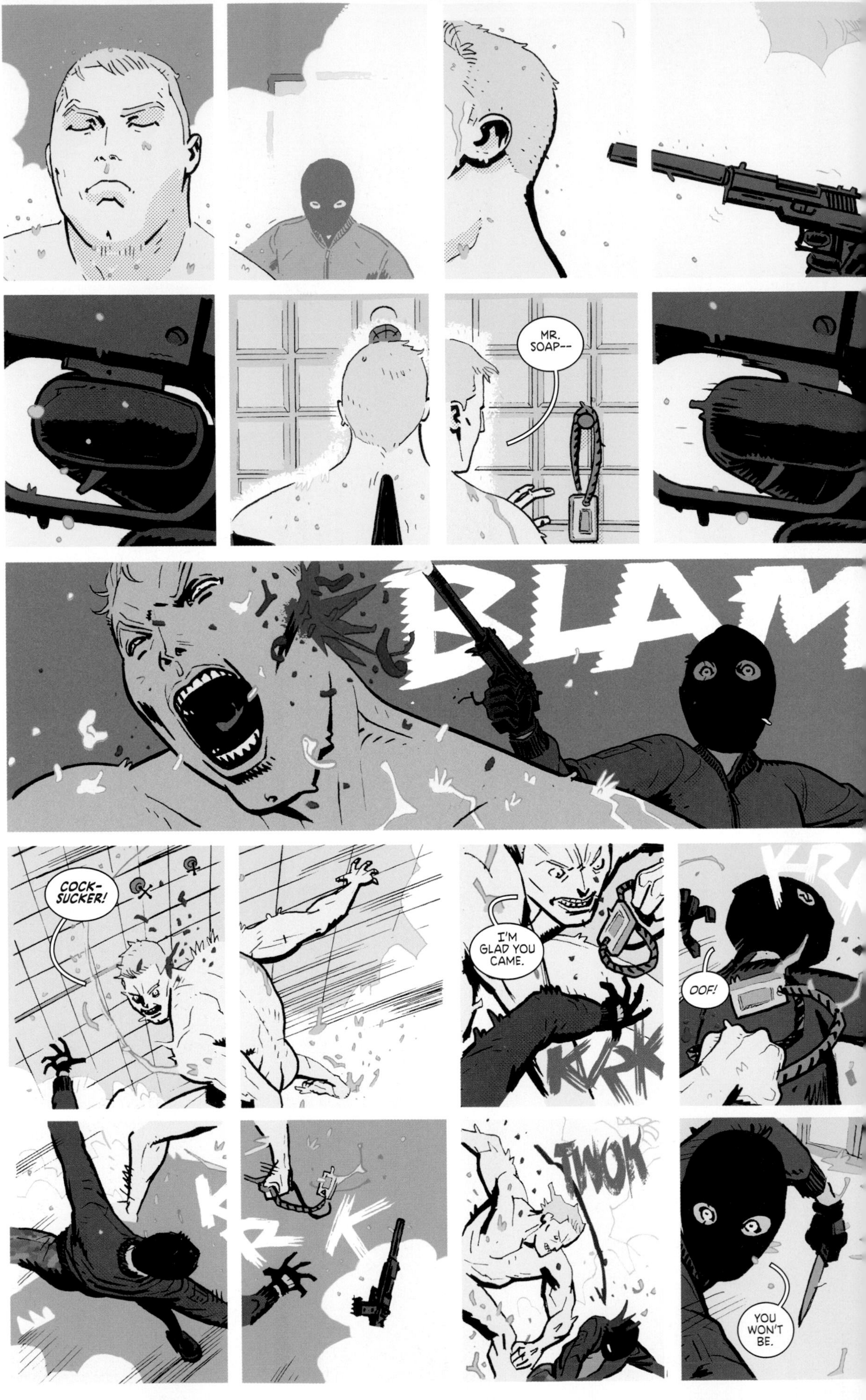
MR. SOAP--
BLAM
COCK-SUCKER!
I'M GLAD YOU CAME.
KRRK
KRA
OOF!
KRK
TWOK
YOU WON'T BE.

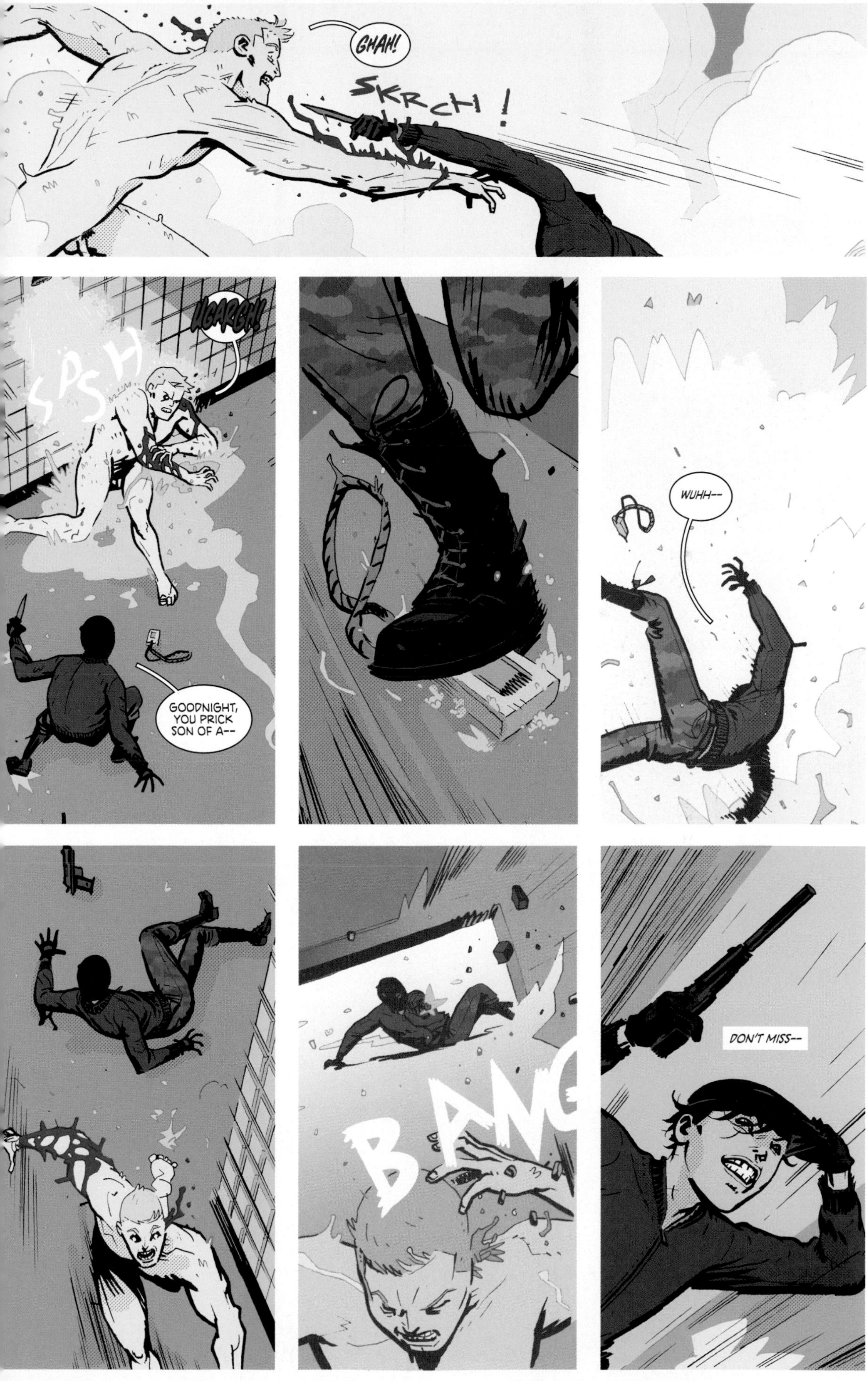
GHAH!
SKRCH!
UGARGH!
SPSH
GOODNIGHT, YOU PRICK SON OF A--
WUHH--
BANG
DON'T MISS--

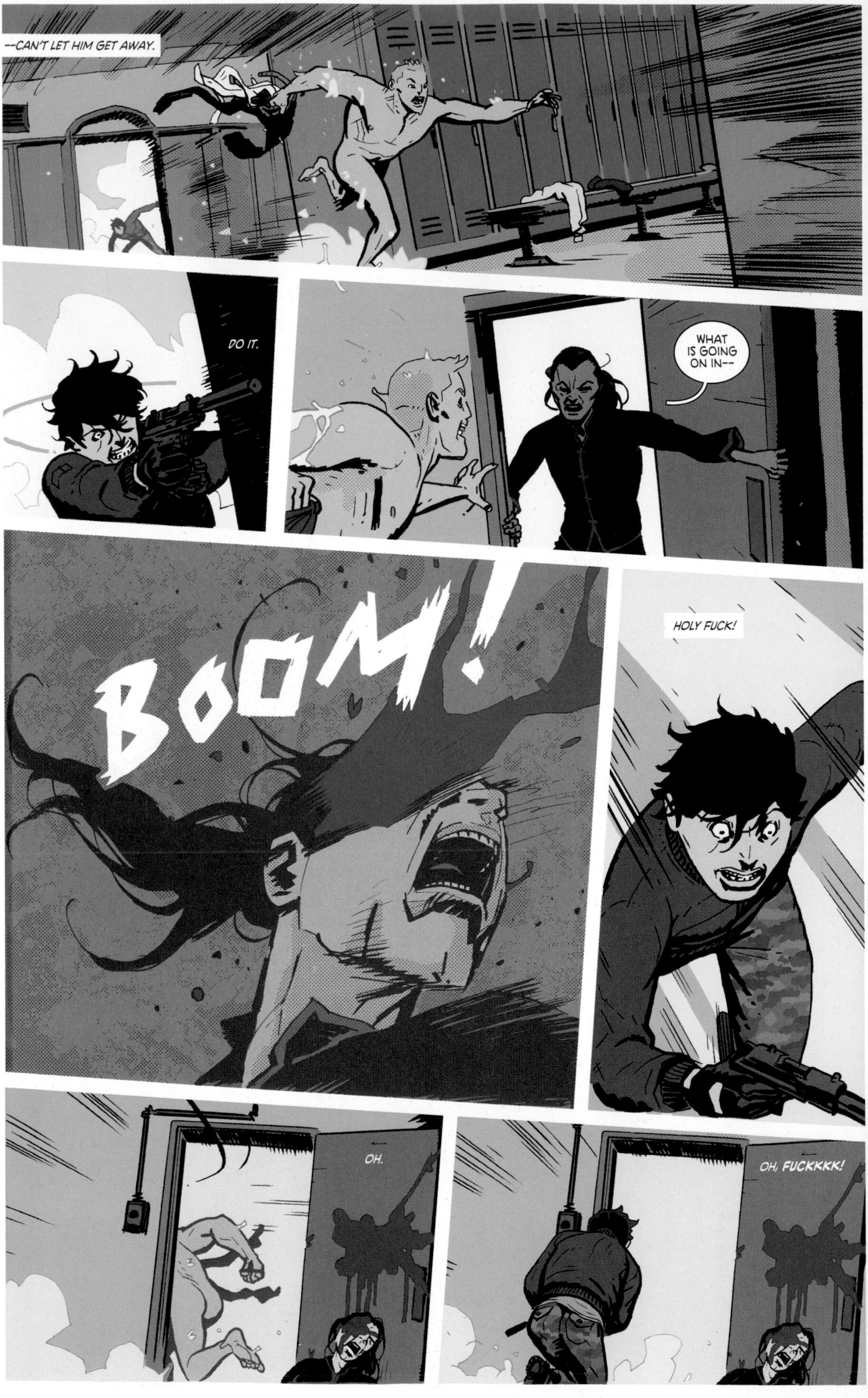

--CAN'T LET HIM GET AWAY.
DO IT.
WHAT IS GOING ON IN--
BOOM!
HOLY FUCK!
OH.
OH, FUCKKKK!

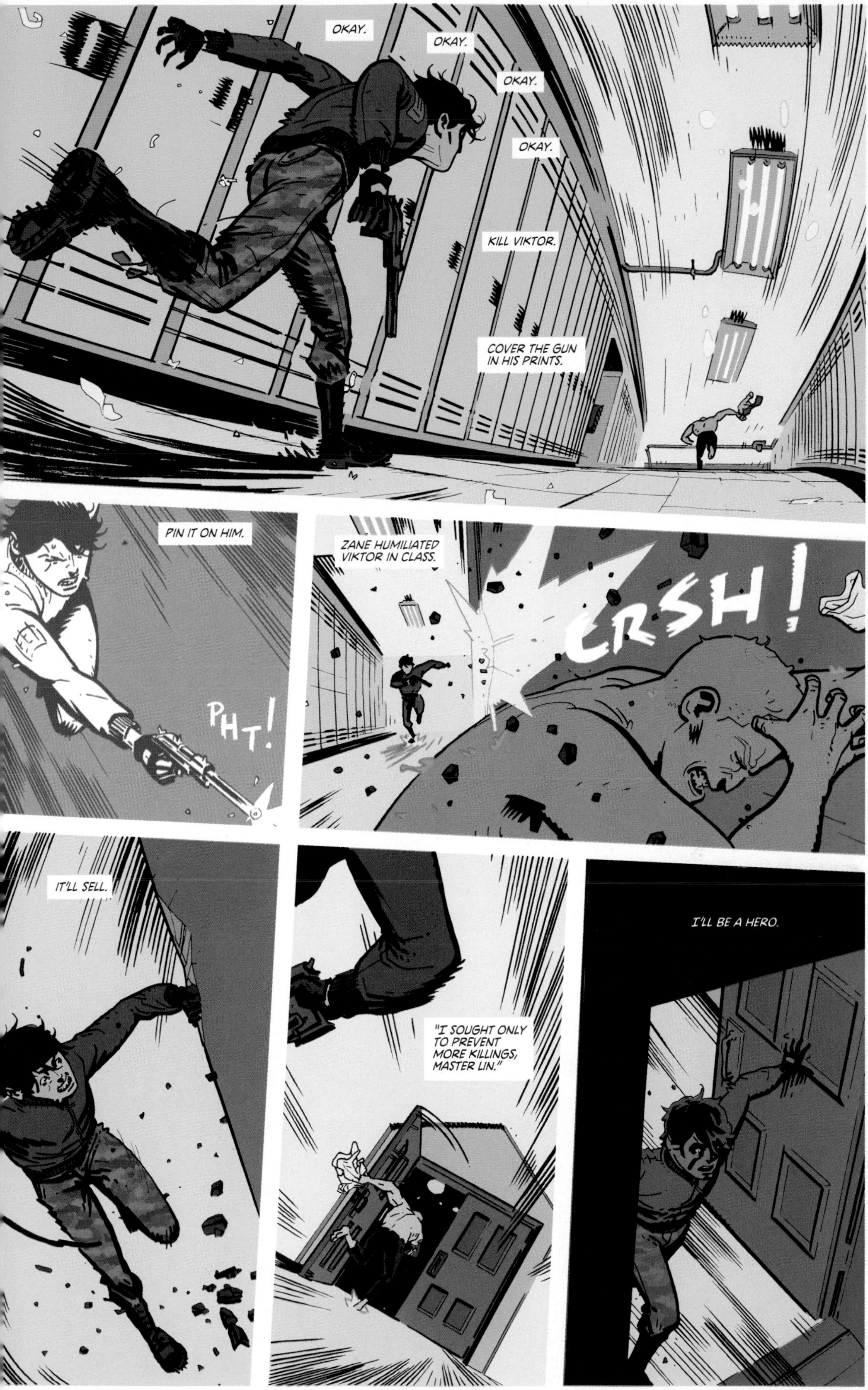
OKAY.
OKAY.
OKAY.
OKAY.
KILL VIKTOR.
COVER THE GUN IN HIS PRINTS.
PIN IT ON HIM.
PHT!
ZANE HUMILIATED VIKTOR IN CLASS.
CRSH!
IT'LL SELL.
"I SOUGHT ONLY TO PREVENT MORE KILLINGS, MASTER LIN."
I'LL BE A HERO.

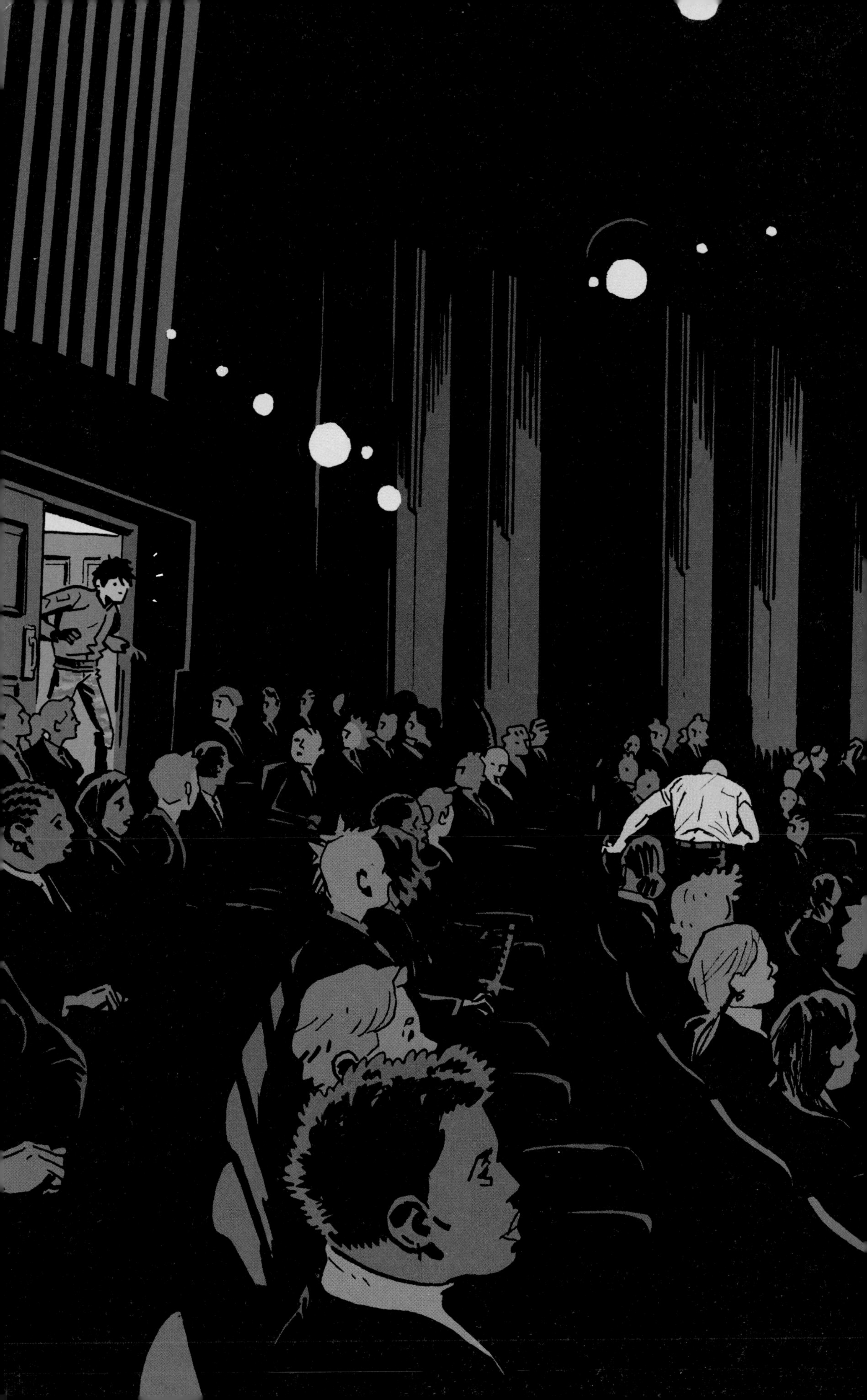

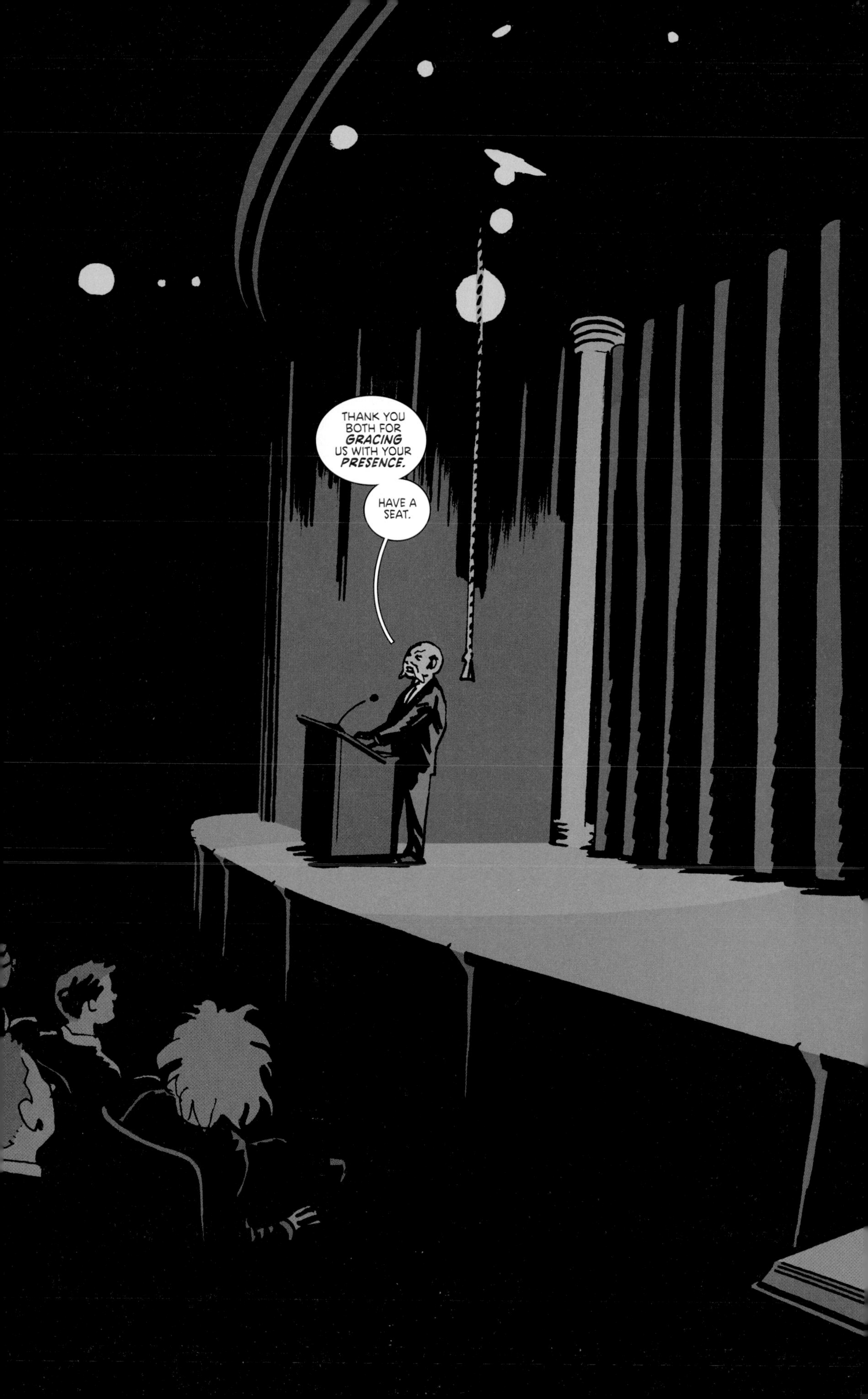
THANK YOU BOTH FOR GRACING US WITH YOUR PRESENCE.
HAVE A SEAT.

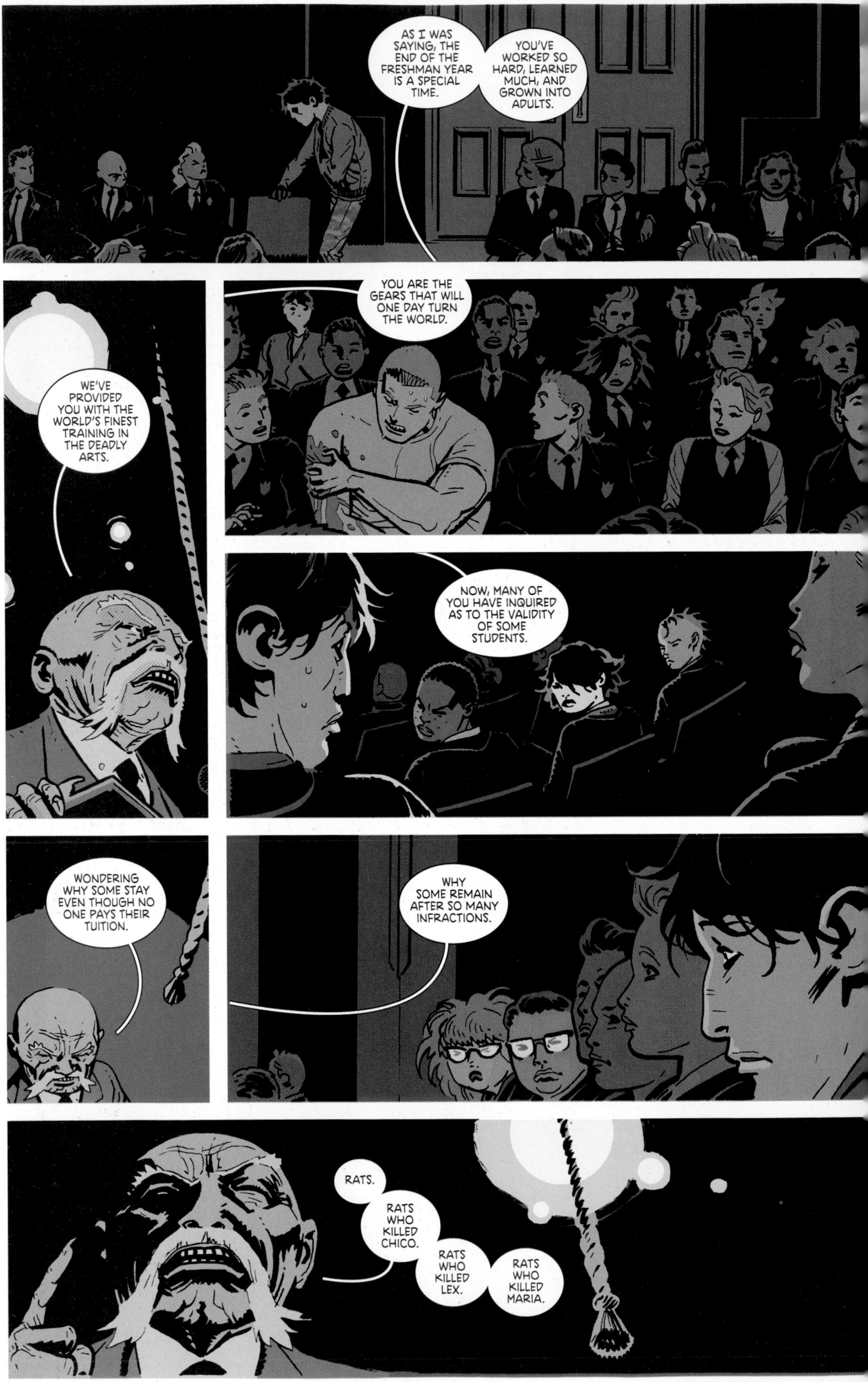
AS I WAS SAYING, THE END OF THE FRESHMAN YEAR IS A SPECIAL TIME.
YOU'VE WORKED SO HARD, LEARNED MUCH, AND GROWN INTO ADULTS.
WE'VE PROVIDED YOU WITH THE WORLD'S FINEST TRAINING IN THE DEADLY ARTS.
YOU ARE THE GEARS THAT WILL ONE DAY TURN THE WORLD.
NOW, MANY OF YOU HAVE INQUIRED AS TO THE VALIDITY OF SOME STUDENTS.
WONDERING WHY SOME STAY EVEN THOUGH NO ONE PAYS THEIR TUITION.
WHY SOME REMAIN AFTER SO MANY INFRACTIONS.
RATS.
RATS WHO KILLED CHICO.
RATS WHO KILLED LEX.
RATS WHO KILLED MARIA.

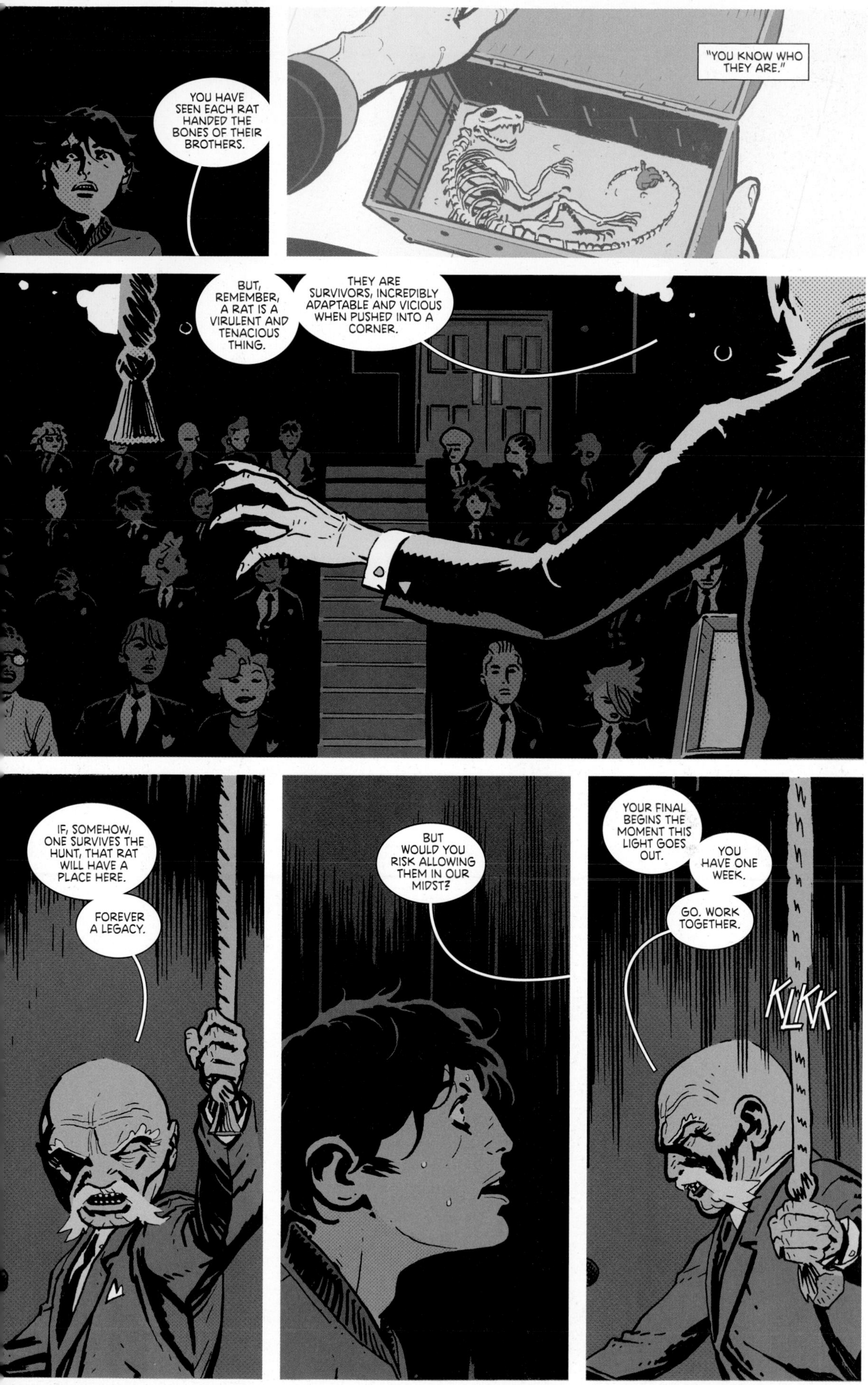
YOU HAVE SEEN EACH RAT HANDED THE BONES OF THEIR BROTHERS.
"YOU KNOW WHO THEY ARE."
BUT, REMEMBER, A RAT IS A VIRULENT AND TENACIOUS THING.
THEY ARE SURVIVORS, INCREDIBLY ADAPTABLE AND VICIOUS WHEN PUSHED INTO A CORNER.
IF, SOMEHOW, ONE SURVIVES THE HUNT, THAT RAT WILL HAVE A PLACE HERE.
FOREVER A LEGACY.
BUT WOULD YOU RISK ALLOWING THEM IN OUR MIDST?
YOUR FINAL BEGINS THE MOMENT THIS LIGHT GOES OUT.
YOU HAVE ONE WEEK.
GO. WORK TOGETHER.
KLIKK

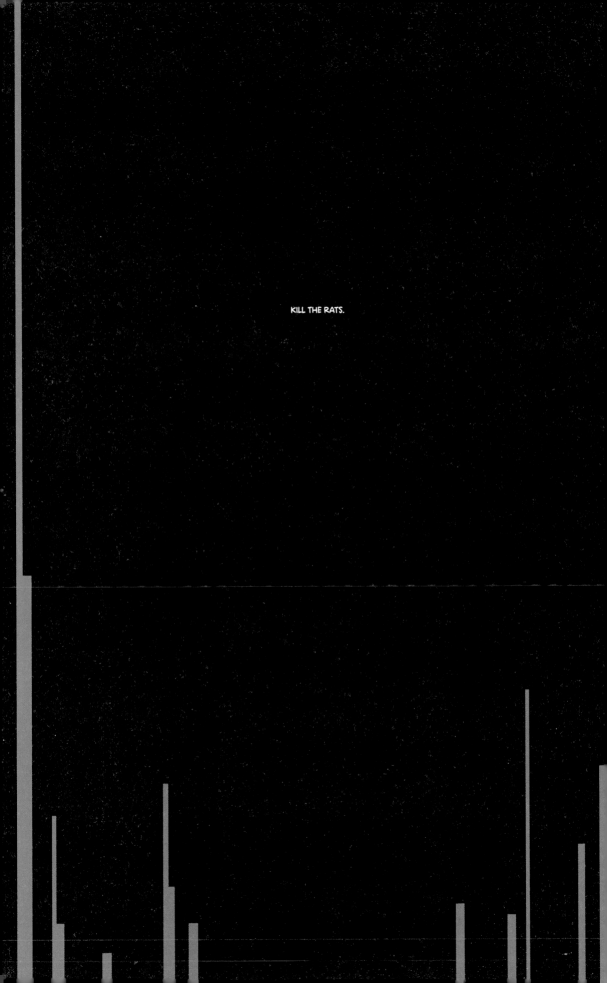

KILL THE RATS.

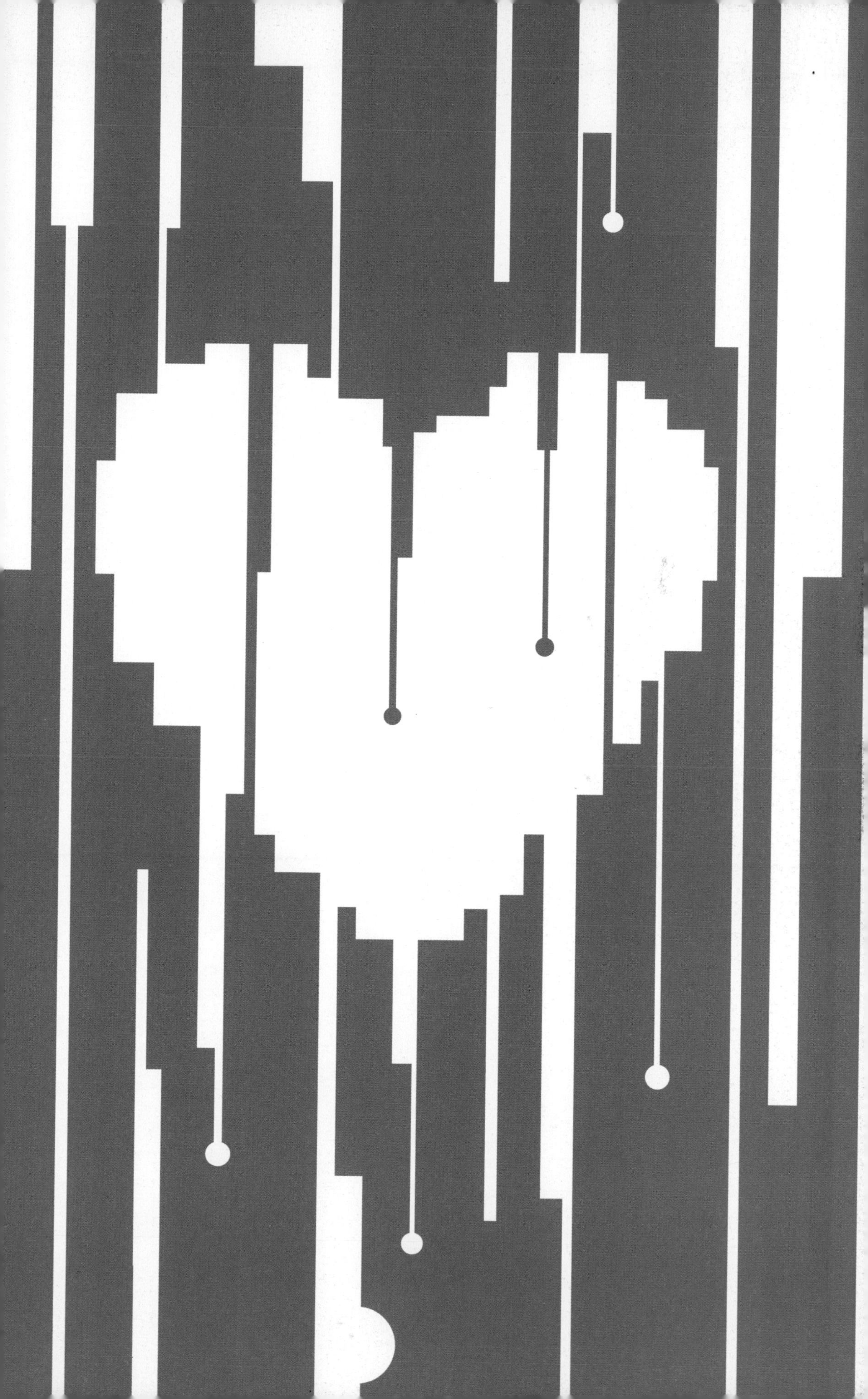

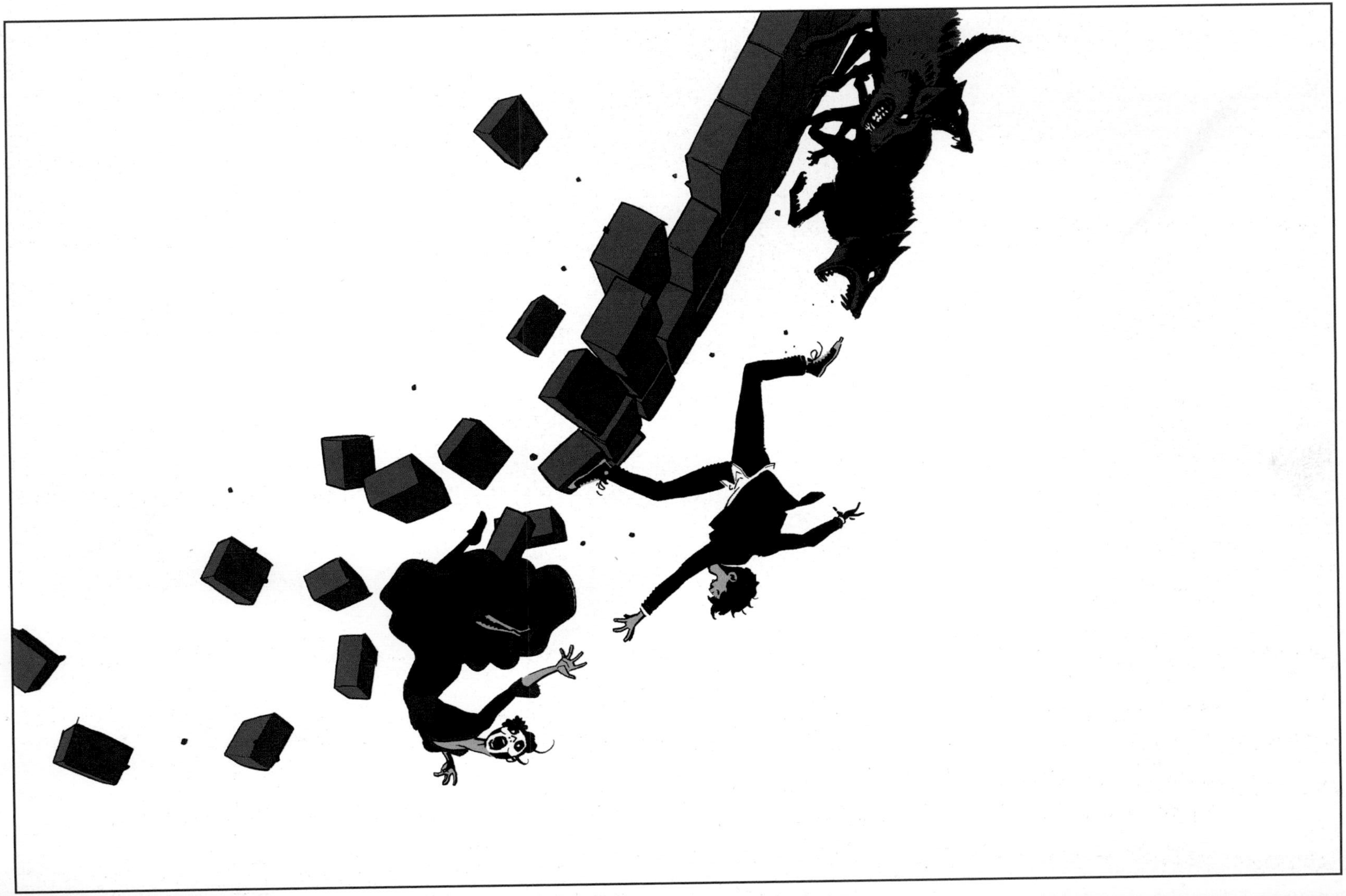

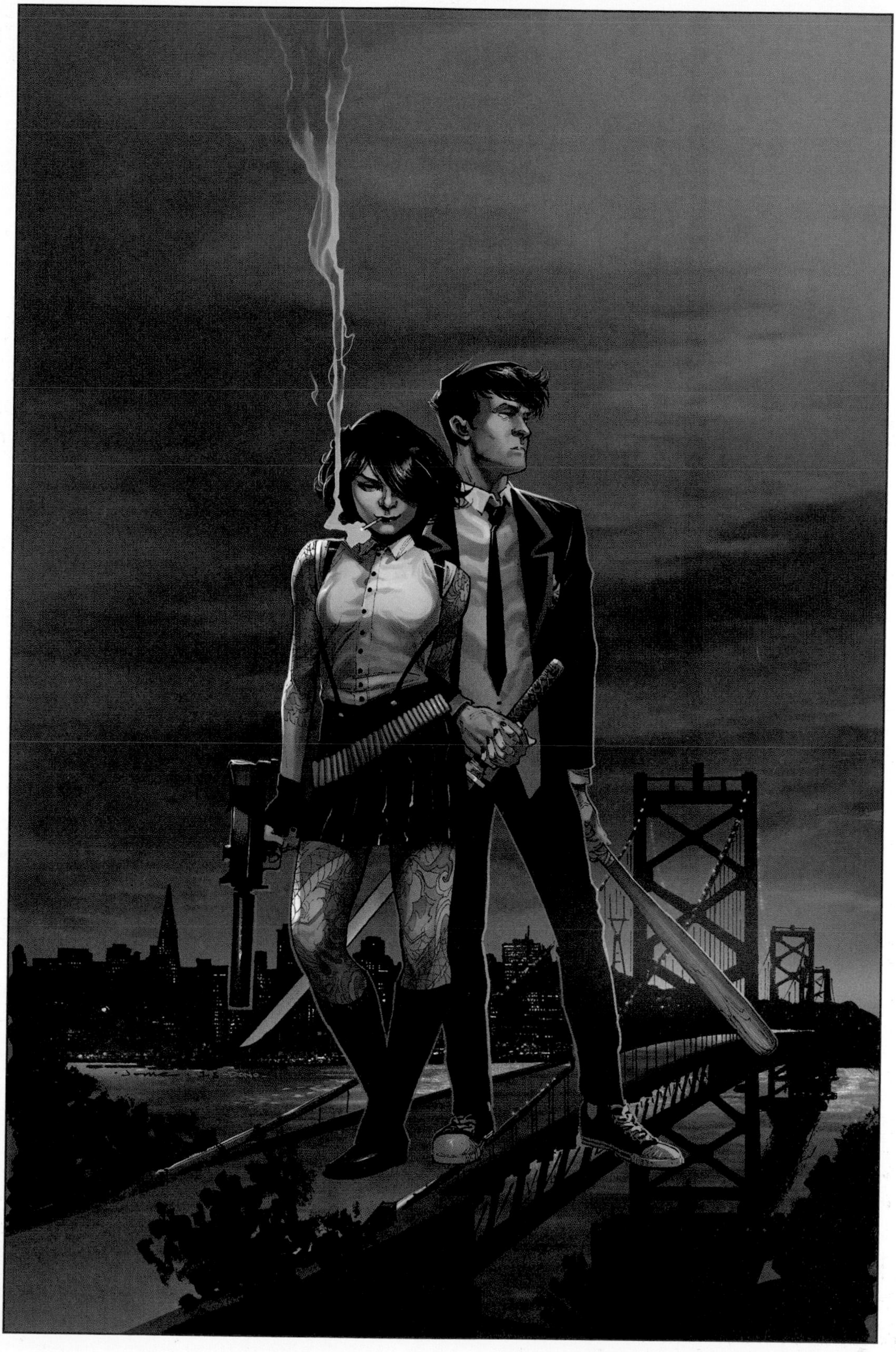

#12 VARIANT BY **JEROME OPEÑA**

#13 COVER BY **WES CRAIG**

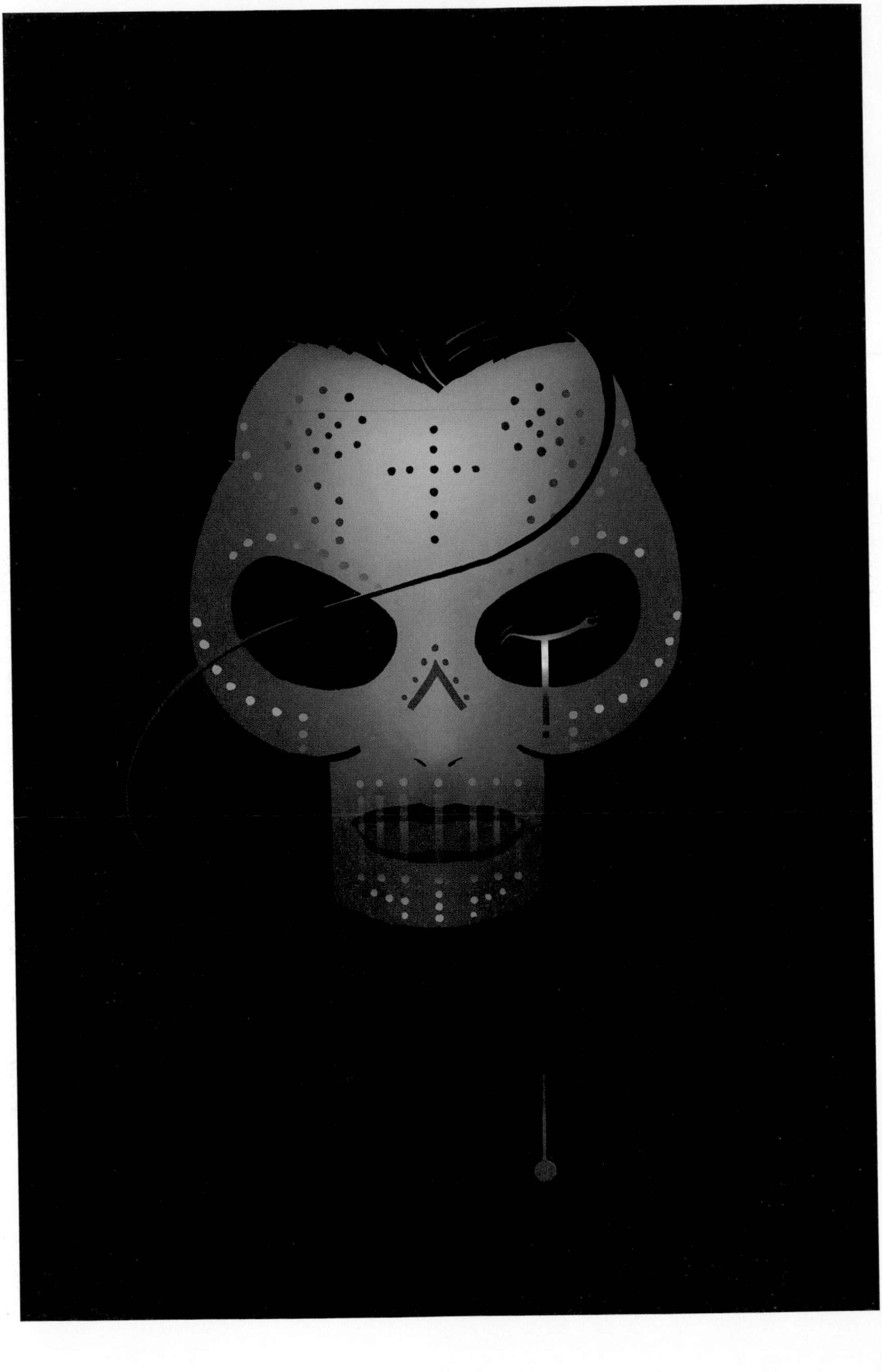

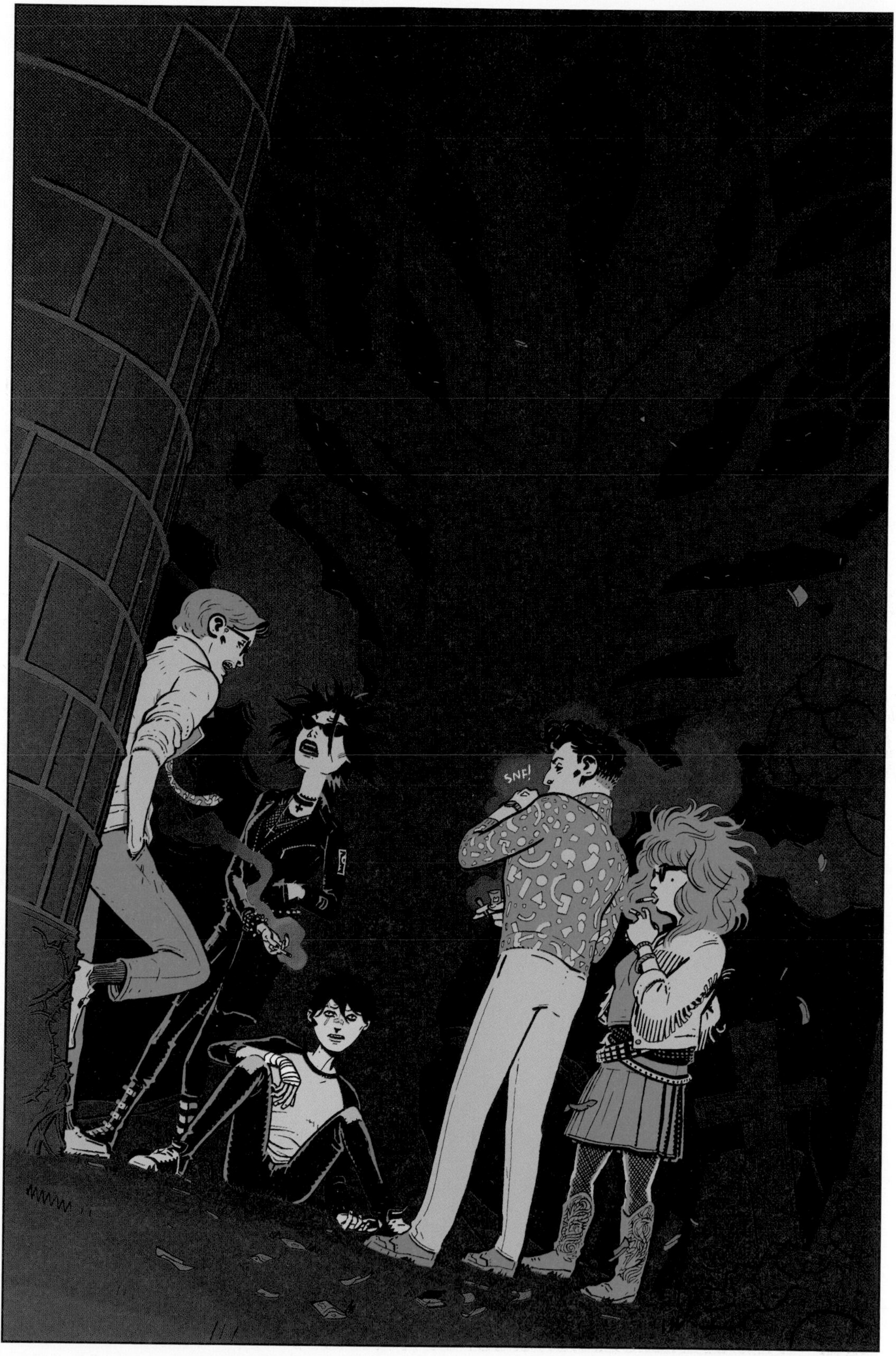
SNF!

#14 COVER BY **WES CRAIG**

#15 COVER BY **WES CRAIG**

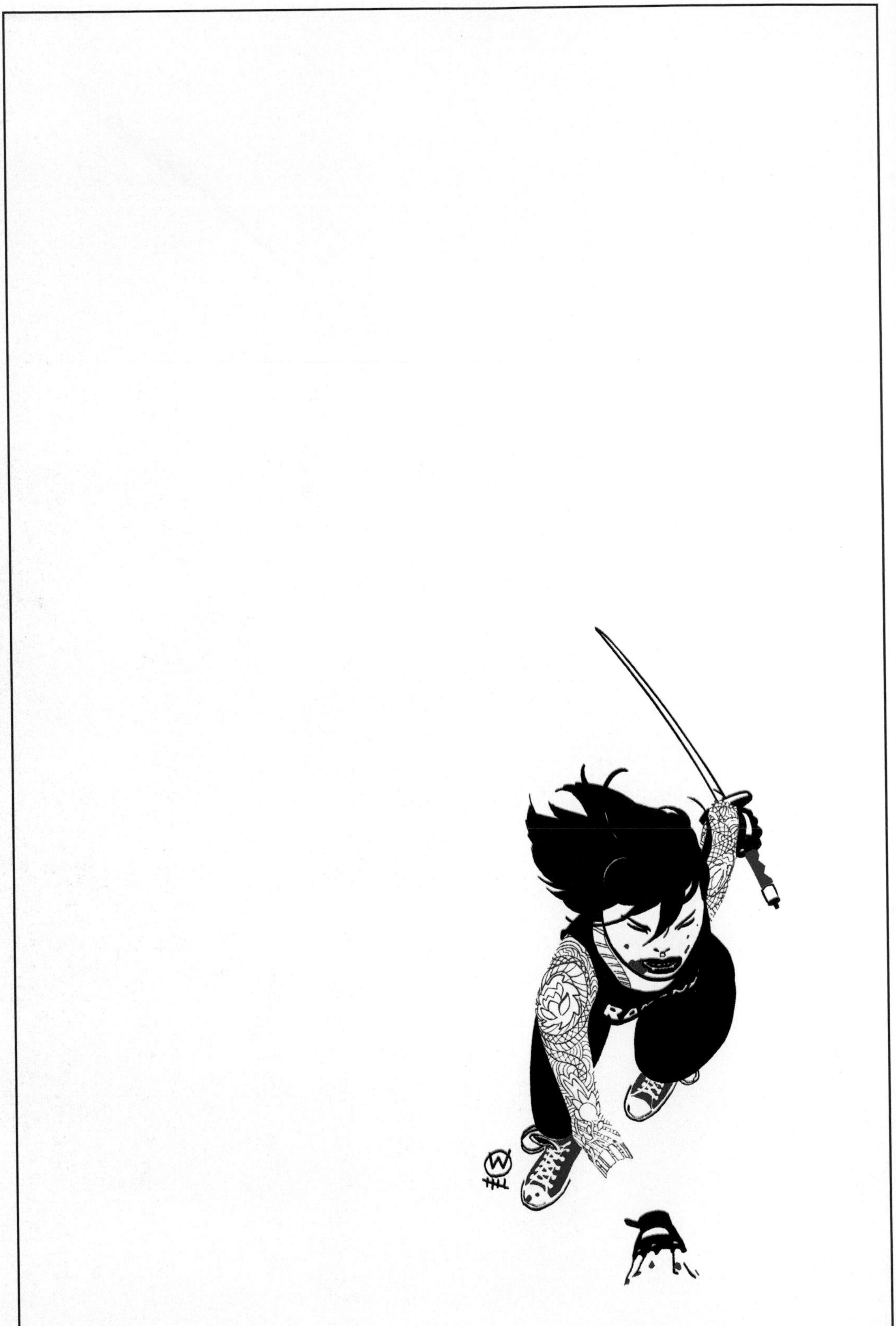

#16 COVER BY **WES CRAIG**

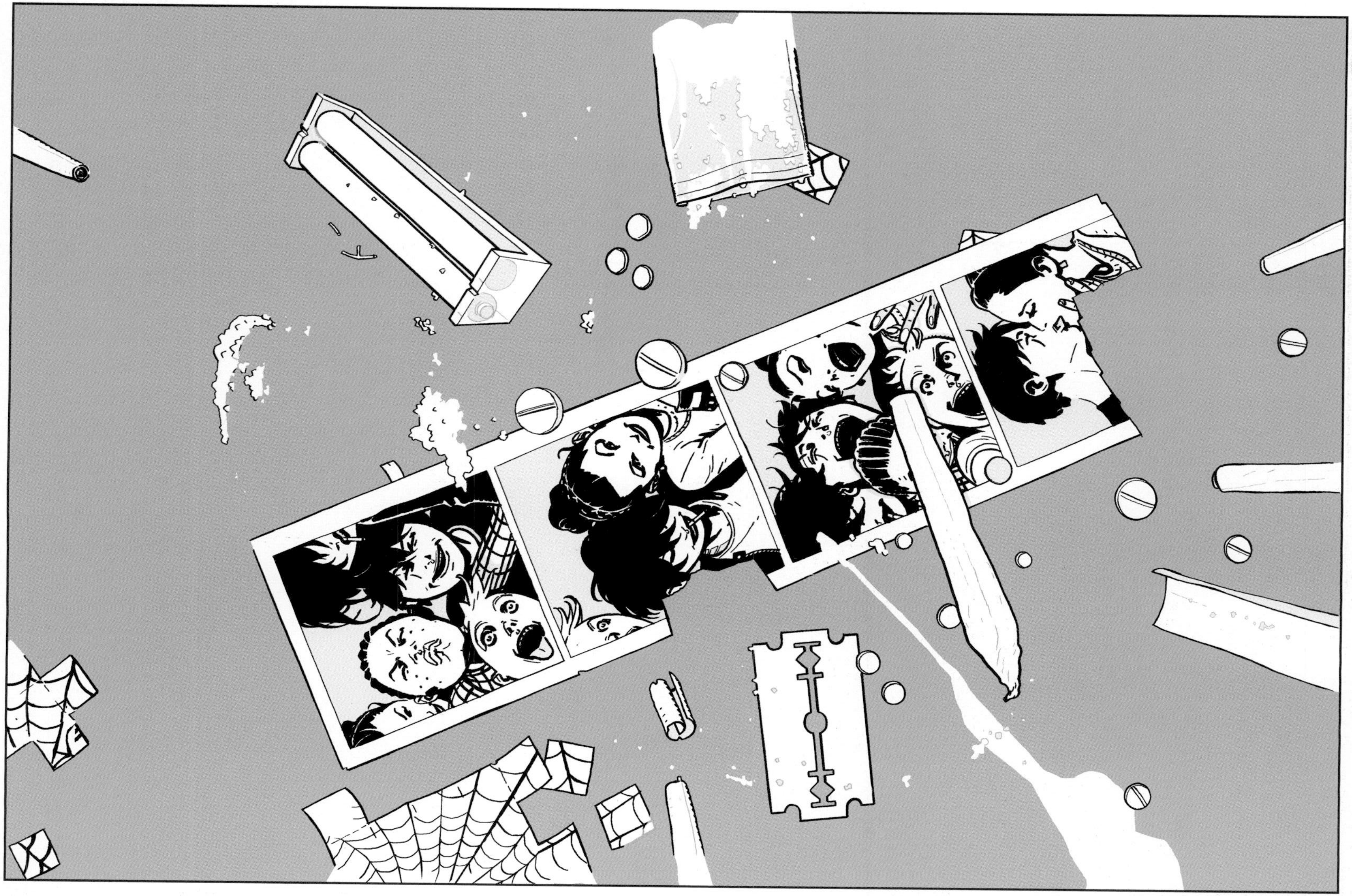

EST
1637

IN VITAM MORTEM